TOT

Get **more** out of libraries

Please return or renew this item by the last date shown.

You can renew online at www.hants.gov.uk/library

Or by phoning   0845 603 5631

 Hampshire
County Council

~ FEB 2014

www.**totallyrandombooks.**co.uk

Also by Mark Frost

THE PALADIN PROPHECY

ALLIANCE

THE PALADIN PROPHECY
Book II

MARK FROST

CORGI BOOKS

THE PALADIN PROPHECY: ALLIANCE
A CORGI BOOK 978 0 552 56533 2

Published in Great Britain by Corgi Books,
an imprint of Random House Children's Publishers UK
A Random House Group Company

This edition published 2013

1 3 5 7 9 10 8 6 4 2

The Random House Group Limited supports the Forest Stewardship Council® (FSC®),
the leading international forest-certification organisation. Our books carrying the FSC
label are printed on FSC®-certified paper. FSC is the only forest-certification scheme
supported by the leading environmental organisations, including Greenpeace. Our
paper procurement policy can be found at www.randomhouse.co.uk/environment

Set in Minion

RANDOM HOUSE CHILDREN'S PUBLISHERS UK
61–63 Uxbridge Road, London W5 5SA

www.**randomhousechildrens**.co.uk
www.**totallyrandombooks**.co.uk
www.**randomhouse**.co.uk

Addresses for companies within The Random House Group Limited can be found at:
www.randomhouse.co.uk/offices.htm

THE RANDOM HOUSE GROUP Limited Reg. No. 954009

A CIP catalogue record for this book is available from the British Library.

Printed and bound in the CPI Group (UK) Ltd, Croydon, CR0 4YY

No one can do it for you . . .

I live my life in growing orbits
Which move out over the things of the world.
Perhaps I can never achieve the last,
But that will be my attempt.
I am circling around God, around the ancient tower,
And I have been circling for a thousand years,
And I still don't know if I am a falcon, or a storm,
Or a great song.

—RAINER MARIA RILKE

ALLIANCE

MARCH

Lyle Ogilvy had trouble staying dead.

During the past seven months, the medical staff had given up on him half a dozen times, only to realize that he was a case for which they could find no precedent in the history of medicine.

They finally had to admit that the question *Is he dead or alive?* had them baffled.

The answer was even harder to come by for anyone outside Lyle's inner circle, as his family and the school had agreed to and honored an ironclad confidentiality agreement about his condition. The mysterious truth was that, since the "unfortunate incident" last fall, Lyle had fallen into a bottomless coma and his vital signs remained a whisper. Six times they'd taken him off life support, but each time they'd hooked him back in because, while nothing they tried would revive him, Lyle's EEGs continued to demonstrate robust brain activity.

The only clue for the rest of the school that the controversial Ogilvy might still be on campus was the frequent, furtive presence of Lyle's parents. They had accepted the trauma team's recommendation that trying to move their son from his secure intensive care suite at the school's medical center could prove fatal. Because Lyle wasn't only a patient; he was also a prisoner, and if he ever did regain consciousness, he faced a long list of serious criminal charges.

So Lyle lay bedridden, as still as a marble replica throughout the winter months and into the spring. His eyes opened periodically, in no discernible pattern, and his pupils responded to light, one of the few encouraging signs the staff could point to.

As expected, with a feeding tube providing his only nourishment, Lyle's bulky overweight frame had melted like wax, apparently wasting away, but closer examination would have revealed that his muscles were growing leaner and more defined. Although the nurses turned him four times a day, because his customized bed was so oversized and they never saw him upright, none of them seemed to notice that the six-foot-two Lyle had grown three inches taller.

Persistent vegetative state, a phrase often used by the doctors when discussing Lyle, didn't come close to describing what was really going on inside him. Lyle's mind had not regained the use of words, but had he been able he might have said that lately he'd grown steadily more aware of his circumstances. He was even dimly able to "see" people coming and going from his room, whether his eyes were open or not.

And as the last of the late-season snows fell and the ice on Lake Waukoma retreated from its shores, something unusual stirred inside Lyle Ogilvy. If he could've settled on just one word to describe what he was going through, it would have been *Change.*

Spring was the growing season, and new life was stirring inside him, assimilating the old Lyle into something far more compelling and powerful. Another perception had recently begun to take shape in his cobwebbed consciousness as well. A rising sensation more felt than known, but Lyle felt it in every cell of his body.

Hunger.

* * *

"How do you feel?" asked the coach.

Numb. That's how Will felt at the moment. And not just from the bitter cold. *It exactly describes how I've felt for the last five months.*

"Do *you* think I can do it?" asked Will.

"I'm not the one who needs to answer that," said Ira Jericho, arms folded, standing back from the edge.

"I know. But your opinion would be useful in helping me form mine."

"Cop-out. Concentrate."

Numb. Overwhelmed. Stuck trying to process and sort through more emotional trauma in one month than he'd been through in his lifetime.

Will and Coach Jericho stood on the eastern bank of Lake Waukoma, halfway through their daily training session, looking out at the water. Most of it was still covered by its winter sheet of ice, with sections of it breaking apart into a checkerboard pattern of isolated floes.

The weak sun drifted low in the west, touching the tree line now. Temperature in the low forties and dropping.

All winter, Will had spent two hours of every afternoon training with Coach Jericho. Like most kids his age, he craved routine and regularity, something that, because of his parents keeping them constantly on the move, had in his life forever been in short supply. After Christmas Will had thrown himself into his first full class load at the Center, the most daunting intellectual gauntlet he'd ever run. When his academic day ended, his training sessions with Jericho presented even tougher physical challenges.

Will had gone dead inside since the scandalous public "deaths" of his parents, and he knew exactly why. It was an involuntary way of protecting himself, maybe even a healthy one, from all the darkness surrounding his early life. So he understood the reasons but hardly felt motivated to change it, particularly during the therapy sessions he'd been required to undergo with Dr. Robbins, the school's psychologist.

Every session with Robbins felt like walking through a minefield, giving her just enough details to suggest he was making progress without divulging any of the secrets he needed to keep to himself. The whole experience left him hardly capable of feeling anything, which made the truth he was hiding easier to bear. He had learned to welcome the physical agony of his training with Jericho as the only sensations he could even experience. At least they let him know his body was still alive.

Will knelt down, stuck a hand in the water, and shivered. "It's about one degree above freezing," he said.

"Fall in, you'd die of hypothermia in less than five minutes," said Jericho. "That is, a *normal* kid would."

"Would you?"

"I'm not stupid enough to try," said the coach.

It'd been forty-two degrees when they left the field house at 3:20. It was overcast and damp, leaving the path through the woods muddy and cold as they jogged down to the lake. An altogether lousy April afternoon.

"But I am?" asked Will, sticking his semifrozen hand under his other arm to warm it back up.

"I didn't say that," said Jericho. "I just said you weren't normal. Can you do it?"

Coach had asked him that question, about so many different puzzling assignments, at least five hundred times during the past few months. The cross-country season was long over, and with most of the team booted out of school because of their involvement with the Knights of Charlemagne, Will had Jericho all to himself. He quickly realized that their daily sessions had been designed to do a whole lot more than teach him better technique on the track.

Each assignment Jericho presented to Will posed an unstated question: Are you strong enough? Are you tough enough? Are you committed enough to (fill in the blank)? Will pushed himself to always answer yes, but Jericho seemed maddeningly indifferent to his efforts, to the point where Will had decided the man was either insane or impossible to please, which only made him try harder. He didn't know what kind of heat he'd get if he said no; he hadn't summoned up the courage to ever do it.

"Yes," said Will. "Yes, I can do it."

Jericho didn't react. He never seemed to react to anything. He just took in whatever Will said and rolled it around in his head, only responding when he had something to say. Most days he seldom said a word, but on occasion, without warning, Coach launched into long rambles outlining his unique philosophy, a mind-bending mash-up of New Age metaphysics and ancient mythology, filtered through the lens of Jericho's Native American lore and legends. The conventional back-and-forth rhythms of social interaction—the polite verbal lubrication that made people feel better about themselves and each other—meant nothing to him.

But what really drives me bat-crap crazy about this guy is that he never answers any of my questions, particularly the ones I most desperately want answers to, like: Why are we doing this stuff? What are you trying to teach me?

Whatever their purpose, Jericho's tasks grew more difficult as they worked through the winter. They were often purely, brutally physical—run from here to there, climb up this hill, jump down from that ledge. Sometimes they involved

5

endurance—balance on this rock on one leg with your eyes closed and listen to the wind, or hold this excruciating posture for an hour until your muscles fail. Other times his "exercises" seemed to have no purpose whatsoever: Sit absolutely still, hold this stone falcon in your hand, clear your mind, and picture an earthen well. Now slowly lower a bucket into it, bring it back up, and drink deeply.

Whatever their purpose, Will grew steadily stronger. Increasingly confident of his unfolding abilities—the uncanny speed and stamina he'd discovered and the startling ways in which he could affect the world and those around him with just his mind.

So what is it going to be this time?

Jericho reached into the pocket of his rain gear, pulled out a shiny silver dollar, held it up for Will to see, and then hurled it as far as he could out into the lake. It landed and stuck in a large floating patch of ice nearly a hundred yards offshore.

"Don't think about it," said Jericho. "Go get it."

Will turned and ran away from the lake for twenty strides, turned back, and accelerated straight toward the shore, nearing top speed with astonishing quickness. As he reached the shoreline—thinking *don't think about it*—he left his feet and soared toward the first patch of ice ten feet out, felt his cleats crunch down into the crusty ice, sensed instantly it would collapse if he gave it his full weight, pushed off, and leaped out to the next patch eight feet to the left.

Another unstable wobble underfoot, but without losing momentum he leaped onto the next patch, and then the next, skipping across the water like a stone. Within seconds he skidded to a halt on the large central span of ice where Jericho's dollar had landed. The floe rocked and swayed as his weight settled.

Will bent down to pick up the coin but the ice floe broke apart under his weight, with the coin on a section that was too small to support him now floating quickly away.

You've worked on this. Don't panic. You know what to do.

Will focused on the silver dollar and held out his hand. He instantly felt a firm connection shoot through the air between himself and the coin.

Just do it quickly.

Will threw all his mental weight at the coin, felt its shape ease into his grasp, then tugged it back toward him. The coin rocked and swayed, then pulled loose from the ice and flew hard and fast toward him, hitting his hand with a loud smack. Will closed his hand around it, then held it up for Jericho to see and laughed, amazed at what he'd just done.

Then he heard a deep muted *twang* echo underfoot, like a string breaking on a huge off-key guitar. He immediately felt a fracture form in what was left of the ice beneath his feet and saw a fault line open at the water behind him, running rapidly in his direction.

"Oh crap."

He looked back at the way he'd come, all his frozen stepping-stones still rocking in the water, drifting farther apart. With no time or space for a full run-up on the return trip, he took two steps and launched off the edge of the floe just as it split in half beneath his feet.

Landing on the nearest fragment, Will rocked and swayed like a novice surfer, only staying upright because his cleats nailed him to the ice. His calculations told him the next chunk was too far away so—again, without thinking—his mind reached down into the frigid water and pulled the ice block toward him. He leaped onto it and continued that way, vaulting from block to block, using his momentum to urge each floating step toward the next, as water washed over his shoes, freezing his feet up to the ankles.

Twenty yards from shore, the last stepping-stone ahead of him, barely a yard across, crumbled apart. In desperation, Will looked at Jericho, immobile on the shore, his whole posture a shrug. Will felt the block beneath him begin to implode, and his mind reached down to plumb and scan the desolate bed of the lake floor below, at least fifteen feet down and quickly running deeper: rocks, dead weeds, sluggish fish.

With the same fierce concentration, Will looked up and a pathway appeared to him, leading toward shore straight across the water. In desperation he flailed out along it, furiously churning his legs, creating so much surface tension that he felt it, just barely, support his weight.

His mind and his muscles sustained the effort to within a few feet of land before he finally plunged down into the water up to his knees and the shocking cold shot through his whole body. He was on the rocky beach a few staggering steps later; then he ran toward Jericho.

His coach had a fire going on the sandbar beyond the rocks. A full, roaring campfire with kindling and split logs. Shivering, Will yanked off his shoes and track pants, sat on a flat rock, and held his frozen feet up near the flames, grateful for the warmth.

How? How did he start a fire like this that quickly?

Coach Jericho never questioned him directly about his powers, how they worked or where they came from. Will wouldn't have been able to answer anyway; he honestly didn't know. Jericho simply accepted what his eyes told him, that Will could do these astonishing things. As they'd worked to develop them, Will came to believe he could trust Jericho to keep his secrets. Coach didn't seem to have a hidden agenda, and Will never worried about him reporting back to anyone about what they were up to.

And as the months passed, in fleeting glimpses that never seemed quite accidental—like the fire that simply appeared on the lakeshore that dreary April morning—Will began to realize that Jericho could do some pretty astonishing things himself.

He always moved silently. Sometimes he seemed to change locations without moving at all. Once he'd shown up at the top of a waterfall about two seconds after Will had seen him at the bottom. And another time, although it came at the end of a grueling session that had Will nearly cross-eyed with exhaustion, he swore he saw Jericho standing in two places at once.

Jericho also insisted that Will always carry in his pocket the small stone figurine of a falcon Coach had given him as a gift. And every once in a while Jericho would order Will to stand still, then pull a handful of feathered sticks out of his pocket and—never explaining why—wave them around Will's head a few times, touching him on the head, neck, or shoulders.

If that was a little oddball, it was a small price to pay for the man's goodwill and mentorship. Will knew that the discipline and intensity of their daily work had become his primary method for coping with all his pain and sorrow. Maybe that was enough?

So Will filed his question about the fire with all the other unanswered ones about his enigmatic coach that he'd accumulated over the past six months. For instance, *Is it really true, Coach, that you're the great-great-grandson of Crazy Horse?*

Oh, and while I'm at it, might as well toss in "How did I run on top of the water?"

"Here's your silver eagle," said Will, and flipped the coin up at Jericho.

Jericho caught it in the palm of his hand. Standing on its

9

edge. He covered it with his other hand and made it disappear with the flourish of a birthday-party magician.

Eyes twinkling, Jericho smiled broadly. A rare enough sight that Will was always amazed the man could actually shape his face into one.

"What did you learn?" asked Jericho.

"Water's wet. Ice is cold," said Will, his teeth still chattering.

"What else?"

Will felt a sudden spike of heat against his leg. He stuck a hand in his pocket and found the stone falcon he always carried. The rock should have been freezing, but it was hot to the touch, almost too hot to hold, like it held a living flame inside. He took it out and stared at it, gripping it lightly between his thumb and first finger.

"It won't hurt you," said Jericho.

Will closed his palm around it, feeling the heat penetrate his skin, but instead of burning him the warmth spread into his fingers and wrist and up his arm. At that moment a falcon's call sounded, somewhere in the sky high above them. Will looked up but couldn't spot the bird anywhere; still, he felt his chest open, cold air rushing in, nourishing him at the deepest levels.

"What else do you know?" asked Jericho, smiling slightly.

"I feel like I'm back in my body," said Will, breathing deeply, feeling the surge of heat shoot into his core and from there down and out through his limbs.

"That means you're healed."

Jericho was right. Will could feel vitality spreading deep into his muscles and bones. His mind tingled. His senses opened up to everything around him. He felt connected to the rocks, the wood, the fire, the sky, the lake. He was alive again.

He was AWAKE.

"So that's what this has all been about?" asked Will. "Me and you. Helping me recover?"

"You tell me," said Jericho.

"Yes."

But there's something more to it than that. Something else going on. You're helping me prepare . . . but for what?

"Tell me what else you feel, Will."

The events of last fall projected through his mind like a scrambled movie trailer: the destruction of his life in Ojai, the kidnapping and disappearance of his parents at the hands of Mr. Hobbes and the Black Caps, the attempt on his own life and those of his friends by Lyle Ogilvy and the Knights of Charlemagne.

"I feel . . . ," said Will, taking another deep breath, a surge building in his chest. "I feel really . . . angry."

"Who are you mad at, Will?"

"The people who did this to me and my family."

Jericho paused. "Hate wears you down and doesn't hurt your enemy. It's like taking poison and hoping your enemy will die."

"I didn't say I *hate* them," said Will, looking right at him. "I just want to take them out."

Jericho smiled his enigmatic smile.

#24: YOU CAN'T CHANGE ANYTHING IF YOU CAN'T CHANGE YOUR MIND.

Returning from the lake, Will burst through the pod door, brimming with energy. Brooke Springer sat at the dining room table, twirling a strand of her long blond curls, reading something on her tablet. She looked up, startled, when he came in, and their eyes met. Will felt an electric jolt but he didn't speak, hoping she'd break the ice first, say something, anything to him . . . a single welcoming word . . .

But Brooke's eyes shaded over and she looked away, with only the slightest nod of acknowledgment. No more than you'd give a total stranger sharing a ride in an elevator.

The same treatment he'd been getting from her since she came back to school three months ago. Will thought *hard* about finally calling her on the distance she'd put between them, the tension and alienation:

Why are you treating me like someone you don't even know when we were so close a few months ago? As close as I've ever felt to anyone not named West.

But if he said one word about this now, he knew his restraint would break and he wouldn't be able to stop until he'd poured out everything he'd been holding inside.

Not the right time.

Will grabbed some water from the kitchen and sailed straight to his room. He closed the door loudly, but with control, then paced around from wall to wall, trying to decide where to start.

He grabbed Dad's List of Rules and opened it randomly, looking for guidance, and the List didn't disappoint. His eyes fell on:

#74: 99 PERCENT OF THE THINGS YOU WORRY ABOUT NEVER HAPPEN. DOES THAT MEAN WORRYING WORKS OR THAT IT'S A COMPLETE WASTE OF TIME AND ENERGY? YOU DECIDE.

Okay, thought Will. *Today let's say worrying works. What do I do next?*

He flipped through the book again, stopped randomly, and landed on:

12

#22: WHENEVER YOUR HEAD IS TOO FULL OF NOISE, MAKE A LIST.

That felt like the best advice Dad had ever given him. His notebook couldn't help him work this out; he needed to go old-school technology. Will locked the door, sat at his desk with an oversized sketchpad, and went to work getting it all out on paper.

And whatever you do, don't *start with Brooke.*

Six weeks remained in the school year; then summer vacation loomed, a yawning void he'd been dreading, with no idea how he'd be able to fill it. *But that could be a plus.* Now that he felt back on his game, he had six weeks to identify what he needed to do and how to go about it. All the unfinished business from last fall that he'd had to hang on a hook, for self-preservation, while his mind, body, and soul knit themselves back together.

Will began writing down questions in big capital letters:

HOW ARE THE KNIGHTS OF CHARLEMAGNE CONNECTED TO MR. HOBBES AND THE BLACK CAPS?

Will had every reason to think the Knights were finished after they'd tried to kill him last November. Ten of the twelve Knights had been arrested. Only the group's leader, Lyle Ogilvy, and Lyle's partner in crime, Todd Hodak, remained at large. Todd hadn't been seen or heard from since the attack. Lyle's whereabouts, a frequent subject of campus rumors, remained unknown. Will knew there wasn't much left of the Lyle he'd known, after barely surviving an attack from the wendigo that he'd summoned to destroy Will.

But can I be absolutely sure *that the Knights were destroyed?*

Will and his roommates had discovered frightening proof of a connection between the men he called the Black Caps—who'd chased him out of Ojai, then kidnapped his parents and made it look like they'd died in a plane crash—and the Knights. They'd found a videotape of a meeting recorded by Ronnie Murso—the roommate Will had replaced in their pod, who'd been missing for nearly a year. A tape that, before he and his father disappeared on a fishing trip, Ronnie had gone to heroic lengths to hide from everyone *but* his roommates, leaving a coded trail of clues to his secret that Will and his roommates had been able to crack.

Ronnie's recording covertly captured a meeting between the Caps' leader, the fearsome bald man Mr. Hobbes, and Lyle Ogilvy. Hobbes could be seen giving Lyle a piece of aphotic technology he called a Carver, a mysterious device that could be used to open a portal between here and a dimension called the Never-Was.

Will had learned (from his dead–undead–badass Special Forces helicopter pilot–guardian Sergeant Dave Gunner) that the Never-Was is a purgatorial dimension where the monsters he called the Other Team came from. A prison where this elder race of beings had been banished from Earth eons ago by the celestial organization that Dave worked for—the Hierarchy. The same group Dave claimed Will now worked for as well, as a low-ranking "initiate." With the treacherous help of human collaborators, like the Knights and Caps, the Other Team had long been planning a jailbreak in order to retake control of the planet, and the agents of the Hierarchy were all that stood in their way.

When Mr. Hobbes, posing as a federal agent, tried to kidnap him, Will also realized that the bald man was some kind of monster/human hybrid himself. Hobbes hadn't shown himself since. How could he and his roommates hope to stop creatures like Hobbes and his minions? He could barely write fast enough to keep up with his thoughts, trying to make sense of all the connections.

THE ABILITIES WE HAVE TO FIGHT WITH

ME:
- Speed (from enhanced fast-twitch muscles, as well as ... ?)
- Incredible stamina (extreme oxygen-binding ability in my red blood cells)
- Amazing restorative ability/self-healing (related to the blood condition)
- Telekinesis: the ability to create energy and apply it to objects or people with my <u>mind</u> (freaky; no idea WHERE this comes from)
- Possibly related: the ability to extend my senses away from my body and receive precise impressions about the world around me. Maybe by tuning in to patterns of magnetic waves? (Don't know if this ability <u>has</u> a name— even in fiction—but I call it the Grid)
- Telepathy: the ability to communicate "thought pictures" and words into the minds of others (likewise, something I've been able to do since childhood but never had a name for it)
- Dad's Book of Rules ... not an ability, really, but a damn helpful ace up my sleeve

AJAY JANIKOWSKI:
- Incredible vision, as good or <u>better</u> than an eagle crossed with a top-gun pilot
- Photographic memory: registers virtually everything he sees (and somehow doesn't suffer from brain congestion)

15

– Total recall: nothing seen by his <u>eye</u> ever gets forgotten by his <u>mind</u> (Where does he put it all? Check to see if he's had brain MRI yet.)

NICK McLEISH:
– Astonishing strength, agility, leaping ability, hand–eye–foot coordination
– World–class fighting skills, champion gymnast, master of half a dozen martial arts
– Heightened sense of direction (an ability shared by—why does this not surprise me—a large number of wild animals)
– Virtually—and perhaps stupidly—without fear (this might be less a "power" than a serious mental deficiency)
Which leads to . . .
– (Nick and Ajay: no sign of telepathy as yet. It's hard enough just <u>talking</u> with Nick.)

ELISE MOREAU:
– Sonic power: able to create, manipulate, and direct sound waves as physical force
– Telepathy: at least with ME, able to communicate without words and over undetermined distances (and getting stronger). Also capable of heightened psychological insights: intuition?
– Precognition and/or remote viewing: Possible intuitive ability to see future events, or ones taking place at far distances (anecdotal; untested and unconfirmed)

BROOKE SPRINGER:
– Incredible beauty (okay, not a superpower, but it might as well be based on how it works on me)

−The uncanny ability to stomp on my heart with the slightest glance

He drew a line through that and aggressively erased it.

− As for more specific powers???? Unknown (and what's up with that?)

He made note of Lyle's powers as well:

LYLE OGILVY:
− Telepathic attacks: ability to exert mind control and mental attacks
− Evil disposition: a possible victim of mind control himself (courtesy of a Ride Along, one of the worst Never−Was monsters)
− Also, bitten by a wendigo from the Never−Was.
Ultimate effects of which are unknown—as are his whereabouts—but what I saw was <u>nasty</u>. Wherever he is, prognosis can't be good.

Will asked himself again, *Where do these powers come from?*

His working theory: *As a result of genetic manipulation performed on us during in vitro fertilization. As part of a secret medical/scientific program called the Paladin Prophecy.*

But it will remain just a theory until we find who did it, and why.

Will hadn't heard a single word or whisper from the one person who might have been able to answer that, his mysterious protector, Dave Gunner. Not a peep since Dave was pulled into a portal to the Never-Was while saving Will's life (for the *fifth* time!). After taking a bite out of Lyle Ogilvy, the wendigo had dragged Dave back into that horrifying place with him. Will had no idea how Dave could have survived. And where he might be now if—big if—he had. Dave had explained to Will that he was already dead—killed in a chopper crash during the Vietnam War—so could anything worse even happen to him? Will kicked himself for never asking Dave if that meant he couldn't be killed a *second* time. Would his guardian angel ever come to his aid *again*?

Because given the immense evil we're about to declare war against, I'll need all the help I can get. So where do we strike first? WHO'S AT THE EPICENTER OF ALL THIS?

Will looked at what he'd written. All the connections pointed to one name:

WE NEED TO FIND MR. HOBBES.

But Will had no idea where to start! Hobbes had always found *him*. They knew Hobbes had been at the Center—on Ronnie Murso's video, six months *before* he'd found Will. And for all they knew, Hobbes could be connected to the mysterious research program called the Paladin Prophecy, but his real role remained a stubborn mystery.

They had one other lead to go on. Will's friend Nando Gutierrez—the taxi driver he'd met in Ojai—had tailed Hobbes and his Black Caps to the Los Angeles Federal Building, tracking them to the office of a seemingly benign academic testing organization called the National Scholastic Evaluation Agency, or NSEA.

The NSEA turned out to be the *supervising agency* that had flagged Will's over-the-moon test scores and brought them to the attention of the Center (Ajay's and Elise's as well).

Not only that, but Will had also subsequently discovered that the Center *owned* the NSEA, through an organization called the Greenwood Foundation.

Will boiled the mystery down to the biggest unanswered questions: WHAT IS THE PALADIN PROPHECY? ARE THE KNIGHTS AND BLACK CAPS BEHIND IT? AND DOES IT INVOLVE THE CENTER?

Will hadn't proved his theory that the strange powers they'd started to manifest during the last year resulted from genetic manipulation performed during in vitro fertilization. But three of his roommates—Ajay, Nick, and Elise—*had* been able to confirm with their parents that, like Will, they'd been conceived and born in the same year as a result of in vitro procedures performed at privately owned fertility clinics in four distant cities.

What odds would Vegas give you on that *being a coincidence? What about after you add in that the Center* owns *the NSEA and all of us end up here fifteen years later, in the same year each of us starts to manifest these strange powers?*

But had all that been done as part of a plot called the Paladin Prophecy? That was THE QUESTION. Which forced Will to finally look at the area that might provide the answer:

He'd spent his whole life believing that he was Will Melendez West, the only son of Jordan West, a low-profile scientific researcher, and Belinda Melendez West, a part-time paralegal. The Wests appeared to be perfectly ordinary, aside from the fact that they'd moved around so restlessly, every fifteen months on average. A puzzling pattern that now appeared to have complicated reasons.

Will had since learned that his father was in fact Dr. Hugh Greenwood, the grandson of Thomas Greenwood, the visionary educator who had founded the Center nearly a century ago. Hugh's father was Franklin Greenwood, only son of Thomas, who had succeeded his father as the school's second headmaster.

Will had cautiously poked around for information about Hugh and learned that he had taught at the Center and that he and his wife had left the school—without explanation—sixteen years ago. Hugh had also graduated from the Center, but all other details of his parents' presence here had been erased, until he'd found a photograph in a seventeen-year-old yearbook. He took out the copy he'd made of it from his desk and looked at it for the thousandth time.

A casual moment of "Hugh and Carol" watching an outdoor student concert, with the following caption: POPULAR SCIENCE TEACHER HUGH GREENWOOD AND WIFE CAROL ENJOY THE ANTICS AT THE ANNUAL HARVEST FESTIVAL.

It was "Jordan" and "Belinda" all right. Many years younger, of course, and their hair looked completely different—Hugh had a crew cut, while Carol wore a long blond ponytail. Hugh was clean-shaven, whereas "Jordan" had always worn a beard, and Will had only known "Belinda" as a brunette. Neither wore glasses or a hat in the photo, something they'd done frequently during Will's childhood, perhaps, he realized now, as part of a disguise.

Why did they go on the run when they did? What made them leave the Center—and the attractions of Hugh's great family legacy—so suddenly? If I have the timing right, that would have been after they'd known Carol was pregnant but before I was born. Was their flight from the Center related to their finding out about that in some way, and if so, how?

Biology had been Hugh Greenwood's subject at the Center, and he was well liked by his students. A trained medical doctor, with a couple of related PhDs, his father's later work as a researcher in neurobiology clearly had its foundation in his earlier life. But did he do it just to make a living, or was there something more to it?

Remember, when the Black Caps not only kidnapped my parents but also when they found us in Ojai, they broke into my father's lab and stole all of his research.

What was Hugh Greenwood working on that scared the Caps into taking so big a risk? And what had Hobbes and his people done with them since?

Two weeks after the plane crash, federal officials claimed they'd identified the bodies in the wreck as those of Will's parents. Will knew better than to believe them because a few days after the crash he'd received a painfully hopeful text message from his missing, and presumed dead, father. And because of a coded message inside it, Will never doubted that Jordan West had written it. He felt less hopeful about his mother's survival, especially after he'd seen her infected with a Ride Along, the mind-control monster that was one of the Other Team's most hideous weapons. His mother might be gone, and he'd come to grips with that over the last few months.

But he believed one hundred percent that his father was *alive,* and that belief alone kept him going. Will had never breathed a word to his roommates about this devastating truth. He was afraid of the many unknowns that might come back to hurt them when they'd been through too much trying to help him already. He couldn't blame them if, just as he had, his roommates had decided to push all this insanity into the background, concentrate on their schooling, go along with the Center's explanation that the worst was behind them, and hope like hell it was true.

But with Will's reawakened attitude, he knew better:

TROUBLE'S COMING BACK WITH A VENGEANCE, BE-CAUSE THIS TIME I'M TAKING THE FIGHT TO *THEM*.

He'd start slowly, with Ajay. They'd follow up on their earlier investigations and then formulate a strategy on how to proceed.

And that's how things went, until 9:14 p.m. on June 3, the last day of their sophomore year.

JUNE

After his last final exam of the year, Will returned to Pod G4-3 in Greenwood Hall, tossed his backpack aside, and was about to enter his bedroom when he spotted a letter, addressed to him, propped up on the dining room table. Hardly an everyday occurrence these days. Postmarked five days earlier, from a handwritten return address in Palm Desert, California, below the name N. DEANGELO.

Will took it into his room, propped up his school notebook, and sat at his desk. His syn-app appeared on the screen of the device, watching curiously as Will opened the envelope and unfolded a single-page letter written in the same neat, feminine hand as the address:

> Dear Will West,
>
> I must apologize for how long it has taken me to respond to your letter of last November. You see, it was sent to my former address in Santa Monica, where I haven't lived in over twelve years, and I've moved twice since then. It's only through the admirable persistence of our much-maligned postal service that it finally reached me two weeks ago.

Will flashed back to the letter he'd written last November to a Santa Monica address that Nando had helped him find. But that was to a woman named Nancy *Hughes,* a navy nurse who Dave had told him he'd known in Vietnam just before he died.

23

Your letter certainly got me thinking. I'm at an age now, recently retired, where you spend a lot of time remembering things. I thought the best way to answer your out-of-the-blue question—"Did you know a man during the Vietnam War named Sergeant Dave Gunner?"—would be to send you a photograph I've kept all these years.

Will found the photo attached to the back of the letter with a paper clip. An aging snapshot, in close-up, of a tanned and shirtless Dave reclining on a tropical beach, holding his sunglasses with one hand and winking, while giving a thumbs-up with the other. Wearing a devil-may-care grin, like he had the world by the scruff of the neck.

Looking *exactly* like the Dave Gunner Will had known, same guy, no question about it. The only difference: no disfiguring scars on his face from the chopper crash. That was yet to come, and apparently soon.

As you probably know, Dave didn't survive the war. In fact, he was killed two days after I took this picture. I was just a kid then, and we only knew each other a couple of days but he certainly made an impression. That's the kind of guy he was. So full of life he could hardly contain it. If anyone had met Dave, then I'm sure they'd never forget him, and his dying when he did, even with all that unimaginable violence going on around us, hit me hard as something senseless and tragic.

"I hear that," said Will softy.

One more point. This is an even harder thing to describe, Will, but since then, more than a few times during my life, hard times, I've had a strong feeling that Dave was nearby. In a good way. I don't know if that sounds too awfully strange to you, but there it is, for what it's worth. It was a long time ago, and I'm married now, happily, to a really great fella, so I'll say no more about that.

But I did hang on to this photo for a very long time, didn't I?

Anyway, I hope I've answered your question.

Sincerely yours,
Nancy (Hughes) Deangelo, R.N., retired

"Yes, you did, Nancy," said Will. "You sure did."

Will folded the letter and looked at the photograph of Dave again.

So full of life he could hardly contain it.

As he stared at the photograph, he felt a strong vibration issuing from his desk. He opened the top drawer, where he kept the pair of "black dice" that Dave had given him. Of course, when Dave used them, they functioned as some kind of holographic database that projected information he requested into thin air, but ever since he'd thrown them Will's way, they'd stubbornly resisted looking or acting as anything other than ordinary dice.

But now the dice were oscillating in place so rapidly he could barely see them, and his whole desk was shaking.

"What's going on, Will?" asked Will's syn-app, looking up from the screen of his notebook, seated at a virtual version of the dining room table, which was also shaking.

"I don't know, Junior. It started after I opened this letter."

Will had grown so comfortable with the constant presence of his miniaturized/computerized double that he'd started calling him Junior.

"May I see it please, Will?"

Will stood, picked up the notebook to stop the shaking, then held the letter up to the screen. "It's from that navy nurse you found the address for last year."

Will held up the photograph, too. Junior stood up and appeared to study them, while analyzing and scanning them into memory.

"That is the same guy, right?" asked Will. "In the other picture you found. That's Dave Gunner."

"Yes, it is, Will. I can definitely confirm that," said Junior. "It really makes you wonder, doesn't it?"

"Yes. It really, really does."

"I wonder what Nurse Nancy looked like way back then."

"Knowing Dave, it's a safe bet that back in the day she looked pretty doggone good."

"I've made a note of her current address," said Junior. "If you ever need to contact Ms. Hughes again."

"Thanks, Junior," said Will.

As soon as he put the letter away, his desk stopped shaking. He opened the drawer to look at the dice, as ordinary as a pair from a Monopoly game again. It suddenly seemed like a good idea to carry them around, so he picked them up and slipped them into his pocket.

He heard the front door slam in the other room and moments later an urgent banging on his door. Will got up and unlocked the door. Ajay rushed in, huge eyes wide, his tiny elfin frame bursting with animated energy.

"Great galloping ghost of Franklin Delano Roosevelt!" said Ajay. "Have I got something to show you."

Ajay swung his immense backpack onto Will's bed, its weight pulling him with it.

"Don't hurt yourself," said Will. "What's the rush?"

Ajay ripped open his bag and rummaged through it, searching for something. "When all that material vanished from the Rare Book Archives about the Knights of Charlemagne, I still felt certain I could put my hands on the information we needed—where did I put it?"

In January, Ajay had finagled a pass into the Rare Book Archive of the Center's library, where they'd hoped to find more about the Knights of Charlemagne, but all references to the Knights had vanished from their physical and digital records. They also checked the field house locker room, where they'd earlier discovered a network of tunnels leading all the way to the island in the middle of Lake Waukoma, but access to them had been sealed off; the door that led down there now ended in a broom closet.

"Put what?"

"No one has even *dreamt* of the firewall that can keep me off a server, but finding an object that has been *removed* in its purely physical/analog form is a more difficult nut to crack—"

"So what did you find, Ajay?" asked Will, moving over to join him.

"Just before all the trouble started, Brooke had located a few articles about the Knights in the school newspaper."

"Ancient ones, from like the 1920s."

"And one from the '30s," said Ajay as he finally fished out the slender folder he'd been looking for. "They've already been plucked from the archives as well, but you'll recall that Brooke showed a single photograph from the library to us when we were online with her, just before Lyle hacked into the call."

"I do remember that," said Will. "A picture of the Knights at a dinner. With some famous politician, wasn't it?"

"That's it! Henry Wallace, the United States secretary of the interior, who was less than four years away from becoming Franklin Roosevelt's vice president," said Ajay as he opened the folder and took out an 8 x 12 black-and-white photograph. "This is the image Brooke held up to the screen while we were watching."

"How did you find it?"

"Well, I'm such a first-class nincompoop, a digital record of the call was backed up on my private server this entire time. When this occurred to me, I went back in, ran a quantum-level search, and found that image on the recording, but it was in appalling shape, terrible resolution, grainy and obscure, so I ran it through a few enhancement renders—"

"Let me see it!"

"There's a *lot* more detail in my version than the one Brooke showed us," said Ajay, laying the glossy black-and-white photograph on the table. "Someone *else* was at that dinner."

It was the same 1937 photo that Brooke had briefly shown them online, but Ajay had completely restored it: the twelve Knights of Charlemagne hosting a fancy dinner in some unidentified dining room for Interior Secretary Henry Wallace.

"Look at it with this," said Ajay, pulling out a magnifying glass.

Will's eye scanned the table until he settled on one of the young men making a toast to Wallace and smiling for the camera—a young student, one of the Knights. The same student, when Will had first seen the photo, that he thought he'd recognized but wasn't able to identify.

"Do you see him?" asked Ajay.

He could now. Solid, built like a linebacker, with unmistakable piercing light blue eyes.

It was the Bald Man, the leader of the Black Caps.

"Oh my God, Ajay, you're *right*," said Will. "That's Mr. Hobbes."

"That's what I was hoping you'd say," said Ajay. "I'd only seen him on Ronnie's video that one time so I didn't want to lead you to it. That is him, isn't it?"

"Yes, this is Hobbes, I'd swear it. He's got hair here, and he's younger obviously." Will scrutinized Hobbes through the magnifying glass. "But not *that* much younger."

"I couldn't help but notice that as well," said Ajay, folding his arms. "So let's ask ourselves, my friend: How is that possible? This picture was taken over eighty-five years ago."

"You remember what he looked like when I saw him through the dark glasses Dave gave me," said Will.

"Of course I do: solid bony exoskeleton, red eyes, like a reptile covered with human skin," whispered Ajay, recoiling from the memory. "Even if I *could* forget details, those aren't the sort of details one forgets."

"He isn't human. Not completely, anyway."

"He'd have to be well over a hundred by now, which should disqualify him for any physical activity more vigorous than shuffleboard."

"Hobbes is some kind of hybrid from the Never-Was. Normal human limits don't apply to him."

Ajay gripped Will's arm. "Now you see why I'm so excited? This is the hard evidence we've been looking for, a connection between the Black Caps and the Knights. Hobbes is *both*."

"So Hobbes was a student at the Center, a senior in 1937, and a member of the Knights," said Will, looking at the photo thoughtfully.

"Which means I should be able to cross-reference his image with existing school records and find out his real name," said Ajay excitedly. "Surely they can't have erased *all* traces of him as a student. And once we have a name, that may lead us to everything else we need to know. . . ."

As Ajay was talking, Will noticed something even stranger in the picture. Ajay must have seen the astonishment on his face.

"What is it, Will?"

Will recognized a *second* student in the photograph, seated across the table from Hobbes. Staring straight into the camera, like the others, raising his glass and grinning. Grabbing the magnifying glass, Will looked closer, and the closer he looked the more certain he became. The photo had been taken before he'd been changed or altered into the twisted, miserable wretch they knew now, but it was him, no doubt about it.

"Hold on to your *huevos rancheros,* Ajay," said Will, then pointed to the other student and held the magnifying glass over him. "We know this guy, too."

Ajay leaned in for a look and then looked at Will, with his eyes open wide, and they both knew he was right.

The second student was the men's locker room attendant:

Happy Jolly Nepsted.

"We need to talk to that man," said Ajay.

#29: YOU COULD ALSO THINK OF COINCIDENCE
AS SYNCHRONICITY.

"We need to find Nick," said Will.

"So what do we think this means?" asked Ajay anxiously, struggling to keep up with Will.

"It means my instincts about Nepsted were right all along,"

said Will, keeping his voice down. "He knows a whole lot more about this place than he says he does—it means he knows who *Hobbes* is, for starters, and that's the biggest break we've had."

They were hustling through the quad, heading toward the field house, where Nick had returned their call to say he was finishing a workout. The campus thrummed with early-evening activity, everyone animated by the summer weather and flushed with end-of-the-school-year fever. Flocks of parents had descended for graduation or to pick up their kids for the summer. Will and Ajay kept their heads down and avoided any eye contact.

"I'm with you, but this is too important to accept without applying anything less than the most exacting standards of inquiry," said Ajay quietly. "For instance, shouldn't we consider that this might be one of Nepsted's ancestors in the photo? Because, like Hobbes, whoever that is would have to be at least a hundred years old by now as well."

"I can't tell you why I'm sure it's him, Ajay. It's more than just what he looks like. It's the look in his eyes," said Will. "And the first time I ever talked to him he said something curious: 'I'm older than I look.'"

Ajay almost moaned. "And it's been so agreeable around here lately. No paranormal calamities, nothing going bump around campus in the night. I'd almost convinced myself we were just normal kids enjoying high school."

"Come on, what fun would that be?"

"Easy for you to say. My palms are sweating and I have that shaky feeling all through my knees and quadriceps again," said Ajay, rubbing his hands on his shirt. "Even my breathing is starting to constrict. I feel I could black out at any moment."

"You just need to burn off some adrenaline," said Will. "Let's run."

As they cleared the crowded quad, Will broke into a trot and Ajay fell in alongside him. "Of course, this wretched timing makes sense. I met the most fantastic girl recently, and I was just beginning to think that she might find me equally interesting."

"Why haven't I heard about this?" asked Will.

"You know I don't like to put my carts in front of my horses, Will. I prefer to lie in wait, an enigma, ever so patiently. Let her grow to believe I'm difficult to reach and deeply mysterious, and then, once she's ripe for the plucking, strike like a cobra."

Will glanced sideways at him. "So she won't talk to you, huh?"

"Wrong, wrong, one hundred percent wrong," said Ajay, offended. "We're exceedingly friendly, and there's little doubt in my mind that we're also one hundred percent pheromone-ally compatible."

"So what's the holdup?"

"I'm still in the intelligence-gathering phase. A wise general plans his campaigns with the utmost care before committing any resources."

"I don't know how to break it to you, Ajay, but advice from Sun Tzu is not going to help you with romance."

"I respectfully disagree," sniffed Ajay.

"Yeah, well, for one thing, Napoleon, your timing stinks. You're about to not see her for three months."

"Ah, but you see, that's where you're wrong, oh ignorant one. She's interning at the science lab during summer school, just as I am."

"Perhaps I underestimated you, Mr. Bond," said Will as they approached the field house. "So who's the target of 'Operation Mongoose'? What's her name?"

"Robyn Banks, from Cincinnati, Ohio. She'll be a sophomore this fall."

"At least you know her parents have a sense of humor," said Will, opening the door for Ajay.

"Whatever do you mean, old boy?"

"Maybe they're related to John Dillinger," said Will, and then, seeing that Ajay still didn't get it, "Robbin' banks?"

"Oh," said Ajay, and then he stopped to think about it. "*Oh.*"

Nick, showing off when he saw two friends enter the gymnastics room, ended his workout on the high bar with a quadruple somersault dismount onto a nearby pommel horse, where he landed on his hands. Then he backflipped off the horse onto a nearby springboard, tumbled twice in the air, and stuck a landing in a *ta-da!* posture right in front of them. The burly, compact, crew-cut blond looked even more pumped than usual.

"Hope you brought me my postworkout snack," said Nick, eyeing Ajay's backpack.

"No, but you just received a nine-point-four from the Martian judge," said Ajay, tossing him a towel.

"Take a look at this," said Will, handing Nick the photograph.

"Whoa," said Nick, glancing at it. "That is a *really* antique snap. You know I never really got how you can take a picture in black and white. I mean it's not like *real life* is in black and white, right? So what is the camera *not seeing*?"

Ajay and Will looked at each other with familiar dismay.

Ajay just shook his head. "Look at the *people* in the photograph, you ape," he said.

After Nick drew a blank, Will pointed directly at Nepsted. "Look at this guy and tell us what you see."

Nick looked closer at it, opening wide and then scrunching up his eyes, while he made a variety of halting sounds, his mind sputtering like a balky outboard engine.

"First time with the new mouth, Nick?" asked Ajay.

Nick jumped to his feet and paced: "Wait a second, don't tell me—dang, I know I know that dude. I've seen him before."

"Yes, you have," said Will. "More than a few times—"

"Got it! Suh-napp!" Nick snapped his fingers and slapped the picture with the back of his hand. "Dude looks *exactly* like this midget wrestler on TV. Actually, little dude's not a wrestler, exactly. He's more like a *gangster-manager* for *another* wrestler, one of the heavyweight dudes who's—air quotes—World Champion, but like the *bad* guy World Champion—they call them *heels*—who's always attackin' and ambushin' the *good* guy World Champion—they call them *baby faces* if you can believe that. I know, strange, right?"

"Are you finished hallucinating yet?" asked Ajay.

"But this little guy wrestles sometimes, too," said Nick, toweling off. "During their sneak attacks. He's got some wicked moves and he's pretty buff for a smallish dude and I'm telling you, this is a dead ringer for—"

"It's *Nepsted*, Nick," said Will, a little sharper than he'd intended.

Nick stared at him, then looked at the photo again. "No way. When was this taken?"

"In 1937," said Ajay. "Somewhere on campus."

"So maybe this is Nepsted's grandpa, or great grandpappy," said Nick.

"Nick, we're pretty sure this is Nepsted *himself*," said Will.

Nick paused, mouth hanging open, then said calmly, "Yeah, I'll go with that."

"And we believe that this other gentleman at the table," said

Ajay, pointing him out in the picture, "is Will's relentless pursuer, Mr. Hobbes."

"Dude, you mean Bonehead? Hold on, hold on," said Nick, putting his hands on either side of his head. "Wait, wait, dudes, oh my God, this could mean that . . . Bonehead and Nepsted *know* each other?"

"Okay, you're all caught up now," said Will, glancing at Ajay.

"This is big. This is unbelievable. This thing is TIGHT." Nick paced around, thinking. "And it means midget *wrestler* dude could be *Nepsted's* great-grandson."

"Remind me why we needed to find Nick again," said Ajay, clamping both hands to his forehead like he was holding back a migraine.

"The squid," said Will.

"Right," said Ajay.

"What squid?" asked Nick.

"*Your* squid. When you got attacked by the *paladin* statue," said Will, taking Nick by the shoulders and forcing him to stand still. "Last fall, down in the locker room, when the *bear* helped you."

"Dude, you expect me to forget a thing like that?" asked Nick, pulling away and putting on his sweatshirt.

"Sit down for a second, Nick," said Will, guiding him onto a bench.

"What are you going to do, hypnotize me?" asked Nick, chuckling until he saw the look on their faces.

"No, that requires a subject with at least a lower primate's level of intelligence," said Ajay.

"I want you to remember another part of this. Think back now," said Will softly. "You told us that when the bear ran off and the statue fell apart . . . a giant squid started talking to you."

"Did I say that? I did, didn't I? Okay. Right. Only it wasn't with words. It was more like thoughts that went right into my *head*, and I'm not really sure this thing was exactly a squid—"

"Maybe it was a rabid woodchuck," said Ajay.

"No, that wasn't it," said Nick, with a faraway look in his eye, moving his arms as he relived it. "It was more like a thousand long pasty dreadlocks came to life underwater, each with a mind of their own, waving around in the air like . . . living underwater dreadlocks . . . and I think they're what killed the statue."

"How?" asked Will.

"By squeezing it to death," said Nick, squinting. "Which, by the way, saved yours truly's bacon, lettuce, and tomato. And then all these little ropy dreadlock dudes handed me the phone, and I think they dialed it for me, too. By which time I was totally messed up."

"You don't say," said Ajay.

"Which phone?" asked Will.

"The one on the counter," said Nick. "Outside the cage."

"Nepsted's cage?"

Nick nodded. "And when I say *dialed,* I mean they only had to push the big C in the middle."

"And where did the dreadlocks come from?" asked Will.

"From behind the cage or . . . *through* the cage," said Nick, and then he gasped. "Wait, so you're saying that if Hobbes is Mr. Bonehead . . . and he's in this picture with Nepsted . . . then Nepsted could be *Mutant Squid-Dude?*"

"Something like that," said Will.

"Awesome," said Nick, grabbing the photograph and heading for the door. "I am all over this."

* * *

They followed Nick downstairs to the vast locker room, nearly empty now that the day was done. Will and Ajay hung back around the nearest corner as Nick approached Nepsted's equipment cage alone.

"Are we absolutely sure letting him handle this is a good idea?" whispered Ajay.

"No," whispered Will.

"And the argument in favor?"

"If Nick really did see Nepsted in Beast Mode, he should be the one to bring it up. Nepsted spooks easily. Better not to confront him with all three of us at once."

Ajay whispered back, "If Nepsted leads us to Hobbes, we can't complain about style points. And Nick is occasionally capable of a certain . . . persuasiveness."

Will remembered something else Nepsted said to him the first time they met:

I'm the guy with the keys.

Will peeked around the corner and watched Nick bang the bell on the steel counter a few times. "Yo, Nepsted! Need a minute of your time, dude!"

After a few moments, Nepsted's squeaky motorized wheelchair rounded a corner into view inside the cage and glided past the deep rows of sports equipment on his side of the counter. His stunted body and withered limbs made him look like an eight-year-old with an adult's head. His hands were the only other grown-up-sized part of him, and his right one, looking surprisingly powerful, gripped the joystick that drove his chair.

"Don't tell me, McLeish," said Nepsted in his high-pitched, wobbly voice. "You trashed another pair of sweatpants."

"I'm not gonna lie to you, man," said Nick, leaning on the

counter and looking him in the eye. "I'm here 'cause I need to talk to you about what went down in this room with us last fall."

"No idea what you're talking about—"

"The rumble in the shower that ended up in here? The details were a tad fuzzy for me when it went down. Multiple blows to the head, massive concussion, right? All I could remember was that the *statue* dude drove the *bear* dude away and it was just about to punch my ticket . . . when some *other* dude came right through this cage and saved my life."

Nepsted's large unblinking eyes widened slightly but betrayed no other reaction.

"How or why this whole deal happened I can't explain," said Nick, leaning in and lowering his voice. "But as more details come back to me, you and I need to chat about it."

"Why should I?"

"'Cause I think you're the only dude who can answer this question: like, dude, WTF, tentacles? I mean, that was you, right? As in, you're the only dude back there."

The left side of Nepsted's face twitched a couple of times, like he was struggling to decide how to respond. Then he nodded, ever so slightly.

"So why'd you stick your neck out like that to help me? Or whatever parts of you that *was* that you stuck out?"

Nepsted still didn't answer.

"Take your time," said Nick. "I'm hanging out all summer. I'll camp right here in front of your cage until you feel like talking."

"I *can't*," said Nepsted in a strangled voice.

"That answer is clown shoes, dude—"

"You don't know what you're playing with!" said Nepsted fiercely.

Nick tried to keep him calm. "Dude, whatever happened, whatever went down around this, whatever kind of trouble you might be in, I promise we can help you."

"WE? Who's WE???!!!"

Nick didn't answer but Nepsted saw him glance ever so slightly over his shoulder.

"You're not alone out there, are you? Who's with you? Who is it? COME OUT SO I CAN SEE YOU!"

Will and Ajay exchanged a worried glance.

"Show yourselves right now, you cowards, or I'll never say one word to ANY of you!" shouted Nepsted.

Will nodded, and then he and Ajay walked around the corner into view.

"West!" snarled Nepsted. "I should have known he'd put you up to this, McLeish. You haven't got the *brains*—"

"You can shout at us all you like, Happy," said Will, sliding in front of Nick. "That's not going to change the fact that we know what we know—"

"You don't know ANYTHING!"

"We know this much," said Will.

He held up the black-and-white photograph close to the cage. When Nepsted saw it in Will's hand, he went completely still, his eyes fixed on the picture.

"We know, for instance, that this is *you*," said Will, pointing to Nepsted in the photo. "And this was taken at the school, so we know you were a student here."

Nepsted only blinked at him.

Then Will pointed to Hobbes in the photo.

"We also know that, just last year, this guy right here—who should be in a *graveyard* by now—terrorized my parents and tried to kidnap me by impersonating a federal officer. For all we know, he might even *be* a federal officer. And you know who he is because you were in the Knights of Charlemagne with him. *In 1937.*"

Nepsted seemed genuinely stunned, staring at Will with his eyes stuck wide open.

"What's this creep's real name, Happy? Tell me who he is, how to find him, and what the hell happened to the two of you?"

Nepsted balled his strong right hand into a fist and banged it down hard on the arm of his wheelchair. On impact, for a brief second, Will thought he saw the fibers and muscles and bones of Nepsted's hand pulsate apart into a hundred separate strands before they coalesced back into solid flesh. Will glanced around and realized that Nick and Ajay saw it, too. When their eyes widened, Nepsted seemed to realize they'd seen it happen and pulled his hand back, covering it with his left.

"I can't tell you anything. You don't even know the kind of trouble you're in—"

"You've got that turned around, Happy," said Will, making an effort to sound calm. "You always try to come off as spooky or mysterious, but here's what's changed—after what I've been through, you can't scare me anymore."

Nepsted gave an abbreviated, heaving sigh that Will thought might have been a sob.

"What did they do to you?" asked Will quietly. "Did it have anything to do with something called the Paladin Prophecy?"

Nepsted put his face in his hands and now the sobs came one after another. *Now's my chance.* Will moved closer to the cage, signaling the others to stay quiet.

"What's your real name, Happy?" asked Will softly.

"Raymond," he whispered, barely moving his lips. "That is, I used to be . . . Raymond Llewelyn."

"What year were you born?" asked Will.

Nepsted looked up at him, tears streaming down his face. "You wouldn't believe me."

"Try me," said Will.

"In 1919," he said.

Ajay saw Nick trying to silently do the math and nudged him with an elbow.

"Raymond, I'm only going to ask you this once," said Will gently, "and I'll assume you know what I'm talking about: Whose side are you on?"

Nepsted looked almost disappointed at the question. "Yours," he whispered.

"Good to know," said Will.

He glanced back at the others, trying to hide his surprise at how unexpectedly easy this had seemed so far. Ajay gestured, urging him to keep pressing their case.

"Raymond," said Will. "We have a lot more questions, about Hobbes and the Knights and the Prophecy, and unless you tell us *everything*, we'll have to go to the headmaster and the police and anybody else who'll listen—"

"And that would be the last mistake you ever make," he said, all the fight gone from his voice.

Will held his eyes, softening his tone to sympathy. "Then I guess you're just going to have to help us."

Nepsted turned away and grew restless, rocking from side to side in his chair like a trapped and wounded animal. He made small snorting and clicking noises and random parts of his body bulged alarmingly out of his skin.

"Uh-oh," said Nick from the corner of his mouth. "Squid alert."

Thin tendrils of pale flesh threaded out from Nepsted's sleeves and collar, lashing around anxiously, grabbing at equipment on the shelves behind him and objects on the counter in front of him and yanking them to the ground.

"Dear gussie," said Ajay, taking a big step back. "We should have brought a tranquilizer gun."

"Raymond," said Will firmly, banging his hands on the cage. "Raymond, look at me. Look at me *right now*."

Nepsted looked up and met his eyes, looking lost, frightened, and hopeless. Will focused and gently pushed a thought picture at him—an image of a lake, clouds, and blue sky—trying to calm him down. Within moments, Nepsted stopped rocking, tendrils retracted, and his body settled back into a solid mass.

"Tell me what we can do," said Will, lowering his voice. "You helped Nick last year and that goes a long way toward helping us believe you're on our side. If that's true, we need to help each other."

Nepsted didn't respond, frozen with fear. Nick then walked past Will to the cage and put his hands up to show he meant no harm.

"You're a prisoner in here, aren't you, Raymond?" asked Nick with surprising sympathy.

Nepsted seemed to shrink down even farther into his chair. All the defiance was now gone from his eyes. He nodded.

"You saved my life here, man," said Nick simply. "You tell us how we can help you, any way at all, and we'll do it."

Tears rolled out of Nepsted's eyes. He made no move to hide them or wipe them away, and this time he didn't look away. Tendrils thrust out of his right hand, snaked out of the cage, and wrapped around Nick's hand. Nick held on to them, even though Will could see it was creeping him out.

"I need the key," said Nepsted in a tiny voice.

"Which key?" asked Will. "The key to what?"

The thin white tendrils crept down and grabbed the massive lock on the outside of the door, holding it up so they could see it.

A long-hasped, heavy-duty security model, to be sure, but far from indestructible.

Acting on instinct, Will took out the special dark glasses Dave had given him when they first met that allowed him to see creatures and objects from the Never-Was. During the winter, Ajay had cut the original lenses down and refitted them into black metal frames the size of small, retro-nerd granny glasses, then used the glass that was left over to make two identical pairs that Will gave to his friends.

Taking their cue from Will, Nick and Ajay put on their dark glasses as well, and all three of them leaned down for a closer look at the lock on Nepsted's equipment cage.

Which now appeared to be like no lock any of them had ever seen, as big as a man's fist, with shifting, multilayered plates of impregnable steel wrapped around a central column that looked like it was fashioned from a solid cylindrical diamond, with no visible keyhole or combination wheel. The whole thing pulsated with some kind of faintly green toxic energy.

"Damn," said Will.

"What kind of lock is *that*?" asked Nick.

"Unless I very much miss my guess," whispered Ajay, sounding a little shaken, "one built by the Other Team . . . with their mysterious and otherworldly aphotic technology."

"And where are we supposed to look for this key?" asked Will, turning back to Nepsted.

"Down deep," said Nepsted, his voice like sandpaper.

"Like, in the tunnels?" asked Nick.

"Deeper. Much deeper. In the cavern at the bottom of the stairs. They used to keep it in the hospital . . . but you can only get to it by going down through the old cathedral." Nepsted slumped over, drained of energy.

"I'm not sure we know what you're talking about—" said Will, glancing at the others.

"That is me in the picture," said Nepsted, tapping it with a tendril. "And you're right about the . . . other student. I did—I do—know him, but I can't say anymore now. Bring me that key first . . . and I'll tell you everything. . . ."

Will turned to look at Nepsted and saw him for the first time through Dave's glasses. The poor pathetic creature that inhabited the chair nearly broke his heart. Raymond Llewelyn was nothing more than a slack lump of pale, shapeless flesh with half-formed limbs, slumped in his chair like a malformed starfish. Nepsted's unmistakable eyes sunk into a melted set of features that passed for a face.

Will quickly took the glasses off, but not before Nepsted caught his gaze and Will sensed that Nepsted knew what they'd seen. He wheeled his chair around and headed toward the back. The overhead lights in the cage blinked off behind him as he went, one by one, until Nepsted disappeared in the gloom.

The boys waited silently until he was gone. Ajay and Nick took off their glasses; Will knew they'd seen the real Nepsted, too.

"What a splendid way to kick off summer vacation," said Ajay.

"That poor bastard," said Nick, shaken to his core. "Did you see that . . . that . . . what he looked like?"

"We saw him, Nick," said Ajay.

"Damn it, what the hell, who did that to him?"

"We can talk about that later, but not here," said Will quietly. "Come with me."

He led them straight to the door in the locker room that used to lead to the auxiliary locker room and the tunnels.

"We need to take another look in here," said Will.

Nick tried the door. Locked. He punched it in frustration.

"Nick, you have our permission to open it," said Will.

Nick whirled and roundhouse kicked it, and the door nearly flew off its hinges.

"Ajay, check the walls. Is there any way we can get through them?" asked Will.

Ajay examined the walls in the broom closet with a device he took from his pocket.

"Solid concrete, sealed off in all directions," said Ajay. "Not a chance, Will."

"Then we'll have to take the other way into the tunnels," said Will.

"From the *island* in Lake Waukoma?" asked Ajay, his eyes widening in alarm. "Will, the last time nearly finished us."

"Dude, Raymond knew Hobbes. They were both in the Knights and he'll tell us the rest if we find that key—"

"Honestly, tunnels, hospitals, old cathedrals, it could be a bunch of malarkey," said Ajay.

"It's all we've got to go on," said Will. "We need to bring the girls up to speed and get their help. We all need to stick around this summer."

Nick raised both hands in frustration and slammed one palm against the broken door, denting the metal.

"Aw, donuts! You freakin' chowder head."

"What's wrong?" asked Ajay.

"I forgot to ask Nepsted about the little *wrestler*," said Nick.

WILL AND ELISE
AND BROOKE

Elise had seemed less affected by the harsh ordeal they'd been through last fall than anyone, but Will knew it was also in her nature to show less than she felt. Elise was all tensile steel inside, not unlike Will.

Not so their fifth roommate: After the incident, Brooke Springer, the victim of the Knights' kidnapping plot who'd suffered the most, had remained at home in Virginia through the holidays and for a month afterward. When she finally rejoined her roommates at the end of January, Brooke had changed. She was subdued and withdrawn, and she'd stayed that way since, never divulging how she really felt.

Elise became convinced Brooke was struggling with the shadows of post-traumatic stress disorder. She'd never told anyone what Lyle had done to her, but Will knew, at the very least, she'd been terrorized by the creep. Whatever dark memories of that day were haunting Brooke, since returning she'd been nothing like her usual bantering, efficient self.

The way she kissed me before she left for Christmas. The way she whispered in my ear: "Don't let an hour go by without letting me know how you are." Then not a word for six weeks. Never answering my calls, emails, or texts. Could that spark have died so quickly? What other answer is there? Since she came back, she treats me like a stranger. The only comfort is she treats all of us that way. But what am I supposed to think?

Either she's not emotionally available, or she's no longer interested. Either totally sucked. To get him through, Will leaned heavily into . . .

#58: FACING THE TRUTH IS A LOT EASIER, IN THE LONG RUN, THAN LYING TO YOURSELF.

So, for the rest of the winter and into spring, Will had offered Brooke his (polite, painfully wimpish roommate-level) friendship and support while she remained maddeningly, mysteriously remote. They almost never found themselves alone together, and if they did Brooke quickly found a reason to leave the room. If he was ever going to break the ice, he'd decided he needed Elise's help.

It was nearing sunset when Will found Elise where he'd predicted, at the piano in one of the practice rooms in Bledsoe Hall. As he walked in, she was playing something jazzy and incredibly complicated with her back to the door.

"Wait till I'm done, West," she said before he could speak.

She didn't miss a note, hunched over, hands flying across the keyboard so quickly he couldn't see them touch the keys until she finished the piece with a theatrical flourish.

Bravo, he thought, pushing an image of a standing ovation toward her. Without turning, Elise bowed with just one arm, like medieval musical royalty.

You are too kind, my liege, she replied, her voice sliding smoothly into his head.

"Nine-thirty on the last night of term," said Will. "Figures I'd find you hard at work."

"Where else would you expect me to be? At the Bonfire of the Swizzle Sticks, singing fight songs with the rest of the J.Crew lug nuts?"

Elise spun around on her bench. Wearing a miniskirt and flats, she crossed her slender legs, cocked her head sideways—her shiny black curtain of hair shimmering in the light—and stared at him with her X-ray green eyes.

A shiver ran up Will's spine. Not an unpleasant shiver, but a shiver nonetheless.

You know something, she said, inside his head again. *What is it?*

Their uncanny ability to speak to each other silently had grown so reliable over the winter that it rarely surprised Will anymore. They'd worked during the last few months on finding the maximum range they could reach across—about fifty yards in most cases—and still make their communication flow smoothly.

At a distance, they'd discovered that using pictures—as Will had learned when he first discovered this ability as a kid—often worked better and more efficiently than words. They'd also learned that, for some reason, sending thoughts that created intense emotion supercharged their connection, making thoughts a lot easier to send and receive.

They'd even spelled out a code of "unspoken" etiquette about their interactions, promising to respect each other's privacy. After an initial "send," the other had to respond in kind before they dove deeper into the other's thought stream. And if either of them preferred not to open up in the moment, all they had to do was answer out loud.

"I hope you haven't finalized your plans for the summer," said Will, out loud.

"My dad's trying to book me a gig on a cruise ship. Is that depressing enough for you?" she asked.

"Yes."

"Wait, it gets worse. Playing seventies cocktail lounge easy-listening top forty for vacationing upper-middle-class baby boomers. They're retired, put out to pasture, watching the glaciers melt from a lame cruise ship like it's some kind of halftime show, and this freakin' generation still refuses to believe they're not the center of the universe."

Will grimaced at the thought. "You're not seriously considering this."

"Nah, I told him I'm holding out for a better offer," she said, playing some dissonant chords. "Mucking out the stables of hell."

"Don't you have other options?"

"Sure. Teaching music to day camp first graders in Seattle for a fraction of the cruise ship scratch. During the course of which I might even learn the top ten ways to remove snot from a flutophone." She played an off-key child's ditty with one hand. "Or I could just drown myself in a swamp."

"What if you just stayed here?" asked Will, trying to sound offhand.

"At the Center? And pay for it how? My parents can barely afford the regular year, let alone summer school—" She stopped playing, turned to him, on alert, and sent a thought request: *Why are you asking?*

Will moved closer, as if someone else might overhear his thoughts, and sent her a compressed mental download of their conversation with Nepsted about Hobbes, the Paladins, and the old photograph. Her eyes closed as she processed it, and when she opened them they lit up.

"This . . . is . . . a *game* changer," she said, as close to awed as Will had ever heard her.

"We're on the same page about that," said Will.

"So what's the plan, Stan?"

"We're staying on campus. Nepsted gave us a lead on the

key to his cage, in the tunnels below the Crag. If we find it, he says he'll tell us everything he knows about the Knights and the Prophecy—and he knows a crap-ton."

Elise gripped his arms and got right in Will's face, her etched eyebrows arched high with excitement. "Listen. I will waitress at a Waffle House or sing happy-hour show tunes at a trailer park rest home, but I promise you I will figure out some way to bank staying here, because you knuckleheads are not going down there this time without me."

"I was hoping you'd say that," said Will with a grin.

"I've been waiting *since Christmas* for this," she said.

Elise leaned in, grabbed Will's face, and kissed him, then leaned back a few inches to gauge his reaction with a sly smile.

"Waiting for what?" asked Will. "To kiss me?"

"For us to get off our butts and put the hurt on these weasels. But you're our leader, right? We figured you needed time to grieve, so none of us wanted to push you. But if you're ready, if you're really ready, then we are with you all the way."

"That's so great," said Will, still holding on to her, their faces inches from each other.

"And, yes, I've been waiting to kiss you, bozo, since you always seemed too paralyzed to bust the first move. "

Will cleared his throat, trying his best not to look or sound awkward. "Okay, then. Uh, so what about Brooke?"

"Really, West? You're going to ask me about Brooke right now? During this intimate thing we're having here?"

"Well, no. First I was going to do this," he said, and kissed her back.

Elise cleared her throat and held up a finger. Her forehead wrinkled, as if slightly puzzled; then she finally opened her eyes.

"Okay, then," she said, and then smiled brightly, as if her

short-term memory had been wiped clean. "What did you want to ask me?"

"Do you think Brooke will stick around this summer and help us?"

"After a kiss like that, mister, you can ask Brooke about that itsy-bitsy detail yourself."

"No joke, Elise, I really need your help. You're closer to her than I am, and she's been avoiding me like I've got Dengue fever."

Elise growled at him, but he could tell she'd do it. Will squeezed her hand and headed for the door.

"You think we can pull this off, West?" asked Elise. "Just the five of us?"

"Hey, it's not like we're your average Breakfast Club," said Will, reaching for the door. "And, between you and me, I've been practicing."

"So have I," said Elise, raising an eyebrow.

With that, she shot an image into his mind. Will staggered momentarily, then looked at her in amazement.

"Now *that*," he said, "I've got to see."

As Will headed back across campus, he realized Elise was right about this much: He *had* been grieving in the months since the accident, but not in any conventional way. He had every reason to believe that his dad, at least, was alive, but he'd never told anyone—not even his roommates—about the text he'd received from Jordan West after the plane went down. He was too frightened that giving voice to that hope might jinx it.

"*Grief is a doorway through which we pass to realize that the sun is always shining.*"

That was the only thing Ira Jericho had ever said on the

subject of his parents' disappearance, and now that he'd snapped out of his dazed state, Will realized he'd been grieving for a way of life that had been lost forever—the blissfully ignorant existence he'd lived before black cars and dead chopper pilots and discovering the elaborate fictions his parents had built around their family. In spite of their lies, he still *missed* them like a phantom limb. All he had left of his fifteen years with them was a single photograph from their wedding and Dad's Book of Rules.

What if my parents were somehow involved with the Paladin Prophecy? How can I miss them so much if I never really knew who they were?

Will's school pager buzzed in his pocket. Someone on campus was trying to reach him on the Center's centralized phone system. He ducked into the nearest building and picked up one of the omnipresent black courtesy phones in the lobby.

"This is Will," he said.

"One moment, Mr. West," said one of the cheerful, ever-present female operators.

Will heard the call get connected.

"Meet me behind Cumberland Hall," said the voice, almost in a whisper. "Five minutes."

Will hung up.

Brooke.

The first words she'd spoken to him in over a month. The first sign she wanted to speak to him in almost half a year. Will felt his heart bonk around in his chest like a pinball.

What did she want?

Cumberland Hall was on the other side of the campus, a small building directly behind the campus's physical services complex. Will turned on the jets and arrived there in two minutes.

* * *

The last glimmers of sunset still filled the western sky. Brooke was already waiting for him behind the building, visible in a soft slice of light from a streetlamp on the corner, highlighting her cameo-perfect profile. She turned when she heard him take in a sharp breath of air. She held out her arms and wrapped herself around him.

It was the first time she'd touched him since December.

She felt soft and warm, and the clean scent of her shampoo—hints of citrus and freshly mown grass—made Will a little dizzy.

"I'm so sorry," she whispered.

"About what?"

"They made me do it, Will. They made me promise not to get involved with you."

"Who did?" asked Will.

"My *parents*," she said, pulling back so she could look him in the eye.

"How?"

"When I was home over the holidays. It ended up being impossible not to tell them how I felt about you, or I guess I couldn't hide it. Besides, they somehow already knew all the details, from the school I assume, and they sat me down and told me they'd decided I shouldn't see you anymore, because of what you'd just been through."

"They decided? Why?"

"They thought you'd be too damaged or unstable emotionally or, to be kinder to them, that we couldn't possibly start any kind of healthy relationship given what you were going through."

Will struggled to take all this in and make sense of it. "Do you always do what your parents tell you to?"

"You don't know him, Will. My father's an *ambassador*, for God's sake. He's a force of nature. They weren't going to even let me come back to the school at all unless I promised. I couldn't stand the thought of never seeing you again, so I went along with it."

"Why wait until now to tell me?"

"Because they have people watching me here. All the time."

Will felt a surge of anger go through him and knew she sensed the tension in his body. "You mean like right now?"

"Right now I don't care if we're onstage at Carnegie Hall," she said. "I just want to do what I've been dying to do for the last six months."

She stood up on her toes and kissed him, and he forgot most of his objections in a heartbeat. Then she hugged him fiercely again.

"I was wrong to go along with it," she whispered in his ear. "I was frightened and so horribly worried about you and I hate myself as a coward for letting them talk me into turning away from you."

And your timing is unbelievable, thought Will, the kisses he'd just shared with Elise still burning a hole in his brain. But it wasn't as if what he felt with either girl was canceling out the other; they were both generating a storm in his circuits at the same time.

"I'm really glad to hear you say that," said Will, wanting to believe her. "So why did you tell me now?"

"Because I simply couldn't stand the idea of not seeing you for another three months without letting you know all this. I wouldn't have been able to live with myself."

"Where are you spending the summer?"

"Here and there, Europe, traveling a lot—"

"Hold it right there," he said, taking her firmly by the arms. "Look, I haven't exactly been myself the last few months, either."

"But that's to be expected, Will, after what you've been through—"

"I know that, but it took my eyes off what really matters. What matters is going forward, finishing what we started. Finding out what's behind everything that's happened here. To us. To all of us."

"I agree with you," she said, looking up at him, her eyes shining in the light.

Believing in me, he thought.

"Brooke, we just broke through on something," he said. "A big new discovery that changes the whole picture and we're going after it. All of us. We're staying here over the summer and we want you to stay with us if you can figure out a way. We need your help."

She looked up at him, her eyes shining brightly in the pale light. "You really want me to? After the way I've treated you?"

"Yes! Of course we do. I do. Want you to."

God, could she hear how awkward that was?

"I'm so happy to hear you say that," she said, and hugged him again. "I can't promise it's going to be easy, nothing ever is with my parents, but I'll do the best I can to work it out."

"Good."

She held him at arm's length for a moment, looking tense and serious. "They're also not done trying to keep us apart."

"How?" asked Will.

"Insisting that I transfer to another pod in the fall—"

"You can't let them do that."

"But this might work for us. If I agree to do that now, I can buy some time, come back to campus for a few weeks this summer. I can be pretty persuasive, too."

Tell me about it.

She was about to kiss him again when from behind them came the crash of breaking glass. Will spun around and saw a window blow out a few stories up in the tall building behind them. A security alarm immediately sounded somewhere inside.

"What the hell—" said Will.

Instinctively, he pulled Brooke into the darkness against the ivy-covered hall behind them.

The air around them grew hushed—Will realized that even the crickets in the area had suddenly gone dead quiet—and he sensed an unsettling presence disrupting the air somewhere near them in the night. Brooke was about to speak when Will put a finger to her lips.

A shadow appeared, curling around the side of the building, distorted by the streetlamp. It kept growing until it looked impossibly tall and then stopped. It was the silhouette of a human figure, wrapped in a long coat or cloak. Its head swiveled slightly, almost mechanically, looking around, or maybe *sniffing* the air.

I know who that is, thought Will. *But it can't be. It's not possible.*

In the distance they heard at least two sirens approaching and the rumble of voices gathering nearby. Lights came on in windows on either side of where the crash had occurred and security lights around the base of the building lit up the elongated face of the glass and steel tower. Will realized they were looking at the medical center.

Will leaned out slightly to chance a look. All he saw was a glimpse of light fabric flapping in its wake as the figure slipped quickly and silently away; when he stepped out to catch a better glimpse, it had disappeared into the night.

"What the hell was that?" asked Brooke.

"Do you know the people who've been watching you?" asked Will.

"A team of three who work for my father. Professionals. You hardly even see them."

"For *real*?"

"I told you, the ambassador does not mess around," she said.

"Could that have been one of them?"

"Not a chance," she said. "They get paid for *not* being noticed, but I'm sure I got out this time without their seeing me."

The commotion continued to grow nearby on the ground, attracting an even bigger crowd. Above them, security people appeared in the gaping hole in the face of the medical building, looking down.

"We'd better get you out of here," said Will.

"We shouldn't be seen together. Let's talk back at the pod."

She started away, but Will caught her arm. "After that I don't think you should be walking around by yourself right now."

"Don't worry. Once they hear that alarm, my minders will be all over me," she said, then lifted up a small black device. "Besides, I just paged them."

Brooke kissed him again, which nearly knocked him over, and then stole off toward the lights in the center of campus. Will headed straight for the medical center. He saw a lot of debris scattered below the hole above—glass, metal framing, even some rebar. An entire double window had blown out along with a sizeable chunk of wall on either side of it. A group of the Center's Samoan security guards were already putting up a perimeter around the front entrance, ushering curious students to the other side of the barriers.

Will spotted his friend Eloni among them, the biggest in the group and the squad's senior officer. As he approached, Will exchanged a glance with him, asking if he could duck inside before they locked down the building. Eloni subtly waved him into the lobby.

Inside, the tumult and confusion were even greater, with equal numbers of medical and security personnel rushing in and out. Will kept to the back of the room, slipped into the nearest stairwell, and dashed up to the fourth floor, where the crash had come from.

He'd never been on this level before; the door was secured with heavy-duty locks and thick wire-reinforced glass in the small slit window. He ducked down as more security brushed past inside, then watched them go into a room about halfway down the hallway.

The room where the wall had exploded.

Will ducked again as the Center's headmaster, Stephen Rourke, came off an elevator in the hallway, flanked by Will's genetics professor, Rulan Geist, and the school's psychologist, Dr. Lillian Robbins. They headed for the same room, stopping in the doorway to survey the damage inside.

A burly security guard burst through the door and headed down the stairs. Will just had time to duck back against the wall behind the door, then reached out and hooked the closing door with his foot.

He let it land softly onto the toe of his shoe, holding it open a crack as he heard more people move by inside—Rourke muttering "Find him!" to somebody—then wedged his body closer and grabbed the door with his hand. Will listened carefully until he heard silence, then moved into the inner corridor.

This looked nothing like the rest of the medical center and more like a high-security prison. He noticed multiple security cameras overhead and he passed two other locked rooms with heavy metallic doors before he reached the open doorway.

A small sliding panel on the wall beside the door had a name written on it: L OGILVY.

Good God.

A huge, heavily mechanized hospital bed filled the center of a large square room, surrounded by monitors, gauges, and instruments scattered around it on the floor. The warm night breeze pouring in through the gap fluttered papers around. Some powerful force had bent or broken the bed's retractable sidebars. Four metallic shackles, attached high and low where a patient's arms and legs would have rested, had been shattered as well.

Cameras had been positioned in each corner, all focused on the bed. Will heard a helicopter approaching outside, and as the sweep of its eye-in-the-sky beam raked across the face of the building and into the room, he retreated back to the hall. He found himself leaning against the room's door that stood open out into the corridor. It appeared, like the others he'd passed, to be made of solid steel. The side that had faced the room was gashed and heavily dented.

Whatever had slammed through the window had tried to get out this way first.

Will heard the elevator door at the end of the corridor open. He dashed away in the other direction, pushed through a door, and launched down a flight of stairs in a single leap to the landing, where he turned the corner and jumped again to the next level. Pausing there, he called up his memory of the medical center's structure and positioned himself on its grid, then located the building's security center and plotted the best route to get there.

Two stories down, through another door, down another

corridor. When he encountered anyone, Will just put his head down and looked purposeful.

#62: IF YOU DON'T WANT PEOPLE TO NOTICE YOU, ACT LIKE YOU BELONG THERE AND LOOK BUSY.

The security center lay ahead on the right. Windows in the hallway looked in on the semicircular space, dominated by banks of monitors on a horseshoe-shaped desk. Two guards and Eloni gathered around them as another guard worked a nearby keyboard. Seeing Eloni, Will pushed through the door into the room almost without thinking because he knew what they were watching and he needed to see what was on that monitor.

It was the recorded feed from the room he'd just left. Lights in the room were low, but the video was high-quality digital that revealed lots of detail. Will entered in time to see a tall raggedy figure with long scraggly hair rip the shackle off one of its wrists.

He felt like he'd been punched in the chest. That face. The way he set his shoulders.

Lyle. Transformed. Taller, leaner, disheveled, but his body language and imperious bearing unmistakably Lyle-esque.

With another yank, the figure pulled its other arm free from the remaining shackle, then moved off camera. A moment later he heard fierce pounding on the metallic door. Then in a blur of motion, the figure formerly known as Lyle Ogilvy reappeared, rushing headlong across the room. It lowered its shoulder like a fullback and crashed into the reinforced windows. The entire section exploded outward and the figure dropped out of sight.

Eloni looked around and realized Will was standing there.

He immediately took him by the arm and walked him out the door.

"You can't be in here, Will," said Eloni urgently. "Not now. Forget you ever saw this."

"He never left," said Will in disbelief. "Lyle was here this whole time? How could nobody tell us this?"

Before Eloni could answer, they heard a mass of people heading their way from the lobby.

"Get out the side door," said Eloni. "Don't tell anyone you were here."

"Not to worry."

Will split through the door behind him just as the crowd came into sight. He thought he saw Headmaster Rourke leading the way. With his thoughts and senses in an uproar, he hurried to a side exit and made sure no one saw him steal back outside.

Almost completely dark now. Slipping on his hood, he walked quickly away from the building, and as soon as he was far enough away that no one would notice, he began to run.

He glanced at his watch: 9:14 p.m.

THE ALLIANCE REBORN

"I know we haven't talked about all this stuff for a while," said Will, pacing around. "I needed some time to get my mind around what actually happened."

"No need to explain, Will," said Ajay.

The five roommates were gathered around the dining table in the pod, each with their tablet workbooks open. It was almost eleven o'clock by the time Will could gather them all together. He'd started by showing the photo of the Knights at their 1937 dinner to the girls and outlined for Brooke the deal they'd made with Nepsted: retrieve the key that would free him, in exchange for what he knew about the Knights and the Prophecy.

"What makes you think the Knights are still active?" asked Brooke, looking uneasily at the others. "Didn't we put them out of commission?"

"That's what we thought, too, until Ajay found this." He pointed at the photograph. "But Mr. Hobbes is a Knight. And Mr. Hobbes is still out there."

"We only shut down the last twelve *student* Knights," said Ajay glumly. "There's no telling how many *alumni* members there might be."

"I think there *is* a way to know that," said Will. "We know from school records they were active until the Center shut them down just before World War Two. They could have revived the Knights at any point after that, but what if they kept it going somehow, secretly, from when the club started in the 1920s until now?"

"That would mean they've graduated twelve Knights a year for almost eighty-five years," said Ajay, doing the math.

"Dude, that's like over two hundred dudes," said Nick, his face in a knot.

"One thousand and twenty," said Ajay.

"*Way* over," said Nick.

"And they aren't necessarily all *dudes*," said Brooke.

"And by now most of them could have attained positions of power in every sector of society," Ajay said. "A network of power, wealth, and influence, united in pursuing their own secret agenda."

The entire group stayed quiet for a moment, waiting for Brooke's reaction. She didn't respond, her eyes downcast, her face hard to read.

"Give Ajay all the credit for persisting and getting to the truth behind that," said Will.

Looking at his friends' faces, Will wondered why he'd even worried about what they'd say; they were the four people he trusted most in the world. He did, however, feel completely paranoid about looking at Brooke for longer than a second while Elise had her eyes on him, remembering, *I don't have to imagine that she can read my thoughts. SHE CAN ACTUALLY READ MY THOUGHTS.*

But so far Elise didn't seem to be picking up any of the wobbly, conflicted feelings thrashing around inside him while in both their presence. They didn't even seem overly aware of each other; both, well, all four of them really, were so focused on him.

"There's more to talk about," said Will. "The other breaking news is that Lyle Ogilvy's been on campus this whole time—"

"Get out of this town!" said Ajay.

"For real," said Will. "The school and the cops had him

cooped up in some kind of secret medical lockdown unit in the medical center, and now he's on the loose—"

"*That's* who we saw?" asked Brooke, her eyes opening wide. Will nodded grimly.

"Wait, you *saw* Lyle?" asked Elise.

"A glimpse of him," said Will. "Near the medical center. He went out through the windows. From his room on the fourth floor."

Brooke drew back, wrapped her arms around herself, turning pale. "There goes six months of therapy," she said.

"Don't worry, kid," said Nick, putting an arm around her shoulder. "We're not letting that bubonic meatbag anywhere near you."

"There've been many rumors about Lyle floating around, Will," said Ajay, looking around the table. "So this is why he wasn't in the hoosegow with the rest of his hooligans."

"Dude, I'd heard Lyle had pretty much turned into a zucchini," said Nick.

"From what I saw happen to him last year, that wouldn't surprise me," said Will. "The wendigo zombified him—not an exact medical term, but I don't know how else to put it."

"So how does a 'zombie zucchini' survive a four-story drop?" asked Elise dryly.

"Good question," said Will. "I snuck in and saw a security video of him making the jump. Lyle didn't exactly . . . seem like himself."

"What does *that* mean?" asked Nick.

"He wakes from a seven-month coma," said Will, "and Lyle's first move is to smash through reinforced glass, jump fifty feet to the ground, and head out for a jog."

"Sounds like *you*," said Elise as she elbowed Nick.

"Yeah, practically my morning routine," said Nick.

"He seems even less human than before," said Will. "For instance, he got taller. By a lot."

"Okay, that's unusual," said Nick.

"So what should we do about it?" asked Ajay.

"Look, the cops are going to be all over this," said Elise, glancing at Brooke. "I don't think any of us has too much to worry about."

"But don't forget Lyle had abilities, too," said Will. "He can influence minds, attack people psychically. His powers were stronger than all of ours before he got whacked. And there's no telling what they've been jacked up into by what he's gone through since then."

Will made a mental note to ask Coach Jericho, *What happens to surviving victims of a wendigo?*

"If you're deliberately trying to freak me out," said Brooke, wrapping her arms around her drawn-up knees, "brilliant job."

"That's not what I'm trying to do—"

"You keep forgetting, Will," she continued, "I *don't* have any abilities like you all do. None I can use against the creep who kidnapped me, anyway."

"No sweat, Brooksie, we got your back," said Nick kind of tenderly, putting an arm around her.

That's what I should have said, thought Will, kicking himself. *And done.*

Then Nick spoiled it by lifting Brooke from her chair with one hand, popping a biceps, and saying, "Check those guns at the door."

Brooke swatted him away. As Nick put her back down, Will got up from the table and paced around.

"I think Elise is right," said Will. "We let the police and the school handle Lyle. Maybe that gives us the cover we need to work our own investigation. And our first order of business is getting back down into those tunnels to find the key to Nepsted's cage."

"Dude, let's go tonight, right now!" said Nick, pounding on the table. "What's stopping us?"

"You mean, aside from how stupid and suicidal that would be?" asked Elise.

"This will require extensive preparations, Will," said Ajay. "We need equipment, resources, and most importantly an excellent *plan*."

"Working on it," said Will.

"I like it!" said Nick, pointing at Will and hitting the table.

"Where do we start?" asked Elise.

"The tunnels under the island," said Will, glancing at Brooke as well.

"The island in Lake Waukoma?" asked Brooke, a little shocked.

"We'll use the entrance behind the castle," said Will. "That's how we got out of there the first time."

"That whole island is crawling with heavy-duty security," said Ajay, starting to pace and wringing his hands. "Let me refresh your memory: Men with sidearms? Angry dogs? We nearly got those rear ends caught in a meat grinder."

"I didn't say it was going to be easy, Ajay," said Will, putting a hand on his shoulder. "I do have a *plan,* but we need to lay some groundwork first."

"Some megabucks guy owns the island and castle, doesn't he?" asked Elise.

"Stan Haxley," said Brooke. "Member of the Center's board and a major school donor."

"A cool ten million to get his name on the medical center," said Elise.

"And as we know," said Ajay, "Haxley doesn't exactly welcome uninvited guests."

"He's going to invite me," said Will simply.

"Huh?" said Nick.

"So we can get into the castle?" asked Ajay.

"And under it," said Will.

"I hope I can help," said Brooke, sighing as she glanced at her watch. "My parents are going to yank me out of here as soon as the school notifies them that Lyle's escaped. And that's already happened."

"Then we'll wait till you're back," said Will. "Ask your father about Stan Haxley, see if he's heard anything on the alumni jungle drum network. We'll get to work in the meantime."

"How much work you got in mind?" asked Nick reluctantly.

"Why do you ask?"

"Dude, they've been crushing us with the books for months. And I wouldn't mind, you know, kicking back with *summer* for about five minutes."

"Okay, well, while you enjoy your umbrella drink down at the cabana, I want the rest of you to think about one more question," said Will. "Have you met anyone else on campus who you think might have qualities, or abilities, similar to ours?"

The others glanced around the table at each other in surprise.

"Other students?" asked Ajay.

"That's right," said Will.

"Similar in what way?" asked Elise.

"In whatever way you might have noticed. Maybe some subtle, almost undetectable thing you've seen them do. Or maybe in some big absolutely unhinged mind-blowing weirdness kind of way."

"Dude, pick any day of my life," said Nick.

"Why are you asking?"

"Something Lyle said last fall got me thinking," said Will. "If the Paladin Prophecy is as big a deal as the lengths they've gone to protect it suggests, do you think the five of us would be the only ones affected by it?"

"No," said Ajay, looking around. "That seems a most reasonable possibility, Will."

"That could mean more kids like us are here already, maybe more than a few, even if they haven't 'awakened' to what they can do. They could be part of the Prophecy as well. That's why it's even more important for *us* to find them before the Knights of Charlemagne do."

The door flung open. Three trim, professional security operatives, two men and a woman dressed all in black, took stances inside the pod with their hands on their shoulder holsters—one covering the door, one covering the roommates, while the third gestured silently for Brooke to join them.

THE TRAIL

By noon of the following day, over three-quarters of the students and their families had left for the summer, emptying the campus. Almost making up for their absence were the state and local police, additional security, and even a few FBI who had poured in to assist with the manhunt for the missing Lyle Ogilvy.

They'd set up a command post on the ground floor of the medical center, and established a perimeter around the building that only something with wings could have penetrated. Additional campus security had been assigned to Greenwood Hall as well. Eloni walked Will and Ajay to lunch the next day. They asked him why, but Eloni wouldn't tell them anything more. Will figured they were worried about Lyle coming back and attacking him again. Eloni was still waiting for them after lunch and as they walked through the quad, Will noticed a small blue and silver Center bus pulling up in front of Berkley Hall, the guest residence hall that parents and family members used for school visits.

The bus stopped, the doors opened, and five people walked off, all carrying their own identical black duffel bags. Three young men and two young women, slightly older than school age, wearing dark glasses and school blazers. All of them tall, athletic, and, each in their own way, striking in appearance. They carried themselves with confidence and self-possession, and none spoke a word to each other. Two security guards were waiting to meet them outside Berkley Hall and opened the doors for them.

"Who are those guys?" Will asked Eloni.

"Recent graduates," said Eloni. "A group comes back every summer. They work as counselors at the school's summer camp."

"For middle-school kids who hope to go to the Center someday," said Ajay. "I attended myself."

"How recently did they graduate?" asked Will, watching the counselors file into the building.

"Last summer," said Eloni.

One of the girls in the group, a tall, athletic-looking brunette, stopped at the door. She took off her dark glasses and looked right at Will. She smiled—a little aggressively, Will thought—showing big white teeth. She touched a boy in her group on the shoulder and pointed Will out.

Will turned away, glanced at Ajay, and knew they were thinking the same thing.

"Let's find out who these guys are," whispered Will.

"Agreed," whispered Ajay.

"And we better find Lyle before he messes up our plan."

"That's your department," whispered Ajay, looking alarmed.

Eloni took them to the door of Greenwood Hall, where Coach Ira Jericho was waiting, stark as an exclamation point in his trademark black sweats. He took Eloni aside and spoke quietly to him. Eloni nodded, then gestured for Ajay to follow him inside, while Jericho walked off with Will.

"Where are we going?" asked Will.

"Training."

"I didn't think they'd let me do that today."

"They will if you're with me."

"Good," said Will. "There's someone we need to find."

Jericho didn't respond. Will walked alongside the tall, implacable man and realized they were walking toward the medical center.

"What do you know about these counselors who come back to school to work with the summer camp kids?" Will asked.

"No more than what you just said."

"You coach any of 'em?"

"Probably. It's a different group every year."

Will waited until no one else was near them to speak again. Jericho's eyes constantly scanned the horizon. *He already knows I want to find Lyle,* Will realized.

"Coach, you're clear on what went down with Ogilvy last fall, right?" he asked, almost in a whisper. "Not the official version, but what I actually saw in that cave?"

Jericho didn't even look at him and never changed expression. "I don't live under a rock."

"So, between us—just in case this might actually be the truth and not some crazy hallucination I had—what happens to somebody who's attacked by a wendigo?"

Jericho glanced at him. "The legends say they die an excruciating death and their soul is condemned to eternal damnation."

Will swallowed hard. "What happens if they *don't* die?"

"Hypothetically? Don't think that happens very often."

"But what if it happened *this time*?" asked Will emphatically.

Jericho stopped; they were near where Lyle had made his leap out of the building. "The legend says that, over time, that person becomes a We-in-di-ko himself."

Will swallowed harder. "Over how much time?"

"These are legends, Will, not bus schedules. They don't come with timetables."

"But how does it happen? I mean, if you could speculate for a second—and I know how much you hate to do that and how annoying all these questions are to you, but I'm asking as a favor, this one time—how would you *describe* what happened to him?"

Jericho turned to look at Will with unsettling steadiness. "I would say that . . . the We-in-di-ko took Lyle's soul from him . . . and left something foul and dark in its place."

Will felt a shiver run from his knees to his chest.

"Hey, you asked," said Jericho.

"What did it leave in its place?"

"For all I know it left a Hello Kitty lunchbox. Was he injured in the fall?"

"You'd have to think so, right? Jumping through plate glass, dropping four stories?"

"So you were there," said Jericho.

Will nodded. "I felt him more than saw anything. By the time I looked around the corner, he was gone. He was wearing a doctor's coat. All I caught was a flash of white."

"Which way did he go?" asked Jericho.

Will pointed toward the woods. Jericho started walking in that direction, waving for Will to follow him.

"Are you going to track him?" asked Will.

"Track him?" said Jericho.

"I mean, you can do that, right?"

"No, but you can," said Jericho. "And you need to find him before he finds you."

They followed a narrow path into the forest.

"Did you bring any weapons?" asked Jericho.

Will rummaged around and showed Jericho his Swiss Army knife. "I left the RPG launcher in my other pants."

Jericho almost smiled.

"What did you bring?" asked Will.

Jericho held up a small stitched leather pouch.

"Great," muttered Will. "Pixie dust."

"Don't knock it till you've tried it," said Jericho, putting it back in his pocket. "Pixie dust is strong medicine."

The air felt saturated with heat and humidity the deeper they ventured into the woods. A heavy blanket of decayed leaves underfoot muted their footsteps and muffled the air. After traveling less than a hundred yards, they'd lost all sight or sound of the campus.

"So how do we do this?" asked Will, scanning the ground as they trudged along. "Search for footprints, broken branches?"

"Do I look like I was born in a tepee?"

"I didn't mean it *that* way—"

"Footprints aren't where the action is. We're after a hairy, ugly-ass freak in a white doctor's coat who's six foot nine. How hard could he be to find?"

As they walked past a tall silver birch, Jericho stopped and pointed to a smeared crimson stain on its bark at about shoulder level.

"Okay," said Will. "As long as you've got a method."

Jericho looked out and scanned the tree line. The forest grew steadily denser ahead of them, the ground rising and falling in small hillocks, in many directions leaving little space to move between the trees. Will waited for Jericho to tell him which way to go next.

"He went this way but you're the only one who knows how to find him, Will," said Jericho. "That is, if you *want* to."

Will burned inside at the provocation in Coach's voice, indignation turning to resolve.

"As a matter of fact, I do," said Will.

He closed his eyes and called up his interior sensory Grid. That extra vision booted up in his mind's eye and as he gazed out ahead of them the woods came alive with patterns and swirls of energy. The world around them went as quiet as a snow globe. He became aware of small animals scurrying and skittering around, emanating flares of nervous system heat. He heard every birdsong, pinging their locations on a three-dimensional, wraparound screen.

A disturbance in the Grid slowly revealed itself, a slightly glowing pathway took shape in the leaves on the ground, leading away from the birch. Will *felt* some quality or feeling lift off the path, and he realized it was as if Lyle had left some energetic trace of himself behind as he passed through—

Ravenous.

The word came into Will's mind. He felt a cold chill.

"This way," he said.

They continued on. Over the next small rise, they came upon the discarded head and chewed bones of what must have been a squirrel. Then, thirty yards on, the remains of a large crow, feathers scattered.

"He's hungry," said Jericho.

"Eating crow," said Will. "Literally."

"Not as much fun as it sounds," said Jericho.

"Why didn't he just head for a supermarket?"

Will was hoping for at least a smile, but Jericho didn't respond. In fact, he looked a little worried, Will thought. Which probably meant he was a *lot* worried on the inside, which was not a warm and fuzzy feeling to have spring up in the middle of these woods. It was early afternoon on a hot sunny day in June, but in here it felt as dark and gloomy as Halloween.

Will heard the hollow keen of a hawk or falcon circling somewhere far overhead. Jericho heard it, too. They looked up—Will could barely see the sky through the trees—then at each other. Will's hand reached for the stone falcon figurine in his pocket, and he felt better as soon as his fingers gripped its familiar contours.

Jericho nodded at him. Will knew exactly what he was thinking: *Your spirit animal is nearby. We're on the right path.*

"If you say so," said Will, under his breath.

Will led the way as they started walking along the "path" ahead of them. He picked up a strong heat signature, confirming that something massive had passed this way, the Grid growing ever more vivid in his mind. They mounted the next rise and discovered that the ground dropped steeply from there into a deep round hollow.

At its bottom, in a shaft of sunlight cutting through the trees, lay the body of a deer, an eight-point buck. On his Grid, Will saw ghostly patterns of movement, streaked and smudged. He realized it was the echo of what had happened here, the energy so powerful that it had imprinted on time-space. It was almost too fast to follow, but he could make out the buck bounding through the woods, spooked and panicked. It stopped for a moment only yards from where they were standing, then was ambushed and dragged down by a large indistinct form bursting toward it out of a thicket.

Sickened by the violence—a quick, savage evisceration—Will staggered against a tree, righting himself before nearly falling over. He didn't want to see the rest of what lingered here, looking over at Jericho and shaking his head.

Will hung back, eyes averted as Jericho examined what was left of the deer's carcass. Not much remained other than hooves and horns, the ground around it black with drying blood. On a nearby branch, Will found a torn patch of white cotton fabric, dyed a deep red.

"He's working his way up the food chain," said Will, breathing deeply to stay calm.

"Fast," said Jericho.

"Still think this is a good idea, Coach?"

"It won't be much farther."

"What won't?"

"Before we find him," said Jericho.

"Or he finds us."

"Why, are you worried we can't handle him?"

"What do you mean 'we'?" asked Will, then pointed behind them back toward school. "I'll be the guy running *that* way."

Fifty yards on they came to another short rise, the forest so thick around them now they were nearly in darkness. From the crest of this rise, the slope fell away into a rocky ravine, about twenty feet deep, carved by a thick slow-moving creek through its center. There, lying facedown half in the water, a still figure in a white coat stood out in the gloom like a patch of snow.

Will and his coach froze. He glanced at Jericho, hoping he'd know what to do, and whispered, "Is he trying to trick us? Playing possum?"

"Only one way to find out," said Jericho.

Coach started down the ravine, holding on to roots pushing out of the slope to maintain his balance. Will didn't follow until Jericho turned halfway down and shot him a withering look. "Coming, West?"

Coach waited for Will at the base of the incline and together they walked cautiously toward the body that still hadn't moved. Will flicked open his knife and held it at his side as they neared.

"Is he dead?" asked Will.

"Well, I wouldn't try to order a latte from him at the moment," said Jericho.

Coach Jericho knelt down next to the body for a closer look. Will peered over his shoulder. Lyle's eyes were open in a lifeless stare. He lay on his stomach, his head turned to the side. His face had taken on a canine cast, almost feral, with elongated incisors that extended past his lips and a starburst crack in his fixed open pupil.

Will's breath caught in his chest. He'd never liked Lyle—in fact, he had every reason to loathe the kid who'd more than once tried to kill him—but the sight of him like this still filled him with pity and horror.

"What are you supposed to do to a dead wendigo?" asked Will, taking a step back.

"You mean to make sure it stays that way?"

"Yeah, I mean, there have to be rules, right? Hammer a stake through its heart or stuff wads of garlic in its mouth—"

"You kids and your damn vampires," said Jericho. "How the hell should I know? I've never seen one of these things before either. And what makes you so sure it's dead?"

"It sure *looks* dead," said Will, pointing to the wet sludgy ground around the body. "With all those . . . fluids and stuff."

"Only one way to find out," said Jericho.

Jericho reached down and turned Lyle's body over, and they realized this wasn't exactly Lyle. More like what would be left of Lyle if you'd sliced him down the middle with a gigantic can opener. A rough flap or seam in his flesh ran the length of the body from his neck to his waist. With Lyle now lying on his back, his chest cavity and midsection looked deflated, as if he'd been flattened by a steamroller.

"What the hell happened to him?" asked Will.

"If I have to guess—which I do—it looks like something that was . . . growing on the inside is now on the outside. And apparently that leaves a mess."

"Wait, so is this Lyle or isn't it?"

"I'd say . . . it used to be."

"So you mean this is more like, what, like a—"

"A snake's skin," said Jericho, standing back up. "Although

you can take it to the bank that when the cops get here they'll decide they've found who they're looking for."

Will peered deeper into the dark woods, intending to scan the tree line for anything lurking out there that might be staring back at them. The frigid fear that stole over him all but wiped out his ability to call up his Grid.

"So this is just an empty husk . . . and Lyle *isn't* dead," said Will.

"Who he *used* to be sure is," said Jericho; then he looked up and peered into the woods himself. "The part that grew inside him, cracked out of his chest, and ran straight down this creek so no one could track it? That part's alive and kicking. And I don't think I'd be calling it 'Lyle' anymore either."

Jericho took out a cell phone and dialed 911.

"Really glad I didn't eat a big lunch," said Will, looking away, seriously queasy.

"Probably not an outstanding idea to talk up our little theory with the police," said Jericho, his hand over the phone speaker. "Or anyone else."

"I hear that."

"We went out for a run, spotted the body from up on the ridge, and called it in. I told you to head back to campus while I came down here to take a look. You never saw any of this. Leave now."

"Coach, are you encouraging me to lie?"

"Let's call it showing you how to survive."

Dad would approve, thought Will.

"I'm good with that."

Will took off running toward school. As he left, he heard Jericho speak to a dispatcher on the other end of the line.

"I need to report a body," said Jericho.

THE BARBERSHOP

The uproar caused by the discovery of Lyle's body lasted three days. Will and his roommates monitored the official statements and coverage closely, and noted that none of the disturbing details Will had witnessed made it into the official version: A severely ill patient escaped from the medical center and died in the woods, apparently breaking his neck in a fall. Whoever was in charge seemed determined to frame the narrative to fit that conclusion, a sad end to the life of a troubled young student turned tragically wrong. The Center also appeared eager to use Lyle's death as a reason to punctuate the end of the Knights of Charlemagne story. Only one report even mentioned that the whereabouts of Todd Hodak, the other major player in the Knights' hierarchy who had disappeared last November, remained unknown.

As the campus emptied, Will and his roommates went to work. Ajay already had his gig in the science lab, and the others quickly secured jobs at the Center through the summer. Elise found work tending horses in the Center's stables and gave piano lessons on the weekends, while Nick landed a job as a lifeguard at the neighboring town's community pool. Once they knew Lyle was "dead," Brooke's family arranged an internship for her in the Center's administrative offices and let her return.

Will was the last to find a job, but for good reason. After researching his target's movements, he'd had to wait another week to put the first step of his plan into action.

#57: IF YOU WANT TO KNOW WHAT'S GOING ON IN A SMALL TOWN, HANG AROUND THE BARBERSHOP.

At Will's direction, Ajay had set up a small surveillance camera outside the school's barbershop, until one particular client arrived for his biweekly shave and haircut.

Will was warming up at the Barn before his daily workout with Jericho when he got the call on one of the black house phones.

"It's time for our study group, Will," said Ajay, using the code they'd agreed on.

Will sprinted the mile from the Barn to the Center's barbershop, arriving in less than three minutes. A part of school lore since the Roaring Twenties, the shop was tucked a few steps below sidewalk level in the southwest corner of Harvey Hall, one of the older ivy-covered buildings in the central quad.

A bell on the back of the door jingled as Will entered. Just as during his one previous haircut, the sights and smells that greeted him inside took him back in time as surely as the school's soda fountain. He'd been in shops like this a few times as a kid—his dad usually cut his hair as he got older—and they had created powerful sense memories. They were his first glimpses of a man's world.

A black-and-white-tiled floor. Two deluxe oxblood leather chairs on chromed hydraulics facing a mirrored wall above two snow-white porcelain sinks. Gleaming clippers and scissors and razors arrayed on a shelf between them like surgical instruments. Combs and brushes marinating in a jar of acrid ocean blue disinfectant. From somewhere the sound of an opera played on a tinny radio. Will caught the tang of hair tonic and the spice of industrial-strength aftershave in the air. A vintage pendulum clock ticked on one wall, alongside framed fading photographs of old sports heroes from the Green Bay Packers, Milwaukee Braves, and one of a horse at a racetrack. A few of the photos had been autographed—Fuzzy Thurston, Joe Adcock, and other names Will didn't recognize.

The man Will was there to see wore a sleek, finely tailored suit and sat in one of the chairs, motionless, fully reclined, with a steaming towel draped over his face. Another man in pressed gray slacks and a clean double-breasted white tunic—the kids knew him as Joe the Barber—walked in from a back room when he heard the bell ring. He was whistling along with the opera and carrying a short white towel over his arm. His hair was jet black and slicked elaborately back with one of his own products. He gnawed at a piece of gum he kept tucked in his rear molars.

"Mr. West," said Joe, flashing a practiced smile. "Good to see you again, sir."

"Thank you, Joe."

"Step right this way, my friend," said Joe, spinning the second chair around as he lowered it by tapping a foot pedal, then slapped the seat with the towel.

Will stepped up into the chair and settled into the old creamy leather. With a flurry of hands as quick and effortless as a magician, Joe picked up a barber's smock from a nearby shelf, snapped it open, spun the chair around to face the mirror, swirled the black smock into place around Will's neck, and fastened the snaps.

"And what can we do for you this fine day?" asked Joe with the clipped nasal vowels of a Chicago accent.

"Coach Jericho said I need a summer cut."

"If the coach so advised you," said Joe, pumping up the chair, "far be it from us to disagree."

"He says I won't like working out with my usual do in this weather."

"You're from Southern California, if I recall correctly," said Joe.

"You've got a good memory, Joe."

"So you're not acquainted with our delightful summer climate," said Joe, holding out and measuring the hair near Will's ears.

"All I know is it's like running in a sauna."

"This is June, pal. Wait till August. You ain't seen nothing yet." Joe popped his gum for emphasis.

Will chuckled politely. He looked over at the man in the other chair, who still hadn't moved since Will came in. Will wondered if he'd fallen asleep.

Joe began by drenching Will's unruly mop into submission with a spray bottle and brush. Hardly a drop touched him anywhere but on his scalp. Joe moved crisply around him, leaving traces of bay rum and his black spicy-flavored gum—Beemans, maybe?—in his wake.

"How long you worked here, Joe?"

"Seventeen years now, Will," said Joe.

"From Chicago?"

"What, the accent give me away?" Joe said, and chuckled.

#52: TO BREAK THE ICE, ALWAYS COMPLIMENT
A MAN'S HOMETOWN.

"Great town, Chicago," said Will. "Second City, nothing. Second to no place, that's what I say."

"I can't help but agree with you," said Joe.

"You still have family there?"

"Absolutely. I get back down at least six to eight times a year."

#53: AND ALWAYS SYMPATHIZE WITH HIS HOMETOWN'S FOOTBALL TEAM.

"The Bears look like they're for real this year, don't they?" asked Will.

"And high time, too. My pop had season tickets the whole time we was kids. He could hardly afford it—city sanitation worker—but he said he'd quit eating before he'd give 'em up."

"That wasn't during the Walter Payton years, was it?"

"You better believe it, baby," said Joe. "Sweetness was the man."

A timer on the shelf behind the chairs dinged.

"What team do you follow, Will?" The voice came from under the towel on the face of the man in the chair beside him. A deep, pleasing, friendly baritone.

Joe immediately moved to the other chair to take the towel from the man as he removed it from his face. He had the generic good looks of a guy who'd play the president in a big budget movie: tall, tan, and fit, probably in his midforties, with a head full of obedient brown hair, grayed so precisely at the temples that it shouted dye job, but if that was the case it was done so expertly you couldn't be sure. Will remembered some vague line from an old commercial: "Only your hairdresser knows for sure." Was Joe that guy? And how much did he know?

"I don't really follow any one team," said Will.

"One of the hazards of living in Southern California, am I right?" said the man, smiling. His gleaming white teeth were as impressive as his hair.

"That's right, sir," said Will. "No one to root for."

"Excuse me a moment," said Joe, who moved to the counter, thumbed some heated shaving cream from a dispenser, and began lathering the face of the man in the chair.

"Oh my gosh, are you Mr. Haxley?" asked Will, as if making a discovery that delighted him.

"That's right, Will," said the man, extending his hand toward Will without moving any other part of his body. "Stan Haxley. Pleasure."

Stan Haxley as in the gabillionaire who owns the castle on the island in Lake Waukoma.

Haxley had a crushing handshake, and Will gave him one back. Joe, standing by with a straight razor in his hand, waited for the handshake to end.

"I recognized your picture from the medical center, sir," said Will. "I have to tell you I think it's really great what you did, giving so generously to build that place."

"Patricia and I have always been very supportive of the Center," said Haxley, closing his eyes and signaling Joe to start his shave.

As if I'm supposed to know that's his wife's name. (Which I do.) Thinks quite a lot of himself, doesn't he?

"They took excellent care of me while I was there, I can tell you that," said Will, sounding as sincere as he could. "I'm very grateful."

"Always glad to hear that," said Haxley generically. "Are you spending the summer on campus, Will?"

"I am, sir."

"What kind of work do they have you doing?"

"Nothing as yet," said Will.

#21: FORTUNE FAVORS THE BOLD.

Go for it.

"Because, actually, I've been hoping, sir," said Will. "Hoping that I might be able to find some way to work for you."

Haxley didn't respond for a second, as Joe had the razor poised directly under his nose. Will resisted the impulse to fill the uncomfortable silence. Joe waited for a signal from Haxley, then finished the stroke and wiped off the razor.

"And what are your interests, Will?" asked Haxley.

"Medicine. Medical research."

Joe waited to see if Haxley would respond before resuming the shave. Haxley finally gestured at him, a little impatiently: *Finish.* Joe moved in for the last few strokes and then wiped off the remaining foam from Haxley's face.

Haxley sat up in the chair, craned his neck around, then leaned back again. Joe applied a splash of aftershave and massaged it into his pink cheeks.

"Medical research is quite a specialized interest for someone your age," said Haxley with a smile. "Why is that?"

"That was my father's field, sir," said Will. "And it's an important way to help people."

Will relied on Haxley knowing just enough of the public version of his parents' disappearance and death to find that irresistibly sympathetic. Haxley sat up as Joe pumped his chair back into an upright position and removed the bib from around his neck.

"That's a very admirable sentiment, Will," said Haxley, adjusting his collar as he rose from the chair.

"It's more than just sentiment, sir. It's the purpose of my life now. Following in my father's footsteps. "

"I'm sure knowing that would make him very proud," said Haxley. "As well it should."

Haxley studied him for a moment with a patronizing

half-smile that said, *You poor little orphan kid*—just the look Will had been hoping to see. Then a business card appeared in Haxley's hand, and he extended it toward Will.

"I'm in town for the rest of the week," said Haxley. "I'd like you to come visit with me at the Crag, if that's convenient, so we can discuss your . . . ambitions."

"What, out on the island?"

"That's right," said Haxley. "Call my office. Use the card. Ask for Barbara. She'll make the arrangements. This evening, around six."

"I really appreciate this opportunity, sir," said Will, standing to shake his offered hand. "I won't let you down."

"Will, you're a very impressive young man," said Haxley, slipping on his sport coat. "Joe here will take good care of you."

Haxley shook hands with Joe—and, Will noticed, smoothly slipped him a hundred-dollar bill in the process—then headed for the door.

"Be seeing you, Will," said Haxley with a parting smile.

The bell was still jingling as Joe went to work on Will with the steady, effortless pace of a lawn mower.

Will studied Haxley's business card and realized it wasn't a traditional printed paper card at all, but a piece of thin flexible metal. Its single image—a 3-D logo of a revolving globe and Haxley's name below it—glowed, all done with some kind of sophisticated micro processing. When Will touched the name, a phone number appeared below it like a hyperlink on the Web.

Joe switched on a pair of electric clippers and buzzed around Will's neck and ears.

"He seems really nice," said Will blandly.

"Very special people, Stan and his wife, Patricia. They built that medical center fifteen years ago. The work they do for people in need you wouldn't believe."

Not to mention that top-secret floor where they kept Lyle, with the rooms that look like prison cells. Haxley built that, too. Wonder if Joe knows about that part of his "philanthropy."

"Try and find me a better human being," said Joe. "You won't. Because you can't."

"When did he buy that place out on the lake?"

"Before I got here. I think about twenty years ago?"

Joe splashed some tonic from an opaque green bottle into his hands and rubbed it vigorously through Will's hair. It had an agreeable minty-lemony scent and made his whole head tingle, electrified, but pleasantly, like his scalp had just been reminded it was alive.

"From who?" asked Will.

"From Franklin Greenwood," said Joe.

"Really? Wasn't he the old headmaster here?"

Not to mention my grandfather.

Joe attacked with a brush and comb now, shaping and pulling, coaxing and stretching Will's hair in all sorts of unexpected directions.

"That's right," said Joe. "He was in charge when Mr. Haxley went to school here. After he made his mark, he could've lived anywhere on the planet. But he came back here. Why? Loyalty. That's what I'm talking about. A first-rate man of wealth and taste. There ain't nobody I respect more than Mr. Stan Haxley."

"He seems like quite a guy," said Will.

"If he takes an interest in you? You are one lucky young man, my friend."

Joe finished setting Will's hair into place with a subtle flourish. He picked up a white rectangular hand mirror and gave it to Will, then spun him around in the chair. When Will lifted the mirror, he could see the back of his collar line in the big wall mirror behind him.

"So how do we like it?" asked Joe.

Will hardly recognized himself. His wild, overactive hair—usually about as responsive to cultivation as a rain forest—had been tamed into the Center's classic prep school look. Parted on the left. Flipped up off the forehead. Trim but full-bodied. Businesslike but still somehow cool.

"I think it's the full Jericho," said Will.

Joe bowed slightly, as if Will had offered him the grandest compliment in the world. Joe loosened the smock and then brushed down Will's face, neck, and shoulders with a large silver-gray brush with the softest bristles he'd ever felt. Joe swept the smock away with one swift practiced move, shepherding all the loose hairs to the floor, then lowered and turned the chair.

Will climbed to his feet. Looked at himself in the mirror. Glanced at the clock on the wall. His entire transformation had taken less than ten minutes.

"How do I pay you, Joe? Do you take the Card?" Will reached for his wallet and the school's black, all-purpose credit card.

"Put that away. For you, Mr. West," he said, offering a sincere two-handed handshake. "This one's on the house."

"I really appreciate that," Will said, and walked outside.

Once Will was gone, Joe emptied the contents of the sweeper—Will's clipped hairs—into a small plastic bag that he placed in a drawer of the cabinet in his back room.

Will found the nearest black phone and left a two-word message for Ajay.

"I'm in."

THE ISLAND

After reporting back to his roommates, Will arrived at the Lake Waukoma boathouse just before six that evening. Stan Haxley's boat was waiting for him at the dock. It was a classic teak and mahogany runabout with twin inboard motors about twenty feet in length. When the driver fired it up, they skimmed across the quarter mile to the island in what felt like a matter of moments. They put in at a long extended dock that was visible from the opposite shore, part of an elaborate landing complex near where Haxley's seaplane was moored.

Two men in black security guard uniforms escorted him from the lake toward the castle. Getting a closer look at the Crag in broad daylight than he had during their nocturnal escape from the island last fall, Will saw that the grounds were extensively gardened and meticulously maintained. At close range the overwhelming size and scale of the castle was much more apparent, by far the largest private residence Will had ever seen. Built with square rough-hewn blocks of granite of a shade Will had seen in the surrounding hills. It must've been quarried locally. Decorative fingers of ivy scaled many of the walls. His escorts led him down a path around the side to a separate entrance, the one Will guessed they reserved for the help.

The door led into a kitchen, or the section of it reserved for staff use, a vast working space designed to handle large numbers of guests, bustling with a dozen people hard at work preparing a meal. The escorts handed him off there to a sturdy man Will assumed was a butler, although he wore a plain black suit, shirt, and tie instead of the uniform Will had seen butlers wear in the movies. The man looked at him with a sneer, oozing contempt, and Will felt an instant dislike for him. The butler didn't say a word as he beckoned him to follow, leading him out through a sequence of impressive rooms—dining room, living room, billiards room—and into a private study.

Bookshelves lined walls that rose to a twenty-foot ceiling and a huge stone fireplace leaned over the room. Buttery leather couches, thick Persian rugs, dark hardwood furniture, and a mighty slab of a desk. A giant globe sat on a massive, curved wooden stand in the corner. The air smelled faintly of spicy aftershave and expensive cigars. It might've been the office of a member of Congress or a nineteenth-century explorer.

The butler backed out and closed the sliding panel doors behind him, leaving Will alone. He glanced around, afraid to touch or even look too closely at anything. He couldn't see a camera anywhere, but felt like somebody might be watching him on video.

Another door on the opposite side of the room opened and Stan Haxley strode in, smoking a cigar and wearing dress pants, suspenders, and a white tuxedo shirt with an undone bow tie around his neck. He seemed animated with a kind of salesman's vitality that Will hadn't seen yesterday.

"You're right on time, Will, and I'm not," said Haxley with a broad smile and a handshake. "Hope you don't mind the cigar. It's the one room in the house where I can indulge."

Will didn't know what to say to that. *No, dude, you can't fire up a fat Cubano heater in your own office.*

"My dear wife, Patricia, neglected to tell me we were hosting a dinner party tonight," said Haxley, pouring himself a drink at a bar behind his desk. "So I'm afraid we'll have to be brief."

Haxley took his drink—single-malt Scotch, according to

the bottle—and perched on one of the couches. He gestured with his cigar for Will to sit across from him, then studied him with a slight half-smile as if amused by some private joke.

Will said nothing.

#12: LET THE OTHER GUY DO THE TALKING.

"I've asked around about you, Will."

Will said nothing.

"There is definite interest here in finding you some work this summer," Haxley continued.

Will nodded but kept quiet. Haxley took a leisurely pull off his cigar and blew a fat smoke ring that hung lazily in the air.

"In fact, I believe I may have a suitable job for you right now. How quickly would you be able to jump in, Will?"

"Tomorrow," said Will.

"I like this enthusiasm! Are you interested in business? That is, as a complement to your worthy altruistic concerns?"

"Are you asking me if I'm interested in making money, sir?"

Haxley grinned. "I suppose I am."

"Well, who isn't?" asked Will, trying to match his smile.

"There's no law against it," said Haxley. "At least, none that states it in so many words."

"So I wouldn't be breaking the law, then?" asked Will, keeping things light.

"That depends on who you talk to—I'm joking of course." Haxley chuckled good-naturedly. "These are complicated times, Will, and whenever that's the case it's best to keep things simple. So we'll start you with some relatively straightforward tasks, see how you do, and then determine where we go from there."

Haxley threw back the rest of his drink, stuck his cigar in his mouth, and stood up. Will stood up, too.

"That's all there is to it, Will," said Haxley, with his politician's grin. "You aced the interview."

The door behind Haxley opened. A man stood in the doorway, backlit, hard to see at first. He wore a tuxedo, like Haxley, although his tie was already tied. He stood tall and straight, on the slender side, loose limbed, long arms hanging at his side. Will's senses went on high alert.

"Will, this is Mr. Elliot. He's a colleague of mine."

Mr. Elliot walked toward Will, extending his hand. When he moved into the light, Will realized he was an older man, somewhere in his sixties, at least twenty years older than Haxley. His face was crosshatched with fine lines, creating a texture almost like parchment, but he moved with vitality and his grip was powerful. He had a full head of thick white hair, wore rimless eyeglasses, and had a pencil-thin gray mustache.

"How do you do, Will?" said Elliot, putting both of his hands on Will's and smiling warmly. "What a pleasure to meet you."

"Pleased to meet you, too, sir," said Will.

Will thought he seemed harmless, but something about him jangled his nerves.

Elliot's pale blue eyes sparkled with delight, and he patted Will's hand a couple of times before he let it go. He carried an air of heavy gravity about him, just about the most "grown-up" grown-up Will had ever encountered.

"Stan's told me so much about you," said Elliot. He had a deep rumble of a voice that almost sounded like a cat's purr, but his words were clipped with precise diction.

Haxley subtly steered them all toward the door. Will heard live chamber music playing in one of the nearby rooms.

"I'd invite you to join us for dinner, Will," said Haxley, "but frankly we don't want to bore you to death."

"No, we wouldn't want that," said Elliot with a soft little laugh.

"That's okay, sir, I forgot my tux anyway," said Will.

Haxley and Elliot chuckled politely.

The kind of laugh you'd give when your polo pony does something adorable.

"Nine o'clock sharp tomorrow morning, Will," said Haxley, and walked off tying his tie.

"We look forward to seeing much more of you around here," said Elliot; then he gave a friendly wave and followed Haxley through an archway.

Will waved back and smiled broadly. *I'm really in. Now to start scouting the place.*

When he turned around, a young woman was standing behind him. In a black cocktail dress and heels, she stood a couple of inches taller than he did.

"What are you doing here, West?" she asked.

It took him a moment to place her—the girl from the counselors alumni group who'd stared him down outside their residence hall the other day. Her dark hair reached to her tanned and muscled shoulders. She had a swimmer's build, legs for days, and startling dark blue eyes that somehow looked familiar.

"I had a meeting with Mr. Haxley," he said. "I'm sorry, do we know each other?"

"My family's heard a whole lot about something called Will West in the last year," she said.

"How's that?"

"You knew my brother."

Then he saw the resemblance. And his eyes landed on the name tag on her blouse:

COURTNEY HODAK

Todd's sister.

"I saw you arriving the other day," said Will when he couldn't think of anything else to say.

Courtney walked around him, looking him over with the kind of superior disdain that reminded him of Todd. "Hard to see what all the fuss is about."

Will felt his anger rise. "You said I knew your brother. Past tense."

"You don't *know* him currently, do you?"

"I don't know anything about him at all," said Will.

"Neither do we!" She almost shouted it, right in his face.

Will worked hard to control himself before responding. "Whatever's happened to him . . . I'm sorry about your brother."

A savage look in her eye, she leaned in almost like she planned to kiss him and whispered aggressively, "Not as sorry as you're going to be."

The butler who'd escorted Will in appeared at the end of the room. He gestured for Will to follow again. As they left, he heard the click of Courtney Hodak's heels as she walked the other way. They skirted the big rooms they'd walked through before. At one point Will caught a glimpse of the cocktail party in another room and saw some more of the counselors Courtney had arrived with, mixing with a dozen adults, including Haxley. Soon after they ended up back in the kitchen, where dinner preparations had ramped up to an even more frantic pace.

The butler opened the back door for him and Will walked outside. The two men who'd led him up from the dock earlier waited for him there. Will noted the time on the kitchen clock—after seven now but the sun was nowhere close to setting yet.

But they didn't lead him back to that landing—Will saw from a distance that guests in formal wear were still arriving there in launches for the party—and instead took him toward a smaller dock on the island's north side where another boat waited to take him across. The dock from which Will and his roommates had escaped during their epic misadventure on the island last fall. Will looked off to the left from the path through the woods and spotted a wooden frame around the hatch they'd climbed out of when they fled from the tunnels. It looked as accessible as it had before.

His plan was working to perfection: He'd found their entry point. His mind raced ahead to the next phase, tomorrow's reconnaissance mission. If that went well, they'd be ready to get down that hatch and start looking for Nepsted's key. And while they were at it, look for a connection between Stan Haxley and the Knights. The presence of Courtney Hodak and the other alums would be a good place to start.

Will gathered the roommates together that night, brought them up to speed about what he'd learned, and told them that if tomorrow went as well as today, they should be ready to go as soon as tomorrow night. They checked and double-checked everything on Will's master list and memorized their timetable, drilling Nick at least five times on his part. Will reminded Ajay to step up his research on how Haxley made his fortune— Ajay said he needed more time to finish—then they turned in early to get a solid night's sleep.

Will was up packing gear he needed in his knapsack when Brooke knocked softly at the door. He let her in, making sure that Elise's door was closed so she wouldn't see them before closing his door after her. She looked worried.

"I didn't want to bring this up in front of everyone," said Brooke, leaning against his desk, arms folded against her body. "Are you sure it's safe for you to go into that place?"

"I don't have any way to know yet," said Will. "It depends on how much Haxley has to do with the Knights."

"He has to know about the tunnels," she said. "I mean, he owns the place, Will."

"I'm sure he knows about them," said Will. "They were there for over a hundred years before he showed up."

"But doesn't it seem like he agreed to hire you a little too easily? What if it's a trap?"

"Come on, give me some credit," said Will. "I stalked him and sold him on the idea. He couldn't resist my big sad orphan eyes routine."

Will clasped his hands in front of him and looked up at her with a pathetic, pleading wide-eyed look. Brooke laughed, but immediately checked herself.

"Come on, Will, this isn't funny," said Brooke. "The Knights tried to kill you."

"More than once," he said, taking her hand reassuringly. "I'll be careful, I promise. And if it goes south, I can always just . . . run back across the lake."

She gave him one of her withering stares and took her hand back.

"You think I'm kidding," he said, deadpan.

"I think you're *crazy*," she said. "What if Haxley's right in the middle of this? What if he wants you working there so they can keep an eye on you, or something even worse?"

"I honestly think he feels sorry for me," said Will.

"That's not a reason to trust him. How do you know what he's got going on over there?"

"That's part of what we need to find out," said Will. "Ajay's running background—by the way, did your father know anything about Haxley?"

"They know each other," said Brooke, twirling a strand of her hair. "Father says he's a good man, very trustworthy. They served on the school's board of directors together."

"Your dad was on the board?" Will asked.

"Yes. I thought I told you that."

"Maybe you did. I forgot."

"It was ages ago, before his last posting overseas. Years before I started here anyway. Speaking of which, my parents are going to make me move to another hall when the school year starts."

"Sorry to hear that," said Will, covering the fact that the news made his heart sink.

"That was the compromise I had to make for them to let me come back this summer," she said, moving to his window and opening it. She leaned out and pointed to Berkley Hall, the second residence down from Greenwood where alumni family kids boarded and where Courtney Hodak and her team were staying now.

"We can signal each other with flashlights," he said. "Morse code."

"It won't be so bad," she said. "Plus if we find out any of those legacy kids are still mixed up with the Knights, I can work undercover. Keep an eye on them."

"Do you know anything about the alumni counselors who work with the summer camp?"

"What about them?" she asked without turning to look at him.

"Ajay and I saw them arrive. They're graduates from a year

ago, the class before Lyle's. One of them is Todd Hodak's older sister."

Brooke turned, alarmed. "Courtney is here?"

"Yeah. I figured you must know her."

"Of course I know her. I grew up with her. She's only a year older than Todd."

Will saw her tense up, her expression suddenly hard to read. "What's her story?"

"She's like every other monster in that family," said Brooke. "Bullheaded. Entitled and egotistical. And they never stop until they get what they want."

"I didn't know any of the others but they all have a kind of Knights vibe about them. They were all at the Crag tonight at Haxley's dinner party."

"What are you thinking?"

"If our theory is right, and the Knights have been graduating twelve people per class for decades, they could be part of last year's class—"

Brooke suddenly turned from the window and embraced him, almost fiercely, a wave of pent-up emotion coursing through her. Will hugged her back, confusion keeping pace with his enthusiasm.

"No matter what happens, I know you're going to be all right," she whispered in his ear.

She kissed him once, quickly, and then she practically flew out of the room, closing the door behind her.

Will sat down on the bed for a second to clear his head. He had a fleeting feeling that someone was in the room with him, watching him. He turned to his notebook, open on his desk. His syn-app was sitting at his virtual desk, twirling a pencil around and whistling.

"What are you looking at, Junior?" asked Will.

"Don't mind me, boss," said Junior.

"What do you make of this? Two girls interested at once?"

"I would make of it," said Junior with a little smile, "whatever I could."

When Will arrived at the lake the next morning, the same launch waited for him at the shore. As they skimmed across to the island, he noticed the seaplane was gone from its mooring near the dock.

Stan Haxley had left the building.

No guards waited to greet him on the landing this time. Apparently he was expected to make his way to the back door by himself, so Will hoisted his backpack, walked around, and let himself in.

The kitchen was quiet, except for the background hum of multiple dishwashers. The same squat butler sat at a plain table, drinking coffee and reading a newspaper. He sighed when he saw Will come in, his moment of leisure punctured, but he seemed more relaxed in general when he stood up and headed into the house.

"Follow," he said.

As they passed through a different set of rooms, Will heard a platoon of vacuum cleaners at work nearby and saw a flock of maids still cleaning up after the party. The butler took him under a flight of stairs and through a door that led down more stairs to a long, straight, subterranean passage of rough concrete lit by bare bulbs. Their footsteps echoed in the cool air.

"Where's Mr. Haxley?" asked Will.

"Away on business," said the butler without turning around. "So mind your own."

Will watched the man's stocky back bobbing ahead of him,

the shaved ramrod neck and his severe haircut. He felt such a visceral dislike for the guy's superior attitude it almost defied explanation.

At the far end of the passage, they reached a circular wrought-iron staircase in a round rock chamber that led up and up, at least four stories by Will's count. Will stayed a few paces behind the butler as he chugged up the stairs without varying his pace. From a landing at the top they passed through a rounded wooden door cut to the shape of its stone frame and entered a vast high-ceilinged room.

They were in one of the castle's twin towers. Tall thin triangular windows graced the circular walls that met at the apex of the ceiling overhead, under the spire. There were no furnishings in the room at all, not a single chair, not even lighting fixtures—the windows let in plenty of natural morning light—just a sprawling spread of dusty boxes scattered throughout. Will estimated there had to be well over a hundred of them.

"We need all these organized," said the butler.

"What, Hercules wasn't available?"

The butler fixed him with a cold scowl. "Shall I tell Mr. Haxley you don't want the job?"

"No, because that wouldn't be true. What's your name?" asked Will.

"Lemuel."

"Lemuel. You don't mind my asking, what kind of a name is Lemuel?"

Now the guy looked annoyed. "It's a Biblical name. It means 'devoted to God.'"

"Really," said Will. "I don't mean to be rude. I've just never heard it before."

"It was more common in the nineteenth century," said Lemuel condescendingly.

Will couldn't resist. "So was smallpox, but they have a vaccine for that now."

Lemuel looked steamed. Will could tell that he was used to playing king of the roost when Haxley wasn't around.

"It is a family name," said Lemuel.

"Understood. Do people call you Lem?"

"You can call me Mr. Clegg. That's a family name, too."

Will thought about it. "Clegg. Hmm." He looked around at the boxes. "Organized how?" he asked.

"Mr. Haxley wasn't more specific."

"By date, size, contents? And just curious, what's in the boxes?"

"Archival information about the Crag. Start by date and proceed from there," said Lemuel, and then headed for the door. "That should be enough to keep you busy for a few days."

This was an unexpected bonus: He could research the Crag while he worked, but he had to make sure Clegg left him alone.

"Is there a bathroom up here?" asked Will.

"At the bottom of the stairs."

"How about water? It's kind of dusty. I'll probably get pretty parched."

"You can walk to the kitchen and get a drink," said Lemuel, then turned to go again.

"And what about lunch?"

"We serve the staff lunch precisely at noon," said Lemuel, even more impatiently.

"But I'm not on the staff."

"Nor will you be for long, at this rate," said Lemuel, his face turning crimson; then he stalked out and slammed the door behind him.

Will moved to the door and heard the man clanging down the metallic stairs. There was no lock on the door, so he waited until Lemuel reached the bottom, opened it a crack, and heard him stomp away down the stone corridor.

Will took one of Ajay's devices from his backpack and used it to scan the room for electronic signals. He detected no cameras or microphones. He moved to the window and took out one of Ajay's compact walkie-talkies from the backpack. After putting an earpiece in his ear, he switched on the device, thumbed the button, and spoke softly into a mic on the wire.

"Yo-Yo Ma," he said.

He heard a crackle of interference, and then Ajay's voice came through, thin and a little scratchy. "What's your twenty, Will?"

"I'm way up in one of the two towers. It's perfect. I have a commanding view of the whole island."

"Is anyone going to walk in on you?"

"No, I made sure the butler won't be coming near me for a while, and this room's clear of electronics." Will took a small pair of binoculars out of the bag along with his notebook, then a sandwich and a big bottle of water. "Are you sure this is a secure frequency?"

"It's UHF," said Ajay. "No one's going to overhear us unless they're a garage door opener."

"Are you in position?" asked Will.

"Yes, we're on the bluff to the north of the lake," said Ajay. "At the base of Suicide Hill. I can just make out the castle towers from here through the trees."

"I'm in one of the windows, the tower on the left. Can you see me waving?"

"Nick, hand me the binoculars," said Ajay, then: "Here, talk to Nick."

"Will, my brother from another mother," said Nick over the walkie. "What kind of serious bouillabaisse have you dropped us into this time?"

"So far, one seriously cheesed off butler," said Will.

"That's it? That's some weak cheddar, bro," said Nick.

"It's only nine-thirty. Give me time."

"What's that, Ajay? . . . Ajay says he can see you waving like an idiot and that you should stop now before any unfriendlies see you."

"Tell Mother to stop worrying," said Will, and stopped waving.

Will heard Ajay take the walkie back from Nick. "Your position appears ideal, Will. Can you see the entrance to the tunnels from there? Over."

Will lifted the binoculars and scanned the roofs of some outer buildings, then tracked a path through a back gate. Twenty yards into the woods he saw a wooden frame. He lowered the glasses until he found the round lid of the hatch.

"We got lucky," said Will. "I can see it perfectly."

"Does it appear to be locked?"

"Can't tell from this distance. The wood looks like it's been reinforced."

"Are there any guards in its vicinity?"

Will scanned around. "Not one. Haxley flew out this morning, so the whole place seems emptier."

"That's great," said Ajay. "Can you determine if the hatch is visible from any of the ground-floor windows?"

Will moved to the next window over to change his angle. "Looks like it might be obscured by a fence and some sheds."

"Good. Can you see the graveyard?" asked Ajay.

Will moved to his right and looked down through another window. "I'm either too close or I don't have the right angle. What about you?"

Ajay paused. "Yes, I can see some headstones in a clearing to the west."

"I'll get over there for a look when I can," said Will. "Are the girls there yet?"

Elise's voice broke through the interference, whispering, "Don't say anything about us you might regret. Instantly."

"I never regret anything I say about girls," said Ajay. "Did you Roger that, Elise? What is your twenty? Over."

"Ajay, are you really going to insist on using that ridiculous military lingo?" asked Elise. "What are we, seven?"

"For God's sake, woman, I'm simply observing a time-honored tradition in covert radio communications." Will heard Nick laughing in the background behind Ajay. "Precision and brevity. Unless, of course, you'd prefer to prattle on incessantly about your new shade of nail polish. Over."

"Nice ad hominem attack, Ajay," said Elise. "Always appreciated."

"Homonym? Doesn't that mean something that sounds like something else?" Will heard Nick ask in the background.

"Yes, *homonym* means something that sounds like something else," said Ajay, off mic, annoyed. "And actually this is a perfect example of it because it isn't what she *meant*. *Argumentum ad hominem* in the Latin means a personal attack used in an argument to undermine the other person's point of view."

A beat. "You lost me at yes," said Nick.

"Let's use plain English," said Will. "Elise and Brooke, where are you now?"

"In the canoe we checked out at the boathouse, paddling across the lake. Or, if you prefer," said Elise, switching to a hoarse, clipped parody of Marines cadence, "our twenty is one-seven-niner degrees of Alphabet Bingo Bango Underwear. On track to reach designated Drop Zone Zamboni on schedule at ninety hundred and fifty-five thousand hours, CDT, BYOB, LOLZ. Over."

"I'll have you know I don't find that the slightest bit amusing," said Ajay, sounding tweeked. "Over."

This time Will heard Brooke giggle in the background. He moved to a western window and spotted their canoe in the northern end of the lake, approaching the island.

"I see you now," he said. "Keep your eyes peeled for security as you pass along the northern shore."

"Maybe try tossing those jamokes a booty shot so they drop their weapons and drool," said Nick.

"Would you please give me that?" said Ajay.

Will heard Ajay wrestle the walkie-talkie back from Nick.

"Remember, this is our scouting run," said Will. "Low profile. We just want to see if they pay any attention to you."

They waited. Will watched them through the glasses as the canoe drew closer. He could make out Brooke in front and Elise steering in back but then began to lose sight of them through the trees.

"The north beach is empty," said Elise, whispering into her mic. "No guards in sight." Will heard Brooke point something out to her. "There's a security camera on a post above the rear dock."

"Is it moving or fixed?" asked Will.

"It's moving. I see it, too," said Ajay urgently. "It's tracking with your canoe, Elise. Don't use your walkie anymore. They can see you."

Will caught a glimpse of the canoe between the leaves, about twenty yards offshore near the dock.

"Four other cameras," said Ajay, lowering his voice. "Five in all, quite compact and attached discreetly to trees. And they're all moving in sync with the canoe."

"Those weren't there last year," said Will.

"They must have added them after our little excursion," said Ajay. "They must be rigged to motion detectors."

"That's why they don't need people watching from ground level," said Will.

"They're probably night vision capable as well," said Ajay.

"And now—for joy—we get to paddle ALL the way back to the boathouse," said Elise.

"No you don't, chick-a-boom," said Nick. "Paddle over here and bring us lunch. Didn't you pack a pick-a-nick basket?"

"You can bet they *do* have night vision," said Will, ignoring him. "We'll have to get down the hatch before dark."

"Will, they must have a control center somewhere inside," whispered Ajay.

"I'm going to look for it right now," said Will, stowing his binoculars.

"Can't we just stash this canoe in the weeds and use it later?" asked Elise.

"And what happens when you don't bring it back to the boathouse at the end of the day?" asked Will.

"We tell them a lake monster chomped our ride in half and we barely escaped with our lives," said Elise.

"Trust me, come back in just your bathing suits and it won't matter what you say," said Nick.

"Stow it, horndog," said Elise.

"Don't worry about getting to the island," said Ajay. "I'll get us across the lake."

"Without a canoe?" asked Brooke.

"Just keep paddling, oh ye of little faith," said Ajay.

"I need to get to work here," said Will. "Head back to the pod and get ready. We're going in tonight."

MR. ELLIOT

Will wolfed down his sandwich, drank half his water, and went to work examining the boxes. He discovered that all of them had dates scrawled on the side, so he cranked up to his highest speed, motored around the room rearranging them, and had them neatly arranged in chronological order in less than twenty minutes. Three equal rows, forty boxes in each, lined up in the center of the room. Some were sealed; most were open. Their weight varied greatly; some were packed solid and heavy with books and ledgers, while others contained nothing but rolled-up maps.

He started going through them, not immediately finding any connection between Haxley and the Knights but he was thrilled by what he did discover. This was a treasure trove; the whole history of the Crag appeared to be in these boxes. In a box labeled CORNISH he found maps of the island dating to the nineteenth century, along with the original blueprints for the castle. Will snapped pictures of those. He also came across a wealth of information about the Center, with records for the school that were as recent as 2006.

That surprised him: He'd been under the impression the Crag had always been a private residence, so it made sense that documents related to the history of the house would be present, but what were all these records about the Center doing here?

There was such a wealth of material that his biggest challenge was deciding where to begin his search. He settled on looking for anything related to one year in particular, the first moment when they knew for a fact that the Knights of Charlemagne and the Black Caps intersected in time: 1937. The year when that photograph was taken, showing Hobbes and Nepsted together, at the dinner given for Henry Wallace.

Will eventually located a couple of boxes with 1937 scrawled on the side. Most of the contents appeared to be mundane paperwork relating to maintenance of the castle grounds. Accounting and payroll ledgers. Books of receipts from vendors. Canceled checks in files, hundreds of them, all drawn from an account for the Greenwood Foundation—the parent organization that owned the Center and its assets, including the NSEA—and for the most part signed by the school's treasurer and accountant.

But not all of them. Paging through the 1937 check files, Will found one written in October in the amount of $315. This "Greenwood Foundation" check was made out to Henry Wallace—who, as they already knew, had been the United States secretary of agriculture.

In the lower left-hand corner was written, *Reimbursement for travel expenses*. That date lined up with the photograph Brooke had found of Wallace at the private school dinner.

Then he discovered something even more curious about it: This check—and *only* this one of all the hundreds he'd gone through—was signed by Will's great-grandfather, Thomas Greenwood, the school's founder and first headmaster.

So it seemed that the Center—and Thomas Greenwood *personally*—had invited Wallace to the school for that event, and perhaps other activities, even paying his way so he could attend.

But why? This certainly seemed to confirm that the Center—and its founder and headmaster—still approved of the Knights at that point in time. It even suggested that, for some unknown reason, Thomas Greenwood wanted a prominent national figure to meet with them.

Will couldn't find any other documents relating to the dinner, but he wanted to check the 1938 boxes to see what he could find there. He checked the time: nearly 11:00 a.m.

Lemuel Clegg would expect him for lunch in the kitchen in an hour. He needed to look for the security center and scout the hatch entrance, which didn't leave enough time to search through any more boxes with the level of detail the job demanded. Based on the small sample he'd seen, there were many things about the Crag and the school in these boxes that they needed to know—maybe really important things—but if he rushed through them, his eyes would cross eventually and he'd stop paying attention and would surely miss something.

This was a perfect job for Ajay. He'd take one look and would retain it as reliably as scanning all this data into a computer.

But how to get any of this to him? Will could sneak a small number of files out in his backpack, but it would take forever to process all this material that way and they didn't have that much time. The other alternative was to somehow sneak Ajay up here, during daylight, so he could buzz through all of it himself, but that presented even more obvious risks.

No solution immediately came to mind.

So, first step: He'd have to stretch out this mundane job so Lemuel didn't stick him onto some other mundane task. With no way of knowing where they'd assign him next, and with Haxley out of town, better that he live up to Mr. Clegg's impression of him as an insubordinate slacker. He quickly disarranged the boxes to make it look like he'd only started sorting them, memorizing the arrangement so he could still track their chronology.

Then he went downstairs to look for the Crag's security control center.

The long stone corridor heading away from the circular staircase led to a number of tributaries, an endless warren of halls, some ending in locked doors, others in dusty storage rooms filled with old furniture and framed paintings. He even found a large vaulted wine cellar with a probably priceless inventory of bottles.

The air in these old halls felt as ancient as the stones in the walls and worn floors, probably the oldest part of the whole estate. He followed the passageways as they meandered around under the entire castle, hoping to find, at some point, that they might connect to the tunnel that led down under the lake, but no luck and, so far, no security center.

Making his way back to the stairs to the main house, Will felt a weird tingling curl its way up his back from the base of his spine to his neck. He stopped and after making sure no one was watching him—which was close to what this felt like—he closed his eyes and tried to track the source of this uncanny feeling.

He'd never tried using his sensory Grid indoors before, and it felt clumsy at first. His image map bumped into walls all around and above him, disrupting the flow, but when he stopped trying so hard—remembering one of Jericho's instructions—all barriers melted away and his senses pushed past them.

He slowly isolated the source of this eerie *watching* feeling. It was emanating from somewhere nearby, on the same level he was on, and it showed up on his Grid as a lambent glow from behind a nearby wall. As he tuned into it and moved closer, he realized it was conveying more than just physical sensations to him; whatever it was had an emotional component as well.

Not fear based. Warm and welcoming.

Someone—something—is trying to say hello to me.

Locking on to that feeling, Will tracked it around a corner and down the passageway toward the source. It drew him to a closed door, halfway down the hall. A worn, wooden door, old-fashioned, rounded at the top. Didn't even appear to have a lock on it.

The sensation drifting from inside beckoned him like a magnet. It felt so agreeable and benign that resisting it didn't even occur to him. He tried the old steel rod handle and it turned with a squeak. He cracked open the door and peered inside.

A long, low room with a couple of dusty landscape paintings on the walls. A single overhead light burning over the only piece of furniture, at the far end—a tall, plain wooden cabinet. Large, clean, unadorned, fashioned from dark sturdy oak.

What was the name for a piece like this, a wardrobe?

It's called an armoire.

Will walked toward it. The pleasant feelings grew stronger as he approached. Something *inside* the cabinet. He thought he could see a faint white glow around the edges of the doors.

I'm supposed to open it.

Will reached for the doors. They seemed to tremble as his hands got closer, as if eager to throw themselves open for him. He could feel them vibrating as his fingers closed around the knobs. They opened smoothly, with a slight creak.

An object sat on a shelf, halfway up, just below Will's eye level. A flat, plain rectangular wooden box, about 12 x 18 inches. No labels or markings on it, the box looked beyond antique, weathered and scratched. Will couldn't resist the temptation to take it into his hands. The wood felt warm to his touch, oiled, dark, and smooth. He undid the simple latch and opened it.

Inside, nestled into a fitted mold lined with wrinkled royal blue silk, rested a circular brass plate, six inches across, etched with complex patterns of straight and curved lines. An ornate configuration of aged and weathered brass discs and circles were arrayed and stacked on top of the larger plate. Some of them formed wheels, half-moons, and curlicues; others ended in sharp points. The round ones were notched, like gauges. Although they were currently locked in place, all these smaller parts appeared capable of independent movement. This was clearly some sort of ancient measuring instrument, but the entirety of the device appeared functional in ways that Will couldn't begin to fathom.

It's an astrolabe.

He didn't know how the word came into his head. He couldn't even remember thinking it. He knew it meant this thing had something to do with sailors and ancient navigation but that was as much as he could recall. He picked it up. The astrolabe felt superb in his hands, a perfect size and balance, weight and shape—he could imagine the powerful attachment some ship's captain from long ago might feel toward an object his whole existence depended upon, but Will couldn't comprehend how anyone could operate any instrument so intricate and complex.

Then something else surfaced below those impressions that made no sense at all. He had the feeling that the object *itself* seemed to *like being held*. That didn't stand up to logical scrutiny. This thing was just cold metal in his hands, not a living organism—

He heard the scuff of a shoe on stone. Will turned. No one in the doorway behind him. But his eyes picked up slight movement: one of the paintings on the wall to his right had shifted.

His hackles rose again. Someone *was* watching him. He kept perfectly still and felt he could almost hear someone nearby *breathing*.

Will carefully placed the astrolabe back in the box. He was surprised to feel a deep twinge of regret as he let it slip from his hands. He closed the box, replaced it in the armoire, and silently closed the doors. He walked out of the room and shut the door behind him.

No one in the hallway. No visible door to any room on the right from where someone could have been watching.

But that didn't mean no one was there.

Will sprinted away down the hall, turning on his speed, taking one turn after another through the twisting basement corridors for half a minute until he was absolutely certain that no one could have followed him.

If his eyes couldn't find the security center, his Grid could. Will went halfway up the stairs, stopped short of the door, closed his eyes, and opened up his senses again.

As he directed the Grid through the rooms above, he picked up the energy trails of the household staff laboring throughout the house—vacuuming, ironing, changing linens, putting away dishes—but kept pressing on, looking for noticeable surges in power.

His perceptions shifted toward a cluster of energy on ground level in the wing of the house to his right, the one he'd already identified as the servants' quarters. This was a lot more than human energy, electrical power in highly concentrated form. He silently opened the door and slipped into the house. Moving to his right, he couldn't find a door that connected to where he felt the power coming from, but he caught a glimpse of the western wing through a rear window.

He closed his eyes again and quickly pinpointed the energetic glow. *There. Right there. In a room on ground level. Accessible through a door on the outside.*

Will walked to the nearest door leading to the grounds in back of the house, trying his best to appear like he was lost and looking for something. He opened the door and waited for an alarm to go off or security guards to come rushing in his direction. Neither happened, so he marched outside, stuck his hands in his pockets, and strolled toward the wall of the western wing. No patrolling guards, no dogs, no trip wires in sight. When he reached the wall, he moved along it until he reached a small steel-framed window next to another door.

Inside, Will saw the castle security center he'd picked up on the Grid. A midsized office with an array of at least twenty-five monitors and stacks of sophisticated electronics and computer towers set against a wall. One young beefy man in a blue blazer and tie sat at a desk in front of the monitors. An earpiece in one ear, a coiled wire disappearing down below his collar.

Will stared at the back of the man's head and sent a thought-form his way: *a clock with the hands spinning around.*

The man looked up at a clock on the wall. Will pushed another picture at him: *a lavish lunch buffet, loaded with delicious dishes, like something out of a commercial.*

The man glanced around, put a hand on his ample stomach, and glanced at the clock again. Ten minutes to noon, not quite time for lunch. Will pushed pictures of a greasy cheeseburger and a pile of fries and a cold soda at him, rapid fire.

The guard's willpower wavered, his sense of duty battling his sudden hunger. Will could practically hear his stomach growling. One more push shoved him over the edge: *a slice of cherry pie à la mode.*

The man stood and bolted for the exit. Will flattened himself against the wall behind the door as it flew open and the guard lumbered off toward the main house, breaking into a jog.

Will waited until the guard moved out of sight, then opened the door and entered. He scanned the monitors—images from all over the property, all of them surprisingly high-def, both inside and out. As he'd hoped, the interior of the tower room with all the boxes was *not* among them.

On one of the cameras he saw the hungry guard rush into the main house kitchen. The help had just finished setting up lunch, and Will chuckled when he saw the guard attack the buffet like a ravenous dog.

Will noticed five monitors in a row featuring views from the five cameras hidden along the island's northern shore, all of them slowly scanning from left to right at different intervals. He studied their pattern of movement, consulting his watch to time their sweeps along the beach, timing a brief pause when they were all turned away from the right side. He also noticed a switch on the console for infrared vision; whoever was monitoring this station would be able to see the entire northern beach just as well in the dark.

One person might be able to sneak on shore unnoticed, if they were both lucky *and* good, but five people crossing the lake on a boat carrying equipment? They could forget about a direct approach. He'd have to make some changes to their landing plan.

He spotted a more challenging problem on one of the other monitors: Another camera, in a fixed position, was focused directly on the wooden structure and hatch leading down to the tunnels. He also realized, at this closer angle, that the wooden hatch they'd encountered last year hadn't just been reinforced but completely replaced by one made out of metal.

And the hatch had a big honking security lock on it, thick and steel-plated.

Will searched the rest of the office for a key that might open that lock. Spotting a square metallic cabinet on the wall near the door, he walked over to open it. Glancing out the small window next to it he saw that the security guard was heading back toward his post. Carrying two plates stacked high with food, the man was speed walking at an almost comic pace, trying not to spill any of his bounty.

Will dashed to the only other door in the room, one that led farther into the building. Locked. Just as the guard pushed open the outside door with his sizeable rear, Will leaped over and stepped behind it as the man backed into the room. Will grabbed the inside doorknob and held it open.

The guard set down his plates on the desk, humming a happy little "I'm about to stuff my face till it hurts" tune. Will leaned out and watched the guard lift a dripping roast beef sandwich the size of a softball, dip it in au jus, and gnaw into it. Will took a deep breath, centered himself, and pushed the first nonsensical image that came into his mind at him: A full-grown Indian elephant appeared on the closest monitor, standing around the corner of the castle's west wing.

The guard looked up at the monitor, midbite, juice dribbling down his chin. He stopped chewing when he "saw" what was there and froze.

"What the hell . . . ," he mumbled.

Will altered the image. The elephant raised its trunk and trumpeted. The guard "heard" it. The sandwich plopped onto the desk as he shot back in his chair, jumped up, and hurled himself outside, activating his comm system while he reached for the pistol holstered on his hip.

"I need backup," he said into the microphone of his communications rig. "Animal on the western edge of the west wing."

He never even noticed the outside door was still open. Will quietly eased it forward, stepped back, and opened the metallic cabinet.

Keys inside, on hooks. All shapes and sizes, some hanging in clusters. Row after orderly row, maybe a hundred of them. Printed labels fastened to the box below each hook, describing each key. His mind quickly tried to process what he was reading as he worked his way down, scanning row after row.

There, near the bottom right: *Tunnel Entrance.*

He wanted to keep looking, but the clock in his head said time was running out. He grabbed the small key ring hanging above *Tunnel Entrance,* shut the box, and jumped back outside, making sure the door closed behind him. He could hear voices around the corner to his right where he'd placed the "elephant" and knew that more guards would soon be on their way. Not enough time to get back inside through the door he'd originally used to leave the house.

Besides, it was opening right now, another guard exiting in response to the alert.

Will turned on his speed and headed for the woods. Once he was far enough in to gain cover, he stopped, turned, and waited to see if anyone had noticed him. He heard voices to his left and saw five guards who'd responded to the "elephant" call returning to the house. The heavyset guard who'd alerted them sheepishly brought up the rear. Once they passed, Will quickstepped to the nearest door on the west wing and reentered the house.

A laundry facility. Half a dozen washers and dryers stacked

against a wall, a few of them churning away. Tables with piles of folded sheets and towels next to a row of ironing boards. No one in the room.

Will moved quickly to an open inner door and listened. Hearing workers down the hall, he leaned out and saw them clustered around a window. Looking out at the security guards to see what the commotion was about.

Will hurried down a rambling hallway to his right, feeling his way back toward the center of the castle. He glanced at his watch: a few minutes after noon now. He needed to get to the kitchen before Clegg started looking for him. Emerging a few doors later, Will found himself back in a marbled hallway of the main residence. He followed that to its end and turned right through a swinging door, instinct telling him that was the way to the kitchen.

He had instead walked into an intimate private dining room, filled with antique furnishings, including a long, magnificent mahogany table. High ceilings, with a fireplace at one end and high, leaded windows. Two distinctive chandeliers rested over the table, heavy black iron with bulbs disguised as candles, with matching candle sconces on the wall.

He'd seen these fixtures before, and then he remembered where. *This is the room in the photograph. Where the Knights had their dinner in 1937 with Henry Wallace.*

On a cabinet straight ahead was what looked like a guest ledger. He walked over and was about to open it when he heard, "Looking for something, Mr. West?"

Will turned. Lemuel Clegg was standing in the doorway, looking stern, arms crossed. Will smiled broadly and crossed to him.

"Boy, am I glad to see you," said Will, falling back into character as a brash, teenage idiot.

"Why is that?"

"Hello, starved? Lost so much weight up there I was about to eat my own foot. I tried to follow back the way you took me up there and got so totally lost."

"Is that so. And how did you end up in the private residential area?"

"Honestly? I have no idea," said Will. "Zigged when I should have zagged about twelve times. Tell me I didn't miss lunch?"

"The kitchen is *that* way," said Lemuel, angrily thrusting a finger at another door. "And if you're unable to find your way in the future, I'll assign someone to escort you."

"Thanks, Mr. Clegg, but I'm good," said Will, walking past him to the door.

"Don't let it happen again," said Lemuel.

"Mr. Haxley must so appreciate your sense of humor—"

"Get!"

After a quick lunch, Will returned to the tower room to discover a tall man standing across the room, his back to the door, looking at a folder he'd apparently taken from one of the boxes. The man heard the door close behind Will and turned.

Mr. Elliot. Haxley's elderly friend from last night. Wearing expensive-looking black wool slacks, a white dress shirt buttoned to the neck, and a gray cashmere cardigan sweater. His finely wrinkled face widened into a toothy smile.

"You've discovered my secret," said Elliot.

Will said nothing, worried that he'd been found out in some way.

"This tower is my favorite section of the house. The entire history of the estate is in these boxes. It's all been sadly neglected for years."

120

"Yeah, everything was in pretty rough shape," said Will, moving toward him.

Elliot smiled again—beamed actually—as Will reached him, and Elliot patted him on the shoulder.

"I'm so delighted that Stan's found the right person to put it all back in order."

"I'm not sure why he'd think I'm the right person," said Will. "I mean, this is a pretty big job, sir."

"Oh, Stan is an excellent judge of character. I trust him to make the right decision about a task as important as this one," said Elliot sincerely.

Will noticed that Elliot was holding the same folder from 1937 that Will had looked through earlier.

Strange . . . What were the chances of that? But Elliot made no effort to hide it from him, so he either didn't know, didn't care . . . or he wanted Will to see it.

"Have you had time to go through any of this material?" asked Elliot, opening the folder.

"No, sir. So far I've just arranged boxes," said Will, straightening one with his foot.

"Perhaps you should organize them by year. Chronological order."

Elliot smiled again, in a way that Will was starting to find unsettling. The man really threw him off balance. *Why is this guy taking such an interest in all this, and in me?*

"I take it you work with Mr. Haxley in some way, sir?" asked Will. "If you don't mind my asking."

"I'm an advisor to him, yes."

"About business."

"About many things," said Elliot, looking down as he paged through the folder again. "Including business."

"I wondered if you might be connected to the school in some way."

"Not in any official capacity. Unofficially, I like to think of myself as its . . . amateur historian."

Will looked around at the boxes. "I guess the history of the school must be pretty interesting."

"History is one of my many interests," he said, still without looking up. "The story of this school fascinates me. You might wonder why there's so much material about the school, stored here in a private residence."

Will didn't know what to say about that, but Elliot seemed to know what he was thinking.

"The Crag was the residence of both headmasters at one time or another. This archive includes many of their private papers."

"I thought they lived at Stone House," said Will.

"You must also be wondering if I was a student here myself," said Elliot, ignoring his question. "If only I'd been so fortunate. The number of extraordinary men who've passed through these halls is remarkable. For instance . . ." Elliot turned around the folder he was holding and showed a picture of—who else?—the thirty-third vice president of the United States, Henry Wallace, one that Will hadn't seen before.

"One of our country's most unusual public figures," said Elliot. "Do you know much about him?"

"I'm afraid I don't."

"You'd do well to study Henry Wallace. You'd learn quite a lot of useful things. Are you interested—may I call you Will?"

"Yes, sir."

"And you may call me Mr. Elliot. Are you as interested in history as I am, Will?"

"I don't know, I mean, I wasn't that much, at least before I got here. Maybe it was the way they were teaching it."

"No doubt. The educational methods employed in most American schools turn good minds to stone. The past has many things to teach us, and we ignore them at our peril. If you don't know where you've been, how can you know where you are?"

Will wasn't sure if Elliot wanted him to answer. "And if you don't know where you are," he said, "how do you know where you're going?"

Elliot beamed at him again. "I couldn't have put it better myself. Mr. Haxley expects you'll do very well here. By that I mean he expects you to do a good deal more than simply arrange the boxes. The material *inside* the boxes needs to be organized as well."

"I see. Mr. Clegg didn't mention that—"

"Mr. Clegg doesn't speak for Mr. Haxley," he said with a slight edge. "The material needs to be organized chronologically. In *all* the boxes."

"That's good to know." Will was secretly thrilled to hear that he'd have more time with this stuff but tried not to show it. "Mr. Elliot, this is such a big assignment I'm thinking about asking Mr. Haxley if I could bring a friend along next time to give me a hand."

"Oh?"

#80: GO EASY ON THE HARD SELL. PERSUASION IS THE ART OF MAKING OTHERS BELIEVE IT WAS *THEIR* IDEA.

"I want to do a really good job," said Will, trying not to sound too enthusiastic, "and I think two heads might be better than one."

"I assume this friend is a student here?"

"One of my roommates," said Will. "And he's really good at this sort of thing. Think I should ask Mr. Haxley about it?"

"He's out of town for a while," said Elliot, pausing to study Will, who tried not to flinch under the pressure of his pale eyes. "But I believe I can speak for him on a matter like this. Let me think about it."

"Thank you, sir."

Elliot kept staring at him, a straight poker face. If he had an opinion about the idea, Will couldn't tell which way he was leaning.

"Why don't you put that back in the box you already started going through," said Elliot as he handed over the folder. "Then come with me for a moment. Speaking of history, I'd like to show you something outside. Won't take long."

Elliot started walking, not toward the spiral staircase but away from it toward the rear of the room. Will stuck the folder back into the 1937 box, but not before sneaking a glance inside; the canceled check written by Thomas Greenwood to Henry Wallace was gone.

Elliot preceded Will through a door that Will hadn't noticed before, seamlessly set in the middle of the dark wooden back wall. Not exactly a secret door—it did have a tiny visible knob—but it was the closest thing to it. They entered a small, windowless vestibule that led to what Will decided was the oldest elevator he'd ever seen.

There were no doors. Elliot slid open a small collapsible steel grating and gestured for Will to enter ahead of him. The inside was paneled with dark wood and banded with cast iron. Elliot followed him in and closed the gate.

"I'm afraid that old staircase is a bit of an ordeal for me these days," said Elliot.

There were no buttons to push. Elliot turned a metallic

crank on a rotating disc—silver and shiny with age, the kind Will had only seen in really old movies—that operated the motor. The elevator, after a fitful start, began to slowly descend. Will could see the rough stone walls of the tower through the grating as they moved down.

"As you learn more about the house," said Elliot, looking up at the ceiling, "you might discover this elevator is one of the oldest still in continuous use in North America."

"That's reassuring," said Will.

The entire car trembled and stuttered every few feet, which Will found quite a bit more disconcerting.

"Don't worry," said Elliot. "It's regularly serviced and in excellent working order. The original owner brought in the sons of Mr. Elisha Graves Otis himself—the inventor of the vertical transportation device—to design and install this one a few years after the estate was built in 1870."

They finally passed a small window, about thirty feet above ground level, and Will caught a glimpse of the island and lake.

Elliot expertly operated the crank as they neared the bottom and feathered the elevator to a slightly bouncy stop at ground level.

"You see, Will, many old things work perfectly well as long as they're properly maintained," said Elliot with a wink as he opened the gate.

They stepped out into a slightly larger stone foyer, and then Elliot opened a door that led directly outside to a terrace on the western side of the castle. Colorful flowerbeds lined the edges of the patio, all of them as meticulously maintained as the rest of the grounds.

"Follow me," said Elliot.

Elliot took a collapsible round white hat from his pocket and carefully placed it on his head. His skin looked almost

125

transparent in the afternoon sun. As he moved away, Will noticed a strange pattern of striated skin—alternating pink and white stripes, almost like peppermint—just behind the man's ears.

It's not a Ride Along scar, but what the hell is that?

Swaying slightly as he walked, Elliot led him along a paved pathway up a slight rise off the terrace. At the crest of the rise, it continued along a flat ridgeline to a grove of maple and box elders, swaying in a slight breeze that moderated the midday heat.

The path ended in a grassy meadow surrounded by the grove of trees, and Will realized they were entering a small graveyard, the one Ajay had spotted from the opposite shore. About a dozen ancient headstones, worn with age and some covered with lichen, scattered over an area about twenty square yards. The carved stones were difficult to read, but Will noticed the name Cornish on a number of them.

"The castle's builder, Ian Cornish, chose this area for his family plot," said Elliot. "The island stayed in the hands of the Cornish family for only two generations, before Thomas Greenwood bought it for the Center just prior to the Great War. That would be World War One to your generation."

Will noticed another more recent stone monument just past the graveyard, set apart by a small black fence. A single large and thick cross on a pedestal, simple and unadorned, with twelve names engraved on its base, and the date May 1938.

"What is this?" asked Will.

"A memorial."

"For what?"

"As I understand it, for the worst tragedy in school history," said Elliot, walking right past it. "A plane crash that took the lives of twelve seniors and one of our teachers."

Twelve victims. In 1938? Will thought about it, his mind racing back to the photograph of the Knights dinner. *That was October of 1937. Seven months earlier. Twelve seniors. The twelve Knights?*

"Members of the class of '38," said Elliot, who didn't seem very interested for somebody who said he was the Center's historian.

In order to keep up with him, Will didn't have time to stop and read the names on the memorial, but now that he knew where it was he vowed to come back, as planned.

Elliot pointed at something ahead and led Will toward two much taller monuments at the far western edge of the grave-yard. They stood at the edge of the ridge before it fell off and ran gently down to the water's edge about a hundred yards away. Quarried from the same stone used to build the castle and turned to the west toward the setting sun were intricately sculpted figures from the school's crest.

A winged angel stood atop an eight-foot-high column, eyes lifted skyward, holding a book in its left hand and a raised sword in its right. Below it, carved as if stepping right out of the body of the column, was a knight, or what Will now realized was more likely a variation of the school's Paladin mascot. The figure struck a defense pose, raising its shield and pointing its sword down at some unseen earthbound foe.

The school's motto was carved into a stone scroll that un-furled at the Paladin's feet: *Knowledge is the Path. Wisdom is the Purpose.*

At first glance the two statues appeared to be mirror im-ages of each other, but the one on the right was a slightly lighter shade of stone that appeared newer, less weather-beaten.

"The resting place of our founder," said Elliot. "And his only son. The school's only two headmasters."

Our founder. *But Elliot just said he was never a student here.*

There were two names engraved in the base of each statue. The ones on the left read:

THOMAS WILLIAM GREENWOOD 1883–1958
MARY FRANCIS GREENWOOD 1890–1962

On the base of the right one:

FRANKLIN WILLIAM GREENWOOD 1920–1995
ELIZABETH HOWARD GREENWOOD 1921–1993

Below both sets of names, a pair of clasped hands had been carved along with the Latin phrase *Requiescat in pace.*

Rest in peace.

Will was looking at the graves of his grandparents and great-grandparents. All those stories his parents had told him about their own parents and how they'd died before he was born. More lies. Lies on top of lies.

He'd never even known his grandmother's real name before. And Franklin's middle name was William.

So William is a family name.

His eyes watered and his whole body felt flushed, and not just from the searing heat. He turned away slightly and had to work hard not to let any emotion show on his face.

Mr. Elliot was watching him closely.

"But Mr. Rourke's the headmaster now," said Will.

"Of course he is," said Elliot.

"You said they were the only two headmasters."

Elliot smiled spookily. "That makes three, then, doesn't it?"

TWO IF BY SEA

Ajay marched into the pod from his bedroom, holding up his notebook in triumph. "It took some elbow grease, because they deploy encryption worthy of the Pentagon, but I've cracked into the Haxley Industries database!"

"Tell us," said Will.

"To paraphrase Gilbert and Sullivan," said Ajay, walking to the table as he read from the screen, "Stan Haxley is what one might call the very model of a modern major millionaire."

"Who's Gilbert O'Sullivan?" asked Nick.

"Gather around, children," said Ajay, waving them to the table. "I've put together a humble presentation."

It was half past six. The other roommates, each laying out equipment they were packing into their backpacks, migrated to the table in the great room. Ajay expanded the screen of his notebook to the size of a wall screen without touching it; then Ajay's syn-app activated a brisk montage of articles and photos about their local magnate.

"According to their confidential files, Haxley runs two enterprises. One, a traditional private equity fund that makes beaucoup bucks by following a well-trod path of rapacious greed and opportunism, using other people's money to buy other people's companies, stripping off the meat and selling the bones."

Photos of Stan Haxley in corny "action" poses like you'd see in a corporate brochure appeared onscreen—Haxley wearing a hard hat, consulting with minions over blueprints, pointing up at a skyscraper under construction.

"I feel a nap coming on," said Nick, yawning.

"Don't mind him. He loses interest if he can't color the pictures," said Elise.

"Haxley also founded a *second* company in 1989, in Chicago," said Ajay, narrating as more visuals appeared. "Much more narrowly focused. Over the next few years it acquired a number of small, often struggling companies around the country—one hundred fifty-seven of them to be exact—all of them involved in areas of scientific research. Specifically genetic research."

That made everyone sit up and take notice. "Now you're talking," said Will.

"This company is privately held, so its true nature remains shrouded in secrecy," said Ajay, "but one can't escape feeling that they're pursuing this strategy toward some unified but unidentified goal."

"What do you think it is?" asked Brooke.

"And why should we give a rat's rear end about another crooked Wall Street bankster?" asked Nick.

"Because of two significant details, my ignorant friend," said Ajay with a secret smile. "Haxley's second in command at this company was Ronnie Murso's father . . ."

"What?" they all asked.

"Wait for it . . . and the name of this covert organization is the Paladin Group."

"No way," said Elise.

Will took some deep breaths to center himself. He looked over at Brooke; every once in a while he had to remind himself that she was more from Stan Haxley's world than theirs. She was listening closely but didn't say anything, her emotions impossible to read.

"And if anyone here thinks that's a coincidence," said Ajay, closing his notebook, "I own a bridge in Brooklyn I would like to sell you."

"How much is Haxley worth?" asked Will, getting up and pacing around.

"As near as I can estimate," said Ajay, checking his screen, "in the neighborhood of seventeen billion dollars."

"Whoa, where do I grab the bus to that neighborhood?" asked Nick.

"He's one of the wealthiest men in the country," said Ajay.

"Who'd run over his own mother if she was standing on a quarter," said Elise. "So for his tax bracket, buying a castle is practically a requirement."

"Okay, so the dude's a Richie Rich dirtbag, but does this mean he's behind the Prophecy?" asked Nick.

"It's a pertinent question, Nick," said Will, then turned to Elise. "Think about what happened last year when Ronnie made that video of Lyle and Hobbes. Elise, you thought that maybe Ronnie showed it to his dad at some point. What happened next?"

"They both vanished," said Elise.

"You're saying Haxley had something to do with that?" asked Brooke.

"It's possible," said Will, his tone urging caution. "What if Haxley and Murso were part of the Knights when they were in school? They were both class of '76. And thirteen years later they start this company, the Paladin Group."

"Keep going," said Ajay.

"Let's give Ronnie's dad the benefit of the doubt. Maybe he didn't know everything about the Prophecy program. Maybe when his son brings him that tape he's so disturbed he decides to confront Haxley. Haxley decides it'd be a lot cleaner if Ronnie and his dad disappeared."

The idea of *murder* with an understandable *motive* injected a chill into the room.

"I would place a Haxley-sized wager that you've hit it on the head," said Ajay.

"Let's hope finding Nepsted's key leads to nailing it down," said Will, fastening his backpack. "Ajay, did you come across anything about an associate of Haxley's named Mr. Elliot?"

Ajay looked up and to the right. A gesture Will knew meant he was accessing his gargantuan, photographic recall "hard drive."

"No," said Ajay. "Why?"

"I met him with Haxley at the castle. They're partnered up in some way but were both pretty vague about it. There's something spooky about this guy Elliot that I can't pin down."

"Did he say something specific that tipped you off?" asked Brooke.

"No, it was something he did. When I was looking through this file for information about that Knights' dinner in 1937, I came across a canceled check written by Thomas Greenwood, the school's founder."

"What's the significance of that?" asked Ajay.

"Don't know yet. The check was written to Henry Wallace, their guest of honor that night, for his travel expenses. So it looks like Thomas Greenwood invited Wallace to be here for the event with the Knights."

"Why would the school's headmaster do that?" asked Brooke.

"I have no idea, but we need to find out," said Will.

"So what was the point you were going to make about the check, Will?" asked Brooke.

"Something strange happened later," said Will. "I found this weird artifact in a room in the basement, an antique astrolabe, in a wooden box. The whole time I had a strange feeling I was being watched. When I came back to the tower after lunch, Mr. Elliot had that *same* file I'd been looking at in his hand. And the check that Greenwood wrote to Wallace was missing."

"So you think Mr. Elliot doesn't want you to know about Greenwood inviting Wallace to the Center," said Elise.

"Maybe so," said Will. "I also found the room in the photo where that dinner took place. It's in the castle, too. And there's a memorial on the island for twelve seniors who died in a plane crash in May of 1938. Anyone want to bet the names on it are the same as the ones who were at that dinner?"

Will waited a moment for all of that to settle.

"Whoa," said Nick.

"But if the ones on the plane were the same group, we know that at least two of them survived," said Ajay. "Nepsted and Hobbes."

"Right," said Elise, thinking it through. "And if they didn't want anyone to *know* there were any survivors, they'd put their names on the memorial with the others."

Wouldn't be the last time somebody survived a "plane crash" around here, thought Will.

"Everything keeps circling back to this one moment in time," said Will, holding up the photo. "Hobbes and Nepsted and the Knights of Charlemagne in the same room with Thomas Greenwood and the country's soon-to-be vice president."

"How do you know Greenwood was there?" asked Nick. "He's not in the picture."

"I'm thinking Greenwood took the photo," said Will.

"There are ten other seniors in that photograph," said Ajay.

133

"I'm still trying to find out exactly who else was in attendance, but all the 1937 yearbooks are missing from the library."

"I think we can get those names off the memorial," said Will.

"Henry Wallace," said Elise, making her own note. "We need to know more about him, too."

"Ajay, I'm also working on permission to bring you up there to go through the boxes."

"I welcome the opportunity," said Ajay, cramming the last few items into his bulging backpack.

Nick picked up a hatchet and a can of lighter fluid Ajay was about to add. "Dude, what are you bringing these for?"

"The spirit of the Boy Scout motto, my good man," said Ajay, taking them back and jamming them into his pack. "For instance, what if we need to start a campfire? *Be prepared.* I fashioned this hatchet in the labs myself, from high-density carbon steel. I believe it could be remarkably useful."

"Guys, we're going in tomorrow night," said Will. "It's Saturday, so they'll be more relaxed about curfew. Let's finish packing and get some rest. We're going to need it."

The others went back to work packing, purposeful and quiet. Ajay shouldered his backpack and staggered around the room. Will figured it must weigh at least forty pounds—Ajay had packed every gadget he owned—but he never complained about how heavy it was.

Will liked what he was seeing; solidifying a connection between Stan Haxley and the Paladin Prophecy had strengthened everyone's resolve.

Seven o'clock Saturday evening. The setting sun still hung a substantial way above the western horizon, but the heat had finally started to ease up as they set out from Greenwood Hall.

They departed in two groups, boys and girls, leaving minutes apart and taking different routes to avoid arousing suspicion. The school's curfews were much less rigidly enforced in the summer months. If any guards bothered to stop and ask, they were headed out for a hike and then a picnic supper down by the lake. Since it would stay light until nearly 10:00 p.m., no one would even question the idea.

The boys struck straight out toward the old field house everyone called the Barn. They passed by the fierce statue of the school mascot—the Paladin—or rather a replica that had recently been installed after the original ripped itself loose and attacked Nick last November.

"When did that go back up?" asked Ajay.

"Last week," said Nick. He eyed the figure warily, and then it triggered a thought. "Hey, I meant to show you this earlier. Check this out. They were passing 'em out at the pool today."

He swung his pack around, rummaged around in the front flap, and fished out a yellow paper flyer, the kind you'd find stuck under your windshield wiper at a mall.

"This is the one I was telling you about," said Nick, pointing to one of the photographs on it. "That's the little wrestler dude who looks like Nepsted."

It was a cheaply thrown together advertisement for a wrestling "extravaganza." Being held next Saturday night at the old armory arena in New Brighton, the nearby town where Nick worked as a lifeguard at the community swimming pool.

Six wrestlers were pictured in corny staged action shots— four men and two women. They wore makeup and outrageous costumes, oversized slabs of beef making aggressively silly faces.

Except for one of the men in the bottom row, a muscular, well-proportioned little person that they called, in big print below his picture, The Professor. Compared to the others, his expression was a portrait in dignified restraint, but apparently that was part of his character. He carried a walking stick, wore a sleeveless cartoon version of a dandy's suit and tie, a jaunty top hat, and a monocle wedged over his right eye.

Will had to admit that, although the photo was a lousy reproduction and the guy was wearing that ridiculous getup, it was clear that the Professor bore a striking resemblance to Happy Nepsted.

"You see? What'd I tell you," said Nick. "Practically dead ringers!"

"Yes, I see," said Ajay. "But what does it mean?"

"I have no freaking idea," said Nick. "But, dudes, next Saturday? We are *so* front row. I already bought us tickets."

Will and Ajay looked at each other, undecided.

"What have we got to lose?" asked Will.

"Only our dignity," said Ajay, waving his hand at the flyer. "Which is, thankfully, much more than you can say for these jokers."

They trudged on, starting down the hill from the Barn toward the woods.

"Awesome," said Nick. "Now I just have to work on the girls."

By 7:30, they reached the observation point Ajay had established earlier in the day. Elise and Brooke arrived fifteen minutes later, following a path along the lake from the east. So far they were completely alone in the woods and no one had seen either group arrive.

So far, so good.

Will and Ajay took a long look at the north shore of the

island. Once again, there were no guards in sight. Ajay didn't even need his binoculars to confirm that the five tree-mounted security cameras were still making their regular sweep of the shoreline.

"Let's motate, dudes," said Nick, bouncing around with excess energy. "What are we waiting around for?"

"For the sun to drop below the tree line," said Will. "Then you'll go across first."

"That's cool," said Nick. "Whenever. I'm ready, Freddy."

Nick stripped down to the swimsuit under his shorts and took flippers, a mask, and a snorkel from his backpack.

"Stand by for the gun show, ladies," said Nick, then arranged his arms in a bodybuilding pose.

"And me without my air sickness bag," said Elise.

They waited behind the thicket until the sun finally slipped behind the trees to the west at 8:10 and twilight filtered the world around them to a uniform slate gray, reflecting the shade on the surface of the lake. A light breeze tickled the water, but conditions remained calm.

"I was just thinking," said Nick, concentrating intently.

"Did you hurt yourself?" asked Ajay.

"About what?" asked Elise.

"Seriously, the totally worst time to have a stroke? Has to be during a game of charades."

Will checked his watch again. "Time to go, Nick," he said.

"Catch you on the flip side, kids," said Nick.

"Be careful, Nicky," said Elise.

"She cares," said Nick, folding his hands under his chin like a lovesick goof. "She really cares."

Elise slugged him in the arm. Nick crouched around the thicket and snuck down to the water's edge while the others watched the island shoreline a couple hundred yards away. Nick reached the last bit of cover before the beach and looked back for a signal; Will gave him the thumbs-up.

Nick slipped into the lake without a ripple. He put on flippers, mask, and snorkel and immediately used a dolphin kick to propel himself below the surface and out of sight. About fifty feet from shore, the tip of the snorkel appeared briefly, just long enough for Nick to take in a breath, then submerged again.

"Good gracious, look how far he's gone already," said Ajay, watching him closely. "He swims like a seal."

"Toss him a fish and he'll balance a ball on his nose," said Elise.

"There's someone on the shore," said Brooke, peering through her binoculars.

Will trained his glasses over to where she was aimed.

A guard was walking along the rocky beach, heading directly for the section of beach where Nick was supposed to make land.

"What's he doing?" asked Elise.

Will watched the guard stop near the water and take out a pack of cigarettes and a lighter, looking around a little furtively as he lit one up.

"He's sneaking a smoke," said Will.

"Nice to know," said Elise dryly. "Even the bad guys discourage smoking."

The tip of Nick's snorkel surfaced again, almost halfway to the island this time.

"He's going to see him," said Ajay, eyes wide with alarm. "We have to warn Nick!"

Will and Elise glanced at each other, thinking the same thing.

You want to try? Will asked her silently.

Elise tilted her head to the side and replied, *Heck, if it works on my family's golden retriever, I ought to be able to get through to Dolphin Boy.*

She lowered her binoculars, closed her eyes, and concentrated.

Will trained his binoculars back on the lake. He saw Nick's snorkel poke to the surface again about fifty yards offshore. It ducked under again briefly, then came up a moment later, in the same spot.

Elise opened her eyes and winked at Will.

"What's happening?" asked Ajay.

"He's treading water," said Brooke. "Nick must've spotted him."

"Why does that blasted guard have to smoke so slowly?" moaned Ajay. "Is he trying to catch cancer from a single cigarette?"

"Don't worry, Nick can probably only tread water for about a month," said Elise.

"Out of curiosity, Ajay, can you tell what brand he's smoking?" asked Will.

Ajay opened his eyes wide and looked at the guard, without binoculars. "It's filtered, but he's already burned past the label. And he's put the pack back in his pocket."

"You can see that kind of detail?" asked Brooke, lowering her binoculars. "Without *these*?"

Ajay hemmed and hawed. "Well, you know, from this distance I just made an educated guess—"

"Yes, he can see that far and that well," said Will. "You're among friends, Ajay. We're not going to tell anybody."

"But I thought your big whoop was *remembering* everything you see," said Elise.

"That's correct," said Ajay.

"Plus he can *see* everything," said Will.

"Within reason," said Ajay.

"How many fingers am I holding up behind my back?" asked Brooke.

"I can see things at a distance," said Ajay. "I never said I could see *through* anything."

"So, for instance, you can't see our underwear right now," said Elise, deadpan.

Ajay blushed and giggled, and then stifled his giggle with both hands and turned away.

Brooke gave Elise a low five.

Will looked at the guard through his glasses again. He put out the cigarette, sat on a rock, and unwrapped a candy bar.

"Great," said Will. "Now he's having a snack."

"Snickers," said Ajay. "To be precise."

Can you nudge him? Will heard Elise ask in his head.

Will didn't think he could push a suggestion over that distance, but answered, *What the heck, time's a-wasting. Worth a try.*

He focused on the guard's head, closed his eyes, and pushed a word picture at him: two other guards talking near the castle: *Is that idiot sneaking a smoke again? Somebody check down by the lake.*

The picture took a while to reach the guard—over three seconds—but when Will raised his glasses again, he saw the man react like he'd just been caught shoplifting. He glanced back at the castle, hastily flicked his candy wrapper toward the water, and hustled back into the woods.

"He's gone," said Will.

"And he's a litterbug," said Ajay.

A few moments later Nick's snorkel peeked out of the water again. His head surfaced as he took a quick look and saw that the guard was gone. He went back under, and ten seconds later Nick crawled up on the beach. At first he lay flat to look around, but once he saw the cameras had rotated away from him, he scampered up the rocks to the edge of the tree line.

Will found Nick through the binoculars, signaling a thumbs-up back in their direction.

"He's across," said Will, looking at his watch. "Get ready to roll."

Will stood up and waved his arms in an arc toward Nick. Nick waved back, then hustled through the woods toward the tree holding the security camera that was farthest to the left. He shimmied up the trunk to where it was hidden, staying behind the lens.

Will spotted him through the glasses again. "Nick's in position. Hit it, Ajay."

Ajay waddled down to the water's edge under his heavy pack and shrugged it off near the waterline. He took out a heavy, compact black cube from the pack, about a foot square, set it on the sand, and yanked a rip cord that extended out of the cube's center. A whoosh of air rushed into the cube and it began to rapidly expand and unfold. Within seconds the cube had re-formed into an entirely new shape: an oblong black rubber raft about six feet long and three feet wide.

Will, Brooke, and Elise took out and snapped together collapsible paddles. Will put together a second one from Nick's pack, and then they all sprinted to the lake.

As soon as Nick saw them appear on the shore, he clamped one hand around the security camera and began to slow down its arc from right to left. Will noted the time on his watch. They had three minutes before the next camera would sweep over far enough to see them.

Wading in to his ankles, Ajay positioned the raft in water

just deep enough for it to float. Ajay and the girls loaded in their packs, climbed aboard, and took their assigned spots. Will tossed Ajay the second paddle, shoved the raft into the lake, and jumped in. All four started paddling toward the island.

"Good job, Ajay," whispered Will, sitting next to Brooke in the back.

"She's holding together fantastically well, don't you think?" said Ajay, smiling with pride.

"How did you make this?" asked Brooke.

"A latex mold I fashioned surreptitiously in the lab, patterned after the Zodiac rafts used by Navy Seals. I simply added a self-inflating friction intake valve for the bladder powered by pulling the rip cord—sorry, I don't mean to bore you with the details."

"No," said Elise dryly. "Pray continue."

"Anyway, I couldn't be more tickled with the results—"

"Less talking," said Will, "more paddling. Sound carries over water."

"By the way, why is a boat a 'she'? Why isn't it an 'it'?" whispered Brooke.

"Quite an interesting story, actually," Ajay whispered back. "In ancient times, sailors named ships after various goddesses, an appeal for benevolence during perilous journeys—"

Elise scowled over her shoulder at Brooke: "You had to ask."

"—and the custom continues to this day when captains name ships after wives or girlfriends; in fact, ships remain one of the only *gendered* inanimate objects in the English language, which is ironic since having a *real* woman on board is considered bad luck."

At that moment the boat sprang a leak near the front, spouting water right in front of Brooke.

"So I guess that doubles down with two of us on board," she said.

"Why don't you fix it with your hatchet?" asked Elise.

"Very funny," said Ajay. "As it happens, I have a patch kit here in my bag."

Ajay knelt down to repair the leak and nearly tipped over into the lake.

"Take it easy, Ishmael," said Elise, steadying him.

Will looked toward the shore. They had made it nearly two-thirds of the way across, and he could see Nick in the tree restraining the camera from swinging over far enough to spot them.

Will looked over at the next camera, on a tree twenty yards to the right of Nick, which had begun to slowly turn back toward them. With Ajay working on the patch and only three of them paddling, Will realized they'd now be caught in its sights before they made it to the beach.

"It's going to see us, isn't it?" said Brooke, watching Will's eye line.

"Hold on a second," said Will.

It was one thing to push a suggestion to someone across a lake, and quite another to affect an object physically over that kind of distance. He'd never tried anything close to this before. Will set down his paddle, focused on the second camera, narrowed his eyes, and concentrated ferociously, blanking everything else out of his mind the way Jericho had taught him.

"What are you doing?" whispered Brooke.

Lost in concentration, unable to answer, Will felt the fingers of his intention rush out across the water toward the second camera, and this time his mind's eye traveled with them. All of a sudden he was "seeing" the camera from midair, right next to that tree. He "wrapped" his fingers around the armature that attached it to the tree, applied resistance, then felt the camera's motor protest as its arc slowed to a crawl.

"Paddle," grunted Will, teeth clenched, sweat dripping down his forehead and neck. "Hurry."

Ajay finished patching the leak and picked up his paddle, and the others dug away at the water, coordinating their stroke to Brooke's whispered count. Will "held" the camera for as long as he could, letting it go just as the hull of the boat scraped bottom on the rocky beach.

They all jumped out and dragged the raft toward the tree line. Nick hopped down from the tree and ran to help them. They yanked it out of sight and dove for cover just as both cameras swung around to their side of the beach.

They waited until the cameras swiveled back the other way, then worked to conceal the raft with loose branches. Will felt a rush of light-headedness and slumped to his knees, heaving for breath after his double exertion. Brooke saw him go down and knelt beside him, concerned.

"Your heart rate's sky-high," Brooke whispered, taking his hand. "And your pulse is erratic. Are you all right?"

Will nodded, still unable to speak.

"Take a deep breath," she said quietly.

Will took in a full breath and felt his heart decelerate out of the red zone. He felt instantly calmer. "How did you know my heart rate before checking my pulse?"

Brooke thought about it a moment. "I don't know. I wasn't wrong, was I?"

Will shook his head.

She took his hand again. "It's slowing now. But you were up near two hundred a minute before, and your blood pressure was sky-high. What did you do to yourself on the raft?"

Will didn't want to answer—Brooke had never seen him use his telekinetic ability, and they'd never talked about it—but before he could respond, Elise cleared her throat, drawing their attention. She and the others were crouched behind them, watching and waiting. Brooke withdrew her hand. Will avoided meeting Elise's eye.

"Do you think their control center noticed those two cameras slow down?" asked Ajay, glancing nervously toward the castle.

"They probably would have reacted by now," said Will, climbing back to his feet. "But let's make sure."

"Dudes, it was the coolest thing," said Nick, putting his clothes back on over his suit. "I'm hauling butt, right, way under water, when all of a sudden I just *know* I gotta stop. So I surface and sure enough there's this guard dude smoking on a rock. I totally had a precondition about him."

Elise and Will glanced at each other and had to suppress a smile.

"Precognition," said Ajay. "Not precondition. *Stupid* is a precondition, which you also have."

"Dude," said Nick. "You need a checkup from the neck up."

Everyone shouldered their bags and followed Will into the woods. He found a simple footpath, little more than a deer trail that led toward the castle. No one spoke, and Will used hand signals from in front to direct them. The woods thinned out about a hundred yards on and Will took his bearings off the rear, guiding them toward the wooden structure over the hatch.

The whole stretch of open area behind the house was empty. They heard no sounds coming from the castle and few lights were on. When Haxley was away, Will figured the staff probably retired to their wing by early evening. When the rear door came into view, he signaled, everyone dropped to a crouch, and he scanned the windows with binoculars.

Under a bright hanging lamp, Lemuel Clegg sat at the kitchen table, hunched over paperwork, his back to the window. Will saw no one else inside or out.

"Hunker down here for a minute," said Will. "I'm going to go check out the graveyard."

Ajay handed him a small pen. "That should do the job nicely."

Will made a dash to the left, away from the house, circling back through the woods. Turning up the speed and relying on his memory of its location to guide him, Will soon spotted the old graveyard.

He hopped the fence around the 1938 plane crash memorial and took out the pen Ajay had given him. Removing the cap, he revealed the lens of a hidden digital camera. Will focused it on the list of names engraved on the base and snapped four pictures, a tiny LED flash illuminating the letters. He wasn't able to read all twelve names in the gathering darkness, but in the momentary flash his eye caught the one he'd been hoping to find. Will pocketed the pen and retraced his path back to where his friends were hiding.

"Any luck?" whispered Ajay.

"Raymond Llewelyn is on the stone," said Will.

"So Nepsted's story is righteous," said Elise.

"As far as someone at the school at that time having that *name* is concerned, yes." Will took the stolen key ring out of his bag and handed it to Nick. "Let's move. It's all clear."

"Which key is it?" asked Nick. "There's five on here."

"Don't know. Try 'em until you find one that works."

"Everyone please activate your communications system,"

said Ajay, fine-tuning the controls on his belt. "And put in your earpieces."

They all turned on walkie-talkies attached to their belts, plugged in Bluetooth earbuds, and switched on. Ajay tested the system with each of them, then handed a small handcrafted device from his bag to Nick, a black box the size of a cell phone with an exterior armature.

"I designed this specifically for the job," said Ajay, "but the dimensions are only estimates. You'll have to adjust the arms once you fit it onto the frame."

"I got it, I got it," said Nick. He slipped the device in his pocket and gave them both a wink and a cocky grin. "Showtime."

Will checked his watch. "Go."

Nick crabbed his way toward the hatch's wooden structure, about fifty feet away.

"Is that gizmo going to work?" asked Elise.

"It worked in prototype," said Ajay. "But since Tarzan of the Apes is using it, past results do not guarantee future performance."

"Elise, watch Nick through your glasses," said Will. "I'll keep an eye on the guy in the kitchen. Ajay, you scan the whole area in front. Brooke, back toward the lake."

Nick made slow progress, staying low so the camera poised above the hatch wouldn't spot him. When he got close, he couldn't resist a couple of gymnastic tumbles that brought him to the back of the structure.

"How's it looking?" Nick whispered over his walkie.

"Clear," said Will.

Nick eased around the structure; this would be the most vulnerable moment, in plain view if anyone passed by or looked out a window and completely out of his roommates' sight. If anyone in the control center happened to glance at the camera over the hatch at that moment they were screwed.

Nick took out Ajay's device, opened the armature, and attached it around the frame of the security camera that was pointed at the hatch. He unfolded it the rest of the way, positioning the black screen directly between the camera and the hatch.

"Done," said Nick, whispering into his mic. "Fits like a glove."

Ajay smiled at Will. "Now take the picture."

Nick touched a button on the device, and an image of the hatch appeared on the screen.

"Got it," said Nick.

"You are exceeding my expectations," whispered Ajay, watching him closely. "Now reverse it and push the other button."

Nick pivoted the screen around in its frame so it was now pointing toward the security camera, with the image Nick had just taken of the hatch still on the screen.

"Is this going to work?" asked Brooke.

"One minute," said Will, looking at his watch. "If no guards head our way we'll know."

They waited. Elise peered out, scanning both sides of the house.

"No one's coming," she said.

"Okay, admit it," said Ajay with a cocky grin. "I'm a little bit of a genius."

"Try the lock, Nick," said Will into his mic.

Nick moved out of their sight. "I'm there," they all heard him whisper. "It's a big fat sucker. Trying the first key . . . no go. Now the second . . . ix-nay on the econd-say. Third . . . dude, key slipped right in, turning, and . . . winner, winner, chicken dinner. Hatch is open."

"Close it and get back behind the structure," said Will. "Everybody switch your headlamps on."

Nick rolled back into sight to the rear of the structure. They all took out an elastic strap with a small LED light attached and put it around their foreheads.

"Nick, I'm coming to you," said Will. "Head down the ladder, one at a time, in the order we discussed."

Will hurried forward and joined Nick behind the structure, leaning against it, shoulder to shoulder.

"On three," Will said to Nick.

Nick gave him a thumbs-up. Will counted with his fingers: on three they moved around opposite sides of the structure. Will lifted the hatch and Nick stepped inside, found the ladder, and quickly lowered out of sight. Will set the hatch down and scurried back behind the structure. Brooke was waiting there for him.

"You good, Nick?" asked Will.

"Hanging in there," said Nick. "Send the next victim."

Will turned to Brooke, who looked nervous, and put his hands on her shoulders. "Hold on to the rungs with both hands. Don't look down. Nick's there to spot you. You'll be fine."

"I'll be fine," said Brooke, steadily meeting his eye.

"You're sure you want to do this?" he asked, taking her hand.

"A little late in the game for second thoughts, but thanks for asking. And yes, I'm sure."

"On three," said Will into his mic.

They moved around the structure together. Will lifted the hatch and saw Nick's headlamp illuminate the top of the ladder. Brooke dropped to her knees, turned, found the first rungs, and climbed out of sight. Will lowered the hatch and hurried back behind the shed.

Elise knelt there waiting for him, eyes alert, on edge but in command, riding her adrenaline like it was one of her horses.

"I love that we're doing this," she whispered, with an all-world smile.

"Me too," said Will, feeling the same kick as he lifted his hand to count. "On three."

"Someone's coming," they heard Ajay whisper in their ears. Will and Elise froze.

"Who is it?" asked Will.

"A guard—no, two guards. And they have a dog."

"Where?" asked Will.

"It's a very big dog."

"Where *are* they, Ajay?"

"They're rounding the side of the house nearest to you," said Ajay. "Looks like a regular patrol and . . . oh dear . . ."

"Oh dear *what*?"

"The dog appears to be a Boerboel."

"What's a Boerboel?" asked Will.

"An exceptionally large and relatively rare South African mastiff bred exclusively for home protection on the veldt and renowned for its ability to hunt and kill lions—"

"Got it, Ajay," interrupted Will. "Do they know we're here?"

"Not yet," said Ajay. "The breeze is predominantly from the west, so I don't think the dog smells— Sorry, I spoke too soon."

"What?"

"The dog has just caught your scent and it's leading them in your direction. Did I mention the breed's extraordinary sense of smell?"

Will turned to Elise and knew she was already thinking what he was thinking.

"We'll take care of it," said Will.

"And, Will, even by Boerboel standards, this appears to be an *exceptionally large* Boerboel," said Ajay.

"Do I need to come back up there and kick its tail?" asked Nick over the system.

"I said we'll take care of it," said Will. "Where are they?"

"Rapidly approaching your position, about fifty feet to your right," whispered Ajay.

Will chanced a look around the edge and saw the guards and their dog heading straight toward them, flashlights cutting through the deepening twilight.

"That is a really big dog," whispered Will to Elise.

Want me to try first? she asked silently.

Will nodded.

Elise eased to the edge of the structure and opened her mouth. Will couldn't hear anything, but he knew she was putting out sound on a frequency that humans couldn't hear.

"The dog's stopped," said Ajay. "It hears something—hold on. Check that. Actually it's going bananas, bucking around and yanking at the leash. The guards are freaking out."

Will leaned around the edge and pushed a picture at the dog—he hadn't tried this on an animal since the first time he figured out he had the ability at five years old, but why not?

A lion. On the other side of the island, down near the main landing. Raising its head and letting out a roar like that old movie logo—

"Oh, this is very good. The dog's broken free," said Ajay. "It's tearing off in the other direction, toward the dock, and the guards are chasing after it."

Elise looked at Will with a crooked smile.

A lion? she asked.

Will shrugged. Elise had to stifle a laugh.

"Shake a leg, Dr. Doolittle," she said.

They hustled around the side and in five seconds Elise was down the hatch. Five seconds later Will was back behind the wall beside Ajay, wide-eyed, breathing hard.

"I don't have fond memories of that ladder, Will," said Ajay. "I know you wanted me to take the next spot but would you mind letting me go last so I can descend at my own pace?"

"I need to close the hatch, Ajay," said Will. "Don't worry about pace. Just picture a Boerboel breathing down your neck."

Will peeled around the side and opened the hatch. Ajay dropped to the ground and slowly slid backward until his feet found the rungs.

"Why on earth did I agree to this?" moaned Ajay. "I possess the proper technology. I could've monitored this whole operation from the comfort of my quarters."

"Piece of cake," said Will. "You got this."

Will held Ajay's arm until he found and gripped the ladder with both hands. Will reached down and switched on Ajay's headlight.

"If I fall, at least I'll end up on the girls," said Ajay with a weak smile, and then disappeared down the hole. "A much more agreeable place to land, wouldn't you agree?"

Will slithered in after Ajay. He half closed the hatch, turned himself around, found the ladder with his feet and one hand, then replaced the lock on the hasp—without fastening it—and slowly lowered the hatch after him with the other.

TEOTWAWKI

Everyone climbed down in calm and orderly fashion. Their headlamps provided ample light and not even Ajay panicked. When he finally set foot at the bottom, they realized why he hadn't complained about anything during the descent.

"Three hundred and thirty-nine rungs," said Ajay. "Twelve inches apart, so I estimate we're currently three hundred and forty-three feet underground, but let me confirm that. . . ."

As Ajay took out a small, multipurpose GPS device from one of the many pockets on his vest, Will jumped down the last few feet and landed beside him.

"We must be even deeper than the lake," said Brooke.

Ajay held up his GPS. "Three hundred and forty-*four* feet to be exact. Around the island—the shallow end of the lake, as it happens—the bottom is sixty feet at its deepest. So, yes, Brooke, we are considerably below the bottom of the lake."

Everyone took out powerful, compact flashlights from their bags and switched them on.

"We're in the same rough-hewn rock-walled chamber as before," said Ajay, turning his light around the room. "And that tunnel, the only way out, leads south toward the lake."

"Nothing's changed," said Nick.

"Only one thing." Will shined his flashlight up to take one last look at the ladder. "This time no one knows we're down here." He took the lead. "Let's get moving."

Will led them out of the chamber into the tunnel, with Nick bringing up the rear. Elise trailed a hand along the walls.

"The rocks are sweating," she said.

153

"That's the lake's downward pressure," said Ajay. "Seeking the water table below us."

"That's ridiculous," said Nick.

"How so?"

"You can't make a table out of water," said Nick. Then a moment later, "A bed, maybe."

The tunnel sloped gradually lower, at least another twenty-five feet, its walls shored up with massive, weathered slabs of timber. They heard the steady *plink* of water dripping all around them, and the floor of the tunnel underfoot grew slick with moisture.

"Now we're directly under the lake," said Ajay, nervously glancing at his GPS.

"You can feel the weight of it," said Brooke.

"This tunnel's been here a really long time," said Elise, shining her light around the timbers.

"At least one hundred and fifty years," said Ajay. "You may recall my theory that the tunnels were dug out by the same man who built the castle."

"I found a book about him in the library last year, remember?" asked Brooke.

"Mr. Elliot mentioned him yesterday," said Will. "His name was Ian Cornish."

"Ian Lemuel Cornish," said Ajay.

"His middle name was *Lemuel*?" asked Will, whipping around toward Ajay.

"Yes, why?"

"That's the first name of Haxley's butler. He told me it was an old family name."

"Gots to be *his* old family, then, dude," said Nick, shaking his head. "*Lemuel?* What were *they* smokin'?"

"Could just be coincidence," said Elise.

"Or a descendant of the Cornish family is working as a *butler* in the house his great-great-something-or-other built," said Ajay.

"Which would explain why he acts like he owns the place," said Will. "Give us the download on Cornish, Ajay."

"Ian Lemuel Cornish, a Boston weapons manufacturer, specializing in rifles and ammunition, who built a tremendous fortune during the Civil War," said Ajay as he stopped and looked up to the right. "Heartbroken when he learned his beloved son Josiah had been killed at the Battle of Appomattox Court House the day before the war ended, he took a long trip through Europe. When he returned, Cornish moved west to Wisconsin and built this castle, patterned after one of the romantic follies he'd seen in Germany while sailing down the Rhine."

"Who needs the Internet," said Nick. "We have *him*."

"Did he have any other heirs?" asked Will.

Ajay continued. "Cornish's only surviving son—*Lemuel*—sold the castle to Franklin Greenwood in 1932, seventeen years after his father Thomas founded the Center."

"True," said Will. "Mr. Elliot told me that yesterday."

"So what did he need these tunnels for?" asked Brooke.

"Sorry, I don't have that information," said Ajay.

"Do you think Cornish might have been a Knight?" asked Elise.

"It's possible," said Will. "We know the Knights are using the tunnels now."

"But for what?" asked Brooke.

"Duh," said Nick. "To get to the 'hospital' and the 'old cathedral,' whatever those are."

"Nepsted will tell us all that if we can find his key," said Will. "And there's a whole box about Ian Cornish in the tower you can check out later."

"Now there's a job I'm actually suited for," said Ajay. "Instead of wasting my time down here in the bowels of the earth."

The tunnel began sloping back up, at the same angle and grade it had previously descended. The rock underfoot was drier here, and the tunnel began to gradually narrow.

Ajay consulted his GPS again. "We've cleared the lake. We're under the southern shore now."

"We should be coming up on the T intersection we saw last time," said Will, shining his light ahead.

They turned a shallow corner and fifty feet ahead another corridor split off to the left at ninety degrees, while straight ahead it turned and dropped around a corner to the right. Will stopped and shined his light down the narrow, rocky passage to the left.

"This is the way we came in last year, remember?"

"Yes, that tunnel leads back to the auxiliary locker room," said Ajay, holding up his GPS.

"What's this way?" asked Elise, pointing straight ahead.

"Never got a chance to scope that out," said Nick. "This is where the Knights went all Wile E. Coyote on us and we had to *meep-meep*."

"Well, if you know what's *that* way, let's go *this* way," said Brooke, and she started walking straight ahead.

"Wait," said Will.

Something washing around in his thoughts came into focus. This tunnel. This particular corner. A double déjà vu sense of familiarity overwhelmed him until he realized, *I have another memory about this place. Not just from when we were here last year. Where is this coming from? Did I have a dream about being down here? Was that it?*

No, that didn't feel right. Will put a hand against the wall, closed his eyes, and tried to bring the vision closer.

"I know what's down there," said Will. "To the right."

"Dude, I just *said* we were in this exact spot last year—"

"No, I mean around the *corner.* I saw it in a dream or . . . something else, I can't explain."

No, not a dream. The closest Will could come to explaining it to himself sounded too loopy to repeat out loud: *Somebody is pushing pictures into* my *mind.*

But who?

"What are you seeing, Will?" asked Elise, moving beside him.

"There's a pair of huge, heavily secured doors around to the right," said Will, pointing straight ahead. "And there's something written on them. Ajay, none of us looked around that corner last time, did we?"

"We didn't have time," said Ajay. "They started chasing us."

"Let's test this, then," said Will. "I need to know how real it is. Go take a look."

"Okay," said Brooke warily.

Brooke, Nick, and Ajay quickly trotted around the corner. Elise stayed with Will.

"Are you seeing any of this?" Will whispered to Elise.

"No."

"I don't have any idea where this is coming from—"

He was interrupted by the others banging on something solid and wooden. A moment later Brooke ran back into view with a look of grave concern.

"I'm not saying there *is* and I'm not saying there *isn't,* okay, but do you recall what—if anything—was written on this alleged door?" said Brooke, slightly out of breath.

"Or carved!" shouted Nick from around the corner.

"Don't give him *clues*," said Ajay.

They all returned a moment later. Will closed his eyes again, leaned back against the wall, and pictured the door in his vision: thick, massive, built from towering timbers.

Two words swam in front of his eyes—one of them crudely etched into the wood, as if with a knife—but he couldn't make them out completely.

"The first one's a slightly shorter word and starts with a *C*, all in caps," he said. "And the second one is below it, and it starts with a *T*."

"Now you are seriously disturbing me," said Ajay warily. "Did you make another trip down here we don't know about?"

"Of course he didn't," said Elise, watching Will with concern.

"And I'm naturally inclined to believe him," said Ajay. "Will, can you by any chance peer back in time and see *who* carved the words?"

"Sorry," said Will, opening his eyes as the vision faded. "That's all I've got."

"Wow, that is so deeply disappointing," said Nick.

"So what are the words on the door?" Will asked.

"Come take a look," said Brooke.

The tunnel widened and the ceiling rose up above them as soon as they turned the corner. The wooden doors blocked the path before them, fashioned from huge, roughly hewn vertical timbers, standing eight feet wide and fifteen feet high. A barely visible seam ran down between them. Will saw that one of the words from his vision was carved carefully and evenly, above eye level, about a foot high, all in capital letters:

CAHOKIA

Below that, scrawled much more hastily, and recently, almost gouged into the wood:

TEOTWAWKI

"Teotwawki . . . and Cahokia," said Ajay.

"Mean anything to you?" asked Elise.

"No," said Will.

"Rings no bells for me either, I'm afraid," said Ajay.

"Dude, it's not somebody's *name*, is it?" asked Nick, staring at the words.

"Are you serious?" asked Elise, making a face.

"Yeah, it could be like Norwegian, right?"

"Of course, Cahokia Teotwawki, the great Norwegian opera singer," said Ajay, rolling his eyes.

"Really?!" asked Nick eagerly.

"No."

"Well, if you're going to be *mean*, I'm not gonna play anymore," said Nick.

"They kind of sound like Native American words, don't you think?" asked Brooke.

"Maybe," said Will. "I'll ask Coach Jericho about them."

"Elise, you study calligraphy and typefaces. What do you think?" asked Ajay.

Elise was already scrutinizing the letters up close. "Whoever carved this took their time with *Cahokia*. It looks official—see how it's centered in the middle? Like someone in charge put it there. And it's definitely nineteenth century, with all these serifs."

"Did whoever built the doors also put the word there?" asked Ajay.

"I think so," said Elise.

"What about the other word?" asked Brooke.

"Different," said Elise, tracing the carving with her fingers. "This came later. The scars in the wood look newer. *Teotwawki.* Written fast, scrawled even, as some kind of comment about the first word. Almost like graffiti."

Nick hopped to his feet, retreated up the tunnel, sprinted back toward the door, jump kicked it with both feet, and bounced back onto the ground. The wood didn't give even a fraction of an inch.

"And, in case you're wondering, these puppies are locked down tighter than a hatch on a nucular sub," said Nick, examining the edges.

"Nuclear," said Ajay, aggravated.

"No knobs, handles, keyholes. No way to get leverage. Nothin'."

"Hinges must be on the inside," said Ajay, measuring one of the walls with another small device from his vest. "And according to my density reading, this wood is massively thick, at least ten inches. Probably reinforced on the other side as well."

"It looks like this is as far as we can go, then," said Brooke.

"We have to get through," said Will. "Nepsted's key is somewhere on the other side."

"Stand back," said Nick. "I got this."

Nick stepped close to the door, spread his arms open wide, and shouted, "Friend!" Nothing happened. "Amigo!" Nothing, then he turned to the others and whispered, "What's another foreign word for *friend*?"

"*Mon ami,*" said Brooke.

"*Mon ami!*" Nick shouted at the door.

"What are you doing?" asked Elise.

"Trying to bust a move from outside the box," said Nick, and when she rolled her eyes: "Hey, it worked in Lord of the Rings."

"Dumber than a can of paint," said Ajay, shaking his head. "Perhaps I should take my hatchet to it."

"And you didn't like *my* idea?" asked Nick.

"Hold on," said Will, holding up a hand, asking for silence.

He closed his eyes. Another image came floating into his mind. Another *picture*.

"There's something else," he said. "Something back this way."

He led them back up the tunnel to the T intersection. Will backed into the smaller corridor, keeping his eyes fixed on the wall straight ahead of him. Nick tried to follow, but Elise jerked him back out of the way.

"Give him room, dodo bird," she said.

Will opened and closed his eyes a few times, trying to line up the picture that had materialized in his mind with the actual wall in front of him.

"What is it, Will?" asked Brooke.

"There's something buried in the wall," said Will, walking slowly forward to it. "Covered over with rocks or mud or moss. Eye level. Somewhere in here."

Will took out his Swiss Army knife, flipped open a blade, and scraped four sides of a square on the wall. The others pointed their flashlights at the two-foot square Will had outlined.

"Want me to use my hatchet?" asked Ajay, reaching into his backpack.

"No need, little buddy," said Nick behind Ajay as he took a sheathed bowie knife from his pack. "Let's see what a real knife can do."

Nick pulled out a wicked-looking foot-long blade and dug in along with Will as the others lit up the square with their flashlights. After they'd hacked away chunks of rock for nearly a minute, something glinted underneath, reflecting back a flash of light. Nick flipped his knife around and stabbed at the spot. They heard a solid *thunk* of metal on metal.

"That's it," said Will.

They doubled their efforts, quickly scraping mud and dirt off a rusted metallic surface—dull brass, a foot square, deeply embedded in the rock.

"It's some kind of metal plate," said Nick.

Will pulled away a final slab, revealing what looked like a large, old-fashioned keyhole in the center of the plate.

"No," said Will. "It's a lock."

They cleared away the last of the rocky debris, then stood back and studied it.

"Fifty bucks says it opens that door," said Elise.

"Right, like I'm gonna take *that* bet," said Nick.

"Hand me the keys, Nick," said Will.

Nick handed over the tunnel keys and Will picked through them. None of the five keys on the ring looked anywhere near big enough to fit inside the lock.

"That figures," said Nick, kicking the dirt in frustration.

"You think if somebody builds a super-super-triple-secret door they're going to leave the key hanging on a hook?" asked Elise.

"We don't even know if there is a key for this," said Will.

"I could whack it with my hatchet," said Ajay.

"Not your best suggestion," said Brooke.

"Looks like we're stymied, then," said Ajay. "Hardly the time or place to call in a locksmith."

Will turned to Nick. "That's your cue, bro."

"Riiiight," said Nick, then quickly rifled through the outer pockets of his backpack.

"What are you talking about?" asked Brooke.

"You already gots a lock-meister in your midst, *mis amigos*," said Nick, opening his bag. "And you're looking at him."

"Nick picked up a few . . . miscellaneous skills growing up," said Will.

"One of the accidental benefits," said Nick, retrieving his ring of professional lock picks, "of a misspent youth." He pronounced it *yout*. "Give me some light here, peeps."

The other four centered their lights on the brass plate. Nick focused his headlamp on the keyhole, then went to work with a lock pick and tension wrench. As he probed the interior with the curved picks, they heard clicks and whirrs inside the lock that sounded promising. Followed immediately by a much less promising series of crunches and grinding of gears that yanked the picks right out of Nick's hands into the hole, followed by the sound of shattering metal.

"The damn thing ate my picks," said Nick, astonished.

"What do you think, Will, is this some kind of aphotic technology?" asked Brooke.

"It's worse than that. It's freakin' *carnivorous*," said Nick.

Will took out his dark glasses, put them on, and looked closely at the plate. "I don't see anything—"

"I paid thirty-nine bucks for those picks," said Nick.

"At where, Thieves Are Us?" asked Elise.

Nick banged his fist on the plate in frustration. Everyone else took a step backward, like it might hit back.

"This isn't aphotic," said Will, putting his glasses away. "But let's think this through. If it *is* some kind of lock, whoever installed this here must have put it in at the same time they built the doors, right?"

"I don't know," said Ajay. "It would have taken ages for the plate to get covered up like that by any natural geologic process, unless . . ."

"Unless what?" asked Brooke.

"Unless the rocks were added artificially," said Will. "As camouflage. Which makes more sense."

"Maybe it's a trap," said Nick. "Maybe you open that door and a monster bites your head off."

"Yes, perhaps we should leave well enough alone," said Ajay, taking tentative backward steps toward the exit. "After all, we need to be back in the dorm before curfew—"

"Buck up, little cowpoke," said Elise, hooking Ajay by the elbow and holding on. "It's only nine-thirty and we've just begun to fight."

"Yeah, you think we want to go through another ambiguous landing all over again just to sneak down here?" asked Nick.

"Amphibious," said Ajay.

"Maybe the key's stashed somewhere nearby," said Brooke. "You know, like a spare key in a potted plant on the back porch."

"I note a distinct absence of potted delphiniums in our immediate vicinity," said Ajay.

"Good idea, Brooke," said Will. "Let's look around."

They spent five minutes scouring every inch of the intersection, all the way to the door and back, searching every nook and crevice.

No key. Nothing.

"I have a question," said Brooke, raising her hand.

"Yes, Miss Springer," said Ajay.

"Not trying to be a wet blanket here, but are we absolutely sure we *want* to open that door?" she asked.

"Dude," said Nick impatiently, pointing toward the doors. "Nepsted's key?"

"But isn't it worth considering that maybe this door wasn't built to keep people out," said Brooke. "Maybe it was built to keep something, on the other side, *in*."

They all considered the idea. Ajay wiped sweat off his forehead with a handkerchief.

"Look," said Will. "Nepsted says there is a key—way down deep, at the bottom of the stairs—that will open the magic lock on his cage. And he won't tell us what he knows about the school and the Knights or anything else until we do."

"And, trust us, he knows a *lot*," said Nick.

"So I'm not leaving until we open those doors and find what we came here for," said Will.

Elise made a gesture with her hands, as if weighing the two ideas. "Yeah, okay. We're opening the door."

Another idea whispered its way into Will's mind. He gave up wondering where they came from and walked over and spoke softly to Elise.

"Sing to it," he said.

"Are you serious?" asked Elise.

"I don't even know why I think that's worth trying, but I do."

"You mean sing . . . like a song?"

"No," said Will, trying to be discreet. "Not a *song* song. One of those *other* skills you said you've been working on."

Elise got the message. She walked over to the plate, took a deep breath, closed her eyes, and brought her hands together in a yoga pose, centering herself. A moment later she stepped into a martial arts stance, drew her head back, and opened her mouth.

A clear, high sound, like a bell ringing in one continuous

peel, filled the enclosed space. She raised her hands and moved them in front of her and the quality of the sound changed, as if she was bending and shaping it or . . .

Sharpening it. The sound grew taut and tangibly powerful. Elise directed the sound—Will swore he could almost *see* it moving through the air—toward the plate in the wall. When it made contact with the plate, a second note arose—in harmony with the first—as the brass resonated. Vibrating, slowly at first, then at an increasingly high rate of speed, filling the air with sound.

The others edged away, alarmed. Nick actually covered his ears, but Will moved closer to get a better look.

This is amazing. She's got so much more control now. Like she's mastered an instrument . . . only she's the instrument.

Elise refined the sound, narrowing it down until it focused to a fine beam—Will could see the brass oscillating wildly, like it was being pounded by a drill press—and then she moved her hands to position the beam of sound over and right into . . .

The keyhole.

The sound vanished up into some supersonic range outside their hearing, swallowed up inside the lock but creating a lot of heat and noise inside.

Elise glanced over at Will, her eyes looking wild, needing to talk but too focused to speak out loud. She had closed her mouth, as if she were whistling a laser beam.

What now? she asked him.

"What do you mean?" he asked.

What am I looking for in here?

"Nick, how do you pick a lock?" asked Will.

"I don't know, it's a feel thing, dude."

"Okay, so what do you feel for?"

"It's sort of hard to describe."

"Trying right now would be excellent," said Will, waving him over to the wall and Elise. "Over here. Tell *her*."

"So there's like this round thing, okay?" said Nick, using his hands, vaguely, to make the shapes he described. "And it has a bunch of, what do you call 'em, tiny little sharp thingies that stick down from it?"

"You're looking for a *cylinder*, with a series of *pins* descending through its middle," said Ajay.

"Yes, thank you—pins—what *he* said," said Nick.

Elise asked Will for help again with her eyes.

"So what should she try to do to them?" asked Will.

"Raise the pins to specific heights, and in the correct sequence," said Ajay, "which will allow the cylinder to rotate freely and release the locking bolt—"

"Okay, shut up and let me concentrate," said Elise through gritted teeth.

Elise struggled to maintain the pressure of her sound beam inside the cylinder. She was somehow able to control her breathing to such a degree she could still generate sound while she inhaled, but Will could see the effort was starting to sap her strength. He glanced over and noticed Brooke, standing back and staring at Elise like she was an alien who'd just bungee jumped in from a mother ship.

"It's most important that you maintain consistent torque on the cylinder so the pins you've pushed up don't fall back down," said Ajay. "Then you pull the latch—"

"Stop helping," said Will to Ajay.

Elise glanced at Will: *Don't know how much longer I can keep this going.* Her whole body was shaking with effort now, sweat dripping down her forehead.

I feel something. Listen. I'm going to try to pull it.

Will moved closer to the keyhole. He heard the sound beam

thrumming away inside, hissing with tension, then a sharp click, and a whirring of gears that stopped abruptly.

"That's it," said Will. "I think you almost have it."

Elise summoned up the last of her strength and doubled the pressure. Will felt the brass plate grow burning hot to the touch, its whole surface vibrating. Then, a louder click, a nerve-racking pause, and finally a sustained unwinding of gears from behind the plate.

Elise slumped to the ground. Nick slid over and caught her before she landed and gently lowered himself to the ground with Elise cradled in his arms. She was semiconscious, her eyelids fluttering, her arms hanging limply.

Will looked at Brooke sharply, asking for her help. She knelt down beside Elise and put a hand on her arm.

"She'll be all right," said Brooke, studying Elise intently. "She's exhausted, not injured."

"How do you know that?" asked Nick, puzzled.

Before Brooke could answer, they heard a massive rumble issue from around the corner, building in volume and intensity.

"The doors are opening," said Ajay.

And at that moment Will was struck by another impression he couldn't confirm with his senses or track to its source. He stared into the corridor behind them, both the direction they'd come and the tunnel to the locker room. He didn't see or hear anything, but his senses were still sending him the same message.

Someone, or something, was following them.

PALADINS

While Brooke and Nick saw to Elise, Ajay and Will hurried around the corner to take a look. The gigantic doors had split along that seam down the middle, and the two halves were opening outward, but ever so slowly, inch by inch, accompanied by the grind of immensely heavy gears meshing and turning.

They trained their flashlights on the gap as it widened, but the beams barely dented the deep, forbidding blackness on the other side. Air wafted toward them from within, almost a slight breeze, conveying suggestions of dampness, ruin, and ancient dirt.

"How long do you think it's been since they last opened?" asked Ajay, blinking rapidly.

Will pointed his flashlight at the ground, where the bottom edge of both doors scraped slightly along the ground as they opened, tracing etched grooves in the dirt along their elliptical path. Will went down on one knee to examine them.

"Doesn't look like they've been opened a lot," said Will. "Over time they would've carved a trench in the floor."

"Will, have a look at this," said Ajay.

He was pointing his light at the backs of the opening doors. They were covered with heavy steel plates, at least an inch thick. Random patterns of heavy gouges crisscrossed the face of the steel on both sides.

"What do you think made these?" asked Will, moving closer to study them.

"They don't look like the work of a tool or machine, do they?"

"No. I'd say that something . . . organic made these. Maybe Brooke was right." Ajay stopped in his tracks. "I don't mean to alarm you, but there's something—*perhaps someone*—standing farther down the tunnel."

Will whirled and joined his light with Ajay's, but the beams faded into the gloom. "Where? I don't see anything."

"Well, I can see *everything*," said Ajay. "Wait for your eyes to adjust."

Will waited. By now the doors had opened enough to create a gap of nearly four feet. Slowly a shape appeared in that opening, floating out of the gloom, at an indeterminate distance from the door. Will found it almost impossible to estimate how far away it was.

"What is it?" he asked.

"It's not moving," said Ajay, still whispering. "It's too big for a human figure, but it's shaped like one. And it's glowing, uniformly, with some kind of phosphorescence. Switch your light off."

They both did, plunging them into pitch-blackness. The heavy grinding of the doors' mechanicals continued and sounded even louder in the dark. Will still couldn't see a thing.

"Do you see better in the dark, too?" asked Will.

"Naturally," whispered Ajay.

"Important question," whispered Will. "Can it see us?"

"It's not moving or appearing to react in any way."

Lights and voices came from around the corner behind them: Nick, Brooke, and Elise, back on her feet.

"Dudes, what's happening?"

"Be quiet!" Ajay barked back at them in a harsh whisper. "Turn your lights off. Use one headlamp to light the way. Slowly walk up to where we are and stop."

The others did as he instructed, joining them. Will's hand

found Elise's and squeezed. *Are you all right?* he asked her silently.

I'm okay. Just don't ask me to sing along with the radio for a while.

The doors stopped abruptly, about halfway open, with a loud, rusty creak. The breeze blowing toward them out of the opening picked up enough to rustle the girls' hair.

"Smells like we just cracked open one of the pyramids," whispered Brooke.

"In a way," whispered Ajay, "that may be *exactly* what we've done. I want you all to point your flashlights ahead of our position, right where I aim mine, and turn them on when I give the word." He waited for them to get ready before he said, "Now."

All five lights switched on, pointing straight ahead, and the others quickly lined their beams up with Ajay's.

They couldn't see its face because it was turned away from the door. A statue, standing fifty feet beyond the doors, dead in the center of the corridor. A human figure, as Ajay had suggested. Depicting a man at least fifteen feet tall, muscular and broad shouldered. Fashioned from some metallic alloy with a dull greenish cast that reflected back almost none of their beams.

"Let's take a look," said Will.

"Do you really think that's wise?" asked Ajay. "What if we go in and the doors close behind us?"

"I'd say that's worth thinking about," said Elise.

"I'll go in, then," Will suggested. "I could make it back way before they close."

"*Nobody* is going in there alone," said Brooke definitively.

"I hear you," said Will, unsure of how to proceed.

"Hang on," said Nick. "Wait here."

Nick dropped his pack and jogged back around the corner

out of sight. A few moments later they heard him grunting and struggling with something. They heard rocks sliding down; something hit the ground with a loud thud and then something dragged along the ground.

"What the heck is he doing?" asked Elise.

"Before anybody gets all bent about it," said Nick as he walked back into sight, dragging one of the heavy timbers from the tunnel walls, "this one was already loose and it didn't cause a cave-in or anything."

Nick dropped the timber on the ground. The post was square, like a railroad tie, six by six inches wide and six feet long. Will helped him wedge it into place between the split doors, perpendicular to the walls. From there they were able to leave a gap of less than an inch on either side.

"If they start to shut, that oughta hold 'em for a while," said Nick.

Will felt uneasy about leaving the doors open. He stared back at the empty tunnel behind them, hooked Nick by the arm, and whispered, "Did you see or hear anything back there?"

"Nah, dude. Nothing, nobody. Why?"

"Just trying to be careful," said Will; then he turned back to the others. "Let's go in."

Everyone moved through the open doors. Except Nick. Will turned back to him.

"Aren't you coming?"

"I had a fairly recent bad experience with a, uh, you know, statue," said Nick uneasily.

"Of course you did," said Will. "We totally understand. Wait here if you like."

Nick hesitated. "Nah, what if it starts throwing down? What are *you* guys gonna do, bore it to death?"

Nick joined them and they edged cautiously forward. The

floor, walls, and ceilings on the far side of the door were paved with some kind of closely stacked earthen bricks that were gray, dusty, and worn with age. The whole shape of the tunnel turned more circular and symmetrical.

"A completely different style of construction," said Ajay, flashing his light around.

"Strange," said Elise, "doesn't look anything like what we've seen so far."

"Word," said Nick. "It looks like a freakin' subway tunnel."

The walls widened out an additional ten feet by the time they reached the statue, forming a slightly rounded alcove around it. The figure stood on a simple square pedestal of rough rock, about three feet high. They edged around it, light beams moving up and down its length as they got their first good look at it.

"Look familiar?" asked Ajay.

"The Paladin," said Will. "A modern version of the Paladin."

It held the same posture as the school's mascot, weapon raised, staring vigilantly into the darkness ahead. But instead of a medieval knight carrying a sword and shield, this was a uniformed American soldier wearing a bucket helmet and holding a rifle.

"What is this?" asked Brooke.

"A World War Two infantryman," said Ajay, shining his light to various points. "Enlisted man, a private by rank. Note the single stripe on his sleeve. He's carrying an M1 bolt-action semiautomatic Garand rifle, the standard-issue weapon for the US military."

"Does that matter?" asked Elise.

"Here's why. The M1 was put into service in 1939. The M1 *carbine*, fully automatic with a larger clip, wasn't introduced until 1942. So this weapon tells us when the statue was built."

"Or you could just look at the date carved in the base here," said Brooke, pointing her light at a small Roman numeral in the upper right-hand corner.

"Built in 1939," said Will, shining his light on the number.

"I'm feeling fairly good about my original estimate," said Ajay with a proud smile.

"So people *have* been in here," said Will. "At least in 1939."

"It's made from cast bronze," said Elise, who had climbed onto the pedestal to take a closer look at the rifleman. "They'd have to make something like this in a foundry."

Brooke joined her on the pedestal. "The big question is how they got it down here."

"The biggest question is what it's doing here," said Will.

"Dude, it's so obvious: standing guard," said Nick.

"Against what?" asked Elise.

"What, too hard for you?" Nick turned and pointed his light into the vast darkness in front of them. "Something out *there.*"

At that moment the light breeze easing through the chamber picked up and moaned ever so slightly. Which didn't do much for anyone's nerves.

"So who put it here and why?" asked Brooke, visibly shivering.

"Can't answer that yet," said Will, squinting to see farther down the tunnel.

"Let's deduce what we can," said Ajay, his voice wavering a bit. "This is a modern variation on the original Paladin statue, which was originally put up outside the Barn in 1917."

"Agreed," said Will.

"The Paladin is the Center's mascot," said Ajay, "but the Knights of Charlemagne were also originally known as

Paladins. Can we therefore assume this has something to do with either the Knights or the Center?"

"Or both," said Will. "But we still don't know why."

Elise and Brooke hopped down and they started forward again as a group. As they left the alcove, the tunnel narrowed to its previous dimensions.

"Now turn the lights off and look back," said Will.

They all did. The statue of the soldier, about twenty-five yards behind them, was glowing brightly in the dark, pointing its gun at them, an eerie and forbidding specter.

"Our lights recharged the phosphorescence," said Ajay.

Will still couldn't shake the feeling that something was farther back in the darkness behind the statue, either watching or stalking them, but he kept it to himself.

"I think we can hazard a guess about what the statue's for," said Ajay, his voice shaking even more noticeably. "To scare the pantaloons off whoever or whatever sees it."

"Dude, I told you," said Nick. "It's a sentry, standing guard."

"But against what?" asked Brooke, turning to look behind them.

No one answered, but the others quickly turned around and switched their lights back on, the beams swallowed by the Stygian darkness ahead.

"Let's keep going," said Will, swallowing his fear and taking the lead.

"We're dropping, subtly, in elevation," said Ajay a few moments later, studying his GPS device. "And we're heading, even more subtly, to the left, or southwest."

They picked up their pace. With the combined lights illuminating the entire tunnel around them, they realized they were turning to the left as they continued to descend.

"Hold on," said Ajay. "Turn your lights off again."

Everyone did. Ajay took a few steps forward and peered ahead.

"There's another statue down there," he said. "Also glowing in the dark."

They inched up beside Ajay but had to advance another twenty yards before a second figure slowly appeared out of the darkness, shining pale luminous green, probably a hundred feet ahead and slightly below them. They switched their lights back on and jogged forward. The corridor widened again, creating an alcove identical to the last one around the figure.

Just like the last one, the statue stood on a pedestal, facing away from them. Another soldier, of similar size, fashioned from alloyed metal. They moved around, examining it from every angle. An identical pose to both the GI and the original Paladin, poised for action, rifle at the ready.

"This one's from World War One," said Ajay, eyes wide, taking in details. "Enlisted man, also infantry, private by rank, in the same defensive posture, but carrying a British Enfield rifle, which means it dates from—"

"Nineteen-seventeen," said Elise, shining her light on another Roman numeral on the corner of its base.

"If he's American, why's he carrying a British rifle?" asked Brooke.

"The Enfield was a standard British forces weapon," said Ajay, "but it was used by American doughboys because we didn't have enough rifles when we entered the war, but the *American* version was two inches longer and nine-tenths of a pound heavier than—"

"God, you could *so* design an app for insomnia," said Nick.

"Thank you, Ajay," said Will.

"This one's older than the last," said Elise, scraping at its leg. "Made from cast copper and a lot more corroded."

"But, dude, how are these dudes *glowing*? I thought that was some kind of modern Halloween technology."

"I would say they were all alloyed with a phosphorous compound," said Ajay.

"Let's keep going," said Will.

They found one more glowing statue in another alcove a few hundred yards farther down the tunnel. This variation depicted the Paladin figure as an infantryman from the Civil War, armed with a musket, pistol, and hand ax. Elise thought the statue was made from cast iron since it appeared cruder than the others.

"This pedestal has no date," said Elise, examining the base, "but the initials I. L. C. are carved in the corner."

"Ian Lemuel Cornish," said Will.

"If Ian Cornish put this here," said Ajay, "it dates to the late 1860s."

"I'll ask again," said Brooke, standing back. "What are these for?"

"They're all soldier dudes," said Nick. "Sentries."

"Versions of the Paladin, updated every time they stuck one down here," said Will, thinking it over. "American versions."

"In the form of whatever figure represented the warrior archetype of that era," said Ajay.

"And I think Nick's instinct is right," said Will. "They're sentries, standing guard."

"Like scarecrows," said Nick. "Really stiff ones."

"So for the last one hundred and fifty years someone's gone to considerable effort to place these here," said Ajay. "That rules out the Center. This started five decades before the school opened."

"The Paladin was the symbol for the Knights of Charlemagne for a thousand years," said Elise. "If it wasn't the school, it had to be them, don't you think?"

"We know Cornish put the first one here," said Will. "So either the Knights continued the tradition—"

"Or Ian Cornish was a Knight," said Ajay.

"What if Cornish was the first modern Knight?" said Elise. "Maybe he revived them."

"We know he built the tunnels, at least as far as the doors," said Brooke. "But did he build *this* tunnel?"

A clear, intuitive response came into Will's mind as he looked around.

"No," said Will, examining the construction of the alcove. "This section beyond the doors was here *first*. It's a *lot* older than these statues. At some point when he was digging out there, Cornish punched through into here."

"So Cornish put up this first statue," said Elise. "And for some reason built the doors?"

"I still don't understand how they're supposed to act as sentries," said Brooke. "What good could they actually do?"

"I have a thought about that," said Ajay, pacing around the figure. "This could be a modern variation on an ancient tribal tradition that was common practice all over the world."

"Such as?" asked Elise.

"The gargoyles you find along the outer walls of Gothic cathedrals like Notre Dame, or the angels armed with swords that flank the entrance to the hall of the Great Buddha of Nara in Japan. They're spiritual guardians, placed to protect important sacred sites."

"Protect them from what?" asked Nick.

"Some theories suggest they were put there to ward off demonic entities from other realms," said Ajay, glancing at Will.

"The Never-Was," Will said, as it all came together for him. "These statues were put here by people who found out about the Other Team."

"Where the monsters come from," said Elise, meeting his eye.

"Wait, so you're saying there's one of those portal-doorway thingies to Monster Central down there?" asked Nick.

"I don't know," said Will. "But we won't find out by standing here. The answers are that way." He pointed ahead, just as a whispery wind moaned from somewhere far below. Will felt it blow a chill into his soul. He shook it off, wandered a few yards into the dark, and pointed his light ahead.

"The right wall of the tunnel falls away here," he said. "Looks like there's some kind of drop-off. Everybody shine your lights down this way."

They joined their lights together to form a single beam that pierced the blackness. They couldn't see anything at all in that direction, but all felt the vertiginous, almost sickening disorientation of staring into a void.

"I'm done dancing in the dark, dude," said Nick. "Time to break out some daylight."

He extracted a couple of thick red flares from his pack, pulled on a pair of thick leather gloves, then ripped off the flares' caps and fired them up. The alcove and tunnel in both directions filled with bright red light. Nick hopped up and jammed one of the flares into a gap between the statue's rifle and hand, then jumped down and held the other flare aloft.

"I brought a crap-ton more of these if we need 'em, a flare gun, too," he said. "Enough to give us over an hour of light. That enough to find Nepsted's damn key?"

Ajay looked at his watch. "It's just after ten."

"That's about as long as I want to spend down here," said Will. "How about you guys?"

They were all in agreement.

Nick advanced cautiously until he could see the edge of the drop-off with his flare. Even with its brighter light shining down, they still couldn't make out anything in the darkness below.

"Hold this a second," said Nick, handing off the lit flare to Will.

Nick took out the flare gun, cracked it open, and dropped in the plug of a flare capsule. He aimed it out just above shoulder level and fired. The flare arced up and out, tracing a line at least a quarter mile into the air before it detonated and transformed the darkness with the white light of a sudden full moon.

The overhead burst revealed the void confronting them as a domed rock cavern, at least a mile wide and half a mile deep. The flare descended slowly, as if by parachute, and eventually lit up the ground far below them.

"What does that look like to you?" asked Nick, pointing down toward the flat base of the cavern.

"It looks like a city," said Will.

CAHOKIA

From this distance, by the light of the flare, they could only see shapes—Ajay identified them as rooftops—but they filled a sizable portion of the gigantic cavern below, and the scale of the place looked vast. They encountered no more statues. Avoiding the open side of the wall, they descended steadily for ten more minutes along the winding path until they reached the top edge of a broad, steep stone staircase carved out of the rock, open to the void on either side as it descended into darkness. They stopped, raised their flares, and couldn't see the end of them.

"Remember what Nepsted told us," said Will.

"The key's in the cavern at the bottom of the stairs," said Ajay.

"Well, we found the stairs," said Nick as he fired another flare into the air. When it lit up above them, they could see that the stairs dropped for at least a quarter of a mile before reaching level ground at the floor of the great cave.

"Nepsted's buildings must be down there," said Will. "The cathedral and hospital."

They'd dropped so much in elevation that the city was no longer visible, something huge and gray obscuring it about a mile away across a flat plain.

"Watch your step," said Will. "We don't know what kind of shape they're in."

Nick took the lead, setting a slow pace, making sure everyone took their time; the stairs were uneven, cracked in many places, completely eroded in others. It took twenty minutes to pick their way to the bottom. The staircase narrowed abruptly just before it ended in a rocky chamber, a vaulted archway being the only way forward. They cautiously stepped through it, reaching the perimeter of the plain leading to that gray obscurity in the distance. The air felt still and cold, so they paused and put on additional layers from their packs.

"Look, you can see where we were," said Brooke, pointing up and behind them.

The light from the flare they'd stuck on the statue appeared as a faint red glow far above them and to the right, which allowed Ajay to obtain their bearings with his GPS.

"Anyone want to holler how freaky this is?" asked Nick. "Never mind, I just did."

Will closed his eyes, called up his Grid, and thought he saw a brief flash of heat at the top of the staircase; it vanished and didn't reappear. A trickle of sweat ran down his back.

"Give me two more of those flares," said Will.

He pulled on a pair of leather gloves as Nick lit them both for him. Will raised the flares high and stepped forward. A carpet of dust three inches thick covered the ground like gray snow for as far as they could see, and stirred up into small clouds with every step. Its uniform gray surface glowed an eerie shade of crimson in the flares' light.

In the distance they could make out what had obscured their view of the city: A high wall filled the entire horizon ahead. The monochrome flat gray plain made it hard to determine how far away or tall it was, but it extended out perpendicularly, curving away in either direction as far as they could see.

A walled city.

Will blinked, summoned up his Grid again, and surveyed the landscape ahead, looking for signs of life. Nothing. Gray and arid as the moon. He cleared a space in the dust with his feet and dropped one of the flares on the ground.

"This will help us find our way back," he said. "Let's move."

He didn't want to alarm them by saying he also wanted it there to see if anyone followed them onto the plain. He lifted the other flare like a torch as he set out, and the others followed closely behind. They walked slowly, in silence, too overwhelmed to speak, the shuffling of their feet in the dust the only sound.

"What is this place?" whispered Brooke.

"Jericho said something to me last year, in the trophy room," said Will, his voice a whisper. "A Lakota legend about an ancient race that lived in the area long before the human race appeared."

"Lived where, here?" asked Ajay.

"Whoa, as in *Wisconsin*?" asked Nick.

"He said 'on this same ground,' so maybe that includes 'way down under it.'"

"We're at least a mile below the surface," said Ajay, his eyes glued to the readout on one of his meters. "Could some of these 'legends' have made it to the surface?"

"Or the other way around," said Will as he shuffled along. "There are lots of caves in the area. Maybe the Lakota found this place or some artifacts they left behind."

"Or, dude, maybe some *dudes*."

"What happened to this older race?" asked Brooke. "According to the legend."

"Jericho said they were destroyed by— Wait, that wasn't it. He said they destroyed *themselves*. Through some kind of madness or . . . disharmony."

"Looks like something a whole lot worse happened than singin' out of tune," said Nick.

"Did he mention if this race of ancient underground denizens were . . . p-p-people like us?" asked Ajay, for once not even bothering to react to Nick.

"He did not."

"Well, *that's* helpful," said Nick.

"How do you think this relates to what we're looking for?" asked Brooke. "Does it have anything to do with the Knights or the Other Team?"

"I don't have the slightest idea how this fits in yet," said Will, raising the flare.

"Well, I'd say this could be very, very good," said Nick. "Or it could be very, very bad."

"Thanks for your expert analysis," said Elise.

"As far as I'm concerned," said Nick, rummaging in his pack again, "we're down here to find Nepsted's key. And the sooner we do that, the sooner we can get the h-e-double-hockey-sticks out of this dusty hellhole."

"Why bother to spell *hell* if you use it five words later?" asked Ajay.

"Ex-squeeze me?" asked Nick.

"Ajay, can you see an opening anywhere in that wall?" asked Will.

"I was just about to help you with that," said Nick.

Nick raised his arm and fired another flare into the air over the top of the wall. When it combusted, the whole area lit up like daylight.

"Are you out of your *mind*?" said Brooke, grabbing Nick by the arm. "What if we're not alone?"

"Don't make me laugh," he said. "Look around, Brooks. This joint's a dead zone."

Will glanced back at the flare they'd left at the stairs. He thought he saw a shadow pass between him and the flare but maybe his eyes were playing tricks. When he turned back, Nick's overhead flare revealed that much of the wall ahead had been damaged by erosion and gravity.

"There," said Ajay, pointing to a section to the left. "I see a break in the wall there."

They turned slightly as Ajay guided them toward the opening. The journey took much longer to complete than Will would have thought; it was impossible to judge distances over the featureless dimly lit plain, and as they shuffled closer, the wall turned out to be much bigger than it first appeared. Well over fifty feet high at the top of its undamaged sections, forming a defensive rampart wide enough to drive a truck around. They were near enough now to realize it had been built from the same earthen bricks that lined the tunnel. But where the tunnel was still intact, the wall was a crumbling ruin, with more advanced decay and disrepair revealed as they moved closer.

"What do you see?" Will asked Ajay, who was staring hard at the wall.

"A number of jagged scars in the bricks that I wouldn't attribute to the ravages of time," whispered Ajay. "Multiple places, halfway up and higher, smashed in by what could have been projectiles."

"Which you interpret as . . . ?" asked Elise.

"It appears this place came under siege at some point. Like a medieval walled city."

"Maybe that's why it's deserted," said Will.

"Let's *hope* it's deserted," said Brooke.

"All along the watchtower, princes kept the view," said Elise softly, looking up at the crumbling line of the wall.

"Jimi Hendrix," said Nick.

"Bob Dylan," said Elise.

"There must be some kind of way out of here, said the joker to the thief," said Will. "My parents had that record."

"Dylan wrote it," said Ajay.

"Yeah, but Hendrix crushed it," said Nick.

"Let's hope there's a way out of here," said Brooke.

"Are you quite finished?" asked Ajay, and drew their attention back to the wall. "These marks are distinctly different from the gouges we saw on the backs of the entrance doors."

"Gouges? You didn't say anything about gouges," said Nick, worried. "What gouges?"

"Don't get too close yet," said Will, ignoring the question. "Head for that opening."

They tracked farther left until the opening Ajay had spotted came into focus for the rest of them as a large gaping black hole.

"Fire another flare," said Will.

Nick sent one up directly overhead, and as it blossomed, revealing the gap before them, they saw what had happened. Two gigantic metal gates had fallen, or collapsed, or more likely been battered in. They'd landed inside the wall, dented and gashed. Massive iron hinges that had once suspended them stuck out from the edge of the portal, wrenched and twisted out of shape.

"What did this?" asked Nick.

"It looks like some kind of war took place here," said Elise as they all stared at it in awe.

Something Dave said once came back to Will, and he heard it in Dave's voice: *"A war between the Hierarchy and the Old Ones, the corrupted Elder Race that had ruled and ruined the planet. Until the Hierarchy drove them back through the Gates of Hell."*

Could this be that place?

"You really think we should go in there?" asked Brooke.

"We've come this far," said Will.

"Hey, nothing's eaten us yet," said Nick.

"Such a confidence builder," said Elise.

"If anyone wants to turn back now," said Will, "just say so."

No one responded.

"Feel free to lead the way, Will," said Ajay, hanging in but hoping someone else went first.

"Once we're inside, don't touch anything," said Will, drawing them together. "Stick together, keep your voices down, and be ready to run. If we have to jam out of here, head back to the stairs and up to the tunnel."

Will raised his flare and led them toward the gates, while Nick took the rear. The light from Nick's last overhead flare faded, leaving them inside a traveling bubble of bright red light.

They reached the fallen gates, each at least fifty feet high. Fashioned from thick solid metal, with great expanses of steel banded and riveted around the edge, they bore the scars of a furious assault; rends, deep dents, and scars defaced their surface.

"Different marks than the ones we saw on the doors upstairs," said Ajay.

"You mean the gouges?" asked Nick.

"Yes," said Ajay.

"There's something engraved on the gates," said Elise, shining her light on one and then the other. "Take a look."

Her beam traced a gigantic indecipherable letter or glyph stamped into the metal.

"Welcome to Cahokia," said Nick, hopping up on the gate and spreading his arms. "Tourist capital of the underworld."

"This is one of the greatest archeological finds in human history," said Brooke.

"I wouldn't be so fast to attach the word *human*," said Elise.

They continued past the gates. Inside, the damage didn't appear to be as devastating, but the same thick blanket of dust lined the ground as far as they could see. Although many interior walls were crumpling into ruin, enough remained that they could make out the patterns of a city grid. A network of paths and lanes trailed off from both sides of the main wide avenue that led in from the gates.

Will saw Brooke fold her arms around herself and draw inward.

"Are you all right?" Will whispered.

"So empty and cold. Like a graveyard, on another planet. Doesn't feel like there could ever have been life here."

"Hold on a second," said Elise as she stopped and waited for the others to do the same. "Talk about exactly how we plan to find this key. For instance, what does it look like?"

Will wondered if her irritation stemmed from seeing him whispering with Brooke.

"We don't know anything else about it," said Will, "except that it's some kind of aphotic device and that Nepsted said we'd find it in the cavern at the bottom of the stairs."

"Cavern, stairs, check," said Nick.

"And that it was inside the hospital," said Ajay. "Which you could only get to through the 'old cathedral.'"

"I don't suppose you asked him if he had a tourist book," said Elise.

"Look, landmarks like that shouldn't be difficult to find," said Ajay. He gestured in front of the GPS screen in his hand; the device projected a 3-D map into the air in front of them, and each stroke Ajay made with his fingers added more detail to it.

"Primitive cities evolved along logical lines, with a practical place and purpose. There would have been a marketplace, for example, near a major entrance, with residential areas on either side, and a neighborhood for the various crafting professions would've grouped together to practice."

"Practice what? We don't even know what kind of people lived here," said Elise.

"If they were people," said Brooke.

"The *scale* of what remains of these buildings appears somewhat oversized for people," said Ajay, walking ahead with his GPS map, forcing the others to follow him. "Based on what we've seen, I'd estimate this was a community with a population of over fifteen thousand . . . whatever they were."

"You are aware that you always reel off a bunch of facts when you're scared, right?" asked Elise.

"And what do you do, criticize others?" he sniffed.

"No, she does that *all* the time," said Nick.

"Manage your anxiety your way, I'll manage mine," said Ajay; then, without missing a beat: "And since Nepsted mentioned a cathedral, it suggests that the inhabitants observed some communal form of worship. Given the importance of spiritual matters to advanced social organisms, it follows that the seat of such observances would have been accorded a prominent and visible location . . . for instance, the tallest point in the city. . . ."

"Like over there," said Will, pointing to a shadow in the distance.

Nick fired another flare in that direction. About two hundred yards ahead, the broad avenue they were on opened into a commons area or square. As they reached the square, the avenue diverged into three separate pathways. One branched left into a tangled warren of small, twisted streets; another turned right and led to a symmetrical pattern of spacious avenues—a residential area, possibly.

The third path continued straight ahead, and fifty yards past the square culminated in a broad flight of stairs that climbed twenty feet to a plaza that wrapped around the most impressive structure they'd seen inside the walls. It had suffered extensive damage. Will thought it looked like one of those hollowed-out husks from the urban bombings of World War Two.

"Cathedral, anyone?" asked Elise.

As they approached, four peculiar objects came into view at the base of the stairs leading to the cathedral. Tall, thin, winding shapes that rose out of the ground for about ten feet and then branched up into large irregular spheres.

"Those look like . . . trees," said Ajay.

"How is that possible this far underground?" asked Brooke. "Without light or water?"

"I have no idea," said Will.

But Ajay was right. The objects did look like trees, with something like a trunk growing out of the ground, and a complex bower of bare, fingery branches above. As they shined their flashlights on them, the branches sparkled, refracting the beams into colorful shards like abstract chandeliers. Moving closer, they saw that all the limbs were riddled with elongated holes and looked more like glass than wood, as if they'd survived but been encased by the passing of a ferocious ice storm.

"They look more like jewels than trees," said Brooke.

"If these are trees, they're as old as a geologic age," said Ajay. "Like fossils in the Petrified Forest."

"Maybe they did have light and water here," said Elise. "Once upon a time."

"I'm just asking: did we find Hell?" asked Nick, moving around restlessly. "'Cause whoever came up with that whole 'Hell is a fiery pit with a bunch of devils jumping around' totally missed the boat."

"Let's check out the church," said Will.

"Yeah, suddenly I got the urge to light a candle," said Nick.

Nick started up the stairs. The stone steps felt soft, almost crumbling underfoot. Will brought up the rear. At one point he thought he heard something soft and rustling behind him. He turned to look and held up his flare.

Nothing moved in the relentless gray, but he felt a vague disquiet, his nervous system registering something he couldn't see. Will called up his Grid to scan the landscape around them. No signs of heat—or life—registered, but he picked up a slight movement.

The trees at the bottom of the stairs. Their branches were swaying, as if stirred by a gentle breeze.

Will hadn't felt any air moving since they entered the gates. He figured the walls were acting as a windbreak, since they'd felt a steady breeze in the tunnel earlier. And the tree's branches were twenty feet aboveground, where they wouldn't feel the wind.

He caught up with the others as they reached a broad colonnade at the stop of the stairs, punctuated with the ruins of a row of thick pillars that might have once held up a portico. Only two were still partially standing. Beyond the columns, an ugly jagged gap led to the building's shadowed interior.

Something about the hole reminded Will of a gaping mouth with broken teeth. He could feel his pulse rising, and as he glanced around, he realized they were all uneasy. Except, maybe, for Nick, who looked like a kid lining up for the teacups at Disneyland.

"You're sure we have to go down *through* the cathedral to get to the hospital?" said Elise.

"Yes," said Will. "I can't picture what he meant by it, but it's what Nepsted told us."

"And this is no time to be deviating from his directions," said Ajay.

"As the only Catholic in the group, I'll go first," said Nick. "In case there's zombie priests inside, which I'm almost hoping for, since there's some padres at St. Francis Elementary whose necks I'd like to snap and this might be the closest I get."

He lifted up his flare, whistled "Onward Christian Soldiers," and marched through the hole. They waited until Nick signaled all-clear and then followed him inside, Will bringing up the rear. He glanced back one last time and thought he saw a tall, shadowy shape slip behind a crumbling building in the distance. Will quickly stepped inside.

Seen by the light of their flares, the place fit Nepsted's description as a "cathedral"; the room was immense and space soared above them just as a central hall of worship would. Most of the high ceiling had collapsed, but a few intact beams spanned the gap above like exposed ribs. Rows of thick stone benches, many broken or overturned, lined either side of a central aisle and faced a raised stone dais where the aisle ended.

As they passed down the aisle, Will realized the benches weren't built to a human scale. They looked between four and five feet high, which suggested anyone sitting in them would have been at least seven feet tall.

Will glanced over at Ajay, who was looking at the seats on the other side. Will held his hand up, about a foot over his head, and Ajay nodded.

"Welcome to the church of the NBA," said Ajay quietly.

Four tall stone steps led to the dais. Nick climbed it first and called the others to come take a look. A square, empty stone platform the size of a boxing ring, about two feet higher than the dais, occupied the middle of the rise.

"This must be an altar," said Elise. "Or something like it."

Directly behind the altar stood a rectangular stone structure about twelve feet long and five feet high. A carved stone slab covered eighty percent of it; the rest had crumbled, leaving an opening on top. Nick hopped onto it and made his way toward the opening.

"What is this?" asked Elise, shining her light around the sides.

"It looks like a crypt," said Ajay.

"Yeah, baby." Nick pointed his flashlight down inside. "Uh, Will?"

Nick held a hand down and pulled Will up to join him. Both directed their lights at the interior.

Amid crumbled debris and other unidentifiable decomposed materials, a massive skeleton rested inside. All they could see was its huge, misshapen head, a bulbous oblong spheroid the size of a beach ball with four empty eye sockets and a gnarled set of fangs that spanned the entire width of the skull.

"What is it?" asked Ajay, looking up at them.

"The tomb of Pope Putrid the First," said Nick, grimacing. "Dude had to be eight feet tall."

"That's why he got the best tomb," said Will.

"The Mac Daddy Monster. Take some snaps of this dude's melon," said Nick as he pulled Ajay and Elise up to take a look. "And I used to think *you* had big brains."

"Oh my God," said Elise. "They're aliens."

"They're not aliens," said Will.

"You're not going to tell me that's *human*," said Elise.

"Extraordinary," said Ajay, immediately snapping pictures. "You really ought to see this, Brooke."

"No thanks," said Brooke, keeping her head down.

"They're not humans, but they're not aliens," said Will.

"How is that possible, Will?" asked Ajay, taking more pictures.

"They're not from someplace else," said Will. "They're from *here*."

"Here? Where here? Where how?" asked Nick.

"Earth. They were here before," said Will. "These must be the 'Old Ones' in the Lakota legends. Or maybe, just maybe, part of that ancient race that's trying to come back to earth, the Other Team. And it's possible they're both."

Will saw Brooke wandering away, folding her arms around herself. He hopped down and hurried over to her.

"Are you going to be all right?" he asked.

Brooke refused to look at him. "I don't think we should be here. At all. I think we should leave now."

"They were here before *what*, Will?" asked Elise, a little more insistently.

"Before us. Before *humans*. A long time before. Thousands of years."

"Considering all this," said Ajay, looking around, "the timeline seems plausible."

"How do you know all this, Will?" asked Elise, her gaze narrowing sharply.

"Good question," said Nick. "Wassup with that?"

Will watched Brooke carefully—she still wouldn't meet his eye—then turned back to the group. *Change the subject. Not the right time to drop the whole "Dave and the Hierarchy" number on them.*

"From what Jericho told me, connecting the dots. Does anybody see any other way in or out of here, besides the one we came through?"

Nick jumped down and scoured the perimeter of the cathedral. No other entrances or exits.

You need to stand on it.

The words slipped into Will's mind just as easily as before, but this time he recognized a familiar tone and rhythm. Did he suddenly know where these instructions were coming from, and whose voice this might be? When he took a moment to think about it, it actually made sense, or as much sense as anything did in his life these days.

Will stepped onto the altar and examined it. Its entire surface was lined with chiseled grooves, worn smooth with time, a patterned latticework of them all running slightly downhill toward a round hole, about three feet across, in its center, big enough to fall through.

"Everybody come up here," said Will.

Everyone but Brooke joined him.

"Come on, Brooke."

"I want to go officially on record and say this is a terrible idea," she said.

"And then . . . ?" asked Elise patiently.

"We'll take a vote," said Will. "Either we keep looking for Nepsted's key or head back. Who wants to keep going?"

Everyone but Brooke raised their hands. She sighed and stepped up onto the platform with them.

The platform jolted sharply and then, accompanied by a sound of heavy chains rattling, the whole altar began to slowly descend.

"You gotta be pooping me," said Nick, laughing.

"Would anyone *else* like to change their vote?" asked Brooke, annoyed.

Ajay jumped off the moving platform, which had lowered

until it was just level with the dais itself, and it came to a sudden stop.

"For goodness' sake, people," said Ajay. "May I ask, Will, what is the purpose of throwing ourselves into this hole?"

"Nepsted said we had to go *down* through the cathedral," said Will.

"I'm perfectly aware of what Nepsted told us, Will," said Ajay, folding his arms.

"We took a vote, Ajay," said Elise.

"And, dude, we're not *throwing* ourselves," said Nick.

"I'm sorry but this constitutes changed circumstances," said Ajay. "I did not have all the information required at the time to make a fully informed decision."

"Don't filibuster us now, buddy," said Elise. "We obviously don't have enough weight to activate this thing without you."

"I feel the need to point out that our progress will not be adversely affected by pausing for a last moment of self-reflection," said Ajay. "Before we recklessly ride a descending stone platform adorning the middle of some godforsaken ruin of demonic worship into the lower precincts of the underworld."

"Hang on a second," said Nick, fishing through his pack. "Sister Mary Margaret makes a fair point. Let me rig something."

Nick took out a long coiled rope and secured one end to a short stone pillar on the corner of the dais, then held on to the other end and jumped back up on the platform.

"I got a hundred feet of rope here. Feel better now?" Nick asked Ajay.

"Brooke?" pleaded Ajay.

"In for a penny," she sighed, resigned.

Will looked at his watch. "Take your time," he said, without looking at Ajay.

Ajay held out for another few seconds before he said, "Oh fiddlesticks" and then stepped cautiously back onto the platform. Another jolt and it immediately began lowering again.

"Yee-haw," said Elise quietly.

As they passed down through the floor of the altar, Nick knelt near the center of the platform, shining his light through the hole.

"This is so awesome," said Nick.

"What is?" asked Ajay.

"I can totally see a huge pile of bones down there."

"Dear God, if there actually is a God, please let me die quickly and painlessly," whispered Ajay, while sinking down onto his hands and knees.

No need to get your knickers in a twist, said the voice in Will's head. *Those bones are as old as the Himalayas, mate.*

No question about it now. The voice was Dave.

THE HOSPITAL

The altar descended at the same steady pace for what Will estimated to be somewhere between fifty and sixty feet.

Dave, hey, Dave? You there?

Will repeatedly *thought* a response to Dave, but the voice didn't respond.

The five of them huddled together toward the center, staying away from the edges. Shining their lights around, they realized they were dropping down through a narrow chamber of rock that appeared to be man-made, or at least not a natural formation. It widened slightly as they neared the bottom, and the platform came to a sudden stop a yard from the floor.

The ground around their stopping point wasn't just littered with bones; it appeared composed entirely of a vast pile of them. Pale, dusty, and compacted together. What appeared to be a path or clearing through them led away to their right.

"If we step off this thing, is it going back up without us?" asked Elise.

"Only one way to find out," said Will.

"Let me make sure we're ready for that," said Nick.

He pulled a piece of climbing gear from his pack—a section of strong fabric straps that formed a seat—and threaded the end of his rope through it, then dropped it down the hole in the center of the platform.

"If it goes back up, I'll climb the rope. You take turns in this seat and I'll pull you up," said Nick as he worked.

"Step off one at a time to test it but stay close," said Will.

"Nick, grab the rope and hang on in case it goes back up on some kind of delay. If it doesn't move, we'll continue on."

"Sounds like a plan," said Nick. "Actually, it sounds like *my* plan."

They stepped off one at a time. Nick went first, reached under the platform, and grabbed the rope. Will went last, bones crunching underfoot as he landed. They waited a full minute, in tense silence, but the altar never budged. Keeping an eye on it, Will led the others away, turning their attention to their new surroundings.

Their lights picked up bones everywhere, piled high all around the moving platform in a chamber that appeared to be the size of a football field. The air around them felt dead and carried the slightest suggestion of decay.

"A cave under a cave," said Nick, lowering his voice. "There must be a word for that, right, like *under-cave*?"

"It's an ossuary," whispered Ajay. "And I have to say that's a word I never thought I would have occasion to use."

"What's it mean, egghead?" asked Nick.

"A receptacle or vault for the bones of the dead," said Ajay. "Or a cave containing deposits of ancient carcasses resulting from carnage. Emphasis on *ancient*."

"Memorizing the dictionary again?" asked Elise.

"The Oxford," said Ajay. "I'm halfway through the *T*s."

"I'm leaning toward something in the *A*s," said Elise. "Like *abattoir*."

"When you two are done playing smarty-pants ping-pong, let us know," said Nick.

"That means 'slaughterhouse,'" said Elise.

"Great. *Abattoir*. My new word of the day," said Nick. "Now let's abattoir to find that key and get out of Dodge."

199

Will led them single file, following the narrow path through the piles. As his light flashed off the bones, he saw shapes and sizes of all kinds—double-skulled heads, spines twelve feet long, arms with reptilian pincers, more than a few suggestions of wings. Many reminded him of the various creatures that had pursued him last year, things Dave had called gulvorgs or lamias. *Maybe what we've found is the Other Team's home, or some kind of lost colony.*

"There's violence here," said Brooke, shivering as she looked around. "Terrible violence."

"Ya think?" asked Nick.

Will elbowed him sharply.

"Doesn't take an archeologist to track that to the source," said Elise. "Part of the services offered upstairs. Start with a few inspirational hymns, a thoughtful Sunday sermon from Cardinal Watermelon Head, and then, to round out the festivities, three hours of human sacrifice."

"Stop saying *human*," said Brooke.

"I'd like to analyze some of these bones so we know exactly what they are," said Ajay.

"You can pick up a souvenir on the way out," said Will.

"Too bad we don't have a dog," said Nick. "A dog would go animal crackers down here."

Will checked his watch. "Let's stay focused."

He hadn't heard anything more from Dave, but he couldn't figure why he was hearing him again. Maybe this place put him physically closer to wherever Dave was, or enabled some kind of stronger connection to the Never-Was. Will tried asking more silent questions to see if his missing "guardian" would respond from, well, wherever he was: *How long ago did the Other Team live down here? Was Cahokia their headquarters or some kind of capital city? Is this where your final battle with them took place?*

Nothing. Dave didn't respond.

"Dudes, so I think I figured out what the hole in the center's for," said Nick as they continued following the path through the bones. "It's like a garbage disposal after they're done at the chop shop upstairs. And when the platform gets too jammed, they could just ride it down, dump the whole load, hose it off, and head back up for more."

"Okay, you can put your imagination back in its box now," said Elise, grimacing.

"But it's true that most ancient civilizations depended on sacrifices of one kind or another," said Ajay. "That was how they reached out to the spirit world for assistance. They most frequently sacrificed animals, but a lot of societies didn't stop there by any means."

"Could be worse," said Nick. "Maybe they were cannibals."

Will took a worried look at Brooke. She was still shaking and seemed overwhelmed. Will put an arm around her and spoke softly: "You're picking up too much," he said. "Can you try to shut it out?"

She shook her head. "It's overwhelming."

"We're going to be fine. This all happened a long, long time ago, and I think you can control what you're feeling more than you know."

She managed a slight smile. "I can try."

Nick took the lead, holding up his flare. "There's some kind of light up ahead. Maybe a way out."

They trudged in silence for a while, accompanied by the dry rattle and crack of the bones, until that stopped and they realized they were walking on rock and dirt again. Heading for the glow in the distance, they followed the path down a short slope to a long horizontal gap in the rock wall. It was about six feet high with sharp edges that looked as if they'd been cut into the stone with precise tools. They ducked under it, passed through a short passage in the rock, and came out into another large, high-ceilinged chamber, onto a ledge overlooking the cave's floor twenty feet below.

A building sat in the chamber's center about thirty yards away. Intact, made of concrete, modern, or at least midcentury, like an office building. One story, long and wide, with a flat roof. The wall facing and nearest to them had floor-to-ceiling windows, lit up inside with a warm, amber light that imbued the surrounding darkness with a ghostly glow.

"That's got to be the place Nepsted described," said Will.

"The hospital," said Ajay. "And it's got power, all the way down here."

"Totally nutso," said Nick.

"So Nepsted wasn't lying," said Elise.

"Kill the lights and the flares," said Will. "Everybody stay low."

Nick discarded their flares and they knelt down behind a cluster of rocks. Will took out binoculars, and Ajay did the same. Will scanned the glass wall. It looked like some kind of administrative or reception area. He saw desks and chairs and doors inside, and what appeared to be a linoleum floor, but no people—or creatures—anywhere in sight.

"See anything moving?" Will asked Ajay.

"Not even a mouse," said Ajay.

Ajay widened the scope of his search while Will blinked and summoned up his Grid, looking for heat signatures. Neither detected living creatures anywhere around or outside the building.

"What do we do?" asked Elise.

"Look, dudes, we didn't come this far down the rabbit hole

to stop on the one-yard line in the middle of like Nazi head-quarters," said Nick. "Did we?"

"No, but if you tried, you could probably mix a few more metaphors," said Elise.

Will looked at his watch. "How many flares did you bring, Nick?"

"Plenty to get us back topside," said Nick.

Will thought about it for a second.

#56: GIVING UP IS EASY. FINISHING IS HARD.

"Nick's right," he said. "Switch your lamps back on and follow me."

They picked their way down from the ledge along a narrow rocky shelf, which put them on the level of the building, about fifty feet away, directly facing the glass wall. The inside looked like a still life or a diorama in a museum. Will directed them around the left side so they never passed directly in front of the windows. The building was much bigger than it first appeared, extending back hundreds of feet, never rising above one story. The walls were plain cinderblock, painted dark industrial green. Before long, they came to a regular-sized door. Will turned the knob. Unlocked. He turned off his headlamp and the others did the same.

"Stay together," Will whispered. "Single file. No free-lancing."

He opened the door and stepped inside. The same soft amber glow filled the corridor inside from hidden fixtures above. Cheap, industrial linoleum lined the floor between wood-paneled walls, and a slight hum oscillated from somewhere beyond the walls. They edged down the hallway to an intersection and turned right, heading for the area they'd seen through the windows. They reached it after passing through one more door.

The room looked as if it had been abandoned in the middle of an ordinary day's work. Chairs had been shoved back from desks. Papers, pens, and open books sat on the main counter, next to an empty coffee cup, everything covered by a heavy layer of dust. Phones but no computers or printers; nothing that modern. A clock on the wall was still audibly ticking, the second hand advancing in small spasms around the dial. One of the fluorescent bars in the hanging fixtures above flickered, casting a fractured strobe effect around the room.

Ajay moved to the main desk, blew the dust off the pages of the largest book on the counter, and examined it.

"This is some kind of ledger," he said. "Dates, initials, in English, but with lots of strange abbreviations."

"Do you see a year?"

"Looks like 1938," said Ajay; then he rapidly paged back through the book. "And it goes back from there about six months to, guess what, late 1937 . . . then it skips a lot of pages . . . and there's another section toward the back from 1935, written in fountain pen. Letters and numbers, arranged cryptically. I'm guessing it's some kind of code."

"Take some pictures," said Will, tossing him the pen-camera.

"I won't have any trouble remembering—"

"For me, not you," said Will. "Everybody, check all the drawers and cabinets."

"Doesn't really look like a hospital," said Nick, looking around.

"If you were a key, where would you be?" asked Brooke.

She opened a small closet and found an assortment of white coats on hangers and a box full of construction hard hats.

"Make sure we leave no trace of our presence," said Ajay as he finished taking pictures.

"I don't know why," said Elise. "No one's been in this room since about forever."

"What do you think it was used for?" asked Nick, opening the drawers in a desk.

Elise reached past him into one of the drawers and took out a handful of empty HELLO MY NAME IS _____ stickers. "Maybe a reception or visitor center, where they processed people in and out of whatever this is."

Will found a calendar for 1938 with pictures of farm machinery in another drawer. "Built in the 1930s. And this part of it, at least, was abandoned not long afterward."

"Really?" asked Nick. "How'd the people who used it get to work?"

"And what kind of work were they doing here?" asked Brooke.

Will opened a small box behind the counter and found a ring of keys on a hook.

"Let's find out," he said.

He grabbed the keys and led them back into the corridor, then down the hall past the door where they'd entered. The corridor continued deeper into the building for thirty paces, where it ended in a perpendicular corridor that took them right. Occasional doors led to smaller rooms on either side, empty or small clerical stations that didn't seem worth exploring. But one opened into a larger space that looked like a barracks, with twin rows of cots lining the walls. Two doors down from that they found a corridor with a row of six barred cells.

"This looks like military construction," said Ajay, examining the craftsmanship. "Fast, sturdy, relatively inexpensive. The army put up barracks like this by the thousands all over the country during World War Two, and through the Cold War, almost overnight."

"A mile underground?" asked Elise. "Next to an ancient alien city?"

"And was that on purpose or an accident?" asked Brooke.

"Not sure," said Will, "but there has to be some connection."

"But how could they have done it?" asked Brooke. "How'd they get everything you'd need to build this down here?"

"There must be some other way up to the surface that we don't know about," said Will.

"You'd be amazed at what a few billion dollars can do," said Ajay.

That corridor ended at a solid concrete wall, with a heavy, steel-reinforced door in the middle. The number 19 was stenciled on it in red paint. Will tried the door. Locked.

He sifted through the key ring he'd picked up in the office and found one attached to a metal-lined cardboard disc with "19" written on it in red ink. He inserted the key, the lock gave way, and he opened the door.

The lights were off on the other side. Will turned on his flashlight and found a light switch by the door. He flipped it up. Fluorescent fixtures flickered on overhead and the room filled with harsh white light. They had entered a newer, entirely different section of the building.

The flooring was a white, high-gloss tile. Stainless-steel cabinets and metal lockers lined the walls. There were slots for nameplates along the top of the lockers but the plates had been removed. Brooke opened the lockers; there were red scrubs inside all of them.

"It's a doctors' dressing room," said Brooke. "These are surgical scrubs."

"Why are they red?" asked Nick, fingering one of the sleeves.

"So blood doesn't show up," said Brooke.

"Oh," said Nick, gingerly replacing the scrub in the locker.

"There's no dust anywhere," said Elise, running a finger over a cabinet. "This room's clean."

"We've found the hospital," said Will.

He opened another locker and saw round tin film canisters, rows of videotapes, stacks of DVDs.

"What's all this?" asked Nick.

"Cans of film," said Will, looking through them. "Dated from the thirties and forties."

Nick sifted through the rest. "The tapes are from the eighties, the DVDs from the nineties."

"Put everything back the way we found it," said Will, replacing the cans.

"There's air circulating through the room," said Ajay, holding up his hand to an overhead vent. "A working filtration system."

"Whatever it's for, this section is still being used," said Will.

"Considerably more modern," said Ajay, studying the doors. "More substantial style of construction. Postwar definitely."

Will opened a door at the far end and led them into the next room, a spacious laboratory outfitted with computers, servers, and every technological gadget you could think of.

"Electron microscopes ... advanced cyclotrons ... ," said Ajay, walking through. "It's as well equipped as the school's labs."

"Suitable for genetic work, gene splicing, that kind of thing?" asked Will.

"More than suitable."

"When do you think they put this part in?" asked Elise.

"Probably 1980s," said Ajay. "At the earliest."

Next to a workbench, Ajay opened a large storage compartment. Inside they found rows of sealed glass containers, most holding a variety of bones suspended in a clear liquid. One held a skull, similar to but smaller than the monstrous one they'd discovered in the cathedral's crypt.

"I have an idea why they built this place," said Will.

"Who's they?"

"The Knights," said Will, pointing to an insignia on the door, an image of the Paladin. "They found Cahokia and wanted to study it. They punched into the bone room from this side of the cave, not the other way around. That's what the older section was for, built in the thirties, a command center for the dig."

"So why'd they build the hospital section?" asked Nick.

"For when they stopped studying," said Will, shining his flashlight through a door he'd opened into the next room. "And started experimenting."

Lights switched on as they entered, activated by sensors. This room had a higher ceiling and was perfectly round, with elevated seats surrounding a space with that same shiny, spotless white flooring. An adjustable stainless-steel table, surrounded by medical equipment, stood in its center. Spotlights were suspended over the table. Everything looked immaculately clean.

"An operating theater," said Elise.

Nick looked more closely at the table and lifted some straps at the corners that ended in complex shackles. "Is it normal to lock people down during surgery?"

"Of course not," said Brooke.

"Didn't think so."

"Who were they operating on?" asked Ajay.

Will didn't answer. "Let's keep moving," he said.

Nick led them through swinging doors at the far end of the surgical theater, feeding into another corridor, this one all white, floors, walls, and ceilings. The electric hum they'd heard since they arrived grew steadily louder here; they were moving closer to whatever its source was.

At the end of the corridor they reached another metallic door, stenciled with a red number 9, in the middle of a solid, poured concrete wall. Will found the corresponding key on the chain and unlocked it. He flicked on some switches to the side of the door and lit everything up.

The square space in front of them was the largest and deepest they'd encountered in the hospital complex. Halfway across was a wall with three equidistant glass doors, which divided the area. There was only darkness behind the door to the left; the pulsating hum they'd heard, much louder now, was issuing from in there. The door appeared heavily secured.

There were lights on inside the door on the right; looking through it they saw a large wall on the room's right side, which rose out of sight and the ceiling along with it. Set into that wall was a pair of large dark steel doors—ten feet wide, eight feet high—and an operating panel with small lights to the left of them.

"What does that look like to you?" Will asked the others.

"I don't know," said Brooke.

"Nothing I've ever seen before," said Elise.

"Like massive steel doors in some super, super top-secret evil scientific laboratory?" asked Nick.

"Hard to top that description," said Ajay, his eyes opening wide. "But perhaps the entrance to a freezer? There are digital readouts on that panel that could be related to temperature."

Will turned his attention to the middle section, walking to the solid glass door. Behind it was the smallest room of the three, rectangular, low ceilinged, painted all white. Overhead lights revealed the only two objects in the room—identical bright steel cylinders, shaped like two strangely formed, elliptical beer kegs, in the center of the room.

"Let's look in here," said Will.

The thick glass door to the central room wasn't locked. They pushed inside for a closer look at the two cylinders. They stood five feet high, fashioned from a glossy metallic substance that reflected so much light they were almost painful to look at. No straight edges or corners anywhere on them, every angle rounded and smooth.

"Is it just me, or do these things look aphotic to you?" asked Ajay.

"Totally," said Nick.

The three guys took out their dark glasses for a look, but aside from a strange white glow emanating from both cylinders, they didn't notice anything different about them.

"See if you can find a way to open them," Will asked Ajay, putting his glasses away.

Ajay walked all around and studied each object carefully from every angle. "The metal appears to be seamless," he said.

Ajay took another small electronic measuring device from his vest. He turned it on and it emitted beams of light that he shined up and down along the object on the left; then he did the same to the one on the right.

"They're slightly different," he said. "The one on the left is denser. There seems to be more mass inside it." He ran his hand over the top of the cylinder. "And there's something odd here. The very slightest indentation . . . it almost feels like . . . the shape of a hand . . . one a lot bigger than mine."

Put your *hand there,* said the voice in Will's head.

Will stepped forward and placed his hand on top where Ajay had indicated. He felt around until he found the described pattern of fingers and palm. It was a tremendously subtle depression, but his hand was a perfect fit and as soon as he locked in on it, he felt the cool metal under his skin warm up and start to yield, almost as if it were melting slightly to his touch.

"Something's happening," he said.

"I think you unlocked it," said Elise.

A razor-thin seam opened along the front of the metal, running up and down simultaneously until it split the entire cylinder. When the halves started to separate, Will moved his hand away and the others stepped back. The two halves of the cylinder folded back, and a single shelf slid out and fanned open into a half-circle tray. Fashioned from the same metallic material, it appeared to be floating in air. Will looked closer and saw the shelf was attached to the cylinder by a single joint at the back.

There were three indentations on the shelf for three distinctly different objects. All three slots were empty but retained the shapes of the things they were designed to hold: a depression on the left, about a foot across, then a hook-shaped hole next to it that held something like a gun and a spray nozzle, and the last a perfect square about four inches wide and high.

"The Knights must have built this place," said Will, running his hand over the shapes. "Probably to keep devices they use in here that they either made or brought across."

"Aphotic devices," said Ajay. "From the Never-Was."

"You've seen more of these than we have," said Brooke. "Do any of the shapes look familiar?"

"The middle one," said Will. "I never held it in my hand, but that thing Lyle used to open the portal to the Never-Was would probably fit here. It was like a gun."

"You mean the thing we saw Hobbes give to Lyle on Ronnie's tape?" said Elise.

"Yes. Hobbes called it the Carver," said Will.

"Where is it now?" asked Nick.

"Damn, I hadn't even thought about this," said Will. "Lyle threw it into the cave after the wendigo came through."

"You think we could still find it there?" asked Ajay.

"We better try," said Will. "Before they do."

"What do you suppose these other shapes were holding?" asked Elise, running a hand over the indentations on the shelf.

"Either objects that they found in the ruins or ones they brought across from the Never-Was, I'm not sure," said Will. "But this tells us there's at least two more of these gizmos around that I'd like to get a look at."

"Maybe they're in here," said Nick, knocking on the other cylinder.

"Why would they hide something in *that* one that they're supposed to keep in *this* one?" asked Ajay, annoyed.

"I don't know, dude. Why does any of what these dudes do even have to make sense? Everybody keeps saying they're not *human*."

"Humans built all of this, Nick," said Will. "Humans that are helping the Other Team. That's what this whole place is for."

Will noticed Brooke looking at him intensely. "If the Knights built it, then why did *your* hand open it?"

"I have no idea," said Will.

"Well, then, see if you can open this one," said Elise, looking at the cylinder on the right more closely.

Will moved to the other cylinder and ran his hands along the top, looking for another depression. He couldn't feel anything there, but then he slid his hand along the side. About halfway down he felt the same hand-sized pattern in the metal.

Nothing happened when he fit his hand to it, so he ran his left hand down the other side and found another pattern for that hand.

As soon as both hands were in place, Will felt an energetic jolt shoot through the metal. The cylinder started to move, this time splitting in four equal quarters all the way down, sliding slightly away from each other. Will quickly yanked his hands away because once the pieces had completely separated, they turned to face each other and began to rotate clockwise, rapidly picking up speed. Within seconds the sections were spinning around in a tight circle so swiftly that all they could see was a blur.

What they *could* see was a still object around which the panels were spinning: suspended in midair in what would have been the middle of the cylinder was a slender, featureless bright metal tube, about six inches long.

Will quickly threw on his dark glasses—Ajay and Nick did the same—and saw the now-familiar aphotic glow emanate from the silver tube, along with a series of complex studs and buttons that rhythmically emerged from the metal and then liquidly merged back into it.

"If that isn't Nepsted's key," said Ajay, "I'll eat my spectro-magraphic topometer."

"I beg your jargon?" asked Nick.

"I think you're right, Ajay," said Will.

"That's great, but how do we get it out of there?" said Nick, sharing his glasses with Brooke and Elise so they could see it.

Will took a piece of paper from his bag and extended it slowly toward the spinning sections of the cylinder. The whirling blades instantly shredded the paper.

"Can't you reach in from the top?" asked Elise.

Will, the tallest in the group, stepped closer and raised his

arm above the center to reach down in for it. Sensing movement, the blades adjusted position, two now spinning directly
above the silver tube. Brooke pulled his hand back protectively.

"Be careful, those things could take your hand off," said
Brooke.

"We're not leaving without that key," said Will, his mind
racing. "We need to attack this together."

A plan took shape in his head and he gave instructions to
the others. Brooke was the only one puzzled by his suggestion,
but she said she'd give it a try. Four of them stepped back and
took positions, waiting for Will's signal. Nick put his heavy
leather gloves back on and moved closest to the cylinder. Ajay
knelt down and stared intently at the spinning blades. Brooke
stood next to Elise, raised both her hands next to Elise's back,
and waited.

Will nodded at Elise, then walked back to the end of the
room.

Elise took a few deep breaths and then summoned up a
rumbling, low-frequency stream of sound that took shape like
a transparent cloud, distorting the air in front of her. She slowly
eased it forward into the path of the spinning blades, creating
resistance. They started to slow, but the effort of sustaining it
against their brute force almost instantly drained Elise of most
of her strength.

"Now, Brooke!" said Will.

Brooke closed her eyes and placed her hands on the center of Elise's back, supporting her. Elise looked revived and the
power of her vocal projection received an instant boost: now
the blades slowed enough, almost by half, so you could almost
see them.

And Ajay could see them quite distinctly.

"Now, Nick!" said Ajay, staring at them intently.

Nick reached down and grabbed the edge of the nearest blade, planted his feet, put all his leverage into it; all the blades slowed another twenty percent, but their force dragged Nick partway around the floor.

"Now, Will!" shouted Ajay.

Will took two steps and dove up and over the cylinder. Once over it he reached down in between the slowed blades. Before they could react, he snatched the silver tube, then tucked and rolled onto the ground on the other side.

"Get away from it!" he yelled.

Nick let go of the blade, Elise dissolved her sound cloud, and all of them were knocked back by an energetic concussion as the blades resumed whirring. Will looked at the tube in his hand, intact, glowing with a slight pulsation of light. It felt almost weightless, as if it might float away if he didn't hold on to it.

The sections of the cylinder stopped moving and reassembled into one solid piece with a loud clank. The metal changed color, turning from bright silver to a dark shade of crimson.

"That can't be good," said Nick, shaking his hands in pain as he took off his gloves. "It's never good when stuff turns red."

"I don't know," said Will.

"Your fingers are bleeding," said Elise.

"Lucky for me we're in a hospital," said Nick casually as Elise examined the cuts.

Brooke moved to Will, took him aside, and spoke in an urgent whisper. "What did I do just then? How did you know I could do anything like that?"

"Something I noticed earlier," he said. "We don't have time to talk about it right now."

She looked frightened. "But it means—"

"I know what it means," he whispered, trying to smile.

"Don't worry, you're okay. The good news is you don't have to feel left out anymore."

"Will, look behind you," said Ajay, pointing.

Will turned. The wall on the left side of the chamber had a window in it. Overhead lights had dimmed in the next room, allowing them to see inside. By far the largest of the three chambers, it was also the strangest.

Two orderly rows of large metallic canisters, a dozen of them about ten feet high, took up most of the room that they could see. Stacks of advanced electronics and technological devices and monitors surrounded them.

"Will, we got what we came for," said Elise, grabbing him by the shirt, whispering fiercely. "Let's get out of here."

"We need to look in there first," said Will.

HOBBES

The others followed Will as he hustled out of the cylinder room and moved to the door of the chamber on the left. They couldn't see much through its front glass wall, even with lights on inside, because this glass turned out to be clouded and opaque.

"Can you see anything?" Will asked Ajay.

Ajay pressed his face up against the glass and opened his eyes wide. "Nothing moving. All I can make out are large, stationary pieces of equipment."

Brooke asked Will to wait, long enough to dress some bandages from her pack onto Nick's hands. He looked like he'd tried to grab a bacon slicer, but once she'd cleaned them, the cuts turned out to be superficial. When she finished, he slipped his leather gloves back on.

"Good to go," said Nick.

Will put his dark glasses on and examined the external lock hanging on the room's door. It had a complex, unearthly appearance similar to the one on Nepsted's cage, fingers of steel slithering around a central gemlike shaft as if the whole thing were alive, glowing with a ghostly green nimbus. Will looked over and saw that Ajay had put his glasses on as well.

"I think it might work," said Ajay.

"Let's give it a try," said Will.

Will lifted the silver key and held it next to the lock, and the device came alive in his hand. Fingers of liquid metal extruded from the body of the tube, reached out, and interacted with mobile parts of the lock in a complex dance, twisting and merging while changing colors rapidly, all in a way that seemed organic, a process that Will could somehow sense was the key persuading the lock to yield.

The interaction ended with a satisfying *clunk* as the bolt opened. All the moving parts of both devices instantly withdrew back into their original forms, and the sickly green light drained out of the lock. As soon as it was completely inert, the door gave way and swung open as if an unseen hand had pushed it.

Will eased it open the rest of the way and stepped inside. Ajay and Elise followed him, but Brooke stopped on the threshold.

"What's wrong?" whispered Will.

"I don't know." She shook her head. "I can't go in there."

"Stay with her, Nick," said Will.

Nick signaled that he would. Will, Ajay, and Elise moved inside. Huge stacks of equipment, most rising to the ceiling in a strangely haphazard way, generated a disabling drone that overwhelmed all sound and made it hard to even think.

Will looked at Elise and asked silently, *Can you do anything about the noise?*

I can try.

Elise concentrated for a moment, opened her mouth, and emitted a high note beyond Will's hearing, but when he activated his Grid, he could see it energetically deploy throughout the room like an opening parachute, neutralizing the din, dampening its disabling effects by half.

"Remind me to invite you to the prom," said Ajay as he moved past her, taking readings with one of his devices.

The canisters stood on raised concrete platforms, three feet high, spaced far enough apart to create an aisle between the two rows. The three friends moved slowly down the aisle. Each canister had an aphotic lock near its base similar to the one on the door. They weren't solid metal, as Will had first thought; each had a riveted panel of curved glass in front, about five feet off the ground. They were pitch-black inside, but they could see just enough to realize that all of the tanks were filled, at least to the level of their window, with some kind of dark liquid.

"There are numbered plates on the base below each container," said Ajay, pointing out small pieces of brass attached to the concrete. "One through twelve. Followed by letters . . . two apiece . . . all these same initials were on the page from 1937 in that ledger up front . . ."

"These last two tanks are empty," said Will, reaching the end of the row. "But the plate on number twelve has initials like the others—E. S."

"Number eleven, too," said Elise, reading the plate on the next to last canister. "R and L."

A chill run up Will's spine. "Ajay, pull up that picture I took of the plane crash memorial."

"Give me a moment," said Ajay, taking out the camera pen.

He transferred the digital image to a handheld device that projected it into the air nearby. Will turned to Elise, eyes wired by what was in his mind, and sent a quick picture of what he was thinking—knowing she was strong enough to handle it, and she was.

I need your help, he said.

I'm right here with you, she answered.

"Read the names, Ajay," said Will, standing by the first canister. "In order."

"Gerald Alverson . . . Thomas Bigby . . . Thornton Cross . . . Jonathon Edwards . . . Professor Joseph Enderman . . . Carl Forrester . . . George Gage . . . Richard Hornsby . . . Robert Jacks . . . Theodore Lewis . . . Raymond Llewelyn . . . Edgar Snow."

Will and Elise traveled down the rows, checking initials against the names.

"The Knights of Charlemagne, class of 1937," said Elise quietly. "Ten of them anyway."

"Twelve students and one teacher went down on that plane," said Will, looking at the photo of the memorial. "Abelson, the teacher, isn't here. Neither are two of the students."

"Edgar Snow and Raymond Llewelyn," said Elise. "Aka Hobbes and Nepsted."

They heard a distinct splash in one of the tanks, somewhere in the middle of the row, next to where Ajay was standing. All three of them froze.

"What was that?" asked Ajay, his voice very small.

Will and Elise locked eyes and knew they were thinking the same thing. They swung their flashlights up and trained them on a tank in the center of the left row, taking a couple of steps toward it.

Another splash from inside the tank. Turning toward Will and Elise, Ajay's eyes looked big enough to jump out of his head.

Will sent a word to Elise: *NOW!*

They switched on their flashlights and pointed at the glass panel on the front of the tank. The liquid inside, dank, yellow-green, and thick with sediment, was sloshing around.

Ajay still hadn't turned to look at it, but he did now, slowly, when he saw the flashlights come on.

Something slapped up against the glass right above Ajay. A large, misshapen melted mass that reminded Will of a cluster of kelp washed up on a beach, pale and sickly, and somewhere in the middle of it they could make out a pair of distended, almost human eyes. A keening wail issued from the tank that froze their hearts.

And then, all around them, fluid stirred in the rest of the tanks. Other terrible things inside began throwing themselves at the glass. Will averted his eyes but still picked up impressions: paddles, fins, eyes, sacks of mottled flesh. Other sounds, equally piteous and strange, cried out to them, a chorus of ungodly voices.

They ran on blind instinct, picking up Ajay along the way, carrying him out the door, his eyes shut tight, trying to catch his breath, paralyzed with horror. Will slammed the door behind them, which didn't do enough to kill the haunting voices trailing after them. The aphotic lock reengaged as the door closed.

Brooke and Nick weren't in the vestibule where they'd left them.

"Nick!" Will shouted.

"Over here!" Nick answered.

They ran to the room on the far right, dragging Ajay with them. Nick and Brooke stood in the open doorway, looking at the panel beside the big steel doors. Lights flashed intensely; the whole room was humming from some kind of machinery behind the doors.

"Dude, it's not a *freezer*—"

"What?" Will could hardly think straight.

"It's an *elevator*," said Brooke.

Will looked up; the whole wall was starting to vibrate, the sounds getting louder.

"And it's coming *down*," said Nick.

Will took Brooke aside, grabbed her hands, and put them on Ajay's shoulders. He was moaning slightly and still hadn't opened his eyes.

"Help him," said Will urgently. "We won't get out of here in time if he can't move."

"What happened?" she asked.

"He's in shock. I can't explain now, and I'll try to help; just *do it.*"

Brooke nodded, closed her eyes, held on to Ajay, and concentrated. Will went to work at the same time, pushing a thought picture at Ajay: *The room with the tanks. Nothing in them. Empty.*

Ajay slumped forward. Will and Elise caught him. Ajay opened his eyes a moment later. He looked himself again, but confused and still wobbly on his feet.

"What happened?" he asked.

"You blacked out for a second," said Will.

"How odd," said Ajay calmly. "I don't remember—"

"Time to go, pal," said Will.

Will glanced back again. The steel doors and the entire wall around it were rattling now, as whatever was descending down the shaft dropped closer to them.

"By all means, we'd best vamoose, then," said Ajay.

Elise and Brooke took him by the arms to steady him and they ran toward the exit. As he followed, Will saw that Nick had wandered over near the door to the tank room.

"Nick!" shouted Will.

"But I heard something in here—"

"Not NOW!" shouted Will and Elise in unison.

Nick hurried after them, the last one out the steel door they'd entered through.

"Close every door behind us," said Will.

Nick slammed it shut. Will thrust in the right key from the ring and turned it. They followed the others back through the operating theater and then out the entrance to the hospital section, Will stopping to lock each door he'd opened behind them.

As he pulled the key from the steel door labeled 19, a

tremendous thud shook the entire building: The elevator had landed.

"They're here," said Will. "Hurry!"

They hurtled back through the paneled corridors, even Ajay keeping pace, running without prompting now. They were in such a panic Brooke and Ajay ran past the door they'd used to enter the building; Will whistled at them, and they spun back and followed the others outside.

"Head back up to the ledge where we came in," said Will, pointing. "Get behind those rocks. Keep quiet, stay off the comm system, and no flashlights."

Nick led the way and Will brought up the rear, glancing back at the building, looking for signs of pursuit. He saw bright flashes of light coming from the back of the hospital and wondered if they'd used another way to get outside. When they were halfway back up the rocky path to the ledge, the whole cave around the building filled with an overhead canopy of light. Will looked up and realized a flare had been fired.

They scrambled behind the rocks on the ledge and took shelter, just as the light billowed and spread throughout the chamber, bright enough to cast moving shadows.

"Stay low," whispered Will. "When I give the word, head back to the stone platform."

"And hope it goes up," said Nick.

"Remember it won't move unless all five of us are on it."

"Who is it, Will?" asked Elise. "Who's down there?"

"I'll hang back a second and find out," said Will. "Go now, Ajay with Elise, then Nick with Brooke. Stay off the walkies unless you hear from me."

Will watched the building as Ajay and Elise scampered up the path and through the carved passage leading to the bone room.

"Don't be late," said Nick, patting Will on the shoulder.

Brooke squeezed Will's hand and hurried off with Nick. Will picked out his binoculars, scanned both sides of the building, then trained them on the lit-up reception room.

Four men burst into the room, guns drawn. Dark Windbreakers and hats: the Black Caps. Will felt something vibrate in his pocket. He took out the pair of black dice; they were vibrating wildly with some kind of internal energy. A moment later a fifth man appeared in the reception area. He wasn't wearing a cap and his bald head gleamed in the amber light.

It was Hobbes. And he looked *furious*.

At his direction, the others searched the room quickly and efficiently. Hobbes moved to the window, staring out at the cave, and spoke into a microphone fastened to his collar.

For the briefest moment Hobbes glanced up toward the ledge. Will ducked out of sight and lowered the glasses. With his head down, he summoned up his Grid, waited for the light from the flare overhead to fade, then glanced over the rocks again.

He picked up about fifteen heat signatures spreading out from either side of the building, slowly and methodically scouring the grounds. Will looked back at Hobbes in the window.

The moment he raised his head, the aura of heat around Hobbes, five times stronger than any of the others, flared up around him in a corona of fiery red and orange. He raised his right arm, holding something in his hand and pointing it in Will's direction.

Which led Will to ask himself, *Can Hobbes see me like I can see him?*

The answer came quickly: Hobbes burst right through the window, shattering the glass, and started running toward the ledge, barking instructions. Will shut down his Grid, turned, and ran up the path to the passage.

Dashing through the hole in the wall, Will switched on his flashlight, then powered up to the hill of bones and sped along the path. He spotted flashlights darting around ahead, and within moments caught up to Nick and Brooke, moving so fast he sped ten feet past them before he could put on the brakes.

"They're coming," he said, circling back.

They both ran faster and he did what he could to help them through the uncertain footing. Glancing back, Will didn't see any lights behind them yet. They reached Ajay and Elise moments later, just as they climbed onto the stone platform.

"Get on, fast," said Will. "Lights off."

Nick lifted Brooke up onto the platform. Will ran the last few paces and jumped up after her. Nick leaped up after him with a single springing bounce, and as his weight hit the platform, they felt it jolt, heard the rattle of chains, and the platform began to ascend.

"Stay low," said Will. "Don't say a word. Hobbes is back there, with a squad of Caps."

Everyone but Nick exchanged worried glances.

"Hey, we're good," said Nick, unconcerned. "How are they going to follow us up here?"

"Maybe they have others up there already, waiting for us," said Ajay.

"Mr. Optimism," said Nick.

"Maybe they know how to work this thing," said Brooke.

Will shushed them. The platform had risen about fifteen feet when they saw the first flashlight beams crisscross the far end of the bone cave. Will found himself next to Elise; she stared down at the advancing lights with a dark and dangerous look in her eye.

"I want to blow it up," she said coldly. "I want to rip this whole place apart. All of it."

Will turned to all of them, cold and determined. "If we're right and the Other Team is behind this, all we've seen is one small slice of what they are. Keep that in the front of your mind. In case we ever need to be reminded why we have to stop them."

Elise gripped Will's arm, fingers digging into him, and locked on to him, her eyes staring deep into his. Words from her mind, amplified by fierce emotion, seared into his: *I am making you a promise, right now. And you'd better do the same for me.*

Will nodded. *Whatever you want.*

For what they did to those wretched souls back there? We are going to find who's behind this and we are going to hurt *them.*

"Promise," said Will.

They didn't spot individual beams of light moving toward them down the path in the chamber until just before the platform passed up through the floor of the cathedral. Just then Will saw a bright burst of light from the person leading the way—Hobbes, he assumed.

"Jump off, fast," said Will. "Get outside and wait for us. Ajay, I need something from your pack. Nick, stay with me."

Will pulled the can of lighter fluid and a lighter from Ajay's pack.

"You're sure you don't want to use my hatchet?" asked Ajay, offering the handle.

"Dude, enough with the hatchet already," said Nick.

"Go!" said Will.

They stood and jumped to the ground as the platform came level with the cathedral floor. Ajay and the girls ran down the aisle toward the opening they'd come in through.

"Tear up your shirt," said Will. "Make a torch out of it."

Will sprayed the stone platform with lighter fluid while

226

Nick tore off his undershirt and knotted it up. As Will expected, moments later the platform began to descend. Will sprayed fluid on the rags, then flicked on the lighter. He waited for the platform to drop a third of the way, then lit the undershirt and dropped it down onto the platform. The platform erupted into flames.

"Suck on that, Hobbes," said Nick, looking down.

They hurried outside to join the others waiting on the plaza in front of the cathedral.

"The good news is we set the platform on fire," said Nick.

"The bad news is it's going down again," said Will. "Let's move."

They ran out of the cathedral. That moaning wind had kicked up again, now whistling through the ruins, much stronger than before, whipping around the spindly limbs of the four sparkling bare jewel-like trees at the base of the stairs.

As they hurried down the long broad steps in front of the cathedral, the trees bent down toward them, more flexible than any tree should be. What followed happened so fast that Will barely had time to register it. With loud crackling sounds from the thick tangle of their boughs, individual branches snaked out from the trees toward each of them, unfurling and extending like cables at lightning speed.

"Look out!" Will shouted.

One of them shot in front of Ajay, tripping him as he ran, and as he hurtled forward another branch gripped him by the arm, then a third wrapped around his ankle, catching him before he hit the ground and raising him into the air.

Other branches shot toward the rest of them. Will put on a burst of speed and outran a cluster of the things grasping after him. He heard a strange snapping sound, looked down, and realized the ends of the branches had openings—he didn't know what else to call them but *mouths*—lined with rows of vicious black teeth.

Hearing Will's warning, Brooke dodged a thick branch that shot toward her knees; then she dove and rolled out of the way of another. Will pulled her out of the trees' reach.

To their left, a branch caught Elise by the arm, spinning her around, but she broke free, and when two more whipped in around her waist, jaws about to bite, she let out a short, lethal burst of sound that shattered them like glass.

Nick tumbled over the arms reaching for him, then saw the branches that had snared Ajay, lifting him into the air and drawing him backward toward the stairs. Nick ran straight at the nearest ones, jumped up, and ran along the branches toward Ajay. When he reached him, Nick became a furious blur of feet and hands, fending off the branches that kept trying to grab him while he snapped the ones wrapping themselves around Ajay. For every two he broke, another one snaked in, but he was finally able to snatch Ajay with one hand and toss him to the ground.

Ajay rolled out of the way of another branch. Brooke and Elise pulled him out of its reach. Will stomped on it, pinning it to the ground, and Elise shattered it with a deadly burst of sound. Ajay pulled out his hatchet, but nothing attacked him, so he spun in place wielding it.

Nick kept fighting, but the remaining branches focused in on him now and more kept slithering his way. He held his own but Will knew he wouldn't last much longer against their superior numbers.

Will ran back toward them, shouting, waving his arms, until the onslaught about to envelop Nick turned their attention toward him. He picked up speed, dodging, weaving, and jumping, in range but eluding every attempt to grab him, as one branch after another slithered after him.

"Keep going!" Will shouted back at the others. "To the gates!"

With their focus elsewhere, Nick shattered the last few branches snaking around him, then ran right at the thickest branch and up it; he pushed off and somersaulted back, landing on his feet and bounding out of range. Will saw him land safely and dodged two more assaulting limbs. He turned, dug in, and sprinted, almost instantly outrunning the last snaking branches.

He hooked up with Nick and they set off after the others, using their flashlights bobbing up ahead in the dark as a beacon.

"You okay?" asked Will.

Nick, winded, nodded as they ran. "Freakin' *trees,* man."

"Those weren't trees. They're some kind of watchdogs from the Never-Was."

"I don't give a rat's bee-hind what they were . . . I am so coming back down here . . . with a chainsaw."

As they neared the gates where the others were waiting, another flare shot up into the air from somewhere behind them, lighting up the dead city around them, creating ghostly, threatening shadows in every corner.

"Crap, they made it up on the platform," said Nick, glancing back.

Will slipped his pack off his shoulder. "Head for the stairs. That flare we left at the base should still be burning."

"And what will you be doing?"

"I'll slow them down, but I need you to get ahead of me," said Will.

"I'm not leaving you alone, dude, forget it."

"Nick, you know I can catch up to you. The others need you right now more than I do. Give me a couple of flares, then get moving."

Will slowed as Nick handed him two of his last three flares and reluctantly ran on ahead. Will tucked the flares in the back of his belt, pulled his binoculars, and trained them on the far end of the city. Under the light from the flare, he saw movement on the steps of the cathedral. Then a bright flash of light shot up into the sky and pinwheeled out in every direction.

The light revealed Hobbes standing on the broad stairs on the far side of the square, surrounded by a large group of Black Caps. The light issued from something he held in his outstretched palm. It was so blindingly bright Will couldn't see its source, but it conformed to the shape of a cube.

Beams of light from the cube wheeled above them and then focused down on the four hideous trees, creating dazzling patterns as they flashed through their crystalline hides. The beams penetrated the glass, then circulated down through the branches into the ground. Bright flashes shot up from the earth, breaking through cracks around their trunks, and all four of the trees bent their branches down, pressed against the ground to create leverage, and with straining effort yanked their roots—immense thickets of wild growth, gnarled and twisted and dark—right out of the ground.

"Not good," said Will.

The moment the creatures freed themselves, Hobbes pointed the cube in the direction of the gates. The beams shot out toward Will, glancing off the fallen gates, and he realized Hobbes was painting a target for the things he'd let loose.

A cube. Like the dice Dave gave me. And the same shape as one of the empty forms we saw in the metallic cylinder.

All four trees gathered themselves up, re-forming into huge spheres fifteen feet high, and began rolling toward Will's position, picking up speed, like gigantic nightmarish tumbleweed.

"Hey, Dave," whispered Will, gripping the dice and the falcon in his pocket for luck. "Wherever you are, now would be an excellent time to send help."

Will stowed the glasses and sprinted out of the gates. In the distance ahead he could vaguely make out the red glow of the flare they'd left at the base of the huge staircase. He ramped up his speed and carved a winding, S-shaped path back and forth through the thick dust, kicking and churning it off the ground. Will soon raised a choking cloud that hung in the air behind him, as high as the ancient walls. He kept up the pattern, extending the cloud away from the gates, building it thicker and taller, all the while staying ahead of it so he could see and breathe.

The long stairway came into view ahead, and he could just make out his friends gathered by the flare. Will switched on his comm system and spoke into the mic.

"Get up the stairs. I'll meet you at the top," he said.

"You okay?" asked Nick.

"Yes. But hurry."

When he saw the red flare begin bobbing and rising up the stairs, Will darted left, away from his friends. He reached into his pack and took out the can of lighter fluid.

Will heard the things before he saw them. A grinding, spinning sound like an immense pack of cyclists wheeling out of the cloud a hundred yards behind him. Then, one after another, the immense rolling trees broke out of the dust, heading toward him, not fooled by his change of direction. Like other creatures he'd encountered from the Never-Was, they seemed able to track him by scent. He knew he was faster and more agile but there were four of these things, all bigger than monster trucks. He needed to execute his plan perfectly.

He pulled the top off the lighter fluid, cornered around, and ran straight back toward the advancing creatures. They spread out and lined up, coming at him two by two. Will angled sharply left, then as soon as they reacted, he cut back the other way. They tried to adjust but couldn't maneuver as quickly. He tacked left again, and again they were slower to adjust. Trusting he could make this work, Will summoned up his Grid, slowing everything down even as he pushed his acceleration to the max.

Viewed through the Grid, the creatures looked like Ferris wheels of heat. Spikes of individual branches extended out of their margins, halos of writhing snakes. Will could see dark energy coursing through their insane forms as they bore down on him; a core of feral intelligence radiated malice from the center of each wheel, where the heart of the trunks had settled, directing the hunt. That was where he needed to attack. Fighting back his fear, Will stopped thinking and let his senses take over.

Then they were on him. As he darted between the wheels, in, out, and between, dodging the gauntlet of snapping-headed branches that shot out at him, Will fired streams of lighter fluid at the interior of each wheel as they rolled past. Each time one shot by, teeth from their mouths tore at his pants, his shirt, his pack, but he made it through the first pass unharmed, and he'd hit each of his targets, soaking them until he'd emptied the can.

He tossed the can aside as he made a wide arcing turn back to face them, blinked away the Grid, and pulled a flare from his belt. He heard the wheels skidding around in the dust behind him, falling into formation for another run at him.

"Will, what's up?" Nick's voice came across his headset. "We're waiting for you."

"At the top of the stairs?" Will asked.

"Yeah, where are you?"

"You'll see in a second."

Will ignited the flare and ran back toward the creatures hurtling at him at full speed. Learning from their first encounter, they'd spread out so they could target him from different angles. His job was tougher this time, too; he had to get closer to them, close enough to touch.

The creatures spread out as the gap between them narrowed. A single strike and Will knew those snapping branches would swarm over him like a ravenous pack. He blinked up his Grid again, slowing down time so he could anticipate every step. The first creature passed close enough to part his hair, and teeth ripped his shirt and grazed his shoulder, but he touched his flare to the heart of the wheel and ignited the fluid, and fire quickly spread through its center.

The second came at him from a right angle, nearly clipping him from behind; another bite ripped into his pack and pulled it off his back, but he pivoted away, touching the flare to it as he rolled past and it burst into flame.

But he'd lost nearly all his speed now and the third wheel was bearing down on him from straight ahead. He stumbled, lunged to his left, and felt the beast roar just past him. He turned back and tossed the flare at the center of it; the fluid ignited and the middle of the wheel lit up.

Will turned right, reaching for his second flare, but the fourth wheel was nearly on top of him. With no time to react, he was about to get flattened when he heard a high-pitched keening from somewhere above and then something lifted the creature straight off the ground just as it was about to annihilate him.

He felt the turbulence of immense wings and caught a

glimpse of something huge and shining as it swooped over his head, clutching the last of the beasts in giant silver talons. A falcon? Whatever it was rose quickly up and away, carrying the wheel-creature with it out of sight.

"What the . . . ," said Will.

No time to think about it. The other three wheels were all in flames but still rolling as fast as before, and now they all turned and started back toward him. Will fired his last flare and lit out for the stairs, holding nothing back. The creatures couldn't gain on him but didn't lose much ground, trailing by fifty yards, the fires in their hubs lighting up the cavern. He glanced back once and saw individual branches falling away, dying in the flames, but the bulk of the malevolent things kept coming.

Will saw flashlight beams stabbing through the dust and then his human pursuers emerged from the cloud—Hobbes and the squadron of Caps, heading for the stairs, trying to cut him off. One fired a flare into the air above the stairs, turning everything to moonlight.

Will didn't hesitate when he reached the big stairs, powering straight up the steep incline, flicking on his comm system: "Nick, head for the doors now, get them *closed*."

"What about you—"

"I'll be there, just go."

Will gulped in air as he hurtled up the hundreds of steps, his energy starting to fade, forcing himself to press ahead. He looked down and saw the burning wheels reach the bottom of the stairs and roll up after him without hesitation. As Will neared the top, he saw Elise standing on the ledge with her arms spread out, staring down past him. He was about to shout a warning when she shouted at him: "Get behind me!"

Will hurled up the last few steps and dove past her as Elise raised her arms. His ears popped and all sound drained away as if he'd jumped into a vacuum. The air around Elise bent and shimmered with building force as she unleashed what she'd gathered. Will saw a visible shock wave sweep down the stairs. A deafening sonic boom sounded and the three flaming wheeled creatures were swept away, flailing in the air, bursting into fiery debris.

The wave didn't diminish as it reached the ground below, lifting up the dust bed like a tsunami and rippling across the floor of the cavern. Near the base of the stairs, Hobbes and his men scattered like bowling pins. The wave roared on, cresting at the walls of the ancient city, and in the dying light from the flare above, Will saw the tops of them shudder and start to crumble from the impact. Another boom sounded and the echo of it rattled around the great dome of the cavern before ending in startling silence.

When his ears stopped ringing, he heard the ancient walls collapsing in the distance, raising another huge cloud of dust. As he climbed to his feet, an alarming hissing sound issued from below; he picked up and raised the red flare that had fallen nearby.

Three dark shapes were quickly scaling the stairs. At first he thought they were enormous spiders, spreading long slithering scaly legs in front as they advanced. Will blinked on his Grid and realized these were the hearts of the trees, stripped of their branches, reduced to the source of the spiteful intelligence he'd glimpsed inside them. Huge glowing gelatinous eyes in their centers fixed on him and the creatures doubled their speed.

Will found Elise nearby, leaning against the rock wall, nearly out on her feet from the effort of the burst she'd generated. He scooped her up, tossed her onto his shoulder, and hurried as fast as he could up the winding corridor. They passed the first statue, the Civil War soldier, and as light from the flare bounced off the widening alcove, Will chanced a look back.

He couldn't see the creatures yet, but he heard them, their repellent limbs clicking across the carved stone floors, drawing closer. Fatigue exerted a heavy drag. He vaguely heard Nick calling his name on the comm system, but with the flare in one hand and the other holding Elise, he couldn't activate his mic to respond. He also felt the same presence of whatever had been following them from the beginning somewhere nearby. As they passed another alcove, the flare cast a shadow of something inside onto the wall to his right, a ragged figure, tall and lean. He didn't even have time to think about it; all he could do was hope it didn't attack.

They were still a quarter mile from the doors and he could barely breathe, let alone call out to Nick for help.

So it's a race. Races are something I'm good at.

#70: WHEN YOU'RE IN TROUBLE, EMPHASIZE YOUR STRENGTHS.

He stopped listening for the creatures behind them and focused on what he could do about it. Will forced his feet to keep moving. Commanded his legs to keep driving. Regulated and measured his breathing for maximum benefit. As they rounded the turn into the alcove for the second statue, he found his second—or third or fourth—wind. That gave him hope. He got another jolt of it when Elise stirred on his shoulder.

"Elise? Are you with me?"

"Why are you carrying me?" she asked.

"You were out on your feet."

"We could move a lot faster if you'd put me down."

"You think you can run now?"

"Faster than you're going," she said.

"Okay, I'll put you down."

"And, Will?"

"Yeah?"

"Whatever you do, don't look behind us."

Without missing a stride, he lowered her to the ground, and of course he looked behind them. The tree-root creatures were less than twenty yards back, filling the corridor, stretching hundreds of vile clicking limbs out ahead, luminous eyes radiating evil. Slower than before but every bit as malevolent.

Will and Elise glanced at each other and took off with a burst of speed, at least at first, preserving the gap between them and their pursuers.

"Can you—I don't know—fire another blast at them?" asked Will.

"No. I'm weak as a kitten. You think that was easy, what I did back there?"

"I didn't mean to suggest it was *easy*—"

"Because it wasn't."

"I *know*," said Will.

"Okay, then."

Will clicked on his comm system. "Nick, what about the doors?"

"*There* you are," said Nick. "They're closing, dude. All we had to do was kick out the post, so hustle your butts."

"We're hustling," said Will. "And we've got company right behind us."

"Roger that, Will," said Ajay.

Elise stumbled, and Will caught her before she could fall. "I'm not going to make it," said Elise, panting for breath.

"Sure you are."

"How much farther? Is it further or farther? I get those confused."

"Farther," said Will. He put his arm around her waist, urging her to keep going. "It can't be more than a hundred yards."

"I'm seeing spots," said Elise. "And little squiggles and lines. I think I'm blacking out."

"Happens to me in races all the time. You just have to push through it."

"Are they closer?"

"Close enough," said Will, pulling her along.

"Hey, West."

"Yeah."

"In case I don't get another chance," said Elise.

"What?"

"This seems like a good time to tell you I think I love you."

"Wow."

"Wow what?"

"Your timing is unbelievable."

"I don't expect you to *do* anything about it . . . I just wanted you to know. Just in case."

"Okay, then, I'm glad you did," said Will, his stomach flipping around. "And I guess I kind of . . . love you too."

Ahead, a slice of light showed the narrowing gap in the doors.

"They're closing. You go first. I think you can squeeze through."

The gap was less than a foot by the time they reached it. Will pushed Elise through ahead of him and she just made it, falling into the arms of Nick on the other side. Will squeezed through after her, emptying his chest of air and a second later the gap was too small for him to have made it . . .

. . . but not too narrow for one unspeakable barbed limb to slither through after him and grab Will by the ankle, dragging him back toward the closing doors, toward those terrible eyes and snapping maws.

Ajay leaped forward, something sharp and gleaming in his hand, and slashed down, nearly severing the hideous limb with a single blow, and they heard a harsh rasping cry as the broken leg dragged itself back out of sight. Will scrambled out of the gap and the huge oak doors finally shut with an authoritative slam.

Ajay turned to his four friends, a triumphant grin on his face, as he held up his useful tool for all to see.

"I told you I should bring my hatchet!"

NEPSTED

To their surprise, nothing jumped out of the dark or chased after them as they exited the tunnel. No one waited for them or appeared to be following them at ground level, either. The coast was equally clear from the hatch to their raft and not a single dog or guard reacted as they paddled back across the lake. Odd, suspicious even, but they were all so tired no one complained. Halfway across, with the weight of Nepsted's key in his pocket, Will relaxed, and realized he felt exhilarated. It was a warm, windless night, with a crisp mass of stars overhead and they were bringing back their objective after an almost suicidal strike deep behind enemy lines.

Once they made it back to their pod, the roommates took turns crashing, in sleeping bags on the floor and the sofas in the great room. Nick and Will alternated sentry duty, just in case.

Why didn't Hobbes and the Caps come right after us once we were aboveground? Will wondered during his stretch, fighting to stay awake. *Is it possible they didn't know who they were chasing down there? But didn't Hobbes see and recognize me before he crashed through the hospital window?*

By sunrise, Will and Nick agreed they could quit standing guard. Will winked out for a couple of solid sleep cycles. When he finally woke with the key still in his hand, it was after ten, bright sunlight filling the room, and he felt better seeing a normal day dawn after all those hours underground. His mood improved even further when he realized it was Sunday and he smelled bacon and coffee in the air.

Most of his roommates were already up and gone, but as Will shuffled to the table, Nick came out of the kitchen and set down a big mug of coffee and a plate of fried eggs, bacon, sausage, pancakes, and buttered corn muffins in front of him.

"Fuel up, dude," said Nick.

Will realized he was ravenous. "Why didn't you wake me up?"

"Figured you needed the shut-eye."

"Where is everybody?" asked Will, diving into breakfast with both hands.

"Brooke went to work, Elise went to practice. Ajay headed to the labs, working on a bone."

"A bone?"

"He brought one back in his pack," said Nick, stretching the kinks out of his neck. "Something about dates and carbon paper?"

"Carbon dating."

"That's it. So what's next?"

"We get to Nepsted, fast," said Will between bites, holding up the key. "Before Hobbes does."

"Let me see that," said Nick, and they looked at the key together. "Dude, that was one whacked-out night."

"We know a lot more than we did. We're getting close, Nick. Hopefully Nepsted tells us the rest."

"Question then is, how can we help *him*? Think he wants out of his cage?"

"I would," said Will. "Wonder where he'd go."

Nick bent over backward into another stretch, hands flat on the floor, arching his back. "I'm cooking up an idea about that."

"Did you cook breakfast, too?" asked Will, unable to stop eating.

"Got an uncle who owns a diner in Brookline. In case the

superhero gymnast thing don't work out, fry cook is my fall-back," said Nick, transitioning to a one-handed handstand and then springing to his feet.

Ajay burst through the front door, out of breath, wearing large goggles that magnified his eyes while holding something behind his back with both hands. "Good morning, gentlemen. I can report two preliminary findings to you after my initial, albeit cursory, examinations."

"Shoot," said Will, his mouth full of pancakes.

Ajay held out the bone as if he were presenting an award. "Ten thousand years old, minimum. And so far not one trace of genetic material to be found that's even a distant cousin to human DNA."

"Are you surprised?"

"No, I'm delighted. Two reasons. It's proof, for starters, that we're not totally out of our skulls. And if we ever get to the bottom of this dog's breakfast, a Nobel Prize for this discovery is not just a possibility, but it's also practically in the bag."

"Dude, you got my vote," said Nick.

"I've also begun researching Cahokia and Teotwawki. Early results are more than a little startling."

"Tell us on the way," said Will as he pushed his empty plate away, drained the last of his coffee, and belched. "We need to see a guy about a cage."

He held up the silver metal key.

"Cahokia is the name of a significant archeological site in southwestern Illinois," said Ajay, a little breathless, struggling to keep up as they jogged through the campus. "About a hundred and fifty miles directly south of here."

"Wait a second, so there's *two* Cahokias?" asked Nick.

"So it seems. And in its day, Cahokia appears to have been the largest urban settlement in North America."

"What have they found there?" asked Will.

"All that's survived architecturally is a series of ancient earthen mounds, now set aside as a national park, but research suggests that at its peak—a period dating back at least two thousand years ago—Cahokia covered over six square miles . . . larger than any city in Europe at that time, and almost as big geographically as London is today."

Will and Nick stared at each other in astonishment.

"Why do you think they're connected? Do they know who lived there?" asked Will.

"That's the mystery of it: No one knows. But it couldn't have been Native Americans—the settlement predates the appearance of any known tribes in North America. The *name* is Native American, however, from a nearby tribe affiliated with the Algonquin, but that name wasn't given to the area until the seventeenth century by European explorers who were drawing maps."

"Dude, so maybe the *original* dudes who lived there were these same *alien* dudes who lived down *here*."

"They weren't aliens, Nick—" said Will.

"Chill, you know what I mean, the Other Team dudes."

"Maybe. If it was at its peak two thousand years ago, what's the oldest they think Cahokia could be?"

"No one knows that either," said Ajay, "due to the absence of datable artifacts. Many more thousands of years at least. But there's another detail that ties it to our location: The settlement to the south includes extensive sections of sophisticated underground construction."

"You're getting warmer," said Nick.

"So to elaborate on Nick's theory," said Ajay, "what if that Cahokia was actually first settled by an even older civilization? A much older one?"

"One that isn't human or alien," said Nick.

"Exactly! An older race of beings that then established outposts or colonies in nearby parts of the upper Midwest. At least one of which in our neighborhood that has never been officially discovered."

"At the least," said Will, "it means whoever carved *Cahokia* on the doors had the same idea."

"What about that other word, *Teotwawki*?" asked Nick. "Could that be our place's real name?"

"Actually, no," said Ajay. "That means something else."

"What?" asked Will.

"It's an acronym, and I'm a bit embarrassed that I didn't recognize it, as it's something of an Internet meme."

"Like one of those dudes with the white stuff on his face who doesn't talk?"

"That's a mime, you idiot," said Ajay. "TEOTWAWKI stands for 'The End of the World as We Know It.'"

No one spoke for a second.

"Hello," said Nick.

Nick rang the bell on the counter.

"Nepsted! We're back, dude," said Nick. "And we brought you a present." Nick paused, but they heard nothing. "That special thing you asked us to find for you, remember?"

Another ring of the bell. Still no reply. They didn't even hear the squeak and whine of his motorized wheelchair. Nick boosted Ajay up onto the counter and he peered back into the deep shadows of the equipment cage through the steel mesh.

"Nothing's moving," said Ajay. "I don't see him anywhere."

"You think he's okay?" asked Nick, looking worried.

"Let's go in and find him," said Will. "Make sure no one's around."

Nick and Ajay scouted this isolated area of the locker room as Will moved to the cage and put his hand around the lock, testing its strength one last time.

"All clear," said Ajay, returning.

"Glasses," said Will.

They all slipped on their glasses. Will took the key from his pocket. Its restless, animated components extruded out and began their peculiar winding motions. When he moved it closer to the shifting plates of the lock on the cage door, both lock and key lit up with the same sickly green energy. A nest of liquid steel tendrils from the key slithered out and around the lock, merging and flowing into its central jewel-like column.

They heard a complex series of thunks, clicks, and whispers, and then the lock gave way, the diamond shaft slipping out of the plates, letting go. The hasp folded elegantly back into the center and the lock fell to the floor, its toxic glow fading to a dull gray.

Will put both hands on the cage and pushed. Rusty hinges screamed but the gate yielded only an inch. All three put their shoulders to it, a door that hadn't been opened in decades and had been painted over many times, and on the fifth try it gave way just enough for them to squeeze through the gap. Nick flipped a light switch on the opposite wall and pale fluorescent fixtures flickered on all the way to the back of the long, narrow storage room.

Ajay set up a button-sized camera just inside the cage, pointed out through the mesh toward the locker room. He activated it with a small remote control the size of a playing card; an image of the locker room appeared on the controller. Will checked out the image and gave Ajay a thumbs-up.

"Let's go," he said.

"Shouldn't we close it behind us?" asked Ajay, glancing back at the door.

"We can't fasten it from inside," said Will. "But you're right, nobody better see it open. Hang the lock on the door."

Nick slipped the lock back through the slot in the door and they shoved it even with the frame.

Ajay edged cautiously forward into the cage, between the tall aisles of sports equipment. Ten yards in, he pointed out a fixed security camera on the wall near the ceiling. Staying hidden in the middle aisle, Ajay drew a small device shaped like a fat squirt gun from his vest. He pointed it at the camera through a gap in a shelf and pulled the trigger. A pulse of energy shot toward the camera and cracked the lens. Ajay nodded at Will. They continued down the middle aisle.

"Nepsted?" called Nick.

"Raymond!" called Will.

No answer. All they heard until they reached the end of the aisle was their own footsteps scuffing the concrete. When they reached the back wall, they found a low, wide passage that led to the left and followed it to a plain, unmarked door.

"Chez Nepsted?" asked Ajay.

"I thought his first name was Happy," said Nick.

"It means 'house of Nepsted,'" said Ajay.

"His name," said Will as he opened the door, "is Raymond Llewellyn."

A single light shone down from a lamp across a darkened, windowless room. Piles of clutter trailed off in all directions into the shadows. Nepsted's wheelchair stood empty to the left of where the beam of the lamp landed. They moved in a few steps more and there in a pool of light sat Nepsted, or something like him, in a large galvanized steel tub filled with dark, thick liquid the consistency of molasses and the color of plums. Heat burbled up from the bottom as if it were a natural hot spring, trailing vapor into the air.

Nepsted appeared to be floating or hovering in the liquid, on his back and at rest, his stunted body hanging loosely below him. His limbs bobbed up and down, just below the surface, and seemed to slowly oscillate between their solid form and the pale, ropy tendrils they'd briefly seen before. His wide eyes stared blankly at the ceiling, and every once in a while his face seemed to lose its structure, melting into a slack formlessness before phasing back into shape. He seemed to register that they'd entered the room but didn't react in any other noticeable way.

"Hope you don't mind we opened your door," said Will.

"We found the key, dude," said Nick, holding it up.

"I didn't think I'd see you again," said Nepsted, almost vacantly, eyes still fixed on something above.

"It wasn't easy," said Will. "But it was right where you'd said it would be."

"Although, truthfully, your directions might have been a bit more specific—" said Ajay, before Will cut him off with a gesture.

"We found everything, Raymond," said Will. "The city, the cathedral."

"The Tomb of the Unknown Conehead," said Nick.

"The bone yard and the hospital," said Will. "And the room with all your friends in it."

That got his attention. Nepsted's eyes darted to Will. "What else do you know?"

"The dinner with Henry Wallace in 1937," said Will. "The plane crash in '38. We know that Raymond Llewellyn and Edgar Snow were the only two who really survived, because you were part of the Knights and they did something terrible, to all of you, after they found that city down there and built the hospital. We know that Snow goes by the name of Hobbes now, and they've started another research program. And we need you to fill in everything else, before and after."

"Like you promised," said Nick, leaning on the side of the tub.

"Did anyone see you?" Nepsted looked a little panicked. "Did they follow you?"

"They saw us," said Will. "But no one followed us and they're not stopping us."

Nepsted studied Will, as if seeing him for the first time.

"Then I must keep my promise," said Nepsted simply.

"You want us to get you out of here?" asked Will. "If you don't feel safe, we can talk someplace else."

"No. I'll say what I have to say. I've waited a long time for this."

"We'll keep an eye on the door," said Will, then held his hand out to Ajay, who handed him the playing-card-sized screen showing the feed from the camera at the cage.

Will took a look. A still life. Nothing moved in the locker room.

With flicks of tendrils that occasionally peeked out of the murk, Nepsted slowly turned around in a lazy circle as he began his story. At a nod from Will, Ajay activated a recording device—disguised as a pen—in the chest pocket of his coat.

"They made it seem like so much fun, you see," said Nepsted. "The Knights were paragons to us, the envy of the school. The parties they gave. The theatricals they put on. The spirit they embodied—sophisticated, gifted, worldly beyond their years. Everyone wanted to be a Knight, but we knew they only took twelve men a year."

"They weren't a secret society yet," said Ajay.

"Not when I arrived in '34," said Nepsted. "That came later. Everybody knew who the members were then, past and present—the club existed openly. But we didn't know the criteria for membership, or how they made their selections. You just presented yourself in the best possible light and hoped to make an impression. Then one day, late in our junior year, they let us know."

"How?"

"A mask. I found it on my pillow that night. A horse's head. All twelve of us found masks we were required to wear the next night, at our first dinner, when they gave us our names. I was Ganelon the Crafter. From that moment, we had to refer to each other, in private, by our secret names."

Will thought back to the twelve ancient masks and the list of names they'd found in a trunk hidden in the auxiliary locker room last fall.

"We know about those, too," said Will.

"But I don't know if you can appreciate what this meant to us. To be welcomed into the fold of a group like this. The intoxicating sense of privilege it gave us when we learned the history behind the Knights, and our true reasons for being."

"What were they?" asked Will.

"That for a thousand years the Knights had been the secret guardians of everything good and true produced by Western civilization—education, science, medicine, charity, the arts, spiritual enlightenment. They had us believe that the Knights were dedicated to the preservation of those disciplines and its highest ideals, throughout the Dark Ages, the Middle Ages, the

Reformation, the Renaissance, all the way to the founding of America and into the Modern Age."

Will and Ajay exchanged a look. Ajay's eyes opened wide, and Will knew they were thinking the same thing. *This is much older and bigger than we even imagined.*

"My parents owned a hardware store in Columbus, Ohio," said Nepsted. "I was a smart boy, nobody special, but a scholarship student who'd gotten into the Center on merit, not family connections. But the Knights quickly made us believe that we were joining a high moral order that operated at global levels of influence and had served mankind for centuries."

"So you were brainwashed," said Will.

"A real sell job," said Nick, almost muttering.

But Nepsted heard him. "You'd do well to remember, my young friend, how much trouble there was in the world then. The depths of the Depression, a second world war on the horizon that everyone saw as inevitable. A few months later, when they asked us to contribute by making a sacrifice of our own, it seemed the most natural thing in the world."

"Who asked you?" asked Will.

"Our faculty advisor, Dr. Abelson."

Will remembered the name from the monument. "A teacher?"

Nepsted looked surprised again. "Yes. He was the adult in charge of the Order."

"But you called him the Old Gentleman," said Ajay, glancing at Will.

"That's what the Knights have always called the man who holds that office," said Nepsted. "Abelson taught science and philosophy and was chairman of both those departments. A traditional role for the Old Gentleman. The Knights have been associated with a school or academy for over a thousand years, and always one serving in the vanguard of advances in science and philosophy."

"Where was Abelson from?" asked Will.

"He was Swedish, but he'd been educated in Germany," said Nepsted. "You see, Dr. Abelson was instrumental in the development of eugenics. That was his area of expertise."

"Eugenics?" asked Nick, clueless, looking to Ajay for an explanation.

"The applied science of improving a contained population's genetic makeup," said Ajay in a hushed tone. "As a way of increasing desirable traits in its most gifted citizens while at the same time . . . reducing the reproduction of people with . . . less desirable traits."

"Through genetic manipulation," said Will.

"Oh," said Nick quietly.

"But he took eugenics much further," said Nepsted. "Abelson had developed experimental techniques that he believed would prove the theories he'd developed in Germany."

Will felt his guts wrench at the realization. "In Germany," he said. "With the Nazis?"

"We didn't know about that when we joined," said Nepsted sharply. "None of us did. Abelson never spoke of it. If we'd had any idea how twisted he was, this would never have happened."

"Twisted how?" asked Ajay.

"The advancements he'd made meant we no longer had to wait generations, as the limits of eugenics required, to see radical improvements in human potential. Abelson believed his treatments could transform human potential, that healthy, living subjects could be elevated into superior states of physical, mental, and spiritual being in a matter of months. He called this accelerated form of evolution the Great Awakening."

"Good God," said Ajay.

"So Abelson built the hospital down there?" asked Will. "For this."

"I believe that started not long after Abelson arrived in 1932. He told us our class of Knights had been selected for a great honor: the first members of the Order to benefit from his . . . enhancements. The first to Awaken, founding members of the modern order of Paladins. A new breed of warriors in the cause they'd been fighting for for a millennium."

"Abelson did this to you?" asked Nick, furious.

Nepsted nodded.

"Dude, what the hell, so you just went along with it?" asked Nick.

Nepsted seemed frustrated by Nick's outrage. "What can I say to make you see how this happened? We were just boys, stupid, overconfident, egotistical boys. There was nothing rational about it. We believed in him, believed in the glory he was bestowing on us."

"That can't be the only reason," said Nick.

"You're right, Nick. We had a leader of our own, in our class of Knights, who believed in Abelson's Awakening so ferociously that he made saying no seem unthinkable."

"That must have been Hobbes," said Will. "The boy you knew as Edgar Snow."

"No, Will. He was an important member, second in command to the one I'm referring to, but it wasn't Edgar."

"Who was it, then?" asked Ajay.

"Franklin Greenwood," said Nepsted.

Will sucked in his breath hard, involuntarily.

My grandfather.

"Franklin Greenwood, the second headmaster?" asked Ajay incredulously. "Son of the founder of the Center?"

"Frank was in our class of recruits. His name in the Order

was Orlando. Traditionally Orlando plays the role of senior advisor to the Old Gentleman."

Will's mind raced: *My own grandfather was mixed up in this madness? How is that possible?*

"Is he in the photograph of the dinner?" asked Will, slipping a copy from his pocket.

"Yes, of course, Frank was there that night," said Nepsted.

"Show him to me, please," said Will, holding the photo closer to Nepsted.

Nepsted looked at the photo impassively. A tentacle lifted out of the muck and delicately touched one of the figures in the picture that Will had hardly noticed before. A tall, slender boy seated at the end of the table, farthest from the camera. He looked more youthful than the others. Arms folded on the table, leaning forward, smiling vaguely.

But something in his eyes contradicted that smile, and then Will realized he wasn't looking directly at the lens.

Franklin was looking straight at the back of Henry Wallace, seated in the foreground, nearest to the camera, turned in his seat to face Thomas Greenwood, if Will's theory about who took the picture was correct.

When Will really studied him, Franklin looked not only *suspicious,* but also angry.

"Does this means the Center was in on this?" asked Nick.

"No, no, on the contrary," said Nepsted. "The headmaster was aware his son had joined the Knights, but he seemed to think it was no more than a fraternity. Frank helped impose all the secrecy so his father wouldn't find out what we were really doing. He was the leader of our group—a born leader, in his character—and Abelson's Awakening was the path down which he led us."

"But Thomas *did* find out about it," said Will. "Or he had

serious suspicions. Why else would he invite Henry Wallace to the school?"

"They were old, trusted friends," said Nepsted, nodding. "Thomas sensed something was going wrong with his son and the Knights and he asked Wallace here to help him find out what it was. We didn't know that at the time."

"Was he too late?" asked Nick.

"By the night of that dinner, we'd already received the first weeks of treatments. Only injections at that point, but they'd gone flawlessly. We all felt healthy, strong, optimistic. Better than we'd ever felt, honestly." His eyes clouded over with pain. "And Abelson was convinced that Wallace never suspected a thing."

"But he was wrong," said Will, studying him closely. "Wallace *was* on to you, wasn't he?"

Nepsted closed his eyes, his face etched by the pain of the memories. "We were scheduled to begin the final stages. Two weeks of intense therapies that required us to remain secluded, out of sight."

"How did they work that?" asked Nick.

"They created a cover story for our absence. The Knights traditionally took a senior year trip together; we'd be going to Europe, with Dr. Abelson as our chaperone. We staged everything to make it appear real."

"The dinner was part of this?"

"Yes, to commemorate the trip. We packed our bags and the next night threw a farewell party. Over two hundred students came to send us off. The next morning we boarded a chartered plane. An hour into the flight we turned around, landed at a nearby airfield, and snuck back in the dead of night. That's when they took us down to that hospital for the first time."

"On that big elevator?" asked Will.

"Yes. They'd built that to help the construction, with a reception area to make it look normal and put us at ease. But before that, not everything went according to plan. Frank never got on that plane with us," said Nepsted, his face cycling through another set of changes. "Dr. Abelson told us he'd been taken ill."

"That wasn't true?" asked Will.

"No. That was how they got Frank away from Abelson. We never saw him again."

"And you think this was Wallace's doing."

Nepsted nodded. "Henry Wallace helped Thomas Greenwood rescue his son. That's why he came in the first place. But Abelson didn't seem concerned. In fact, he told *us* that Frank had been given a more important assignment."

"If his father knew the score, why didn't he get the rest of you out of there?" asked Nick.

"I don't know the answer. Maybe he didn't know. Maybe it's because we weren't his sons. *Most* of us never saw Frank again."

"Most of you never left that building," said Will.

"What happened down there, Raymond?" asked Nick softly.

Nepsted paused, and the words came much more haltingly. "We'd been in the hospital only a few days. Confined to our rooms. The new treatments were much more painful than before. As it grew worse, they kept us drugged . . . and then the process went wrong. Just one of us at first—George Gage, from Baltimore. We woke up one morning and George was gone. After that the others turned quickly. In less than a month." Nepsted blinked repeatedly, his eyes filled with sorrow. "I saw them, Will."

Will's whole body shook with an anger that he had to work hard to contain. "We saw them, too. They're still down there."

255

"I know," said Nepsted.

"Saw what?" asked Ajay blankly. "How could you have seen them?"

"Dude, were they in that room with those big *tanks*?" asked Nick.

"I'll explain *later*," said Will, and made sure Nick got the message before he turned back to Nepsted. "Keep going, Raymond."

"We'd been living in a barracks together, but they separated us in locked rooms like jail cells once the others started disappearing."

"We saw those, too," said Nick.

"They took the others away one by one, until nine had vanished. None of the staff would tell us what had happened or where they'd gone. But I saw George, or what he'd become."

"Until only two of you were left," said Will. "You and Edgar Snow."

"That's right, Will," said Nepsted. "Our cells were next to each other. We could whisper at night through the bars. They kept us for months, watching, testing constantly, but neither of us changed or got sick like the others. In the meantime—I found this out much later—they'd staged the crash to explain our disappearance. They dropped a real plane into Lake Superior, saying it had gone down on its way back from Europe. Of course no bodies were ever recovered."

That sounds familiar, too, thought Will.

"So they put up that memorial," said Will. "And all your families thought you were dead."

"Yes. Edgar and I realized we were prisoners. Locks on the doors now. Then I woke up one morning to find that they'd taken Edgar, too. I assumed he'd gotten sick like the others and if he was still alive that he must have thought the same about me."

"But you were normal," said Ajay. "Nothing had changed."

"Oh yes, perfectly normal. A picture of health." He held up his hands in a mockery of contentment. "I went on living, adjusting as best I could to solitary confinement. I was an only child, never many friends, so I was used to being alone. The nurses brought me my books and let me study, screened movies for me, brought me newspapers, always treated me kindly. But I soon realized that they had no intention of letting me conduct my life as 'Raymond' again. After the 'accident,' that was out of the question. Which I learned a year later, when Edgar came to see me."

"Why?"

"To convince me to cooperate. Show me that the program had been a success after all. Because Edgar *had* changed, finally, but the process hadn't killed or disfigured him. He'd lost his hair, he was much bigger and stronger, but beyond that he looked the same. He showed me these abilities—the things he could do just by looking at something, his strength and physical invulnerability, impervious to pain, disease, or heat or cold—and how he'd learned to control them. Even more striking as far as they were concerned was that Edgar could appear perfectly normal whenever he wanted or needed to."

"He was one of them now," said Will. "A Knight."

Nepsted nodded. "Edgar'd always had the light of a fanatic in his eyes, but it burned brighter than ever now. And why not? His existence meant Abelson's plan had delivered one of the Holy Warriors he'd promised to create."

"For what reason?" asked Will.

"To serve the Knights. They knew better, you see, than

governments or countries. They believed a war was coming that would destroy the world. The Knights would be the only force strong enough to survive and build a new civilization from the ashes."

"So Edgar Snow became the first modern Paladin," said Ajay. "Which made the rest of their failures acceptable."

"And if he'd survived, that meant they hoped the same could happen to you," said Will.

"That's why they kept me down there, Will," said Nepsted.

"Was Abelson still in charge?" asked Nick.

"No, he stopped coming a few months after they took us down here—I never saw him again after that."

"When was this?" asked Will.

"Early spring of 1939. From then on I only saw Edgar. I came to accept that he was in charge. He told me Thomas Greenwood had fired Dr. Abelson when he outlawed the Knights on campus. A few months after he rescued his son. I don't know what happened to Abelson."

"How much did Greenwood know?" asked Will. "He must have found out about the hospital."

"News of what the headmaster did or didn't know, and when he did or didn't know it, never reached me," said Nepsted with a wan smile. "I remained a prisoner down there for the next fourteen years."

"My God," said Ajay.

"And in all that time, I never changed. By that I mean I was *exactly* the same. All through my captivity I'd never been sick, never so much as caught a cold. And I never aged a day."

Again Will remembered some of Nepsted's first words to him: *I'm a lot older than I look.*

This is starting to sound too much like what's happening to us, thought Will.

"So, you see, their treatments had worked after all, just not in any way they'd anticipated. The only thing that changed was my willingness to cooperate. From the moment I saw the first mutations, I refused to be part of it, even if it meant living in that cell for the rest of my life."

"Did they tell you anything else? Anything about the ancient city they'd found?" asked Ajay. "Or the older race of beings that lived there?"

"No. I only knew what I read in the magazines and newspapers they gave me," said Nepsted. "Until 1956. When for reasons I never learned, Edgar told me my captors had been moved by some charitable impulse to let me go. Under certain conditions."

"What were they?" asked Will.

"I would be set up in a different life. Under a new name, in a distant city. Flagstaff, Arizona."

"Why would they just let you go after all that?" asked Nick.

"I think I know why," said Will. "In 1956?"

"That's right."

"That was the year Franklin became headmaster of the Center," said Will. "He must have had something to do with it."

One of Nepsted's tendrils slipped out of the liquid and trailed over the edge of the tank, searching for and then digging out an old notebook, buried among the random stacks of books and debris on the edge of the light.

"I believe you're right, Will," said Nepsted. "I think Frank took pity on me. Perhaps he felt real remorse about all that happened to us, or his youthful role in it."

"What did Edgar tell you?"

"How easily he'd slipped into his new life—he called himself Hobbes now—and that I could do the same. He even offered an apology, that none of this should have happened to us,

259

that the hospital would be destroyed along with all records of these events. I would be free to start this new life, as long as I kept to myself and never spoke about it to anyone."

"And you believed him?" asked Nick.

"What choice did I have? I'd been alone so long I didn't know a single soul on the outside anymore. Hobbes drove me to Flagstaff himself. They'd created a whole new identity for me. He gave me the car we'd used to get there and enough money to start over. About a week later I got a job in a hardware store, the only trade I knew, and it hadn't changed much."

More tendrils flowed down after the first one, helping to lift the notebook, opening it and holding it up so the boys could see inside. It was a scrapbook, with pages of faded snapshots fastened with little plastic triangles at the corners.

Will's eye fell on a yellowing shot of Nepsted standing in front of a sun-drenched hardware store. The cars on the street looked to be from the early to mid-1960s.

"I was thirty-seven years old and still looked like I was eighteen," said Nepsted. "I'd never lived on my own. I hadn't been out in the world in nearly twenty years. Edgar was always kind to me, but he made it clear the Knights would be watching at all times, and if I tried to run or contact my family, or tell anyone about what had happened, they'd bring me back here for good. I never even knew if my parents were still alive. I was so eager to be free I agreed to everything."

Nepsted took in a sharp breath, having trouble containing his emotions. Ajay looked like he was about to cry, too. Will took the scrapbook from Nepsted and slowly paged through the frozen moments of Nepsted's new life.

"And I believed him. That they would know if I ever spoke to anyone about what we'd gone through, but also that they'd put a stop to the program. So I obeyed their rules, and kept completely to myself, for nine years. Edgar never came to see me again, so eventually I stopped thinking so much about the warnings he'd given me."

Will turned the page and saw a photograph of Nepsted in a park with his arm around the waist of a pretty, slender young woman with long brown hair.

"By the time I fell in love with Julie, I scarcely gave what Edgar'd told me a second thought. I stuck to my story, never told her a word about what had really happened. By then it hardly felt like lying. As far as I was concerned, I really *was* Stephen Nepsted, since that's where and when my life had actually started. They started calling me Happy at the hardware store as a joke, because I looked so serious all the time . . . but for a while, after I met Julie, I really was happy."

On the next page Will found photographs of a simple wedding in a small chapel, just Raymond and Julie—in everyday clothes—standing with a minister and a witness.

"Dude, you got *married*?" asked Nick.

"We'd gone together for two years. No one had bothered us, Edgar had never appeared, so the week I turned forty-one, we drove to Vegas and found one of those ridiculous chapels."

One of Nepsted's tendrils tenderly traced another photo of him standing with his smiling bride, who held a small bouquet.

"Julie was twenty-three, but our age difference never mattered to me. In most ways I wasn't really older than I looked, even though I hadn't aged since I'd reached Flagstaff."

The three roommates huddled together, looking at the photos, the only sound in the room the soft burbling of the liquid in the tub. The last photo was of Julie posing in a small bedroom that had been converted into a nursery.

"I'd lied to Julie that we shouldn't have kids, health issues in my family, so we had to be careful. But she got pregnant anyway, and I tried to pretend, I wanted so badly to believe everything would be okay. . . ."

Nepsted couldn't continue for a moment.

"Is that when it happened, Raymond?" asked Will gently.

Nepsted nodded. "The stress brought it on, I think . . . all the terrible fears it brought back . . . what they'd done to me lay dormant all those years, the treatments . . . but then I started to change . . . into this. . . ."

Will turned the page. The rest were blank.

"I tried to hide at first, hide it from everyone . . . and I did for a while . . . but then, in small ways, it began to . . . happen in public. I controlled the mutations as best I could, but after a while my 'normal' body started to change, too, permanently. I couldn't keep my job. I didn't know how I'd support my family when the baby was born. Then one day after work I found Edgar waiting in my car. He never threatened me; he knew I hadn't betrayed our agreement. He said he only wanted to help. But he could only do that by bringing me back here. Where they could give me a place to live and take care of me again."

Tears softly rolled down Nepsted's cheeks. Will noticed Nick wiping the corner of his eye.

"Edgar promised he'd take care of my family, too . . . but they'd have to believe I was dead. I didn't know what else to do. He was right, in some ways. If people found out what I really was, what kind of life could we have had, what kind of future would there be for my wife and son? I had no choice, you see?"

"I guess I do, Raymond," said Will.

"Edgar arranged a life insurance policy. So Julie and Henry would have everything they needed," said Nepsted.

"Except a father and a husband," said Nick under his breath. Will hushed him.

"I had one condition: I told him I could never go back to

that hospital," said Nepsted, shaking his head slowly. "I needed a real place in the world, and a real job that had meaning and contact with younger people so I could . . . have some idea of the life my son might be living."

"You've never even seen him, have you?" asked Nick.

"I left Flagstaff a month before Henry was born. They staged a car accident that even the insurance company believed."

"They're good at that," said Will.

"Edgar flew me here in a private plane at night. Brought me to this room. In 1974. And I've been here ever since. The equipment manager in the boys' locker room."

"Though still a prisoner, Raymond?" asked Ajay.

"That lock was my idea," said Nepsted, shaking his head vigorously. "I didn't want to be tempted to leave. If the kids saw me when I couldn't control my appearance, if they suspected I was anything other than the cripple behind the screen who gave them their sneakers, even this much might get taken away from me."

"So why'd you ask us to find the key for you?" said Nick, puzzled.

"What changed, Raymond?" asked Will.

Nepsted lowered his voice. "I hear whispers. People tell me things or I overhear them. Sometimes I even hear their thoughts. When they look at this cage they don't know how carefully I'm watching and listening. And many years ago, almost twenty now, I realized that the Knights of Charlemagne had come back to the Center."

Will felt a chill run up the nape of his neck.

"In fact, it seems they'd never left. I assumed Edgar was in charge, and had been all along, but I was wrong. He was now taking orders from someone else."

"Franklin?" asked Will.

"No, from everything I've learned, he turned against the Knights, too," said Nepsted. "And Frank died in 1995. Whoever's leading them now is a person with powerful allies."

Haxley, thought Will.

"Three generations of former Knights are out in the world," said Nepsted, "a hidden network of prominent men in positions of tremendous power and influence. Edgar hinted that something new was in the wind, something unimaginable."

"A new program based on Abelson's ideas," said Will, glancing at Ajay and Nick. "Genetic manipulation. It's called the Paladin Prophecy."

"Good Lord," said Nepsted, surprised. "What else have you learned about it, Will?"

"It's heavily funded, well organized, and may involve a lot more people this time. Raymond, is it possible Franklin could have found out the Knights reactivated the Paladin program and tried to stop them?"

Nepsted read the suggestion in Will's eye. "You mean, so they killed him?"

"Yes."

"It's possible. You have to understand—I think you already do—that these people let nothing stand in their way. Is it *exactly* the same program they used on us?" asked Raymond, his voice quivering.

"It's worse," said Will, deciding to hold nothing back. "This time the future of the planet is at stake. They're working with an older race—maybe the ones who built that city down there. Those things were banished ages ago to some other dimension, but they're trying to come back and regain control of the Earth. A war is coming, not between men this time, but men are helping them, men like the Knights, in exchange for wealth, power, advanced technology . . . and a favored position once this older race takes over."

"Yeah, but we're going to stop them," said Nick, without much conviction.

"You three kids?" asked Nepsted.

"There are five of us, actually," said Will.

"Well, thank goodness for that," whispered Nepsted.

"And we're hoping, of course," said Will, "that you can help us."

"So the *objective* of the program hasn't changed," said Nepsted, his voice faltering. "Trying to create a race of advanced beings. Paladins."

"But now the *science* has caught up to their philosophy," said Will.

"So this time they not only possess the knowledge, they also have the wealth, technology, and will," said Raymond, his eyes meeting theirs. "We must do something, anything, to stop them."

"Why didn't you act before, if you suspected something? Why did you wait until now?" asked Ajay.

Nepsted looked right at Will. "I was waiting for you," he said.

Will saw something move in the image on the card-sized screen in his hand, streaming the feed from the camera in the cage at the counter up front.

"Someone's out there," said Will.

THE MANDALA

"I want you all to look away," said Nepsted urgently. "Right now, please, do that much for me."

The three roommates turned their backs and they heard Nepsted hoist himself out of the steel tub, then the wet syncopated patter of a thousand tendrils slapping on the concrete as he rapidly transported himself toward the door.

Will glanced at Ajay and realized that he'd turned just enough to catch some of this in his expansive peripheral vision; his jaw hung agape, his eyes wide. Ajay turned to Will with an expression of helpless astonishment.

Will shook his head: *Don't look.*

Ajay closed his eyes and then clamped his hands over them. They heard a sequence of strange slapping sounds, flesh hitting flesh, tendrils whipping around each other and binding back together.

"Aw, *dude*," said Nick, wincing.

"Thank you," said Nepsted when it was over. "Now come with me."

When they turned back to him, Nepsted was dressed and in the form they'd always seen him in—a small, deformed man seated in his wheelchair, operating its joystick by hand, steering it through the door.

"Could you see who it was?" Nepsted asked Will quietly as he rolled back into the cage.

"No," said Will. "I only saw movement."

"You need to hide. Back here in the aisles where no one can see you."

"We put the lock back on the door but didn't fasten it," said Nick. "We couldn't reach it through the cage."

"I'll take care of that. I hope you disabled that camera on your way in," said Nepsted, nodding up at the security camera near the ceiling, halfway down the aisle.

"I put it to sleep," said Ajay.

"Good," said Nepsted. "That's how they watch me."

"No one saw us come in, I can promise you that," said Ajay.

"Whatever happens, don't reveal yourselves," said Nepsted solemnly. "It's not safe for you to be seen here."

The three of them crouched behind boxes of equipment in the last row to the left while Nepsted rolled down the aisle toward the cage.

"Dudes, I didn't want to bring it up in the room," whispered Nick, making a face, "but oh my bleeping bleepness, what is up with the purple bubble bath?"

"It's got to have something to do with his . . . you know," said Will.

"Squidness?"

"My guess is it serves as some kind of delivery system for nutrients or medications that keep him alive," said Ajay.

"How long do you think he can survive without it?" asked Will.

"I have no idea," said Ajay. "What's the longest you've ever seen him in his regular form?"

Will thought back to their past conversations. "Maybe half an hour?"

"If he wants to leave, it won't be easy lugging that big tub of goo around," said Nick. "What do you think is in it? He's so freakin' old maybe it's some kind of preservative."

Will peeked around the edge of the box and saw that Nepsted had reached the counter.

"Who's there?" they heard Nepsted say.

Will saw a few tendrils slip out of Nepsted's right sleeve, slither toward the gate, and slip through the gaps in the cage.

"He's closing the lock from the inside," whispered Will. He leaned back and held up the small screen so they could all see it.

"I know someone's there," said Nepsted. "Show yourself."

Will noticed a blurry smudge swiftly approaching the counter and then a naked human form appeared in a fragmented flash of light, right in front of the cage, instantly coalescing from a cloud of dust.

It was Courtney Hodak. Tall, preposterously fit, and she seemed completely unself-conscious about her unclothed state. She raised her left hand, grasping a handful of Nepsted's writhing tendrils in a vise grip, sneering at him through the cage.

"I hear this is where they keep the freaks," she said.

"This is the *men's* locker room," said Nepsted, in pain, struggling to pull away from her.

"Are you alone back there, freak?" she asked, looking past him.

Ajay's eyes bugged out. Both Will and Nick covered his mouth with their hands.

"What do you think?" said Nepsted as he finally freed himself, tendrils snapping back through the cage and vanishing up his sleeve.

Courtney turned to the darkness behind her and waved someone forward. The dice in Will's pocket began vibrating again; he had to hold them in his hand to dampen the sound. Wearing his black Windbreaker and cap, Hobbes strolled out of the dark, flanked by two tall muscular guys that Will recognized from Courtney's class of Knights. Hobbes casually held a white shirt and some shorts with a hooked finger and handed them to Courtney as he reached the cage. She slipped them on, taking her time, clearly enjoying how uncomfortable her nakedness made Nepsted.

Nick pulled the screen closer. Ajay tried to take it away from him so he could watch. Will gestured for them both to cool it.

"That's Todd's sister," mouthed Will silently.

"That's *Courtney*?" Nick whispered, looking amazed.

"You didn't recognize her?" Will asked.

"Dude, I wasn't looking at her face." Nick pulled the screen closer for another look and lowered his voice even further. "Totally stark *naked*."

"To be accurate," whispered Ajay, "she was wearing shoes."

"Hello, Raymond," said Hobbes, smiling pleasantly, his strange light eyes glowing.

"Who are your playmates?" asked Nepsted.

"You haven't forgotten the pride of last year's class, have you, Raymond? Misters Halsted and Davis?" said Hobbes, gesturing toward the two boys. "Although of course you wouldn't have seen Courtney before."

"He has now," she said teasingly.

"What do you want, Edgar?" asked Nepsted.

Hobbes leaned forward on the counter, relaxed and amiable. "I came to warn you, old friend. A few young students have taken it upon themselves to pry into our history. Subjects they have no business knowing. That no one but you and I are privy to."

With his left hand, Hobbes reached down and yanked hard on the cage door lock. It rattled but didn't give; Nepsted had succeeded in relocking it just in time. Hobbes smiled again.

"What's that to do with me?" asked Nepsted.

"I believe you know who I'm talking about," said Hobbes.

Will watched the screen intently. Hobbes leaned over the counter; close to the camera, the man's eyes burned with

269

unnatural heat, staring at Nepsted until Happy finally looked away.

"I might," said Nepsted.

"You know how devastating this could be, Raymond. I wouldn't be surprised if these kids try to speak with you about it anytime now. Unless they've been here already?"

Hobbes waited until Nepsted shook his head.

"I don't need to reemphasize how vital it is that you don't share anything with them. Do I?"

"No, Edgar," mumbled Nepsted.

"Because if you require a reminder, there's something I've been meaning to tell you for the longest time but never had a chance, or should I say, a *reason* to, until now."

Hobbes slipped something from the pocket of his Windbreaker and pinned it up against the cage in front of Nepsted. It looked like a photograph, but Will and the others couldn't make it out on their screen.

"Do you know who that is, Raymond?"

"I have no idea."

"Your son, Raymond," said Hobbes. "That's Henry Nepsted, as he looks today. The apple of your eye."

They heard Nepsted choke back a sob. Will felt Nick tense up beside him, anger spiking, and put a hand on his arm to settle him down.

"As you can see, Henry's ... kind of a special person." Hobbes smiled. "Just like his dad."

"How do I know you're telling the truth?" asked Nepsted, his voice husky and strained.

Hobbes seemed genuinely puzzled. "Your question hurts my feelings, it really does. When have I ever lied to you, Raymond? We've always been able to trust each other. Don't you know how much I depend on you after all we've been through together?"

"How do I know that's really my boy?"

"Because I give you my *word*," said Hobbes, not smiling now.

"Where is he?" asked Nepsted after a few moments, sounding weaker.

"Oh, we know exactly where he is—in fact, I took that photograph myself just the other day. I'll leave this with you, if you open your drawer."

A moment later, Will heard the metal drawer in the cage wall slide open. Hobbes dropped in the photo and Nepsted drew it inside. Hobbes leaned forward on the counter.

"Henry's less than half an hour from here, Raymond. But don't worry; he knows nothing about this, or you, or the school, or anything really. He's in no immediate danger. You'd like to keep it that way, wouldn't you? I know what a worrier you are."

"Please . . . ," said Nepsted.

Hobbes modulated his tone again, two old friends chatting over a beer. "You have such an active imagination, Raymond. So I want you to imagine what would happen to your son . . . if you do anything to help these misguided young people. Could I make that any clearer?"

"No," said Nepsted softly.

"What's that, Raymond?"

"I understand, Edgar."

"I'm so thankful for the chance to have this conversation," said Hobbes. "Before things got carried away."

Hobbes smiled, showing his sharpened teeth, stood back from the counter, turned, and walked into the darkness, waving once over his shoulder. The three young Knights trailed after him, with Courtney shooting a last smirk back at the cage as she blew Nepsted a kiss.

Will, Ajay, and Nick didn't move until they heard Nepsted's wheelchair roll back their way and stop nearby. Nepsted looked ashen and wouldn't meet their eyes. He clutched the photo Hobbes had given him in his left hand.

"You have to leave now," he said.

"Raymond, don't believe him. You can't believe a word that guy says—" said Nick.

"Give me the key so I can open the lock and let you out." Nepsted held out his hand, still not looking at them. Will reluctantly gave him the silver key.

"But it can't be true," said Nick.

"Edgar's never lied to me," said Nepsted, turning his chair around, heading back to the gate.

"What should we do?" Nick whispered.

"We should go," said Will. "There's nothing we can do right now."

"He told us what we needed to know anyway," said Ajay.

"But we can't just leave him like this. We need to help him," said Nick passionately.

"We need to leave him alone for a while," said Will. "If Hobbes doesn't find out we were here, he should be okay."

Will got up and the others followed him to the counter. Nepsted had already opened the lock. A cluster of tendrils pulled open the gate, then slithered back up his sleeves. He lowered his eyes as they eased their way past him.

"Raymond, you don't need to do what that guy tells you anymore," said Nick, pleading with him. "We can help you; we can make him stop—"

"Don't ever come down here again," said Nepsted coldly.

With fire in his eyes, he slammed the gate behind them;

then more tendrils shot out through the cage and he used the key to relock the lock. The key clattered to the floor at Will's feet as the wheelchair turned and limped away, one wheel squeaking on every turn.

Will picked up the key and pocketed it.

"What now?" asked Nick.

"Find Elise and Brooke and talk about it. Take the back way, in case they're watching the doors— What's the matter, Ajay?"

Ajay kept glancing at Nick, looking wary. "I caught a glimpse of that photograph," he said.

"What about it?" asked Nick.

"I think I know who Nepsted's son is," said Ajay.

Will's pager went off. He picked up the phone on the counter and the operator connected him.

"This is Will," he said.

"Meet me at the Riven Oak," said the voice.

Coach Jericho.

At first Nick didn't believe it when Ajay told them what he'd seen in Raymond's photo, but once Ajay reminded him why, he and Nick decided to investigate immediately. They snuck out the Barn by the back way. Nick and Ajay headed back to the quad, taking a long route through the woods to avoid detection, while Will headed to the Riven Oak.

Coach Jericho was waiting for him inside the big split tree, leaning against the wood as Will arrived. Coach didn't move, looking cool and relaxed.

"What took you so long?" said the coach, deadpan.

"It's been three minutes," said Will.

Coach Jericho beckoned him inside the hollow of the broken tree, out of sight.

"What's up?" asked Will.

"Jungle drums," said Jericho. "You're stirring up some notice."

"Am I?" Will tried to hide his concern. "Where are you hearing that from?"

"Between the lines," said Jericho, then studied him carefully. "What do you want to ask me?"

Will was about to say, "Hey, you called *me*," then realized he wanted to ask six questions at once but settled for: "You remember telling me once about an ancient race that lived here before your people did?"

Jericho looked even more serious, if that was even possible. "What did you find?"

"Proof that you're right. I'm trying to decide what to do about it. Without 'stirring up too much notice.'"

"How are you going about that?" asked Jericho, staring up into the tree.

"I'm thinking."

"Which mind are you using?"

"I don't understand the question," said Will.

"You have more than one mind," said Jericho, pointing to Will's head, then his heart, then his stomach. "Decide which one to listen to. The higher mind's the one that matters. Then it'll speak to you."

Like much of what Jericho said, Will didn't know what to make of that, but he'd learned he usually had to give Coach's advice time. In this case, time for it to soak down into his "higher mind," he guessed. Without realizing it, he'd taken the stone falcon out of his pocket and was rubbing it absentmindedly like prayer beads. Jericho opened Will's hand and stared at the figure as if he could read it, then looked up at Will.

"Yep," he said. "Falcon."

"Excuse me?"

"That's definitely your spirit animal," said Jericho. "And you saw the We-in-di-ko."

"I did?"

Jericho hesitated. "Unless I'm wrong."

"No," said Will, remembering the shambling figure that had followed him in the tunnels. "I actually think you're right."

"You and Lyle aren't through with each other," said Jericho quietly.

"What does he want?" asked Will.

"He'll get back to you about that. But when the reckoning comes, you'll have more help on your side than you know."

Then he was gone like a puff of smoke. Will wasn't sure he'd ever seen him run before. He wasn't sure he saw him run this time.

Will set off through the woods, staying off the main trails. About halfway back to the quad, his pager beeped, and a beat later he heard Elise's voice in his head.

We need to talk. Disregard the page if you can hear this. Meet me at the art studios.

Will picked up his pace, and after tracking the outskirts of the campus, he made his way to Adams Hall.

The upper floor of Adams housed a series of spacious garrets, with floor-to-ceiling windows and skylights for optimum light, where art students kept their studios. Will found Elise waiting outside the studio she shared with Brooke. She pulled him inside and closed the door.

Will was about to give Elise a hug when he noticed Brooke waiting behind her. It surprised him, but he hoped he didn't look disappointed she was there. He wasn't; he was happy to see them both and to share what they'd learned. So he gave them both a hug—Elise first, then Brooke—making sure he didn't favor one over the other. He was relieved to see neither of them seemed to mind. He brought them quickly up to speed on Nepsted's story and his encounter with Hobbes that seemed to confirm everything Raymond had told them. It worried them but they appeared to take the information in stride.

"So the Knights tried this before," said Brooke. "Genetically altering students."

"That's right," said Will. "Nepsted and Hobbes were the first Paladins."

"Paladins 1.0," said Elise.

"The only ones that survived, anyway," said Will.

"So they rebooted that program as the Paladin Prophecy," said Elise, drumming her fingers. "Fifty years later."

"Once research and technology made it more feasible," said Will. "And, since we seem to be part of it, let's hope less obviously dangerous."

Will reached over and knocked wood. The girls did, too.

"Why'd they do it, Will?" asked Brooke. "Did he know? Did he tell you?"

"No. Personally I think the Prophecy's part of whatever pact they've made with the Other Team. Creating soldiers, maybe, to fight on their side in the coming war."

"But we don't know that for sure, right?" asked Brooke.

"That's the next thing we need to find out—why the Knights pushed the button on this," said Will.

"At least now we know where the idea for what they did to us came from," said Brooke.

"And 'us' includes everyone from Courtney and her class," said Elise, "to Lyle and God knows who else."

"That's right," said Will. "If I had to guess, what they want, probably, is for us to play ball like the others and join their side."

Brooke went pale and sat down, looking like she was going to be sick.

"Presenting the new and improved Paladin 2.0," Elise said in a phony commercial announcer's voice. "Still in the beta testing stage, but so far no crippling side effects."

"Did you say Courtney was *invisible*?" asked Brooke.

"Not exactly," said Will. "We saw something moving through the air before she appeared. Ajay thinks she may have some way of bending light around her."

"She's bent, all right," said Elise. "Her brother's a blunt instrument, but Courtney's a stainless-steel sociopath."

"We've been talking about what's happened to me, too," said Brooke, glancing at Elise. "Those things I didn't know I could do when we were down in the tunnels."

"What'd you come up with?" asked Will.

"For starters, she's what they call a medical intuitive," said Elise. "She can sense people's physical condition with amazing precision using some kind of hands-on diagnostic ability."

"You can also heal, using touch, your hands," said Will. "The two fit together if you think about it. Is that what it felt like to you?"

Brooke nodded, looking at her hands. "I don't know how. It happened so fast. I could sense what was wrong—with both you and Elise. I could see it in your bodies, where the weakness was, and once I had the intention, I directed energy there that helped. I can't pretend to understand how. I don't even feel like I can control it."

"It's new to you," said Elise. "We felt that way, too, at first. Control's something you have to develop or train, like we did."

"There's something else, too," said Will. "I sensed it when we were trying to get the key out of that cylinder. That's why

I asked for your help. And if you think about it, this fits with your other abilities because it also involves touch."

"What?"

"If you use that—whatever you want to call it, healing energy—you seem able to amplify whatever power another person has."

"And that . . . is kick-ass," said Elise, giving Brooke a high five.

"She's right," said Will. "That might even be your most powerful way to use it. You'll just have to experiment and see."

"You can handle it," said Elise, patting Brooke's shoulder. "We know you can."

Brooke seemed overwhelmed. She got up and walked over to the window, looking out at the campus below. Will glanced at Elise.

Is she going to be cool with this? he asked.

Were we at first?

Not at all.

Fact: we were freaked out like our hair was on fire. Give her time.

"At least I don't have to feel left out anymore," said Brooke with a crooked smile.

"That's right, girlfriend," said Elise. "You can hoist your freak flag like the rest of us."

At least this is bringing them back together, thought Will. *That's got to be a good thing. Just as long as they don't start talking about me.*

"Should we show him?" asked Brooke, looking up at Elise.

"Yes. Come over here, West, we've got some 411."

Elise led him across the room past a large square canvas laid out on the floor. It was covered with a huge circle of intricate lines and subtle shades, in swirling, symmetrical patterns.

When he looked closer, Will realized that it was made entirely of dozens of different colors of fine-grain sand.

"What's this?" he asked.

"A mandala. Sand painting," said Elise. "A new form I'm playing around with. I had a dream about it a few nights ago."

"Really," said Will, intrigued. "This looks amazing."

"Glad you like it, but that's not what we need to show you," she said.

On an easel in front of a small couch, Elise and Brooke had their notebooks set up and expanded to the size of a small television.

"Add your notebook," said Elise. "You can copy it onto your drive while we show you what we found."

Will set his notebook on the easel and it merged with the others, expanding the composite screen by a few more feet. All three of their syn-apps appeared on-screen, awaiting orders.

"Show Will what we found on Henry Wallace," said Elise to her syn-app.

Elise's syn-app gestured to Brooke's, who turned on an old-fashioned movie projector. That activated a video file that filled the screen. Junior sat down to watch, while Brooke's and Elise's syn-apps took turns narrating the still photos and newsreel footage that appeared.

"Henry Wallace was born and raised on a farm, 1885, in Iowa. He graduated from Iowa State, where he studied botany and agriculture and became close friends with a graduate student named George Washington Carver. He made another great friend there, a fellow undergrad who shared his interest in education: Thomas Greenwood."

Early film footage appeared of young Thomas Greenwood shaking hands with Wallace as they toured the grounds of the Center where the quad was under construction.

"Wallace served as a private advisor to Greenwood when he founded the Center, and continued in that capacity for many years. During that time, Wallace not only created new, more productive crop hybrids, but he also developed scientific methods of advancing agriculture yields, all of which made him a wealthy and celebrated businessman."

Now they saw Henry Wallace in Washington, meeting with President Roosevelt and other officials, and footage of both men at Roosevelt's first inauguration.

"In 1933, Franklin Roosevelt named Wallace as the United States' eleventh secretary of agriculture. Roosevelt liked and trusted him so much that seven years later he asked Wallace to serve as the thirty-third vice president of the United States."

Footage of Wallace being sworn in at Roosevelt's third inaugural appeared.

"What is this, the History Channel?" asked Will impatiently.

"Hang on, here comes the meat," said Elise.

Film of snowcapped mountain ranges followed—strange, thought Will, they almost looked like the Himalayas—with Wallace taking part in a mountain-climbing expedition.

"The controversial aspect of Wallace's story involves his unusual spiritual beliefs. In the 1920s, Wallace became involved with the Theosophical Society, an early New Age movement. Their central belief is that all of human history, including our evolution, has been secretly directed by a group of highly evolved supernatural beings. These beings supposedly live in the remote reaches of the Himalayas in a mystical valley called Shambhala where they're known as the Hierarchy of the Masters—"

"Stop!" Will nearly shot out of his seat. "Where did you find this?"

"The Library of Congress," said Elise's syn-app as the video froze on the expedition footage.

"What's wrong?" asked Brooke.

Will looked around, a little wild-eyed. "This isn't the first we've heard about this."

"Which part?" asked Elise.

"Shambhala came up before, on Ronnie's secret message, as *Shangri-la,* remember? And this Hierarchy . . ." Will paused. *Could it possibly be . . . ?* "Do you have anything else on it?"

The two syn-apps looked at each other. "No. But one source suggests that Roosevelt didn't disapprove of Wallace's spiritual interests—and in fact may have shared them to some degree. That's the only other reference to it. The rest is about Wallace's political downfall."

"Show me," said Will.

More video appeared, all newsreel footage, and Elise's syn-app continued narrating: "Wallace served just one term as vice president. In 1944 he was forced off the ticket by members of both political parties, who claimed Wallace was unsuitable for the office. He was replaced by a little-known senator from Missouri, Harry Truman. When President Roosevelt died a few months after his inauguration in 1945, Harry Truman became president."

"So Wallace missed becoming president by only a few months," said Will.

"That's right," said Elise, looking concerned by his interest. "Could that have something to do with the Knights or the Paladin plot?"

"Not sure," said Will. "What else do you have on Wallace in the Himalayas? When did he go there?"

"Early 1944," said Elise's syn-app. "He led an extensive expedition through the region for over two months."

More footage appeared of Wallace leading a sizeable group through the high snowy peaks; it ended with a sequence of the vice president being greeted by some Tibetan monks in a high mountaintop lamasery.

"Hold it there," said Will.

The image of Wallace and the monks froze on-screen. As Will studied it, his mind swam with ideas that threatened to overwhelm him. "This happened while Wallace was still in office?"

"Yes," said Brooke's syn-app. "Apparently as some sort of diplomatic mission that the president approved. Something to do with agriculture."

"Whatever it was for," said Elise's syn-app, "this mission seems to have played a large part in why the opposition forced Wallace out before the election later that year."

"What does this all mean, Will?" asked Brooke.

"Start by asking . . . what was going on in America in 1944?" Will said.

"The end of World War Two was approaching," said Brooke. "Less than a year away."

"The Manhattan Project," said Elise, her eyes lighting up.

"That's where I went, too," said Will.

"A crash program to secretly develop atomic weapons," said Elise. "In '44, they were only a few months away from being tested."

"Which Wallace must have known about," said Will.

Brooke was nodding. "After we'd used them in the war and the arms race began, Wallace said on record that atomic weapons represented the greatest threat to the planet in human history."

"And so a few months before they test the first bomb," said Will, thinking as he paced, "Roosevelt sends his vice president to the roof of the world on a phony diplomatic mission."

"But why?" asked Brooke.

Will didn't want to share it just yet—it still sounded nuts, even to him—but based on what he'd just learned, the only explanation he could find struck dangerously close to secrets of his own:

Agriculture might have been the public reason, but if Henry Wallace was working as some kind of go-between to the Hierarchy, what if he was an Initiate himself, just like I am? Maybe his trip to the Himalayas involved Wallace's role in the ongoing battle between the Hierarchy and the Other Team.

"He was worried, for good reason," said Will. "Worried that this weapon could fall into the wrong hands."

"Maybe he was worried that it already had," said Elise, nearly reading Will's mind.

"You mean people in the government?" asked Brooke.

"People in the *Knights*," said Will, with a glance at Elise. "Who had already infiltrated government. Dig deeper and I'm pretty sure we'll find that the forces who ruined Wallace's career were carrying out orders from the Knights of Charlemagne."

"Why?" asked Brooke.

"The next year he misses becoming the thirty-fourth president of the United States by a matter of weeks," said Elise, sitting down to think.

"And a few months later the United States drops two atomic bombs on Japan," said Will. "Weapons with the greatest destructive capacity in human history."

"We've got the chronology down," said Brooke, "but what does it mean, Will?"

Will hesitated. Eventually he'd have to tell his friends about Dave and the Hierarchy and his connection to them, so he might as well ease into one corner of the picture.

"From what he did here, we already know Henry Wallace opposed the Knights of Charlemagne," said Will. "When he helped save Franklin Greenwood and stopped Abelson's experiments, he threw himself into the front lines of a battle that's been going on against the Other Team forever. The same battle that destroyed that city we saw a mile underground. The same battle we're fighting now."

Elise and Brooke looked at each other with rising alarm.

"If that's who Wallace was fighting against," asked Brooke, "who was he fighting *alongside*?"

Will took a deep breath. "I'm going to go out on a limb here and say it might have been . . . this group called the Hierarchy."

"The superevolved quasi-mystical beings who hang out in the Himalayas?" asked Elise skeptically.

Will gestured at the image of Wallace and the monks at the lamasery. "Well, it seems pretty clear he went there to meet *somebody*, doesn't it? And come on, agriculture in Tibet? That had to be a cover story. I mean, these guys with the robes and beards don't exactly check out as lobbyists from the local corn exchange."

"So what was he doing there, then?" asked Brooke evenly.

"It might sound crazy, but carry the logic," said Will. "If there really are 'beings' like this and you're trying to help them save the planet, doesn't it make sense to warn them that this kind of weapon had been developed? A weapon the Other Team would welcome, by the way, because it encouraged our self-destruction, making it that much easier for them to come back and take over."

"TEOTWAWKI," said Brooke.

"So they had to prevent Wallace from reaching real power he could use to destroy them," said Elise.

"That's why they took him down politically," said Will.

One other startling thought tumbled into Will's mind: *What if the connection between Wallace and Thomas Greenwood was even stronger than we know? Maybe my great-grandfather, Thomas Greenwood, was an Initiate, too.*

As if something just as unsettling had occurred to him as well, Will's syn-app, Junior, stood up on the screen and signaled him urgently. "Will, someone is trying to reach you."

"What do you mean, are you getting a text or an email?"

"No, nothing like that," said Junior, pacing nervously. "This is different. Someone's trying to reach you *directly*."

"How do you know that?"

"I can feel it," Junior said, looking alarmed. "Can't you?"

Will stopped, closed his eyes, and tried to sense what Junior was describing—imagining something like when he'd heard Dave's voice while they were down in the tunnels—but he couldn't come up with anything.

"No, I can't."

"This is important." Junior put his hands on either side of his head, as if physically in pain. "You need to try harder."

Will glanced at Elise and she was thinking the same thing he was: *Let's try together.*

He felt her mind reach out for his, and their thoughts swirled around each other like live currents of electricity. As the currents merged, their eyes met and Will knew she was adding her power to his and letting him direct it. He reached out for Elise's hand and when she gripped it, the power intensified again. Will pushed the edge of their combined mentality outward, past the physical boundaries around them, searching and probing to find whoever might be trying to contact him.

Will closed his eyes and became aware of a sound like a voice calling out from a great distance, but it was small, muffled, and he couldn't make out any words. Then he felt another pair of hands settle on top of his and Elise's and opened his eyes; Brooke had added both her hands to theirs, eyes closed in concentration, and the power flowing through the three of them went nova.

The air around them danced with power. The reality of the garret seemed to weaken, objects warping, walls shifting and swaying. Suddenly a shaft of light shot through the space, piercing the mandala on the nearby canvas.

Pulled by some power in that light, the sand on the canvas began to lift into the air, angle into a vertical axis, and spiral around, the mandala animating to life with its round border intact but its shape shifting within like a multidimensional kaleidoscope. Out of the swirling patterns a recognizable shape emerged.

It revealed itself as a face, ten feet high and wide, in three dimensions, fashioned out of the sand and eerily lifelike, and Will knew who this was instantly, even before its blue eyes opened and the scarred lips began to move and he heard its voice speaking to him.

"Can you hear me now, mate?" asked Dave's voice.

"I hear you loud and clear," said Will.

"'Bout bloody time," said Dave. "Not for lack of trying on my part. Which cost me no small amount of blood, sweat, and tears, I can tell you that."

When Will looked around, he realized Elise and Brooke also had their eyes open, and judging by their speechless astonishment, they could hear Dave, too.

"I heard you earlier," said Will. "You know, when we were down in the tunnels."

"That's when I started to get the hang of it from my end," said Dave. "I could tune into you but the signal was fairly dicey."

"Yeah, you were fading in and out a lot," said Will.

"Found out I could boost my signal through your little

computer pal—by the way, you oughta check that thing out. I think it's got some of your actual DNA—"

"You *know* who this is?" asked Elise, astonished.

"This is Dave," said Will, trying to keep it as simple as possible. "He's a friend."

Dave's image rotated to face Brooke and Elise. "Don't give me the cold shoulder, buttercups. Aren't you even going to say hi?"

"Hi," said Brooke, wide-eyed with terror.

"How's it going, Dave?" asked Elise, doing a slightly better job of covering her terror.

"Been worse," said Dave. "Definitely been better."

"I see," said Elise.

"Look, there's nothing I'd like more than chewing the fat with you lovely ladies but time's running short, the kettle's on the boil, and this whole zone's about to go hot as a monkey's doodle-dandy."

"Okay," said Brooke.

"What did he say?" Elise asked Brooke, who shrugged.

"Where are you?" asked Will.

"Where do you suppose I am, mate? You saw me get yanked through that infernal manhole with your own eyes, didn't you?"

"You mean, in the cave? When the wendigo grabbed you?"

"Now you're back on the beam," said Dave. "I've been here ever since."

"Oh my God, you've been in the *Never-Was* this whole time?" asked Will.

"Time has no meaning in here, mate. In fact, all bets are off, to put it mildly. Took me this long just to set my compass and find a way to make contact. Not the easiest job with a wendigo breathing down your tailpipe."

"Where did you meet this guy?" asked Brooke.

"On a plane," said Will.

"Was he made of sand then?" whispered Elise.

"No, he's like a person usually, sort of," said Will, then turned back to Dave. "So the wendigo's in there with you?"

"Old home week for that one. Finally gave it the slip, along with legions of other hideous beasties they've stockpiled in here—by the way, how much time has gone by on your end?"

"Almost eight months," said Will.

"Zounds, this is worse than I imagined," said Dave. "I've avoided capture to date, but they've had me on the run from the moment I landed. Never had anyone from our squad on the inside before, so it's hardly wasted effort—I've got a recon report that'd curl your hair—but if I don't get out and deliver it to the boys upstairs in short order, our goose is collectively cooked."

"What, you can't contact the Hierarchy from in there?"

"No chance, mate. All frequencies jammed. I only got through to you because of the unique nature of the Wayfarer-Client connection."

"Do you have any idea what he's talking about?" asked Elise.

"Uh, yes," said Will.

"I don't know which would be worse," said Brooke.

"Here's the short version, mate, and you'll grasp the urgency: They're massing for attack on this end, something fierce. Unless I miss my guess, they're lining up to launch that invasion we've talked about."

"Really? Then why isn't the Hierarchy all over this?" asked Will.

"They can't see in here for starters, and my guess is they're up to their eyeballs. The OT's sending out skirmishers and scouts all over the planet—feints and distractions, designed to keep our side busy so they can't glimpse the big picture. I don't know how much time we've got. D-Day could be right around the corner. The moment of no return is fast approaching."

"Is he saying what I think he's saying?" asked Elise.

"The Other Team's about to break out of the Never-Was and take over the planet," said Will. "Again."

"Okay, why should we believe any of this?" asked Brooke defiantly. "How do we know this isn't some kind of CGI stunt?"

"What, it's not enough that your boyfriend vouches for me?" asked Dave.

"He's not my boyfriend," both girls hastened to say.

Will didn't know how he felt about that.

Dave turned his eye to Elise. "You're the one who artfully sprinkled all this sand on the canvas. Am I right, ducks? Just the way it appeared in your dream."

"That's right," said Elise, surprised.

"I sent you that vision," said Dave. "Through *your* connection to my young friend here. And I think you know what I'm referring to."

"Oh," said Elise with a glance at Will; then she quickly turned to Brooke. "Okay, he's for real."

"You were on the money, Will. These two are a set of matched pistoleros," said Dave, and then he winked at them, dropping sand at their feet.

"How can we help?" asked Will.

"Job one: You've got to get me out of here," said Dave. "ASAP. So I can warn HQ posthaste."

"Isn't warning HQ something I can do?" asked Will.

"No, mister. As a Level Two dogface, you most decidedly cannot," said Dave.

"Oh, so I'm Level Two now?"

"Field promotion," said Dave. "For general excellence. Had no way to tell you."

Will felt no small swell of pride but had to squelch it quickly. "So how do we get you out of there?" he asked.

"Only one way," said Dave. "You'll have to come get me."

"How are we supposed to do *that*?" asked Brooke.

"For starters you'll need that cosmic can opener your pal Lyle used in the cave."

"The Carver," said Will. "We were just talking about going to find it."

"Well, shake a leg, kiddo," said Dave. "Then assemble every bit of muscle you can scrape together and come on in. You'll need it. It's no company picnic in here."

"I don't know, Dave," said Will. "This sounds like more than we can handle, honestly."

"Maybe so, but what other choice do we have? For what it's worth, I think you're up to it, my lad. And there will be help unlooked for, you can count on that."

"You mean like that silver falcon you sent to help me?" asked Will, lowering his voice.

"Falcon? What falcon?"

"The one in the cave, when the trees were after me."

"Sounds fascinating, but that weren't me, mate. They've got me so harried I couldn't summon an angry mosquito—"

"But if you didn't send it, who did?" asked Will.

"No clue—hang on." Dave's face tilted upward, as if listening to something in the distance. "Damn the luck, they've locked onto our signal. I've gotta scoot, and head's up, Will. Part of whatever they're throwing at me might seep through at you—"

A blinding flash of light filled the room and the sand that had formed the image fell apart and showered to the floor.

Will turned to the girls. They both looked about as stunned as he expected, but Elise was staring up at the skylight, and then a second later she pointed at something.

"What's that?" she said.

Something small and dark was moving—or falling— toward the window out of the sky at a high rate of speed.

THE CAVES

"Get out of the way!" Will shouted.

They scrambled toward the door but the object didn't crash through the glass as Will had anticipated. Instead it stopped short and paused, looking vaguely like a car-sized rain cloud, hovering just above the windows.

Then the cloud collapsed into a thousand fragments—something like oversized raindrops—that clattered on the skylight. Instead of beading up and running off like liquid, the drops stuck where they landed, and from each piece Will felt malevolence radiate. The droplets spread out and covered the entire skylight, blotting out the sun.

"That's not rain," said Brooke.

All at once the droplets turned a darker shade, a sizzling sound filled the room, smoke rose from the skylight, and Will realized they were burning through the glass.

He heard Elise ask him, *What should we do?*

Blast 'em.

Elise took a deep breath and let out a focused sonic blast. The skylight exploded out into the air, carrying the liquid with it.

The three stepped forward, looking up at the hole to the open sky.

"We're going to hear from maintenance about this," said Brooke.

They quickly stepped back as shards of shattered glass fell back into the room. Drops of the strange liquid hit the floor as well, wriggling around as if electrified.

Elise raised her foot to stomp on one of them.

"Don't!" Will shouted, pulling her out of the way. "Don't let it touch you!"

Within moments the loose droplets snaked toward each other in the center of the room, reassembling into something bigger and much more worrying than a rain cloud, something tall and dark and menacing that looked more elemental than humanoid.

Before Will and Elise could react, Brooke walked straight toward the creature before it could completely coalesce and fearlessly laid both hands on it. Ferocious concentration etched her face as she leaned into the thing, and right before their eyes it lost its organizing energy, wilting, falling apart, and within seconds spilling to the floor and dispersing as harmless and inert as tap water.

Will and Elise looked at each other, amazed, as Brooke turned to them, much cooler and calmer than either of them would have thought possible.

"I was thinking about what you said earlier," said Brooke, looking at her hands, "and I figured that if I changed my intention I could . . . reverse the flow. You know, take energy *away* from something, instead of give it?"

"Good to know," said Elise, nodding.

"Very good," said Will, still stunned.

Somewhere in the building they heard an alarm sounding.

"Maintenance really isn't going to like this," said Elise.

"We better go find the Carver," said Brooke. "Before school security or mine shows up."

"Sounds like a plan," said Will.

"And if they grill us about this?" asked Elise, pointing at the ceiling.

"We weren't even here," said Will, heading out the door. "Let's find Nick and Ajay and meet in an hour."

"By the way, what's a 'Level Two dogface'?" asked Elise.

"I'll explain later."

Ajay and Nick responded immediately to Will's page; they agreed to meet at the Riven Oak behind the Barn, each arriving separately but only after making sure they weren't followed. It was just after three when Brooke was the last to arrive and they set out for the caves. She explained it took extra time for her to send her three-man security detail on a wild-goose chase—checking out the attack at the art studio—before breaking away unnoticed.

Nick led them into the deep woods, using less-traveled paths so they didn't see another soul until they reached Lake Waukoma. Afternoon winds had kicked up and the lake was dotted with sailboats, so Nick veered away from the water, cut through a final stand of woods, and skirted the edges of the forest as they climbed to the plateau that led to the cliffs. As they walked, Will brought Nick and Ajay up to date, giving them the same info he'd told the girls about Dave.

"Huh," said Nick.

"Why am I not surprised," said Ajay.

The most exposed part of the hike would come when they left the forest and made for the path to the ridge. After Ajay looked ahead and behind and saw no one following, Will activated his Grid to scan the area and confirm. The sun, filtered through a thin layer of cirrus clouds, felt like a hot wet blanket as they crossed the rocky plateau to the base of the escarpment. Will took the lead now—he remembered every detail of the ascent from last fall vividly—and Nick brought up the rear as they started up.

Dripping with sweat, concentrating on every foothold and handhold, Will glanced back frequently to make sure the others were okay. Everyone climbed in silence, even Ajay, who labored hard and uttered not a single complaint. When they crossed the summit onto the ridge, they took a water break, looking down over the broad river valley and the lake below.

As they studied the openings in the sheer rock wall ahead, Will passed out maps he'd drawn earlier from memory of the three caves on the ridge. He recounted the fight with Lyle and the wendigo—just the memory gave him chills—and pointed to the center cave as the most likely place the Carver landed after Lyle had thrown it when the wendigo attacked.

Will wiped a sheen of sweat off his brow. The wind felt stronger here but did nothing to moderate the intense heat, which reflected off the face of the cliff like a mirror. In case the Carver had been moved, Will sent Nick to search the smaller cave to the left and sent Brooke and Elise toward the one to the right. Will entered the biggest opening in the center with Ajay, where his vision would be best served in the cave where Will hoped to find the Carver.

"All three connect deeper inside," said Will. "Give a holler if you see anything."

They turned on flashlights and comm system microphones and advanced to the openings. Will gripped the stone falcon in his hand, turned on his flashlight, and led the way inside. It had been winter when Will was last here; the cave had felt dead and cold then, almost antiseptic. Now it was moist and hot inside, thick with a rich musk of loam and mold. After the vast spaces of Cahokia, it felt almost claustrophobic. He let Ajay take the lead, scanning the ground, his hungry eyes gleaming in the dim light.

Will turned his light off, blinked on his Grid, and examined the darkness ahead for life or energy, wondering if the Carver might emanate a readable signal. He faintly saw Nick and the girls' heat signature through the wall to either side, but nothing straight ahead. He blinked the Grid down, turned his light on, and searched crevices and small hiding places with the naked eye as they slowly advanced.

"Spot anything?" Will asked into his mic.

The others answered that they hadn't.

About a hundred feet in, the cave widened and the three passages merged. Nick rejoined them first, then Brooke and Elise. Will stopped; this was as far as he'd gone the last time. The single larger passage yawned open before them, snaking around a corner to the right.

"Near as I can remember," said Will, "this is about where Lyle was standing when he threw the Carver."

They trained their lights ahead, spread out in a straight line, and started forward, examining the ground inch by inch.

"What was that?" asked Ajay, stopping suddenly. "I hear something."

They stopped and listened. Slowly the sound of dripping water somewhere ahead, plinking into a puddle, came into focus.

"Water," said Elise.

"There's something else," whispered Ajay.

"What, you got supersonic hearing now, too?" asked Nick.

"If I had a pistol, I'd shoot you," Ajay said, gesturing for silence. "Listen, don't you hear it?"

Will closed his eyes to concentrate. He did hear something else, low and steady, almost below audible range.

"It sounds like breathing," whispered Will.

"Yes, that's it," whispered Ajay. "Acoustics in here may be amplifying it, making it harder to trace its source."

"You guys have gone goofy," said Nick. "I don't hear anything—"

Something burst out of the darkness ahead, straight into where their flashlights were pointed, and it happened so fast they both dropped them in shock. They caught only a glimpse of something that was as tall as the ceiling, long, sinewy, and ghoulishly pale, with eyes like dark shining beacons. It looked toward Will, locked eyes with him for a moment, raised one hairy arm to block the lights, gave out a muffled cry, and then as quickly as it appeared, the specter slipped back into the darkness around the corner.

"Don't anybody move," said Will.

"I may need to, Will," said Ajay, who slumped to his knees. "At least vertically, as it seems I'm having a heart attack."

"It's not a heart attack," said Brooke, putting a hand on his back. "It's adrenaline."

"To be precise, it's called the fight-or-flight response," said Ajay, struggling to breathe. "And I'm strongly leaning toward flight."

They instinctively huddled together, fighting the impulse to bolt toward the exit.

"What the hell was that?" asked Nick. "Bigfoot?"

"No, just another stupid death clown from the Never-Was," said Elise, picking up her flashlight.

"Maybe," said Will as his heartbeat settled into high aerobic range. "But I don't think so."

"Good thing I didn't scream," said Elise. "I'd have blown its head off."

"Why don't you think it's a Never-Was thing, Will?" asked Brooke.

"Because it looked more like a wendigo," said Will.

"Great, I can scratch 'see a wendigo in its native haberdashery' off my bucket list," said Nick.

"Habitat," said Ajay, annoyed.

"But I thought you said wendigos *came* from the Never-Was," said Elise.

"They do, but it looked a lot more human than the one I saw before," said Will, his mind jumping ahead to a conclusion he didn't even want to consider. "And I think that same thing was following us down in Cahokia—"

"Now he tells us," said Elise.

"I'm not finished . . . ," he said, remembering the look in the creature's eye. "I think it might have been Lyle."

"No way," said Nick.

"You may be right, Will," said Brooke, her eyes meeting Will's. "He kind of looked like that when we saw him escape the hospital."

"Only now he's more . . . wendigo-ish," said Will.

"A *lot* more," said Brooke.

"Dude's at least six-seven now," said Nick. "Lyle was six-one. How's that possible, Professor Peabody?"

"Jericho said that if a wendigo bites you and you don't die from it," said Will, "you could turn into one."

"Now I'm sorry I didn't scream," said Elise.

"Okay, if that really was Lyle Crocodile, what's he doing in a cave?" asked Nick.

"My guess is he's living here," said Ajay. "Think about it from a troglodyte's perspective. The cave offers shelter, privacy, running water—"

"A hefty supply of creepy-crawlies to snack on," said Nick.

"And a spacious patio to work on his tan," said Elise.

"Didn't look like he's using that much," said Nick.

"These caves could connect to the ones leading to Cahokia,"

said Will. "Maybe that's how he got down there. Maybe he wasn't following us but just making his rounds."

"Do you think he recognized us, Will?" asked Brooke.

"Hard to say," said Will. "No way to tell how much he even remembers about who he used to be. Plus we had our lights in his face and he's used to the dark."

"Maybe he recognized our voices," said Brooke.

"Maybe," said Will.

"You know what would be really bad?" asked Nick, laughing a little. "If he's like an actual man-eating wendigo now, *plus* he still has all his old bad-ass Lyle mojo."

"Okay, I'll meet you back at the pod," said Ajay, turning to go.

Will put up a hand. "Hang on. We don't know how all these tunnels connect and he does. He might double back and jump us on the way out. We need to stay together."

"Excellent point," said Ajay, immediately turning back to join them.

"We should keep going," said Will. "We have to find that Carver."

"Shouldn't we have seen it by now?" asked Ajay.

"What if Lyle found it and took it back to his ... what would you call it? Where he lives?" asked Nick.

"Pied-à-terre," said Elise.

"What if we run into him again?" asked Brooke.

"He seemed at least as scared of us as we are of him," said Will. "And if he comes back, we're pretty capable of handling ourselves at this point, wouldn't you say?"

"No doubt," said Elise.

"I'm in," said Nick, flexing his fists. "If Yeti-boy tries to throw down now, I can pound him to a grease spot without worrying what the school says about it."

Everyone looked at Ajay, who seemed to have recovered, to see if he objected. "Lead the way, Will," he said.

"Be ready," said Will.

With their lights forward again, Will edged around the near corner, and then another turn after that led back. The mustiness of the cave transitioned to something ranker, which they traced to a small alcove off to the left.

"We must be getting close to his lair," said Will.

"Well, we are *definitely* closer to his bathroom," said Nick.

"I don't hear any more breathing," said Ajay. "Maybe we did scare him off."

They moved cautiously around another turn into a long, narrow, high-ceilinged chamber about the size of a house trailer. Another narrow passage led out of the room at the far end. Some primitive effort had been exerted to make the space more livable; stacks of pine branches laid in one corner formed a long bed, and a big flat rock had been set up between two outcroppings as a kind of table. A thin trickle of running water down one wall emptied into a dank, bowl-sized pool in another corner, and near that were the remains of a fire. Near that was a pile of bones, likely small animals that had been killed and eaten.

"So we found his kitchen, too," said Nick.

"All the comforts of home," said Elise.

"At least it doesn't look like he's eaten any people," said Will, sifting through the bones with his foot.

"Maybe they're not on the menu yet," said Elise.

"I hate Lyle's guts," said Nick. "But I gotta say even I'm bummed to see him living like this."

"Look over here," said Ajay.

He was shining his light into a corner at a squalid pile of what looked like rubbish. Will picked up a stick and sifted through it as the others held their lights on the trash—tin cans, strips of fabric, bits of leather and string, and the torn remains of a few ruined books.

"This has to be Lyle's crib, dudes," said Nick, picking up a limp textbook cover. "Half man, half ape and he's still doing homework."

The beam glanced off something in the pile that threw back a bright reflection. Will shoved away the junk around it, reached down, and lifted out the object. A small grilled barrel widened into an elegant silver handle shaped like a pistol grip. Three small raised buttons with strange glyphs on them lined up on the back. Covered with grime, the metal felt smooth, seamless, and unnaturally cold in his hand.

"This is it," said Will, showing the others. "So Lyle must have found it when he came back up here."

"Amazing he didn't shoot himself in the face with it," said Nick.

"You're absolutely sure, Will?" asked Brooke. "You're the only one who's seen it up close."

"This is the Carver, all right," said Will, turning it in his hand.

Will saw it from the corner of his eye before he knew what it was: something strange happening in the room behind him. He turned. Elise was being dragged back toward the way they'd come in, her legs kicking and thrashing, but she made no sound, and her face looked distorted as if something Will couldn't see was covering her mouth. As Nick turned to look, a feathered dart smacked into the back of his shoulder just to the right of his neck.

"What the hell!" said Nick, turning around, his hand fumbling to find it.

As he yanked it out, Nick took two steps toward Elise, then stumbled, fell to his knees, staggered, and then collapsed hard onto the ground. His eyes were open, but he was either out cold or paralyzed.

Will turned to Brooke beside him and said, "Run!"

Brooke took off through the small exit at the back of the room behind them. Will took a step to block anyone from following her, his mind ramping up to attack. When he turned, he saw Ajay staring at someone, a man, who walked in past the struggling Elise.

Ajay dropped his flashlight, his expression glazed and robotic. The eyes of the man staring at him were glowing like hot cinders.

It was Hobbes. Stark and still, all in black.

Something he can do with his eyes, Raymond had said about him. He could see it in Ajay's collapsed, disjointed posture: some form of deadly mind control. Hobbes had Ajay in a vise grip.

Behind Hobbes, Will saw Elise go slack, and the person grabbing her from behind faded into view.

Courtney Hodak, wearing nothing but her mocking grin.

"Your friends can't help you, Will," said Hobbes calmly. "You want to try—I wouldn't expect less of you—but if you fight or resist me in any way, you'll watch your friends die. So think carefully."

The other two Knights they'd seen in the locker room with Hobbes—Halsted and Davis—stepped into the chamber. The blond one, Halsted, pointed a pistol at him, loaded with another tranquilizer dart. He stopped just outside the range of where Will could reach him before he pulled the trigger. The bigger of the two, Davis, knelt and lifted his arm above the helpless form of Nick on the ground. Davis made a fist, and then his flesh expanded and hardened, gleaming like iron, until it looked as lethal as an anvil poised over Nick's head.

And Hobbes, just by staring at Ajay with those uncanny

burning eyes, somehow lifted Ajay's limp body three feet off the ground.

"Now, very slowly, young man," said Hobbes, "put the Carver on the ground and kick it to me."

Will stood perfectly still. Controlled his breathing so he could think clearly. His mind efficiently ran through his options.

#43: THE BRAVEST THING IS NOT ALWAYS THE SMARTEST THING.

Will slowly set the Carver on the ground and slid it toward Hobbes, who knelt down to pick it up, then slipped it into his pocket as casually as if he'd found a set of keys.

"You've caused a lot of trouble for me, Will," said Hobbes, but he didn't sound angry. "Leading us to this almost makes up for it."

At least Brooke got away, thought Will. *And they don't know what she's capable of now. That could end very badly for Mr. Hobbes.*

"If you hurt my friends, I don't care what you do to me," said Will. "I'll kill you."

Hobbes looked at him with real interest and, Will thought, more than a little sympathy.

"And no one, especially me, Will, as I hope you come to learn, would blame you for wanting to try," said Hobbes.

Hobbes nodded at Halsted, who fired the pistol, and a dart smacked into the meat of Will's left thigh.

Will pulled out the dart as the tranquilizer started to work, dropped to his knees, and threw it back at Halsted. Head spinning, his view of Lyle's wretched chamber grew dim and then vanished.

BETRAYAL

He came out of it all at once, as if someone had pulled a blind-fold off his eyes. Will stood up quickly, looked around, felt his head clear as the last of the drug wore off.

A circular room, wooden plank floor, low wooden ceiling, no windows. Whitewashed stone walls. A bare futon on the floor, that's what he'd been lying on—clean, no sheets—otherwise the room was empty. No, a bottle of water sat beside the bedding, a commercial brand, unopened so he would think it was safe. Maybe it was, but he didn't touch it.

A small mirror hung on one wall. He lifted the frame, nothing behind it but stone. He moved to the room's single wooden door, no handle on the inside. Felt around its edges, put his shoulder to it once, then closed his eyes and used the Grid to analyze it. Thick, substantial, locked—and barred—on the other side.

No way to get through this without alerting them.

His watch was gone. All he had in his pockets were his black dice and the stone falcon. No way to know how long he'd been out, or whether it was day or night, or even the same day.

He closed his eyes and tried to reach Elise. Nothing. A wild spike of anger ran the length of his spine, his power ramping up, urging him to blow this door off its hinges and destroy everything and everyone in his path on the other side.

He gripped the falcon, felt it turn red hot, then slowed and centered his breathing, closed his eyes. Waited for a sense of calm to return.

#47: OUT-OF-CONTROL ANGER WILL GET YOU KILLED EVEN QUICKER THAN STUPIDITY.

Start with the first question: *Where am I?*

Will remembered Jericho's recent advice: *"You have more than one mind. Decide which one to listen to. Then it'll speak to you."*

Before he had another thought, an unexpected peace came over him, his fury melted away, and Will heard a voice in his head that answered with clarity and reason.

We're in the castle.

It wasn't Dave or Elise. This felt like a part of himself. Maybe the "higher mind" Jericho had mentioned?

What does that mean? he asked.

It means they don't want to kill us. They've kept us alive for a reason.

What do they want, then?

Wait. They'll tell you. That's why you're here.

This voice put him completely at ease: Jericho was right. This was a voice he could trust above any other.

Will's eye fell on the mirror and he moved closer to it, peering into the glass. He closed his eyes for a moment, searching inside for the voice's source. When he opened his eyes, there it was in the mirror. A close reflection, but not an exact one, looking back at him: a slightly different Will. Older and calmer, one who seemed to know more than he did.

Why show up now? he asked it.

Because you're ready to listen. All your friends are still alive, too.

How do you know?

These people want something from you. They're using your

*friends to convince you to give it to them, and they can't do that if
your friends are dead or injured.*

That makes sense.

*But something else is wrong. Think about it. Ask yourself the
right question.*

How did Hobbes know we'd be in the cave?

*Yes. You were careful, you weren't followed, but they knew
anyway. How?*

Someone told them.

Who told them?

One of my friends.

I'm afraid so.

Will closed his eyes in pain.

*Think back, Will. Has this happened before? Have they ever
known what we were going to do before we did it?*

*Yes. The other day. Hobbes came looking for us when we
found the hospital.*

*That's right. But we were down there a long time. Why didn't
he show up until we found the hospital?*

I don't know.

*And then Hobbes came to the locker room when we were
there, didn't he?*

Yes, after we spoke to Nepsted.

That's right. Why did he wait until after *we were done?*

I don't know that either.

This has happened before. Last year, when we first arrived.

*Yes. When Lyle came to search our rooms and nearly found
my cell phone. As if he knew it was there. He seemed shocked that
it wasn't.*

That's right.

And when I was at the medical center getting an MRI, Lyle

attacked. He knew I was there then, too. And again, when I went to the cave the first time.

Yes. It's been this way since the beginning.

But who is it? I must have told everybody what we were going to do at some point.

It's not clear yet.

How can I find out?

We'll have to wait.

For what?

Until one of them comes to us. Tries to convince us to cooperate. They'll appeal to our feelings, and also our reason. They'll try to make us see it's the only way we can save our friends.

Will didn't say anything, staring into the glass, his heart pounding.

Whoever comes first. That will be the one who's betrayed us.

Will heard noises outside the door. Locks being opened. Someone coming.

#35: TRYING TIMES ARE NOT THE TIMES TO STOP TRYING.

The image in the mirror faded, leaving Will's younger image. Younger and more vulnerable. Tears forming in his eyes. He wiped them away, trying to erase the emotion from his face before whoever was out there came in.

The door swung open. Mr. Hobbes—Edgar Snow—walked into the room. Sharklike, cool and confident in his black Windbreaker and cap. Will turned, shocked to realize he was almost glad to see him—the man he hated and feared most in the world—because it meant he didn't have to face what he'd just learned.

307

Not just yet.

Hobbes stopped just inside. When he took off his cap, he looked almost friendly. "How are you feeling, Will?" he asked.

"What do you want?" said Will coldly.

Hobbes hesitated. "Just so you know, this isn't how we wanted this to happen."

"I won't fight you now," said Will bitterly. "If that makes it any easier for you."

"You don't have to make it easy for anyone but yourself."

"Why don't you tell me how I can do that, Edgar? And which of my friends or family you'll hurt if I don't."

Hobbes's eyes went cold, but he covered it with a thin, reptilian smile. "If you're sincere about cooperating. Showing us where the Carver was, for instance—even inadvertently—was a step in the right direction."

Hobbes gestured toward the open door. "After you."

Will tried to appear relaxed and confident as he walked through the door. He blinked on his Grid and picked up a heat signature standing motionless ten feet to his left: Courtney.

Better to not let her know I can see her.

Will blinked down the Grid as he walked past her down the hall. Hobbes kept his distance behind him.

"Take the first door to your right, please," he said.

Will walked around a bend and through the next open door into a high and wide room. He had to shield his eyes from bright sunlight pouring in through narrow windows on either side of its high, pitched ceiling. Brick walls, exposed beams, wide planked floor, all painted a gleaming, almost blinding, white. Glancing out a window, Will realized he was in the Crag, in a gallery connecting the two towers of the castle.

A long wooden table ran nearly its entire length, with

twenty high-backed chairs. Two place settings had been laid at the far end, with glasses, a selection of drinks on a silver tray, plates of fruit, bread, and cheese. A low, square wooden box rested on the table halfway between him and the food. It looked familiar but he couldn't place it. Three monitors, fashioned from the same black material as their notebooks, stood on stands near that end of the table.

Hobbes gestured to a chair near the food. "Help yourself if you're hungry," he said.

"I'm not. And I'd rather stand."

"Suit yourself," said Hobbes, perching on the table's edge. He picked up a handful of grapes and ate them one at a time, every move coiled and deliberate, never taking his unsettling light eyes off Will.

Without even using his Grid, Will felt certain that Courtney had moved into the room and was standing a few feet behind him. Will walked to the table and poured himself a glass of orange juice.

"I'm listening," said Will.

Hobbes smiled again, oddly, and pointed his hand at the first screen to the left. He drew his fingers together and then spread them apart. The screen expanded to three times its size and flickered on.

It showed an overhead angle of a closed room that looked like a prison cell. Nick paced restlessly back and forth as the camera panned to follow him; there were bars across one side of the room. He looked like a caged leopard. Based on the look of the stone, Will decided the room must be somewhere in the castle, maybe down in its endless basement.

Hobbes pointed at the middle screen and expanded it with the same gesture. Will recognized the large round room in the tower with all the boxed archives. A high camera looked down on Ajay, sitting cross-legged on the floor, reading a document from one of the boxes.

Hobbes then gestured at the screen on the left, enlarging it as well. It showed a surgical theater, possibly the one they'd found in the underground clinic. Banks of bright overhead lights were on, and directly beneath them, masked medical personnel were strapping someone to the metallic operating table.

Brooke. The team around her buckled her hands to the table, prepping her for surgery.

She hadn't gotten away after all. And what about Elise? Where did they have her?

This was probably all for show—effective stagecraft, something the Knights took perverse pride in—but the implied threat to his friends made Will's blood boil. It took every ounce of self-control he possessed to keep from blasting Hobbes with all the force he had in him. But he had to do something.

He turned and splashed the orange juice all over Courtney, revealing her outline. She sputtered in anger.

"Oh, I'm sorry," said Will flatly. "I didn't see you there."

Hobbes almost looked amused. He picked up a large cloth napkin and tossed it at Courtney, who grabbed it out of the air and stormed toward the door, wiping herself off.

As she left the room, two others came in. Will recognized the first as Davis, Courtney's cohort, the "iron-fisted" one who'd threatened Nick in the cave. It took Will a moment longer to recognize the second; he looked much bigger and bulkier than Will remembered, like an insanely roid-raged NFL linebacker but teeming with the same unstable intensity he'd always possessed. The bulging muscles exposed by his singlet rippled and pulsed with excess energy. His jawline and neck looked cartoonishly big, almost a parody of manliness, but his dark good looks and ruddy complexion were unmistakable.

"Hello, Todd," said Will, trying to sound calm.

Todd's cockeyed grin radiated even more malice than usual. He looked ready to chomp his way through the table to get at Will.

"Scrub," said Todd, his voice an octave lower than Will remembered.

"Long time no see, buddy," said Will, looking him up and down. "Working out much?"

Todd Hodak snorted and took a step toward him, cracking his clenched fists together. They looked like canned hams.

"Keep it civil, gentlemen," said Hobbes sharply.

"So I guess you, what, transferred to gladiator school?" asked Will. "Or did they just grow you in a tank?"

Todd's face flushed with anger.

Some things haven't changed.

"Your turn's coming, punk," said Todd, jabbing a finger at Will.

"Mr. Hodak is going to visit your friend Mr. McLeish," said Mr. Hobbes matter-of-factly, nodding toward Nick on the screen. "Mr. Davis will go with him. They're going to punish Mr. McLeish and they're not going to stop until we get your full cooperation. If he gives up the ghost before you come to your senses, Mr. Davis will visit your friend Ajay."

Davis held up both his hands and his index fingers grew into lethal six-inch spikes.

"He'll start with the eyes," said Mr. Hobbes, setting two grapes on the table.

Davis plunged his spikes through the grapes and all the way through the table. Will worked hard not to react, but felt like his chest might crack open.

Hobbes directed the two toward the door, and Todd and Davis headed out. Hobbes walked over to the third screen, folded his arms, and studied Brooke in the operating theater.

"Or should we have Ms. Springer go first?" said Hobbes casually, as if thinking it over. "I'd hate to see her lose those lovely hands."

Hobbes gestured and Brooke's screen went dark. Will felt like he was about to lose his mind. He had to control himself. *Listen. Watch. Wait. This isn't the time to fight.*

"Here's another possibility," said Hobbes. "What if we do all three of them at once? Would that prove more persuasive? Do I have your full attention yet?"

Why hasn't he mentioned Elise? Could that mean she'd somehow gotten away?

"Leave them alone and tell me what you want," said Will, sounding cold and weary.

Hobbes considered that, his hand tracing a circle on the wooden box on the table. "One of your friends will do that for me."

The door opened again. Courtney, now cleaned up and dressed, and Halsted came in, carrying Brooke between them. They had her in a kind of straightjacket, her hands wrapped around her sides and secured under thick canvas.

So either that surgical theater was right next door, or the image of Brooke on the screen had been prerecorded. For one horrible moment Will wondered if they'd already performed the threatened operation.

They brought her to the table and pushed her down to her knees in front of Will. Brooke didn't appear to even know where she was, possibly drugged. But she didn't look as if she was in the excruciating pain that Hobbes's threatened torture would create.

"We'll let you two get caught up," said Hobbes, signaling the others to follow him out.

Will waited for the door to close before he dropped down beside her. He gently put his hands on her shoulders and waited for her to look at him. Her blond curls fell around her face in soft piles. She looked deathly pale, exhausted and lost, but even with all that her beauty still made his heart skip a beat. She seemed confused until her eyes sparked with tender recognition.

"Will."

She leaned into him, cradling her head on his shoulder as he put his arms around her. Will noticed a series of locks down the back of the straightjacket.

"What happened?" he whispered in her ear.

She leaned back slightly so she could look at him. "I ran back through the cave. I didn't know where I was or where I was going. I must have been lost in there for an hour."

Her lips were chapped and she sounded parched. Will poured a glass of water for her and held it as she took a few sips, then nodded her thanks.

"I saw some light and ran toward it," she said. "They were waiting when I came out." She shuddered. "I don't know what happened after that."

"Did you see any of the others?"

She shook her head. "I woke up in an operating room. Hobbes was there. He told me what they were going to do to us." Her voice trembled with fear. "To each of us. He said it so calmly. How they were going to hurt us . . . what he was going to do to my hands if you wouldn't go along with what they wanted."

Will felt his insides churn, his worst fear curled around his heart.

Not this. Not Brooke.

"Did he tell you what that was?" Will could hardly hear his own voice.

She shook her head. "He wouldn't tell me anything else. Only that cooperating with them was the only way for you to save all of us." She looked up at him, and he forced himself to hold eye contact with her. "Will, I'm so afraid."

Until one of them tries to convince us to cooperate. They'll appeal to our feelings, and also our reason. They'll try to make us see it's the only way we can save our friends.

"I hate to think of you giving in, in any way," she said. "But I think he might be right."

Will stayed absolutely still. "Do you?"

"I don't even know what they've done to Nick and Ajay or Elise or where they are. . . . What have they done to you? Are you all right?"

"They haven't hurt me," he said.

"Thank God."

"Not physically, at least."

He could tell she thought that sounded curious. Just the slightest crack in her elaborate façade, and then she was back on message.

"I'm so glad," she said, leaning her head on his shoulder again. "I was so worried about you."

What should I do? he thought. *How do I move from this moment? How do I ever move on from here?*

#32: EVEN THE SLIGHTEST ADVANTAGE CAN MEAN
THE DIFFERENCE BETWEEN LIFE AND DEATH.
NEVER GIVE IT AWAY.

"They're watching us right now," Will whispered in her ear. "Listening to every word we say."

"What are we going to do, Will?"

"I don't know yet . . ."

Better yet: go on the offensive.

"But I've figured something else out," he said, "and you're not going to like it."

"What's that?"

He put his hands on her shoulders, held her close, and lowered his voice further. "I think it's possible that somebody, one of us, has been cooperating with them all along. Since the first day I got here."

She froze for the slightest moment before responding. "Oh my God, Will."

"You can see how dangerous that could be for us."

"Of course."

"I mean, who can we trust if we can't trust our friends?"

"I can't believe it," she said. "Do you have any idea who it is?"

He lifted her gently off his shoulder and looked her straight in the eyes so he could watch carefully. "I think it might be Elise."

Her pupils contracted, a small muscle twitched just under her left eye—relief—and then she simulated shock, so expertly that it took his breath away. An intake of air, her mouth forming a small O, eyes widening, eyebrows lifting ever so slightly.

And then, the dagger. "Will, I think . . . that's so terrible, but I think you might be right."

"You do?"

"I've suspected something, that something was wrong about her but I couldn't fit my mind around how that could be, for the longest time." She paused, furrowing her brow.

"Really?"

"How could she have fooled us so badly? But if you think

315

about it . . . how else would they have known we were going to be at that cave?"

"Exactly," said Will, hardening his heart.

Don't forget: they know everything she knows. And she knows almost everything.

"I'm sure if we thought it through, we'll come up with other evidence." She shook her head in disgust. "They might even try to make you believe she's in danger."

"They'll stop at nothing," said Will.

"We mustn't say a word to anyone," she whispered urgently.

"I won't."

Brooke stared up at him, the sunlight from the high windows glancing across her cheeks, filtering through her golden hair, angelic. Now even the perfection of her beauty seemed like a lie. A single tear gathered in each eye and rolled gently down her face.

She'll tell me she loves me now.

"I love you, Will," she whispered. "I should've told you before . . . but I've never said that to anyone."

Will cradled her face in both his hands, looked her deeply in the eyes, and allowed himself one truthful moment.

"You'll never know how much you meant to me," he said.

Whatever else they do to me, it can hardly be worse than this.

Then he kissed her softly on the forehead. She raised her face and closed her eyes, ready to be kissed.

The door opened. Hobbes strode back in, followed by Courtney and Halsted. Will stood up abruptly, as if shocked, but he'd expected them. He was actually relieved they'd come in when they did. Now he had to keep selling the idea that he was in the dark about Brooke.

"You leave her the hell alone," said Will, putting himself between them.

"I can arrange that," said Hobbes.

"If you hurt her or any of my friends, whatever I agree to goes away. All bets are off. And from now on that includes Raymond. And I need to know that Elise is all right."

"That sounds perfectly reasonable," said Hobbes.

Will glanced at the screens. He saw Todd Hodak and Iron-Hands Davis step into view near the cage where Nick was being held. Nick stood up, ready for a fight.

"Then call off your dogs," said Will.

Hobbes touched an earpiece in his ear and whispered softly into a mic concealed up his sleeve. Todd and Davis stopped, put hands to their ears to listen, and then moved back out of the frame. Nick looked disappointed, then looked up at the camera, realizing somebody was watching. He flipped off the camera before Hobbes made a gesture that turned off Nick's screen.

Courtney and Halsted helped Brooke to her feet and walked her roughly toward the door. Brooke sought Will out with her eyes. He met her gaze for only a moment, but used it to try to reinforce their "pact" before turning away.

Will pointed to the other screens, at the image of Ajay.

"Once I know they're safe, you can take me to whoever makes the decisions. Because I know it isn't you, Edgar."

"What am I to tell them?"

"That I'll listen."

Hobbes straightened up and looked at Will from a few feet away. Appraising him thoughtfully, without rancor. Hobbes spoke softly into his mic, then gestured at Ajay's screen and it went dark.

"They might be right about you," he said, then headed for the door. "Wait here."

The door closed loudly behind him. Will was alone. He moved to the windows and looked down toward the docks.

Stan Haxley's seaplane was moored offshore again, bobbing in the water.

Haxley is here.

Will wondered how long it would take him to arrive. He must have been watching and listening from somewhere nearby.

How long will they make me wait?

The door opened.

FAMILY BUSINESS

Mr. Elliot had walked into the room. Alone. Dressed in an elegant three-piece tweed suit and a natty bow tie. A smile on his face. He raised his hand in a cheerful greeting as he entered, then folded both hands behind his back, his tall angular frame bent forward as if leaning into a stiff wind.

"Here you are, Will," he said.

Will didn't know what to say.

"By the by, thank you for such an excellent recommendation about your friend Ajay," said Elliot. "What a bright fellow. He's going to be a *lot* of help to you with sorting out all those files."

Will just stared at him: *Is he crazy or senile? Did he just wander in here by accident?*

Elliot didn't seem to notice or mind that Will wasn't responding to him. He puttered over to the table, picked up the old wooden box, and set it down closer to Will.

"Here's something I believe you already have an interest in, Master Will," said Elliot, opening the box. "Come take a look."

Will stepped closer as the lid drew back. The ancient brass astrolabe rested inside. Elliot lifted it out of its crushed velvet bed and held it up for them both to admire its elaborate gears, discs, and levers. Will noticed the faint hum of an energy source issuing from somewhere inside it. All the various pieces of the device seemed to vibrate in gentle harmony.

"Go ahead," said Elliot. "Touch it again if you like. It won't harm you."

This is just too weird.

But Will felt the same mysterious pull toward the object

that he'd experienced when he first found it in the castle's basement. He put one finger on the brass, cool to the touch, but agreeable. He liked the way it felt. A lot. He ran his hand over its smooth, weathered outer ring.

"Hold it," said Elliot, offering it to him. "Both hands. You'll get the hang of it."

Will took it in both hands and felt the weight of his crushing worries and fears melt away. *How is that possible?* This ancient piece of technology—inscrutable and foreign—somehow filled him with confidence and a sense of peace he could hardly begin to fathom.

Some willful impulse of resistance prompted him to set the astrolabe back down in the box, but he found himself instantly regretting it. He wanted to pick it up and hold the thing again, wanted to feel that feeling again.

"I'd like you to have this, Master Will," said Elliot kindly, moving the box slightly toward him. "My gift to you. As a token of our appreciation for the fine work you've done, in helping us organize the archives."

"But I haven't finished yet," said Will, the only objection he could think to offer.

"Don't you worry. I suspect that with you and Master Ajay working together, you'll have the job done in no time."

About time I start working on my own rules, thought Will.

WILL'S LIST OF RULES TO LIVE BY

#1: GIFTS FROM STRANGERS? I DON'T THINK SO.

Will put his hands on the lid and, with a supreme act of self-discipline, closed the box. "I don't know what to say," he said, then forced himself to take a step back from the table.

"That's perfectly natural," said Elliot, smiling benignly. "I daresay we've all felt the same way, in our own time."

"I thought Haxley would be coming to see me," said Will, tearing his eyes away from the box.

"Ah, yes," said Elliot, looking down at him, amused. "I can certainly understand how you might have reached that conclusion."

"But it's not him at all. It's you. You're in charge. You're the Old Gentleman."

All Elliot did was shrug modestly and smile. Relaxed and untroubled.

"Tell me what I'm doing here. What do you want from me?"

"It's not so much a case of what I want from you, Will. It's what I want *for* you. Will you walk with me for a moment?"

Will nodded, then followed Elliot into the hallway. Elliot indicated Will should turn left, and they moved along a windowed passage. Will caught glimpses of the island and other parts of the castle as they proceeded. Sharp beams of sunlight angled down through the windows, bathing the creamy marble with deep rays that seemed to carry an almost palpable weight.

"I certainly have my regrets about how we've come to this pass," said Elliot, eyes ahead. "Apologies are in order, sincerely, no question about that, for lapses in judgment that should never have occurred."

"I'm listening," said Will.

"The late Lyle Ogilvy, for one. Lyle's treatment of you was uncalled for, from the beginning. He was spoken to, reprimanded, warned repeatedly. A severely unstable young man. One always holds out hope you can guide troubled souls back into the full light of their being. Promising as he was, sadly that was not the case with Master Ogilvy."

"What wasn't he supposed to do?" said Will.

Elliot led him up a curving flight of marble stairs, their footsteps echoing.

"He wasn't supposed to try to kill you," said Elliot more plainly. "Heavens no, Will. We gave him a simple supervisory and observational responsibility. Lyle was expressly forbidden, more than once, from resorting to violence. He was never authorized to attack you in any way, far from it. But the person in charge of Lyle failed to interpret the severity of his derangement."

"That would have been Mr. Hobbes?"

"Exactly so, Will," said Elliot, seeming pleased. "You comprehend that situation *precisely* as it is. As if one needed any further confirmation of the acuity of your mind."

"Lyle wasn't the only one who tried," said Will. "Even before I got here, they came after me in the hills outside my house and attacked my plane in midair."

"Tremendously regrettable. How shall I explain?" Elliot looked up, searching for words. "We have *associates* in this enterprise, Will. Distant partners, or independent contractors, if you will. They're unpredictable and not entirely ours to control."

"Because they're not human," said Will.

Elliot looked surprised, as if he hadn't expected Will to know so much.

The Other Team. So Dave was right about them. And if he was right about that, maybe he was right about everything.

"So these 'independent contractors' weren't supposed to kill me either?"

"Heavens no. And once you arrived, believe me, that was immediately corrected."

"So why am I here?" asked Will.

As they reached the top of the staircase, Elliot held up a hand, asking for patience. "Allow me to address that more fully in a moment, but let me say just this much and I hope you'll accept it with a certain amount of faith: Because you *belong* here."

Elliot walked to a nearby door, pausing with his hand on the knob.

"So much happened, Will, before we realized how truly special you were. You see, we needed your father. That's why we were looking for you and your family. Needed him so desperately, we were willing to go to any lengths to bring him back."

"You've been looking for him all my life," said Will.

"Indeed."

"Because he and my mother went on the run, before I was even born."

"Sadly, yes."

"Needed him for what?"

"His work, of course," said Elliot, and opened the door.

Will followed him out onto a spacious roof garden, a surprisingly open space perched on the roof of the gallery they'd been in below. Between the towers, high above the island, was a serene oasis of flowing shade trees, exotic flowers, stands of bamboo, and wild grasses, all possessing an uncommon beauty, bursting with a wild abundance of life. A koi pond bisected the garden, crossed by a filigreed bridge. Colorful songbirds flitted from branch to branch, their musical trills adding graceful notes to the mild breeze modifying the summer heat. Classical statuary had been installed throughout the garden—large Buddhist heads, busts of gods from a dozen ancient cultures. Elliot led them along a grassy path embedded with smooth paving stones.

"Your father is a very proud and extremely stubborn man," said Elliot. "We decided that having you here would be the best way to persuade him to return."

"You mean to blackmail him," said Will.

Elliot smiled in an understanding way. "In time you'll come to see there are less harsh ways to view this. However you wish to interpret it, we learned that as long as your father knew you were safe, he agreed to proceed with the work."

Will had to stifle his anger before he responded. "Then why did he run to begin with? What work are you talking about?"

"You are aware of the work your father was involved with, aren't you, Will?" Elliot looked almost puzzled.

"He never talked about it," said Will. "All I know is it had something to do with genetic research."

"I'm not talking about the insignificant drone he pretended to be for sixteen years," said Elliot impatiently. "I'm referring to the man he was before. I believe you know who I mean."

Elliot loomed over him, hands on his hips, staring at him with a commanding smile.

"His name was Hugh Greenwood," said Will sullenly. "He used to teach here."

"Hugh Greenwood was the finest scientific mind of his generation, Will," said Elliot, lifting a finger. "I'm a little disappointed you haven't learned to appreciate this. His groundbreaking efforts made everything we're doing—all of this—possible."

Will chose his words carefully. "You mean the Prophecy."

"Exactly right," said Elliot, looking pleased. "No one disputes the genius of Abelson's original idea, but his methods were fatally flawed, a disaster when implemented. That is irrefutable. Our finest minds labored for decades but couldn't crack the problems—years of wasted time and effort—until, can you imagine, it turns out that Hugh, and only Hugh, possessed the vision, depth of knowledge, and synthesis of thought to make the breakthrough we'd waited for."

Will's blood ran cold. "You're saying Dad helped you willingly?"

Elliot gave a surprised laugh, mildly amused. "Not to worry, Will. Your father's integrity remains intact. Hugh's gift is in the realm of pure research. He's always lived in and for the theoretical. He never knew what we were using it for."

"So that's why he ran," said Will, feeling relieved. "When he found out."

"Perhaps." Elliot looked inward. "Or you could say he lacked the courage to see his ideas through to their logical and most useful conclusion. When one's given a gift that could make life better for all mankind, can he rightfully refuse to use it?"

They'd come to a bench in the garden, on the far side of the pond. Will sat down, overcome by an immense weight that made it hard to move, struggling to incorporate what he was hearing into everything he already knew.

"Look around you, Will," said Elliot, spreading his arms. "Every species of life in this garden has been utterly perfected by the hand of *man,* not God. Each one the product and beneficiary of your father's insights into the most intricate workings of existence."

He lifted Will by the arm and led him to what looked like a wide window on the far side of the garden, darkened by a shade on the other side. The school's crest was carved into the stone above the sill. Elliot pointed to the words on the scroll below the image.

"Read that for me," said Elliot.

"'Knowledge is the Path, Wisdom is the Purpose.'"

"Wisdom," said Elliot, grasping Will's arm. "To be used

for the benefit and *betterment* of man. This is and has always been our mission. This is why we needed your father to return, under *any* circumstances, to finish and perfect his work."

"Why?"

"Because we're running out of time! The human race as an unregulated experiment in the field has run its course. It's over, Will. Abject failure." He pointed out over the walls of the castle. "You've seen the evidence out there. It's all around us. Look with clear eyes, objectively. Our poor world, despoiled, consumed by the base, parasitic impulses of a greedy, selfish predatory species that's run riot, proliferated to the brink of extinction, and brought us to the dawn of ruin."

"Not all people are that way," said Will.

"*People* are only as good as their *leaders,* and only a higher quality of human being, strong and wise and enlightened, can lead us out of this darkness we've made. *That* is the kind of person we can create now, but it doesn't stop there. We have to mold and prepare and teach them how to save this world, and our species, from destroying itself."

Will was terrified by the old man's passionate zeal, by the too-bright light in his eyes. "So that makes what you've done all right? That justifies cutting a deal with demons that want us dead?"

"Who have you been talking to?" asked Elliot, eyes narrowing. "One of those old fools from the Hierarchy?"

Will tried not to show any surprise and said nothing.

"No, no, they're so very dangerous, Will. You mustn't listen to them," said Elliot, quiet and sincere. "We outgrew the need for those deluded 'babysitters' ages ago. What have they told you? They claim to be responsible for the world's well-being, yes? If you think they're up to that task, look at the state they've left us in. They're the ones responsible for this darkness."

"You've got it backwards," said Will. "The Other Team wants to destroy us, and you're helping them—"

"No, son, listen. We're in charge of our own destiny now—the stakes are too high—we must make alliances however we see fit. They may not be the most savory influence, but we remain in control."

"That's what you think," said Will. "How much does the school know about this?"

"The school? Nothing," said Elliot dismissively. "Why would we want to burden them? This is family business. They work for us, not the other way around."

He's crazy, Will thought. *I should just pick him up and throw him off this roof.*

"Don't you know why you're so important to us, Will? You're living proof. The fact that you're as extraordinary as you are is why we know we can succeed—"

"How can you say that?"

Elliot moved closer, almost whispering, his tone as soothing as a bedtime story. "Because with you on our side, Will, and your father returning to his work, everything is in balance. The Prophecy has come to pass. And that means no one needs to suffer anymore."

"What about my friends?"

"All perfectly safe. Now I need you to tell them what I've explained to you. Tell them you've realized that you made a terrible mistake about us. Because we want them to thrive and prosper, every bit as much as we need *you* to."

Will said nothing, staring at him, paralyzed by the possibility of another way out. No more fighting or struggle. He could save both his family and his friends. Let someone else worry about being in charge.

"Shall I make it easier for you?" asked Elliot kindly. "I know how challenging it is to cross this threshold. Allow me to help."

Elliot knocked on the thick glass of the window. A curtain or blind parted on the other side, and all at once they could see into the room.

It was the surgical theater he'd seen on Hobbes's screen, where he'd watched them strap Brooke to the table. All the lights were on, but someone else was lying on the table.

Elise. Unconscious, most likely drugged. Her head tilted back at a severe angle. Prepped for surgery. Judging by the lines they'd drawn on her neck, they were about to destroy her voice.

But there was more.

The only doctor in the room, standing over her, holding a scalpel, took off his mask and looked toward the window, toward Will, but he didn't react or seem to see anything. Hobbes stood just to the side, holding a pistol to the doctor's head. The doctor wore glasses. Pale and thin, a trim beard. His hair shorter and grayer than Will remembered. The man he'd known his whole life as Jordan West.

Will's father, Hugh Greenwood.

Will banged on the window, shouting his father's name. Hugh didn't react.

"That's one-way glass," said Elliot. "He can't see or hear you, Will. And you have my solemn word that if you just do as I ask from this point forward, no harm will come to him, or Miss Moreau, or any of your friends."

Will's whole body began trembling. He wanted to cry, or kill, anything to stop living in this moment. "Why should I believe you?" he asked, stalling for time. "Why should I believe anything you say?"

Elliot smiled down at him again, the most tender smile, and gently put a hand on his shoulder.

"Because, my dear boy, my name is Franklin Greenwood," he said. "I'm your grandfather."

#100: STAY ALIVE.

Will didn't hesitate and looked up at him decisively. "I'll do whatever you say."

TO BE CONTINUED IN THE NEXT

PALADIN PROPHECY
ADVENTURE

Will lifted the smooth metallic object up to shoulder level, pointing it straight ahead into the darkness of the corridor like a gun.

When he pressed the first button, the device thrummed to life in his hand, powerful vibrations rocking up his arm into his entire body. "Whoa." The end of the barrel slowly energized with an intense white light that spread out ahead of him, piercing the darkness.

"Powering up," said Elise. "Check."

"Second button," said Will, pushing the one with the circle.

The Carver bucked with energy, and he had to grip it hard with both hands just to hold it steady. The white light narrowed down to a single sharp beam and phased through a spectrum of colors, finally settling on gold.

"Would you like me to push the final button?" asked Ajay, watching Will struggle.

"Please," said Will.

Ajay leaned in and activated the third and last button.

Now the Carver emitted a high-pitched keening and Will felt a whoosh of energy ramp up inside it, smoothly this time. The device was suddenly easier to hold and control, but he had the distinct feeling that if he made the slightest slip, disaster might result.

They all focused their eyes on the point in space about twenty feet ahead where the golden beam appeared to stop, hitting nothing but empty air. Sparks flew from that spot, like from a welder's torch on steel, and as Will slowly edged the Carver to the right, the beam looked as if it was creating a seam or opening.

"I think it's working," said Ajay.

"Is that the good news or the bad news?" asked Elise quietly.

"Never-Was, here we come," said Nick, loosening up his shoulders and arms.

"I hope you're not planning on going in there alone," said a voice behind him.

They all turned.

It was Coach Jericho.

#37: COURAGE ISN'T THE ABSENCE OF FEAR. IT'S FEELING AFRAID, AND GOING AHEAD ANYWAY.

Dad's List of Rules to Live By

#1: THE IMPORTANCE OF AN ORDERLY MIND.

#2: STAY FOCUSED ON THE TASK AT HAND.

#3: DON'T DRAW ATTENTION TO YOURSELF.

#4: IF YOU THINK YOU'RE DONE, YOU'VE JUST BEGUN.

#5: TRUST NO ONE.

#6: REMAIN ALERT AT ALL TIMES TO THE REALITY OF THE PRESENT. BECAUSE ALL WE HAVE IS RIGHT NOW.

#7: DON'T CONFUSE GOOD LUCK WITH A GOOD PLAN.

#8: ALWAYS BE PREPARED TO IMPROVISE.

#9: WATCH, LOOK, AND LISTEN, OR YOU WON'T KNOW WHAT YOU'RE MISSING.

#10: DON'T JUST REACT TO A SITUATION THAT TAKES YOU BY SURPRISE. *RESPOND.*

#11: TRUST YOUR INSTINCTS.

#12: LET THE OTHER GUY DO THE TALKING.

#13: YOU ONLY GET ONE CHANCE TO MAKE A FIRST IMPRESSION.

#14: ASK ALL QUESTIONS IN THE ORDER OF THEIR IMPORTANCE.

#15: BE QUICK, BUT DON'T HURRY.

#16: ALWAYS LOOK PEOPLE IN THE EYE. GIVE THEM A HANDSHAKE THEY'LL REMEMBER.

#17: START EACH DAY BY SAYING IT'S GOOD TO BE ALIVE. EVEN IF YOU DON'T FEEL IT, *SAYING* IT— OUT LOUD—MAKES IT MORE LIKELY THAT YOU WILL.

#18: IF #17 DOESN'T WORK, COUNT YOUR BLESSINGS.

#19: WHEN EVERYTHING GOES WRONG, TREAT DISASTER AS A WAY TO WAKE UP.

#20: THERE MUST ALWAYS BE A RELATIONSHIP BETWEEN EVIDENCE AND CONCLUSION.

#21: FORTUNE FAVORS THE BOLD.

#22: WHENEVER YOUR HEAD IS TOO FULL OF NOISE, MAKE A LIST.

#23: WHEN THERE'S TROUBLE, THINK FAST AND ACT DECISIVELY.

#24: YOU CAN'T CHANGE ANYTHING IF YOU CAN'T CHANGE YOUR MIND.

#25: WHAT YOU'RE TOLD TO BELIEVE ISN'T IMPORTANT: IT'S WHAT YOU *CHOOSE* TO BELIEVE. IT'S NOT THE INK AND PAPER THAT MATTER, BUT THE HAND THAT HOLDS THE PEN.

#26: ONCE IS AN ANOMALY. TWICE IS A COINCIDENCE. THREE TIMES IS A PATTERN. AND AS WE KNOW . . .

#27: THERE IS NO SUCH THING AS A COINCIDENCE.

#28: LET PEOPLE UNDERESTIMATE YOU. THAT WAY THEY'LL NEVER KNOW FOR SURE WHAT YOU'RE CAPABLE OF.

#29: YOU COULD ALSO THINK OF COINCIDENCE AS SYNCHRONICITY.

#30: SOMETIMES THE ONLY WAY TO DEAL WITH A BULLY IS TO HIT FIRST. HARD.

#31: IT'S NOT A BAD THING, SOMETIMES, IF THEY THINK YOU'RE CRAZY.

#32: EVEN THE SLIGHTEST ADVANTAGE CAN MEAN THE DIFFERENCE BETWEEN LIFE AND DEATH. NEVER GIVE IT AWAY.

#34: ACT AS IF YOU'RE IN CHARGE, AND PEOPLE WILL BELIEVE YOU.

#35: TRYING TIMES ARE NOT THE TIMES TO STOP TRYING.

#40: NEVER MAKE EXCUSES.

#41: SLEEP WHEN YOU'RE SLEEPY. CATS TAKE NAPS SO THEY'RE ALWAYS READY FOR ANYTHING.

#43: THE BRAVEST THING IS NOT ALWAYS THE SMARTEST THING.

#45: COOPERATE WITH THE AUTHORITIES. BUT DON'T NAME FRIENDS.

#46: IF STRANGERS KNOW WHAT YOU'RE FEELING, YOU GIVE THEM THE ADVANTAGE.

#47: OUT-OF-CONTROL ANGER WILL GET YOU KILLED EVEN QUICKER THAN STUPIDITY.

#48: NEVER START A FIGHT UNLESS YOU CAN FINISH IT. FAST.

#49: WHEN ALL ELSE FAILS, JUST BREATHE.

#50: IN TIMES OF CHAOS, STICK TO ROUTINE. BUILD ORDER ONE STEP AT A TIME.

#51: THE ONLY THING YOU CAN'T AFFORD TO LOSE IS HOPE.

#52: TO BREAK THE ICE, ALWAYS COMPLIMENT A MAN'S HOMETOWN.

#53: AND ALWAYS SYMPATHIZE WITH HIS HOMETOWN'S FOOTBALL TEAM.

#54: IF YOU CAN'T BE ON TIME, BE EARLY.

#55: IF YOU FAIL TO PREPARE, YOU PREPARE TO FAIL.

#56: GIVING UP IS EASY. FINISHING IS HARD.

#57: IF YOU WANT TO KNOW WHAT'S GOING ON IN A SMALL TOWN, HANG AROUND THE BARBERSHOP.

#58: FACING THE TRUTH IS A LOT EASIER, IN THE LONG RUN, THAN LYING TO YOURSELF.

#59: SOMETIMES YOU FIND OUT MORE WHEN YOU ASK QUESTIONS TO WHICH YOU ALREADY KNOW THE ANSWER.

#60: IF YOU DON'T LIKE THE ANSWER YOU GET, YOU SHOULDN'T HAVE ASKED THE QUESTION.

#61: IF YOU WANT SOMETHING DONE THE RIGHT WAY, DO IT YOURSELF.

#62: IF YOU DON'T WANT PEOPLE TO NOTICE YOU, ACT LIKE YOU BELONG THERE AND LOOK BUSY.

#63: THE BEST WAY TO LIE IS TO INCLUDE PART OF THE TRUTH.

#65: THE DUMBEST GUY IN A ROOM IS THE FIRST ONE WHO TELLS YOU HOW SMART HE IS.

#68: NEVER SIGN A LEGAL DOCUMENT THAT HASN'T BEEN APPROVED BY A LAWYER WHO WORKS FOR YOU.

#70: WHEN YOU'RE IN TROUBLE, EMPHASIZE YOUR STRENGTHS.

#72: WHEN IN A NEW PLACE, ACT LIKE YOU'VE BEEN THERE BEFORE.

#73: LEARN THE DIFFERENCE BETWEEN TACTICS AND STRATEGY.

#74: 99 PERCENT OF THE THINGS YOU WORRY ABOUT NEVER HAPPEN. DOES THAT MEAN WORRYING WORKS OR THAT IT'S A COMPLETE WASTE OF TIME AND ENERGY? YOU DECIDE.

#75: WHEN YOU NEED TO MAKE A QUICK DECISION, DON'T LET WHAT YOU CAN'T DO INTERFERE WITH WHAT YOU CAN.

#76: WHEN YOU GAIN THE ADVANTAGE, PRESS IT TO THE LIMIT.

#77: THE SWISS ARMY DOESN'T AMOUNT TO MUCH, BUT NEVER LEAVE HOME WITHOUT THEIR KNIFE.

#78: THERE'S A REASON THE CLASSICS ARE CLASSICS: THEY'RE *CLASSIC*.

#79: DON'T MAKE ANOTHER'S PAIN THE SOURCE OF YOUR OWN HAPPINESS.

#80: GO EASY ON THE HARD SELL. PERSUASION IS THE ART OF MAKING OTHERS BELIEVE IT WAS *THEIR* IDEA.

#81: NEVER TAKE MORE THAN YOU NEED.

#82: WITHOUT A LIFE OF THE MIND, YOU'LL LIVE A MINDLESS LIFE.

#83: JUST BECAUSE YOU'RE PARANOID DOESN'T MEAN THAT SORRY IS BETTER THAN SAFE.

#84: WHEN NOTHING ELSE WORKS, TRY CHOCOLATE.

#86: NEVER BE NERVOUS WHEN TALKING TO A BEAUTIFUL GIRL. JUST PRETEND SHE'S A PERSON, TOO.

#87: MEN WANT COMPANY. WOMEN WANT EMPATHY.

#88: ALWAYS LISTEN TO THE PERSON WITH THE WHISTLE.

#91: THERE IS NOT—NOR SHOULD THERE BE—ANY LIMIT TO WHAT A GUY WILL GO THROUGH IN ORDER TO IMPRESS THE RIGHT GIRL.

#92: IF YOU WANT PEOPLE TO TELL YOU MORE, SAY LESS. OPEN YOUR EYES AND EARS, AND CLOSE YOUR MOUTH.

#94: YOU CAN FIND MOST OF THE WEAPONS OR EQUIPMENT YOU'LL EVER NEED AROUND THE HOUSE.

#96: MEMORIZE THE BILL OF RIGHTS.

#97: REGARDING EYEWEAR AND UNDERWEAR: ALWAYS TRAVEL WITH BACKUPS.

#98: DON'T WATCH YOUR LIFE LIKE IT'S A MOVIE THAT'S HAPPENING TO SOMEONE ELSE. IT'S HAPPENING TO *YOU*. IT'S HAPPENING RIGHT NOW.

#100: STAY ALIVE.

OPEN ALL DOORS, AND AWAKEN.

Acknowledgments

Thanks to Jim Thomas, editor extraordinaire. Ed Victor and Sophie Hicks, agents provocateur. All the great and talented at Random House Children's Books. Susie Putnam, Jeff Freilich, Deepak Nayar, David Lynch, Carolyn Roberts. And Lynn and Travis, first, last and always . . .

ABOUT THE AUTHOR

MARK FROST studied directing and playwriting at Carnegie Mellon University. He partnered with David Lynch to create and executive produce the groundbreaking television series *Twin Peaks*. Frost cowrote the screenplays for the films *Fantastic Four* and *Fantastic Four: Rise of the Silver Surfer*. He is also the *New York Times* bestselling author of eight previous books, including *The List of Seven*, *The Second Objective*, *The Greatest Game Ever Played*, and *The Match*. To learn more, visit ByMarkFrost.com.